2/19/18

Comfort and Joy

By Fern Michaels

About Face • Annie's Rainbow • Celebration • Charming Lily • Dear Emily • Deck the Halls • Finders Keepers • Fool Me Once • Free Fall • The Future Scrolls • The Guest List • Jingle All the Way • The Jury • Kentucky Heat • Kentucky Rich • Kentucky Sunrise • Lethal Justice • Listen to Your Heart • Payback • Picture Perfect • Plain Jane • Sara's Song • Sugar and Spice • Sweet Revenge • Up Close and Personal • Vegas Heat • Vegas Rich • Vegas Sunrise • Vendetta • Weekend Warriors • What You Wish For • Whitefire • Wish List • Yesterday

By Marie Bostwick

Fields of Gold • On Wings of the Morning • River's Edge

By Cathy Lamb

Julia's Chocolates

By Deborah J. Wolf

When I'm Not Myself • With You and Without You

Published by Kensington Publishing Corporation

FERN MICHAELS

Comfort and Joy

Marie Bostwick
Cathy Lamb
Deborah J. Wolf

DOUBLEDAY LARGE PRINT HOME LIBRARY EDITION

ZEBRA BOOKS
KENSINGTON PUBLISHING CORP.

ZEBRA BOOKS are published by

Kensington Publishing Corp.
850 Third Avenue
New York, NY 10022

ISBN-13: 978-0-7394-8871-3

Printed in the United States of America

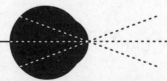

This Large Print Book carries the
Seal of Approval of N.A.V.H.

Contents

Comfort and Joy

Fern Michaels

Chapter One

Angel Mary Clare Bradford, Angie to her friends, looked over at her assistant, who was stacking rolls of colored ribbon onto spindles. Satisfied that the rolls of ribbon were aligned to match the spindles of wrapping paper, she turned away to survey her domain.

The thirty-foot-by-thirty-foot room with its own lavatory was neat as a pin because Angie Bradford was a tidy person. The room she and her assistant, Bess Kelly, were standing in was known as the Eagle Department Store gift wrap department.

Eva Bradford, Angie's mother, had a lifetime lease on this very room, thanks to retired owner Angus Eagle, something that rankled the current young department store head, Josh Eagle, Angus's heir.

Angie and Josh had gone to the mat via

the legal system on several occasions. Josh wanted the lease canceled so he could open a safari clothing department. He claimed the paltry, three-hundred-dollar-a-month rent Angie paid for the gift wrap space was depriving the Eagle Department Store of serious revenue. Another set of legal papers claimed his father had not been of sound mind when he signed the ridiculous lifetime lease.

Angie countered with a startling video of Angus playing tennis and being interviewed by the *New York Times* talking about politics and his philanthropic endeavors on the very day he signed the lifetime lease. In a separate filing, Angie charged Josh Eagle was a bully, and presented sworn testimony that he repeatedly turned off the electricity in the gift shop as well as the water in the lavatory just to harass her. On occasion the heat and air conditioning were also turned off. Usually on the coldest and hottest days of the year.

Josh retaliated by saying Angie should pay for the electricity, water, heat, and air-conditioning. He said there were no free lunches in the Eagle Department Store in Woodbridge, New Jersey.

Judge Atkins had glared at the two adversaries and barked his decision: Josh Eagle was not to step within 150 feet of the gift wrap department. Angie was to pay an additional thirty-dollars-a-month rent for the utilities, and a new heating unit was to be installed at Eagle's expense.

At that point the Eagle-Bradford war escalated to an all-time high, with both sides doing double-time to outwit the other. The present score was zip-zip.

"So, are you going to the store meeting or not?" Bess asked as she gathered up her purse and jacket.

"Nope. I don't work for Josh Eagle or this store. I work for my mother. I'm just renting space from Eagle's. It was toasty in here today, wasn't it?" Angie asked. It had been unseasonably cool for September.

Bess eyed her young employer and laughed. She'd worked for Eva Bradford for twelve years before Eva turned the business over to her daughter, 110 pounds of energy who was full of spit and vinegar, five years ago. Angie had jumped right into the business, played David to Josh's Goliath, and come out a winner. At least in Bess's eyes. With the Christmas season fast approaching, Bess knew in her gut that Josh Eagle would pull out all his big guns to try to get under Angie's skin and make her life so miserable she would give up and move out. She laughed silently. Josh Eagle didn't know the Angie Bradford she knew.

"Come on, boss, I'll walk you out to the parking lot. How's Eva today?"

Angie slipped into her jacket and hung her purse on her shoulder before she turned off the lights. She pressed a switch, and a colorful corrugated blind came down, totally covering the entrance to the gift wrap department. She waited a moment until she heard the sound of the lock slipping into place. She'd installed the sliding panel at her own expense, much to Josh Eagle's chagrin. She then locked the walk-through door to the gift wrap department. Not just any old lock, this was a special lock that Josh Eagle couldn't open with the store's master keys. She'd also installed her own security system with the ADT firm. Josh had taken her to court on that one, too, and lost, with the judge saying Angie was protecting her investment and as long as she wasn't asking him to pay for her security, there was no problem. Back then the score had been one-zip.

"Uh-oh, look who's standing by that big red X you painted on the floor!"

Angie looked ahead of her to see Josh Eagle glaring at her. "You're late!"

He was good-looking, she had to give him that. And he had dimples. Right now his dark brown eyes were spewing sparks. He was dressed in a power suit and tie, his shirt so blinding white, it had to be new. It was all about image with Josh Eagle.

Angie looked down at her watch. "Actually, I'm leaving right on time, Mr. Eagle. My lights are off, the heat has been turned down, the security system locked and loaded, and my door is locked. It's one minute past six. The store closes at six."

"I called a meeting for six-fifteen for all department heads. That means you're supposed to be in the conference room promptly at six-ten. You're still standing here, Ms. Bradford. What's wrong with this picture? Well?"

Angie sighed. "How many times do I have to tell you, Mr. Eagle? I do not work for you. Judge Atkins sent you papers to that effect. I have copies in case you lost yours. What part of I-am-not-one-of-your-employees don't you understand?"

Josh Eagle looked like he was about to say something, then changed his mind. Angie started walking again, and when she got to Josh and he didn't move, she stiff-armed him.

"You touched my person," Josh said dramatically as he pretended to back away.

"Will you get off it already! Do you sit up there in your ivory tower and dream up ways to torment me? I did not touch you. I put my arm out so *you* wouldn't touch *me*. In case your vision is impaired, I have a witness. Now, I suggest you get out of my way and don't come down here again with your silly demands. This shop is off-limits to you!"

"Just a damn minute, Ms. Bradford. If you want to go to court again, I'm your man. I want to know what you're going to do about wrapping my customers' Christmas gifts this year. That's the main topic to be discussed at tonight's meeting."

"We've had this same discussion every September for the past five years. You had the same discussion with my mother for the five years prior to my arrival, and the outcome has always been the same. This year

is no different. Pay me to wrap your customers' gifts, and we're in business. If you
don't pay me, I cannot help you. I'm in business to make money just the way you are.
Try to wrap your feeble brain around that
fact, then get back to me or have your
lawyer call my lawyer. Good night, Mr. Eagle."

Outside in the cool evening air, Angie
dusted her hands together. "I thought that
went rather well." She sniffed the air.
"Someone's burning leaves. Oh, I just love
that smell."

Bess opened her car door. "I think you enjoy tormenting that man. I agree he's sorely
lacking in the charm department, but my
mother always told me you can get more
flies with honey than vinegar. The guy's a
hottie, that's for sure."

"Ha! Eye candy. The man has no sub-
stance, he's all veneer. On top of that, he's
greedy and obnoxious. With all that going
against him, I wonder how he manages to
charm that string of women he parades
around all the time," Angie sniffed.

"His money charms them. Josh Eagle is

considered a good catch. You know, Angie, you could throw your line in the pond. You reel him in, and all this," Bess said, extending her arms to indicate the huge parking lot and the department store, "could be yours!"

Angie started to laugh and couldn't stop. "Not in this life time. See you tomorrow, Bess."

"Tell your mother I said hello."

"Will do," Angie called over her shoulder.

Angie sat in her car for ten minutes while she played the scene that had just transpired back in the store over and over in her mind. Would Josh Eagle drag her into court again? Probably. The man had a hate on for her that was so over-the-top she could no longer comprehend it. In the beginning she'd handled it the way she handled every challenge that came her way: fairly and honestly. She fought to win, and so far she'd won every round. Remembering the look on Josh Eagle's face, she wondered if her luck was about to change.

Well, she would think about it later. Right now she had to stop for pizza and go to the rehab center on New Durham Road, where her mother was waiting for her.

Angie reached for her cell phone to call Tony's Pizza on Oak Tree Road. She ordered three large pepperoni pies and was told they would be ready in ten minutes. That was good, the pies would still be hot when she delivered them to Eva and the other patients at the rehab center.

On the ride to the pizza parlor Angie thought about her mother. A gutsy lady who had worked part time to help with the family bills. Back when she was young, with a family to help support, she'd worked three days a week for Angus Eagle, a man her own age whose wife deplored housework. Her mother had cooked and cleaned for Angus, and in doing so they had forged a friendship that eventually resulted, one Christmas morning, in his turning over the gift wrap department at his store to her with a lifetime lease.

Her mother never tired of telling her the story of that particular Christmas that changed her life, even though Angie, who was fifteen at the time, remembered it very well. Angus's wife hadn't wanted to be bothered wrapping presents for Josh and her husband, so she'd turned the job over to Eva. Each time her mother told the story, she would laugh and laugh and say how impressed Angus had been at her flair for gift wrapping.

It was always at times like this, when Angie grew melancholy, that she thought about her own life and why she was doing what she was doing with it. She'd gone to work on Wall Street as a financial planner, but five years of early mornings, late nights, and the long commute was all she could take. Then she taught school for a couple of years but couldn't decide whether or not teaching was a career to which she wanted to commit herself. Five years ago, she'd happily given it up without a second thought when, after her aunt Peggy got into a serious automobile accident in Florida, her mother suggested that Angie take over the gift-wrapping business. Eva had rushed down to care for Peggy, knowing she was leaving her little business in good hands, and was gone four years.

After her aunt's passing, Eva had remained to take care of her sister's estate, returning to New Jersey only a year ago.

It was nice having her mother home again, in the big old house on Rose Street.

Angie giggled when she thought about all the young guys, the sons of friends her mother had invited to dinner on Sunday in the hopes one of them would be suitable for Angie. So far, she'd made a lot of new male friends, but none of them was what she considered blow-my-socks-off material.

As always, when she got to this point in her reverie, Angie's thoughts turned to her beloved father and his passing. It had been so sudden, so shocking, so mind-bending, it had taken her years to come to terms with her loss. How she missed the big, jolly man who had carried her on his shoulders when she was little, the same man who taught her to ride her first bike, then to drive her clunker of a car. He'd hooted and hollered at her high school graduation, beamed with pride at her college graduation, and could hardly wait to show her the brand-new car he'd bought her. It was all wrapped up in a red satin ribbon. Oh, how she'd cried when she'd seen that little silver Volkswagen Jetta convertible. These days she drove a bright red Honda Civic, but the Jetta was still up on blocks in the garage on Rose Street. She planned to keep it forever and ever.

Angie dabbed at her eyes. It was all so long ago.

Twenty miles away, Eva Bradford sat in the sunroom of the Durham Rehab Center, waiting for her daughter. The television was on, but she wasn't listening to the evening news. Nor was she paying attention to the other patients, who were talking in polite, low tones so others could hear the news. Her thoughts were somewhere else, and she wasn't happy with where they were taking her.

Eva looked up when the evening nurse approached her with a fresh bag of frozen peas to place on her knee. She was young like Angie with a ready smile. "You know the drill, Eva, thirty minutes on and thirty minutes off." The nurse, whose name was Betsy, reached for the thawed-out bag of peas Eva handed her.

Eva wondered if she'd ever dance again. Not that she danced a lot, but still, if the occasion warranted it, she wanted to be able to get up and trip the light fantastic. Knee replacements at her age were so common it was mind-boggling. She looked around the sunroom and counted nine patients with knee replacements, one a double knee, four hip jobs, and two back surgeries. Of all of them, she thought she was progressing the best. Another few days and she was certain she would be discharged with home health aides to help her out a few hours every day. She could hardly wait to return to the house on Rose Street in Metuchen.

Eva turned away from the cluster of patients who looked to be in a heated discussion over something that was going on in the Middle East. She did her best to slide down into the chair she was sitting on so she wouldn't have to look at Angus Eagle who, according to Betsy, had just been transferred from the hospital to receive therapy for a hip replacement he'd had a month ago. She knew the jig would be up when Angie arrived with their nightly pizza. At this moment she simply didn't want to go down Memory Lane with Angus or be put in a position where she had to defend her daughter's business dealings.

She hadn't seen Angus for a long time. At least five years—she really couldn't remember. She tried to come up with the exact year. In the end she thought it was five years ago, the same year her older sister, Peggy, a childless widow, had been in that bad car accident. She'd gone to Florida and stayed on for four years because her sister's health had deteriorated, and with no children to help out, it was up to her to see to her sister's comfort. Then, she'd stayed to handle all the legal matters, sell the house, the furnishings, and the car. She'd been home for a year now. She swiped at the tears that threatened to overflow.

Would Angie take care of her the way she'd taken care of Peggy? Of course she would. Angie had a heart of gold and loved her. She couldn't help but wonder who was going to take care of Angus Eagle. Not that hard-as-nails son whose mission in life was to make Angie give up the gift wrap department. Well, Angus could certainly afford in-home health care around the clock.

Eva looked up to see her daughter standing in the doorway holding three large pizza boxes, one for the two of them and two for the other patients. Angie was so kind. She watched as Angie handed two of the pizza boxes to Betsy and moved across the room to join her mother. Angie hugged and kissed her.

"How'd it go today, Mom?"

"Not too bad. I think I'll be out of here in a few days. Honey, Angus Eagle arrived today for additional therapy. He had a hip replacement a month ago, according to Betsy. He's sitting over there between Cyrus and Harriet. Don't look now."

"And this means . . . what?" Angie asked as she sprinkled hot peppers on the pizza, then handed her mother a huge slice. She chomped down on her own as she casually looked around. She had no trouble locating the elegant-looking Angus Eagle. At seventy years of age, he still looked dashing, with his snow-white hair, trim body, and tanned complexion. It had been a few years since she'd seen him in the courtroom alongside his son. How angry he'd looked that day. Today he looked like he was in pain. A lot of pain.

"Well . . . I don't know. I'm sure he hates us both. He's probably regretting giving me that lifetime lease. You know that old saying, blood is thicker than water. Josh is his son, so it's natural for him to side . . . whatever," Eva dithered as she bit down into her slice of pizza.

"Business is business, Mom. Isn't that what you always told me? Sometimes people make deals that go sour. As long as it's done legally, the way your deal was done legally, you live with it and go on. Josh and I had a rather heated exchange as I was leaving the store this evening. By the way, it's cold out in case you're interested. I think today was the first day that shop felt warm."

"What happened? Wait, look—is *he* eating *your* pizza?"

"Oh, yeah, and he looks like he's enjoying it. What happened? Well, Josh thought he could dictate to me. He called a meeting for six-fifteen for all department heads. I'm sure you remember he does that every September. He wants me to gift wrap his customers' packages. For *free.* I told him if he paid me, I would. It was a standoff. I have an idea. Want to hear it?"

Eva smiled at the excitement in her daughter's voice. She leaned forward to hear what she just knew was going to be a smashing idea. "What's he doing now?"

"Watching us. I am going to decorate the shop like a fairy land. Gossamer, angels,

Santas, sleighs, Santa sacks. I'm going to gift wrap Santa sacks for the kids. I already ordered the red and green burlap. Colored raffia ties for around the sacks. I'm going to suspend some reindeer from the ceiling with wires. Bess said her husband will make us a wooden sled and paint it. The best part is the room is big enough to do all this. We'll get some publicity with the local paper. Parents will bring their kids to see it and, hopefully, shop. Extra business for Eagle's, but Josh won't see it that way, would be my guess. This is the part you might have a problem with, Mom, but hear me out, okay? I'm going to, for a price, agree to wrap purchases from other stores. On a drop-off, pick-up-later basis. I'll hire a few extra people, and we'll do it after hours, when the store is closed. Josh won't have a comeback because I pay my own utilities."

"Can you do that, Angie?"

"My lawyer said I could, so that's good enough for me. Josh will fight me, but that's publicity for me. I'm looking at it as win-win. You look worried, Mom. Are you seeing something I'm not seeing?"

"Well . . . You know me, I'm just a born

worrier. If your lawyer says it's okay, then I guess it's okay."

Angie frowned. What was wrong with her mother? Normally, she'd be up for anything to make the shop prosper. She risked a glance in the direction of Angus Eagle. Caught staring, she offered up a wide smile. To her delight, Angus winked at her. *Now that's something I'll have to think about later.*

"How's that new company doing with your special order?" Eva asked.

"Mom, you won't believe it, but they came through royally, and the price is unbelievable. One-of-a-kind baubles, artificial greenery that looks better than the real stuff, and it's been sprayed, so it even has a balsam scent. I ordered tons of stuff. Their ribbon is satin. Real satin, all widths. Our Christmas packages are going to be over the moon. And it's just a little cottage industry in a small town called Hastings, in Pennsylvania. They're going to start shipping the merchandise to the house next week."

Mother and daughter spent the next hour discussing a real tree versus artificial, paper wrap versus foil wrap, and other unusual ways to wrap gifts.

A bell sounded in the hallway. Betsy appeared to take away the frozen peas. She chatted for a moment, asked Eva if she wanted to return to her room or stay to watch television. "Five minutes, ladies."

"I guess I better get going, Mom. I'll be back in the morning with the order from Dunkin' Donuts. Two dozen donuts, right? Same number on the coffees?"

Eva smiled. "Plus one more for Angus."

Angie picked up her jacket and purse before she hugged and kissed her mother good night. She was almost to the door when she saw Josh Eagle standing in the doorway staring at her. She was about to move past him when a devil perched itself on her shoulder. "Spying on me, Mr. Eagle? Or are you *stalking* me? Shame on you!" She said it loud enough so everyone in the room could hear.

"Don't flatter yourself, Ms. Bradford. I'm here to see my father."

Angie whirled around and pointed to the clock. "Well, that figures! You have three minutes to visit. Oh, is that a gift for your father? A Hershey's bar! How kind of you. Money-hungry jerk," she hissed, before she sailed through the doorway and down the hall.

"Witch!" Josh hissed back, but loud enough to be heard by the patients. "Hey, wait a minute, you forgot your broom!"

Angie stopped in her tracks and turned around. "What did you just call me, you pompous, money-hungry, no-good piss-ant?" Venom dripped from Angie's lips as sparks flew from her eyes.

Josh Eagle immediately regretted his words, but he couldn't back down now. "I called you a witch and said you forgot your broom. You called me a money-hungry jerk. So now I'm a pissant. Well, it takes a pissant to know a pissant."

The captive audience gasped as they watched the scene unfold in front of them. Even Betsy, mouth hanging open, could only stare at the two hissing enemies.

"I called you that because I was too polite to call you what you really are. Now, if you don't get out of my way, you are going to be minus a very important part of your anatomy." To her chagrin, Angie realized her voice had risen several decibels. Stricken, she looked around at the patients staring at her. All she could think of to do was wave.

As one, the rapt audience gasped. They returned her wave, even Angus.

The final bell for visitation rang.

"Looks like you have to leave now, Mr. Eagle. You better stay 150 feet away from me, or I'll have you arrested," Angie said coldly.

"Oh, yeah?" Josh blustered.

"Yeah!" Angie shot back. She flipped him the bird before turning on her heel and marching down the hall.

The audience gasped again.

"I'm afraid you have to leave now, Mr. Eagle," Betsy said. "Try to come a little earlier tomorrow. You better wait a minute—Miss Bradford did say 150 feet. She looked to me like she meant business. It won't look good for the center if she calls the police." Betsy eyeballed the distance down the hall. "Okay, you can go now." She reached out to take the Hershey's bar, but Josh shoved it into his pocket.

Eva did her best not to laugh out loud. She turned around when she heard something that sounded like hysterical laughter. Angus Eagle was laughing so hard one of the aides was clapping him on the back. She was stunned to hear him shout, "You got yourself a spitfire there, Eva!" She wished he would have said something she didn't already know.

The score for this round, if anyone was counting, was one-zip, with the point going to Angie.

Chapter Two

Josh Eagle, his shoulders slumping, entered the house through the kitchen. Delectable aromas wafted about the kitchen, thanks to Dolores, the day lady who had been with his family for the past twenty years. He knew his dinner was warming in the oven, but for some reason he wasn't hungry. The fact of the matter was he was too damn mad to eat.

As he yanked at his tie with one hand, he opened the oven door with the other and set his dinner plate on the kitchen counter. Maybe he'd eat later. First he needed a beer, and he needed to calm down. He carried a beer from the fridge and swigged at it as he made his way to the second floor. He stripped down. Within minutes he was in sweats and slippers. It took him a minute to realize he was cold. He marched out to the hall to turn the thermostat to eighty before he made his way downstairs to grab another beer.

Heat gushed from the two vents in the kitchen. At least he would be warm while he drowned himself in ice-cold beer.

Josh sat down at the kitchen table and propped his feet on a chair as he swigged from the bottle in his hand. Who in the damn hell did that female think she was? He answered himself by saying she was the female who had him over a barrel. He stretched out a long arm to snag a chicken leg off his dinner plate and was just about to bite down into the succulent-looking piece of chicken when the phone rang.

Josh eyed the phone suspiciously. He didn't know how he knew, but he knew it was his father on the other end of the line. He might as well get it over with. He was a small boy again when he picked up, knowing full well his father was going to have something very profound to say. Something he wasn't going to like.

Josh looked at the caller ID. He squared his shoulders, clicked the ON button, and said, "Hi, Dad."

"Good evening, son. I'm sorry we didn't

get a chance to talk this evening. I was looking forward to a long chat."

"I'm sorry, Dad. I had a meeting. I'll come earlier tomorrow. Do you need anything?"

"No, I don't need anything, Josh. Is there anything you want to talk to me about?"

Well, hell, yes, there were at least two dozen things he wanted to talk to his father about, but the old man only pretended to listen to anything he had to say. Josh threw caution to the winds and said, "Since when do you ever listen to anything I have to say? So, the short answer is, no. Is there something you want, Dad? Like maybe my hide, a pint of blood? Name it, and it's yours." His voice was so bitter that Josh could hardly believe it was his own. He heard his father sigh. He always sighed when Josh let loose with his feelings.

"You were pretty hard on that little gal, weren't you?"

"If you say so, Dad. Is there anything else? If not, I'm going to turn in early."

"Okay, I'll see you tomorrow, son."

"Actually, no, I won't be stopping by. If you need something I can have someone from the store drop it off. But now that you've brought it up, there is something I've been meaning to say. I guess this is as good a time as any to tell you that I'll be leaving the first of the year. I'm moving to London. I got a job at Harrods. I leave New Year's Day. You can have Eagle's back. I guess I'm not really giving it back to you since you never really relinquished your interest in the store to me the way you agreed to. The way I figure it is this: you'll probably have a week in January before you have to close Eagle's doors for good. Good night, Dad."

Josh tossed his beer bottles into a wire basket in the laundry room. As he made his way up the stairs he could hear the phone ringing. He knew it was his father calling back because he was in shock over his son's cold announcement. "It's been a long time in coming, Dad," Josh muttered as he settled himself in his small home office. He clicked on the computer and ran some stats. Nothing had changed since earlier in the day. Eagle's was still at the bottom of the list. Just a few months until Eagle's would have to close their doors. Well, come the first of the year, Eagle's Department Store would no longer be his problem. He was sick and tired of battling his father, sick and tired of batting his head against a stone wall. Eventually he would get over the shame of failing. He had a job waiting for him at the prestigious Harrods in London, where his expertise would be appreciated.

The phone at the end of the long second-floor hallway continued to ring. "Give it up, Dad, I have nothing more to say."

Josh climbed into bed and pulled up the covers. Then he climbed back out of bed to turn the thermostat down to sixty degrees. Back in bed, his last conscious thought before drifting off to sleep was that he had to apologize in the morning to the witch with the broom.

Eva knew that Angus was coming up behind her. She could hear his walker on the tile floor. Then again, they were the only two patients in the sunroom, so who else could it be? She steeled herself for Angus's sharp tongue and whatever he was about to say. She clicked the OFF button on the remote control. What was left of the evening news report disappeared.

"Do you mind if I sit down, Eva?"

"Not at all. It's nice to see you again, Angus. It's been a long time, five years if I'm not mistaken. How strange that we should meet up like this after so long."

Because she was a nurturer by nature, Eva wanted to get up to help Angus ease himself into the chair across from her, but these days it was a production to get herself up and moving. "Are you in pain, Angus?"

"A bit. How about you?"

"At times. I try to ignore the pain and just use the frozen bags of peas. They really do help. Other than the hip replacement, how are things?"

"Are you asking to be polite or do you really want to know?" Angus asked.

Eva thought she'd never heard a sadder voice. "Is there anything I can do, Angus?"

"Not unless you have a magic potion that will turn my son into a charming young prince. What was that all about earlier?"

Eva decided not to pretend she didn't know what her old friend was talking about. "Rivalry would be my guess. Two strong, bullheaded people pushing each other's buttons. How is the store doing, Angus?"

"According to my son, not well at all. He blames me. Says I'm an old fuddy-duddy. He says I have no foresight. He claims I'm locked in the past. He said the last time I had an idea was the day, almost twenty years ago, when I gave you the lifetime lease on the gift wrap department, and from that day on, it was all downhill. He doesn't like me much, Eva. Yesterday he called me a meddler."

Eva threw her hands in the air. "What did you do? Or should I be asking what *didn't* you do? Josh was always such a wonderful young man. How did it all go wrong? I don't understand any of this, Angus."

Angus leaned forward. "Look at me, Eva. I have something to tell you that is going to affect you as well as your daughter. My son just told me a few minutes ago when I called him that he's leaving the store the first of the year. He's accepted a job at Harrods in London. That means the store will be closing. He's been telling me that for the past year but I . . . I just blamed him for not knowing what he was doing. I was . . . I was cruel about it, saying things like I made a mistake when I turned things over to him, that he wasn't up to the job."

"Oh, Angus, how could you do something like that?" How was she going to tell her daughter they would both be out of a job after the holidays with only her Social Security coming in?

"Because I'm a horse's patoot, that's how. Josh has been telling me for years that we had to streamline the store, we had to keep up with marketing trends. He wanted to hire new buyers, be more mainstream. I fought him every step of the way. He wanted to restructure everything. That meant layoffs. I didn't want to deal with it. One time he actually called me a dried-up old fart and told me I deserved whatever happened with the store. He was right and I was wrong. And I'm not going to lie to you, Eva, but the gift-wrapping shop was always a thorn in Josh's side. He thought, and I'm sure he still thinks, that you and I had an affair that is ongoing. I think that's another reason he keeps going to the mat with your daughter."

Eva's thoughts were all over the place as she stared at her old friend. "I thought the store was doing well. How could I have been so wrong? What are you going to do?"

"What can I do? Josh's mind is made up— he's leaving because he's fed up. I have to admire his spunk. He gave it his best shot, and I just kept fouling up everything he did.

Now all my chickens are coming home to roost."

"For heaven's sake, Angus, Josh is your son. You can't let him leave under these conditions. You have to make this right. There's nothing in this world more important than family. If you don't take a stand now, you'll never get Josh back. What's so hard about saying you're sorry, that you made mistakes? You can't just let Eagle's close their doors. Eagle's is an institution in this town. Shame on you, Angus Eagle. I'm going to bed now. I don't want to talk about this anymore. I have therapy at seven o'clock."

"Eva, wait. Help me out here."

"Oh, no. It doesn't work that way. You're the only one who can make this right. I'm willing to cancel that lifetime lease and renegotiate a new one. In fact, I insist. I'll call my lawyer in the morning."

"That's a drop in the bucket, Eva. The gift-wrapping shop was never about money. In the beginning it was a courtesy to our customers. You're the one who turned it into a moneymaker. Then Josh wanted to use the gift wrap department space to outfit a safari department. He said it was the 'in' thing. I'm ashamed to admit I laughed at him. Two days later, I heard a group of men on the golf course talking about all the gear they'd just purchased because they were going on safari. One of the men poked my arm and said Eagle's didn't even know what a safari was. Even then, I couldn't see it. I guess I *am* a dried-up old fart, just like Josh said I was."

"Yes, Angus, I guess you are just one big gas bubble. I certainly don't envy you."

Eva struggled to her feet as she leaned heavily on her cane. She knew she'd been sitting too long. She could hardly wait to get to her room so she could ring the nurse to ask for a bag of frozen peas. She moved off as she tried to figure out how she was going to tell her daughter what Angus had just shared with her.

Christmas this year was going to be bittersweet, she thought.

When Eva woke the following morning the first thing she saw was Angus Eagle standing in the open doorway. "How long have you been standing there, Angus?" she gasped.

"About an hour. You snore. I thought only men snored. Can I come in and sit down? I didn't sleep all night. I've been walking up and down the halls and I'm getting tired."

"For heaven's sake, come in and sit down. For your information, everyone snores, even children." Eva pushed the button on the remote to raise her bed. She wished she had a cup of coffee.

"I asked a nurse to bring us some coffee. I hope that was okay. Listen, Eva, you were always so grounded. I assume you still are. That's one of the things I always admired about you. I need your help and I'm not ashamed to be asking, either. For me to give in now, to give up total control when we're just months from closing our doors seems a bit silly to me. Josh won't buy into it. You know that old saying—too little, too late. You know as well as I do that the Christmas season revenues can carry a store for a whole year. We depend on that revenue. What should I do?"

"Angus, I know nothing about the retail business. My only claim to fame is I know how to gift wrap packages. I think you should talk to my daughter. She seems to have an eye and ear to the business. In the past she spent hours and hours telling me all the things wrong with the store. And I know for a fact she dropped dozens of suggestions in Eagle's suggestion box on the second floor because she thought if you had more foot traffic, she would have more gifts to wrap. We had a really bad summer, everyone was buying from the discount houses. That's something else you didn't take into consideration. They popped up all over town like mushrooms. For the record, all of Angie's suggestions were ignored."

Angus's voice was desperate when he asked, "Will your daughter talk to me?"

"Of course she'll talk to you. What kind of child do you think I raised? It's your son she won't talk to. But when I tell her he really isn't her enemy, that you are, well, I don't know for sure. There's no doubt about it, Angus, you're standing knee-deep in a mess. Of your own making, I might add."

"I know that, Eva. Help me out here."

"Put yourself in your son's shoes. What would you like your father to do? How would you handle it?"

Angus shrugged. "Josh said I never listened to him. It's true. All of a sudden, I'm going to listen now, when it's too late?

Maybe there's a way to help him without him knowing I'm helping."

"Spit it out, Angus. How? I suspect you have some groveling to do first, my friend. Call him at the store. Ask him to come here to see you. That's a first step. By the way, Angus, how long are you here for?"

Angus grimaced. "Today or tomorrow. I've been here a week but I stayed in my room because I didn't want anyone to know I was here. I simply didn't want to socialize. I wish I had known you were here, Eva. When are you leaving?"

"Tomorrow, I think. I'll have a home health aide for two weeks. She'll come by three times a week and help with my therapy. The rest is up to me. We can talk on the phone if you like."

"I'd like that. I really would."

"How are you going to get home, Angus?"

"I'll call a car service. I don't want to bother Josh. I'm surprised he hasn't moved out of the house. I'll have to stay out of his way."

"This is not right, Angus. Angie is going to come by this morning with donuts and coffee. She does that every morning. She can give you a ride home if they discharge you today. You can talk to her then."

Eva almost felt sorry for her old friend as he made his way to the door. Almost. Angus looked back, his face filled with pain. For some reason Eva thought the pain was more mental than physical. Once, this wonderful man had literally saved her financial life. Maybe with the help of her daughter, she could return the favor. How that would come about, she had no clue. *Well,* she thought briskly, *I can think about that while I'm having my therapy. Perhaps thinking about Angus will help to alleviate the pain of therapy.*

By nine o'clock Eva had finished her therapy, eaten a light breakfast, and showered before she slowly made her way to the sunroom, where she flopped down on a chair, her forehead beaded with perspiration from her efforts. She could hardly wait for Angie and the delicious coffee she was addicted to. Not to mention the donuts.

Eva looked around, acknowledging the other patients who were waiting for their turn in the therapy room. There was no sign of Angus. She didn't know if that was a good thing or not. She leaned back and closed her eyes, her thoughts going in all directions.

Fifteen minutes later, Eva's eyes popped open when she felt a light touch to her shoulder. "Morning, Mom. Did you have a good night?"

"I did have a good night. Angie, I need to talk to you. Pass out your donuts and coffee and hurry back here." Seeing the alarm on her daughter's face, she hastened to add, "It's not about me. I'm fine. Hurry, Angie."

A few minutes later, worry lines were etched on Angie's face as she settled herself next to her mother. She shook her head when her mother offered her a jelly-filled donut. "What? Tell me, Mom."

"It's the store, Angie. Angus and I spoke last night after you left. When I woke up this morning, he was standing in my doorway waiting for me to wake up. It's not good, Angie. Let me tell it all to you the way Angus told it to me. Don't interrupt me, either."

Angie listened, her facial expressions going from anger to disbelief to sadness. When her mother finished, the only thing she could think of to say was, "We can't let that happen, Mom. Eagle's is an institution. We can renegotiate the lease. Oh, God, I need to think about this. I thought Angus Eagle was a nice man. How could he have sabotaged his son like that? I feel terrible about the way I treated Josh. I need to give Mr. Eagle a piece of my mind."

"You need to do no such thing. What you will do is give Angus a ride home. He's finished with his therapy today and was going to call a car service. I volunteered your services, dear. You can talk to him on the way home."

"Mommmm!"

"Sweetie, we're all in this together. I don't want Angus to lose his son, and that's what will happen. Both of them have too much pride to admit when they're wrong. Because we're women, we can fix that. At least I think we can. All right, we're going to *try* to fix things. All those wonderful suggestions you had over the years might come in handy now. All you have to do is get Josh to think they're his ideas."

"Mom, you can't undo years of being in the red in a few short months. Yes, profits are greater during the holiday season, but that alone can't ward off the inevitable."

"I'll settle for a reprieve. For now, the gift wrap department belongs to Eagle's. We'll take 20 percent and the store takes 80 percent. This is just for now. I'll call our lawyer today to discuss it. We have two short months to turn things around before the shopping season begins."

Angie offered up a bitter laugh. "Mom, Eagle's merchandise is archaic. Where can they get new stuff in two months?"

"Where there's a will, there's a way. Think about something people can't do without. Then stock up on that. Fire sales, get rid of the junk they're stuck with or donate it somewhere. Get some glitter and sparkle in there. I know you'll come up with something, dear."

"Mom! When was the last time you experienced a miracle? That's what it's going to take to get Eagle's to soar again. I'm not . . . I don't think . . ."

"I don't want to hear anything negative. From here on in, we think positive. I know we can at least get it off the ground. If we can do that, then it's up to Josh to follow through. Now run along and pick up Angus and take him home. He is a nice man, Angie. He just didn't know how to let go, and he didn't trust his son enough to let him run with the ball. Unlike me, who trusted you completely. Angus is a man," Eva said, as if that was the only explanation needed.

Angie bit down on her lip. "Okay, Mom. I'll do what I can. I'll see you tonight. What do you want me to bring?"

"A hoagie would be nice."

"You got it." A moment later, Angie was gone. Eva closed her eyes and sighed mightily. She couldn't help but wonder if there was a miracle in Eagle's future.

Chapter Three

The following morning, Angie dressed with care. It was still cool, so she decked out in warm clothes—a plum-colored suit, sensible heels, and a crisp white blouse. Light makeup that her mother said she didn't need, a spritz of perfume and she was ready to go toe to toe with Josh Eagle. There was no point in kidding herself. She was nervous about the confrontation. More so since driving Angus Eagle home yesterday, a drive that had been made virtually in silence. Twice she'd bitten down on her tongue so she wouldn't say something her mother wouldn't approve of. Back in the recesses of her mind Angie wondered, and not for the first time, if Angus and her mother had ever had an affair. Lifetime leases didn't happen for no reason. No one was that kind, that good-hearted. Or, were they? Well, it was none of her business, so she needed to stop thinking about it. Easier said than done.

Angie ran her fingers through what she called her wash-and-go hairdo. A month ago her mother had finally convinced her to cut off her long, curly hair in favor of a more stylish cut. Her mother said the new hairdo was becoming, and mothers never lied. Well, almost never. After two weeks of staring at herself in the mirror, she agreed with Eva's assessment.

Angie realized she was postponing the moment when she had to leave and get on with the day. For all she knew, without an appointment to see Josh Eagle, all this anxiety she was experiencing might be for naught. For naught—such an old-fashioned term. One her mother or Angus Eagle would use.

On the ten-minute ride down Route 1, Angie thought about her own precarious position at Eagle's. If the store closed, she would be out of a job. It might be months before she found another one. Being self-employed, she wouldn't be able to collect unemployment insurance. Her mother would have to start pinching pennies because the medical bills would be coming in shortly. Even with Medicare, her mother would be paying them off for months. With only Social Security coming in, their meager savings would be gone in the blink of an eye. Well, she couldn't let that happen. She'd always been an idea person, according to her mother. If there was ever a time to come up with a dynamite idea, now was it.

Angie slowed for a traffic light, then made a right onto Woodbridge Ave. She drove down to the mall lot, left her car, and entered Eagle's through one of the back doors next to the loading platform. Instead of going straight to her shop, she walked the floor. There were no customers in the store that she could see. The sales help were standing around chatting with one another. She wondered what happened to the rule of look busy even if you aren't. She winced again as she surveyed the merchandise, which looked like it had been hanging on the racks forever. Hopelessly outdated.

Was it too late to save this store? She glanced around again and nodded to herself. Well, she'd never been a quitter. But, as Bess would say, there's a first time for everything.

Angie walked back to the end of the store to the gift wrap department, rolled up the corrugated shield, unlocked the door, and turned up the heat. In the little alcove at the far end of the room, out of sight, was a little station where she kept a coffeepot. She filled it and waited for the hot water to drip into the little red pot. She couldn't do anything until she had a cup of coffee. Coffee fortified her, made her brain cells do double-time. The moment she finished her second cup, she would march herself to Josh Eagle's office on the second floor. She had no clue what she was going to do or say when she got there. She'd always been pretty good at winging it. There was a lot to be said for spontaneity. She didn't believe it for a minute.

At the same time as Angie was waiting for the coffee to brew, Josh Eagle was pacing the confines of his office. He hated that he had to go down to the first floor and apologize to the witch with the broom. She looked like the type who might take a swing at him. His stomach started to curdle at the thought. Still, there was no reason for him to

behave the way he had at the rehab center
the other night. He should have sloughed it
off and ignored the young woman with the
sparks in her eyes. And, she was pretty. He
told himself she could be pretty and still be
a witch.

Josh diddled around for another twenty
minutes before he squared his shoulders,
straightened his tie, and shook down the
cuffs of his shirt. Now he was ready. His
heart was beating way too fast. His mouth
felt dry.

His cell phone rang, jarring him from what
he was feeling. He looked down at the caller
ID and saw that it was his father, who had
come home yesterday and was asleep
when Josh got home. He'd said everything
he had to say to his father the night before.
It was much too late to hear his repeated
apologies of *I'm sorry, son. I didn't know,
son.* Then a few more I'm sorries. No sense
beating a dead horse. He ignored the insistent ringing and left his office.

He met her a foot away from the huge red
X. He'd gone ballistic the day he'd seen that
red X for the first time. The witch's biting
words at the time still rang in his ears to this
day. *Step one foot over that X, and I'll have*

you arrested! He knew she meant every word of it. And that was three years ago. To date, he'd never stepped beyond the X. How childish was all this? Damn childish.

Josh took the initiative. "Ms. Bradford, I came down here to apologize to you for my rude behavior the other night. Not that I'm defending my rude behavior, but I have a lot on my plate right now."

"I know you do. I was on my way to your office to apologize to you. Would you like to . . . uh . . . go out to the food court and get a cup of coffee? Neutral ground, so to speak. If you're busy . . ."

Josh stared at the young woman. Did she just invite him for coffee? "Sure," was all he could think of to say. How brilliant was that?

They walked around the corner, down one of the long halls until they reached the food court, which was virtually empty this early in the morning. Neither said a word on the short journey.

"How do you take your coffee?" Josh asked.

"Black. It's not coffee if you doctor it up with cream and sugar."

"I feel the same way. Take a seat, I'll get

the coffee." A black-coffee drinker like himself. Who knew?

The moment Josh sat down, Angie leaned forward and said, "We're going to cancel the lease. We can renegotiate it again after the first of the year if the store is still open. Until then, Eagle's gets 80 percent of the take, we get 20 percent. Look, let me finish what I have to say before I lose my nerve. My mother told me what you told your father. You're leaving the first of the year. I guess I more or less understand that. Speaking strictly for myself, I've never been a quitter, but that's me and, like you said, you have a lot on your plate.

"Your father . . . well, he's been wrong. Older people have a hard time . . . What they do is give generously and then they realize they lost their control. It's hard for them to accept the aging . . . Help me out here, Mr. Eagle."

"First things first, let's stop with the Mr. and Ms. I'm Josh, and you're Angie. Okay?"

Angie smiled. Josh suddenly felt his world rock. "I . . . I know what you're saying. For the last ten years I've battled my father. He's stubborn as a mule. I had so many plans for the store, but he shot me down each and every time I presented something. I finally got to the end of my rope. There's nothing more I can do."

Angie sipped at the scalding-hot coffee. "Sure there is. Where are all the suggestions that were in the suggestion box? I used to slip one in that box once a week."

"You're the one who . . . I still have them all in my office. They were good suggestions. I ran each and every one of them by my father, but he vetoed all of them. I'm being kind when I say he's in a time warp."

"I know. I drove him home from the rehab center yesterday. He didn't say much to me, but he did open up to my mother, who in turn passed it all on to me, and I am now telling you. What a round-robin. Why can't people just say what's in their minds and hearts?"

"Why are you telling me all this?" Josh asked, suspicion ringing in his voice. "I thought you hated my guts."

Angie looked genuinely puzzled at his remark. "I don't hate you personally. I don't even know you. I hate what you did. I guess I should say I hate what you didn't do, but I didn't understand what was going on. I have ideas," she said quietly.

"It's too late, Angie. The store needs mega revenues for the Christmas season or the doors close in January. Dad . . ."

"You scared the devil out of your father, according to my mother. He's onboard now. You have carte blanche to do whatever you want. I have ideas," she repeated.

In spite of himself, Josh was intrigued. "It's the middle of September, Angie."

"That's almost two months until the Christmas season kicks off. If we hunker down, with no interference, I think we might be able to make this a banner season. I'm game if you are." Angie waited, hardly daring to breathe, waiting for Josh's answer.

"I guess I owe my old man one more shot at it. If nothing else but to prove I wasn't a know-it-all. If, and it's a big *if,* we pull it off, I'm still leaving for London after the first of the year. I committed, and I never go back on my word."

"That's your decision, Josh. I, for one, would never try to talk you out of something if your mind is made up. I guess that's a holdover kind of thing from when I was a kid. I have a ton of stuff to do today. How do you feel about getting some Chinese at the Jade Pagoda this evening after the store closes? We could talk in detail and make a plan. That's if you're serious. If you are, check all those suggestions I bombarded you with. There's a game plan in there."

Josh propped his elbows on the table. "Did you just ask me to dinner? A date?"

Angie laughed. "Well, yeah," she said. "Now that we're . . . uh . . . friends, I thought . . ." She flushed a bright pink when she caught Josh smiling at her. "I never asked a guy for a date before. It's a little embarrassing."

Josh threw his head back and laughed, a sound that sent shivers up Angie's back. "Now you know a guy's worst fear. Asking a girl for a date is traumatic. I accept. I'll meet you by the loading dock at six-ten. Does that work for you?"

"Yes. I want you to think about something today. I'd like to see you close the store for two days. Get rid of all that outdated merchandise on the floor. Close off the second floor until we can decide what we're going to do, what we're going to specialize in. Like I said, I have some great ideas."

Josh felt his throat close up. "Close the store! In the middle of the week? That had never happened in the lifetime of the store. Are you sure you have a plan?"

"I do. It will work, too, as long as you don't fight me. Look, I'm giving up the lease. It's all yours. That alone should prove I'm on your side. Besides, I hate the thought of going job hunting. Do we have a deal?"

Josh gulped but nodded. Angie's hand shot out. He reached for it, marveling at how soft her hand was in his.

Josh smiled.

Angie smiled.

Throw your line into the pond and reel him in, Bess had said. Angie giggled all the way back to the gift wrap department, which she'd just given away.

The first thing she did when she walked behind the counter was to call her mother. "Josh said okay, but he's still leaving in January because he committed to Harrods. I'm hoping he might change his mind. We're in business, Mom. Listen, I'm going to have Bess pick you up and take you home. I have tons of stuff to do. You can work the phones when you get home. You okay with that? Okay, now listen up . . ." She went on to detail the outline of her plan.

"Yes, honey. It all makes sense. I just hope

you can do it all in two months. The vendors aren't all that cooperative at this time of year. Is it okay to tell Angus?"

"Sure. Your job is to make sure he doesn't waffle on us. Talk it up real good, Mom."

"Okay, honey. Congratulations!"

"Bess, instead of taking me home, take me to Mr. Eagle's house. It's just a few miles out of your way since it's on the corner of Plainfield Road and Park Avenue. Angus has a ramp, so I won't have a problem with the steps. Angie can pick me up later."

Bess raised her eyebrows but only nodded. Something was going on. She wondered when Eva or Angie would confide in her. She didn't like being kept in the dark. And now this visit to the Eagle home. Something was definitely going on.

"Just park in the back, Bess. The ramp is by the kitchen door. At least it was years ago, when Angus's father had to use a wheelchair. No, no, don't help me. I have to do this myself. I have my cane. Thanks for bringing me here, Bess. You're a good friend."

"Is there anything I can do, Eva?"

"Not right now, but very shortly there will be plenty for you to do. Have a nice day now. Go, go! I'm fine."

At the kitchen door, Eva used her cane to rap on the glass pane. When there was no response, she opened the door and stepped into the kitchen. She took a moment to look around. She'd spent a lot of time in this kitchen, catering to Mrs. Angus Eagle. The truth was, as Angie pointed out more times than she wanted to remember, she spent more time here than she did in her own kitchen. She suspected Angie still held that against her.

It was all so long ago.

"Angus, it's Eva," she called out. "Are you here?"

"I'm in the den. What in the world are you doing here? Are you all right? How did you get here? Good Lord, Eva, are you sure you should be out and about? Come in, come in. Sit down."

Eva could hardly wait to sit down. Once there she wondered how she was going to get up out of the depths of the deep, comfortable couch. She'd worry about that later. "I suppose I could have called you when I got home, but for some reason I didn't want to be alone. I thought since I'm clumsy by nature, I might fall or something. So I decided to come here. You're stuck with me until Angie can pick me up, which won't be till later this evening. Or, I can take a taxi."

"Nonsense. I'm grateful for the company. I was just sitting here thinking about how badly I've fouled things up. Josh still won't take my calls, and I was asleep when he got home last night. I've been calling him since eight this morning. My son can be very unforgiving. Is your daughter like that?"

"At times. When I was standing in your kitchen I was thinking about how angry she got when I had to cook dinner for your family. Then I would rush home and cook dinner for my own family, and it was always late. Then I had to rush back and clean up because your wife wouldn't do it. That meant Angie had to clear up my own kitchen. It's one of the reasons why she doesn't like you. She thought you took advantage of me."

Angus looked dazed. "I didn't know that, Eva. What I mean is I didn't know you went home to cook for your family, and then came back here. You should have said something. I would have cleared the dishes myself. There's no point now in me trying to make apologies to you for my wife. But I am sorry, Eva."

Eva stared at her old boss. "Angus, who did you think cooked my family's dinner those days?"

Angus threw his hands in the air. "I guess I never thought about it. You should have said something at the time. What do you want me to say?"

Eva snapped her fingers in Angus's direction. "Earth to Angus! Your wife told me if I complained to you, she would fire me. I needed the job. She was so demanding. I wanted to quit so many times, but my family needed the money I brought in."

"Eva, I am so very sorry. I didn't know. If there was a strain between you two, then why would my wife insist I turn over the gift wrap department to you? It doesn't make sense."

"She didn't want me around in the afternoon when she ... when she ... entertained. It was to ensure I never said anything. Fill in the blanks, Angus, and I am never going to talk about this again. Are we clear on that?"

"No, we are not clear on anything. When

you imply something like that you need to . . . to explain *exactly* what you're saying. We're talking about my deceased wife here. Eva?"

"How many ways are there to say your wife entertained in the afternoons while you were at the store and your son was out somewhere or away. She did not entertain women with tea parties. I only ever saw one man and that was quite by accident, so I cannot give you a name. That's it, Angus. Now, leave it alone."

Angus rubbed at his jaw. By the stubborn set of Eva's chin, he knew she had said the last word on the subject. "I didn't know. Something like that never occurred to me."

Eva picked up her cane and waved it around. "I didn't know, I didn't know. That's all you've been saying for several days now. What *did* you know, if anything?" she asked sourly. "Look at the mess you're in, and now I'm in the same mess because my daughter is going to be out of a job, and I'll be losing my share of the profits. 'I didn't know' is not good enough, Angus."

Angus felt his shoulders start to shake. He choked up and turned to Eva. "It's my only defense. I was so obsessed with the store, keeping it going, trying to stay ahead of all the upstarts coming into town. I didn't want to fail my father. I see now where I was wrong. I'll be honest with you, Eva. I don't know what to do. 'I'm sorry' more or less falls into the same category as 'I didn't know.' Can you help me?"

Eva leaned her cane against the sofa. "Was that so hard, Angus? Asking for help? This is the same position your son finds himself in right now. With a slight difference. He had the good sense to ask you for help, but you stomped on him. He's the one you have to talk to, not me. If you don't, you're going to lose him. Open your heart and your mind, and if he calls you an old fart again, suck it up. We're supposed to be older and wiser, the ones our children come to in need. I think that little ditty just reversed itself."

Angus forced a laugh. Eva thought it the saddest sound she'd ever heard.

"How'd you get so smart, Eva?"

"By trying not to do the things you did. I had to think about my family. We weren't well-off like you were. We struggled for everything. More than once Angie had to wait weeks when she needed new shoes.

There were a lot of things she couldn't have when she was younger because they cost too much money. My husband worked on an assembly line. We had a mortgage payment, car payments, appliance payments. Then we had to save for college. Until you leased me the gift wrap department, we barely made ends meet. I don't want to talk about this anymore, Angus. I want your word that you are not going to interfere with the kids when they do whatever it is they're going to do. Your word, Angus, or I'm leaving and will walk home, at which point I will collapse and my condition will be on your conscience."

"You drive a hard bargain, Eva. You have my word. I'm not going to like what they're going to do, am I?"

"Not one little bit!"

"Can you give me a clue, a hint?"

"Try this one on, they're going to close the store and get rid of all that stuff that came over with the ark."

"The merchandise? That represents money. What . . . What are they going to do with it?"

"My guess is there's going to be one heck of a supersale followed by a bonfire somewhere real soon. Like I said, Angus, get over it."

"What the hell, okay. Want to stay for dinner? Dolores is still with me, so you know there's something delicious waiting."

"I'd love to stay for dinner."

"Do we have a date, then?"

"We do indeed have a date. Speaking of dates, Angie and Josh are going out for Chinese this evening. I rather imagine the two of them will be venting to one another about the two of us," Eva said.

"Imagine that!"

"I think the two of them think you and I had an affair years ago," Eva said, her face taking on a rosy hue.

Eyes twinkling, Angus said, "Imagine that!"

Eva laughed. "Yes, imagine that!"

Chapter Four

The Jade Pagoda was bustling when Josh held the door for Angie. They were shown to a table into the back section of the room that was separated from the other diners by strings of silver beads—beads that tinkled as the servers walked in and out. It was a pleasant sound, as was the fountain that trickled over lava rocks in the middle of the room. A smiling Buddha holding a fortune cookie sat atop the fountain, welcoming all guests.

"I come here sometimes just to relax," Josh said, waving his arm about. "Win Lee told me if you rub the Buddha's belly he'll bring you good luck. For some reason, that little fat guy never worked for me."

Angie smiled. "Maybe it's because you aren't Chinese."

"Do you think?"

"No! I just said that to have something to say."

"Do you come here often?"

"After my father died Mom and I used to come every Friday night. When she went to Florida to help my aunt I stopped coming, mainly because I don't like to eat alone. When Mom finally came back we just never picked up where we left off. I agree with you, though, it is soothing and peaceful in here. People seem to whisper when they're here. Then again, they might have some top-of-the-line acoustics."

Josh held a chair for Angie before he took his own seat. "My mother wasn't one of those warm, fuzzy mothers. I used to hang out at friends' houses because I liked the way they interacted with their mothers. It sounds like you and your mother had a good relationship."

"We did. Sort of. Kind of. I hated you and your family for a long time," Angie blurted. "That . . . That probably colored my deter-mination to fight you on the lease."

Josh looked so shocked at her words, Angie hastened to explain. "My mother spent more time at your house than she did at her own. Every time I needed her, she was at your house. Back then I didn't understand my family's need for money. I also didn't like it that my mother cleaned your house and cooked for you. Our dinners were always late. Then my mother would go back to your house to clean up after your dinner while I was the one who cleaned up ours. I wasn't always as kind as I could have been to my mother. Of course I regret that now. My dad did his best."

Josh blinked. He struggled to find something to say. "I guess I would have felt the same way. As a kid you just more or less take things for granted. I'm ashamed to admit I never thought about Eva in terms of having a family to take care of. She was just there sometimes. I'm sorry if that hurts your feelings, Angie."

"Well, that was then, this is now. We were both kids back then. You know what they say, you can't unring the bell. Isn't it ironic that we've come together like this? Your father with his hip operation, Mom with her knee replacement. If it weren't for that, you and I would still be battling one another. I guess everything happens for a reason."

"So we have a truce. At least for now."

"Yes. We have to make it all work. I think

we can. Did you look over the suggestions I put in the box?"

"I did. Most of them are really good. I particularly like your idea to turn the gift wrap department into a Christmas wonderland. But the retail side of me can't quite accept the idea that for a fee you're willing to gift wrap merchandise from other stores."

"The idea, Josh, is, those customers will browse the store and buy point-of-purchase merchandise with the money going into Eagle's coffers. The gift wrapping is not going to be cheap, I can tell you that. Most of that money will now go into your coffers, too."

Josh nodded as he motioned to the waitress. He told her that they were ready for some green tea. "I sent out memos today. We'll close the store this weekend for two days. Three if we need an extra day. I also made arrangements for everything on both floors that has been marked down twice to go to Goodwill. Everything else will be sold below cut-rate to two different discount stores. This will get underway Friday night after the store closes. You might want to walk through the store to see if you think there's anything we can salvage."

"Get rid of it all. We're starting fresh. No

holdovers. You also need to get an electrician to install some better lighting. A nice new, shiny tile floor will work wonders."

"I'm not a miracle worker, Angie. Two days, even three, it's a monumental task."

"Offer a bonus. Tap into your workforce. The salespeople have spouses who might like to make some extra money. Your new motto from here on in is, 'The Eagle Soars.' Start running ads in the local newspaper. Get some flyers made up. Hire some kid to put them on the windshields of the cars in the parking lot. Have a raffle every day. All entries have to have a sales receipt attached. That kind of thing. In order to make money, you have to spend money. You might need to close for two *weeks*."

Josh brought the little cup of tea to his lips. His gaze locked with Angie's. "Two weeks! Young lady, you're scary!"

"I'm going to take that as a compliment. A scary compliment. What did you do about laying off your staff?"

Josh leaned back in his chair. "It was hard, but I did it. I think a lot of the staff were more or less relieved. I laid everyone off for three weeks except for a few I knew we would need. I don't know why, but I thought some, if not most of them, welcomed the decision. Some of the staff are my father's age. Past retirement age, but Dad wouldn't let me lay them off. I checked all their files, and none of them are in dire need of money. They work to have something to do. I can't fault them for that."

"You might be able to use the grandmothers to man the day care I want to put in on the second floor. Think about it, Josh. Mothers dropping off their children so they can shop! At thirty dollars a day with lunch and snacks, it would be a bargain. Of course you'd have some moms who just might want a few hours at a time. We'd work out a reasonable fee. I can see you taking in a couple of thousand bucks a day. The more activities you have for the kids, the more demand for the service. The kids would get a day with a real grandma who will read them stories, sing songs with them, rock the babies. Your dad and my mom will be perfect if we can get them to agree and at the same time still be in the loop. I already earmarked all the things on the floor that could go into the day care. I have a lot of friends whose kids have outgrown many of their things. I can ask to borrow them. Next year, if this all works, we could really do a bang-up job, but for now, I think this will work."

"My father is going to go nuclear!" Josh laughed. "Day care! Never in a million years would I have come up with that idea. You're right, you are an idea person!"

"Thank you, sir!"

The waitress showed up to take their order. Angie ordered a dish called Volcano Shrimp, while Josh ordered a sizzling seafood platter. Both now crunched down on hard noodles, a bit more relaxed with one another.

As Angie munched, she asked, "What did you think about my idea of having a really huge live Christmas tree in the middle of the floor? And the Santa with his sack of toys?"

"Great idea, but it will seriously deplete floor space. I'm still waiting to see what kind of merchandise we're going to be selling. Not to mention where we're going to get that merchandise. Vendors are notoriously cranky and in no hurry to get the deliveries to you during the year. They're worse over the holidays. I hesitate to ask this, but is there a Plan B lurking anywhere?"

"Plan B? More or less. Incentives. Cash on delivery. If the merchandise angle falls short of my expectations, I think we could more than make up for the revenues with services, like cooking lessons, knitting lessons, all kinds of hourly lessons. Kind of like the YMCA. I think I'd like some Chinese beer now."

"You like Chinese beer! Imagine that! I like it myself." Josh signaled the waitress and placed the order. When it arrived, he held up his bottle to clink it against Angie's. "What should we drink to?"

"To success, what else?"

Angie drank from the bottle, ignoring the glass sitting on the table. Josh seemed mesmerized by his dinner companion as she kept upending the bottle. He'd never dated a girl who really liked beer, much less drank it from the bottle. He grinned from ear to ear. He took a moment to wonder what it would be like to kiss those full red lips. He just knew in his gut he'd soar like an eagle.

Angie and Josh were the last to leave the Jade Pagoda. With way too much Chinese beer under their belts, Josh called for a taxi. "We can pick our cars up in the morning."

"What time is it?" Angie mumbled as she looked at the array of beer bottles on the table.

Josh peered at his watch. He knew he was snookered when he couldn't read the numbers. "Late," he said triumphantly. "Do you have to be home before . . . before . . . the moon comes out?" Damn, he was witty tonight. And charming.

"I was . . . I think I was supposed to . . . Maybe I wasn't . . . Where is my mother, do you know?"

Angie was looking at him like he had the answer at his fingertips. He didn't want to disappoint his new friend. "I'm not sure. I'll help you look for her."

"That's wonderful. Thank you. I think she might be . . . you know, pissed that I forgot about her."

Josh pulled himself up to his full six-foot-two-inch height and said, "We *were* busy."

"Yes, we were. Why don't we walk home, Josh? We might see them on the way. Oh, I remember now, my mother is keeping your father company. That's not good. Oh, shit! My cell phone is off."

Josh burst out laughing and couldn't stop. Suddenly this peppery young woman he'd dined with, drunk with, was all too human. "How many times did she call?"

"Well, guess what, Josh? I can't really see

those itsy-bitsy little numbers. A lot. And who's paying for this taxi?" Angie asked as it pulled up.

Josh stepped up to the plate. "Eagle's," he said smartly.

"Tell him to take us to your house. Then he can take me and my mother home. She is going to be so . . . so . . ."

"Pissed?" Josh asked, howling with laughter. "My old man is going to go through the roof. I need to move out and get my own place. I think he needs me, and that's why he likes me living with him. I bet your mother feels the same way. They're old. Old people think like that."

They got into the cab and Josh gave the driver his address.

"Nah, it's all a game to keep us in line. Those two are more independent than either one of us. If you had your own place, I could visit you."

Whoa. Josh leaned over and kissed her ruby-red lips. At least he thought they were ruby red. He didn't care if they were ruby red or purple.

"You're a good kisser," Angie said a long time later. "I think the driver wants you to pay him. Are we at your house? Time does fly when you're having fun, doesn't it? Yesireee, you are a good kisser."

"Damn straight I am. A good kisser. Not because I had . . . have a lot of practice," Josh said, handing the driver a twenty-dollar bill for the five-minute ride. "Keep the change," he said magnanimously.

"Wait for me, mister, I have to pick up my mother."

Walking up the driveway, Josh stopped and reached for Angie's arm. "Should we have a story? You know, why we're so uncaring, so negligent, so . . ."

"Drunk?"

"Egg-zactly," Josh said, roaring with laughter.

"No defense is the best defense. I don't really care. Do you care, Josh?"

"I don't think I do. Tomorrow I might."

Josh was about to open the kitchen door when it swung open. He looked up to see Eva Bradford glaring at him. His father's face defied description. A sappy expression on his face, Josh said, "Good evening, everybody." He made a low, sweeping bow. Not to be outdone, Angie did the same thing and almost fell on her face.

"They're both drunk," Angus said.

Josh straightened his jacket and looked over at Angie. "They're worried about us while they've been here . . . noodling . . . canoodling . . . Oh, shit, messing around. Hrumph!" he sniffed. "Your chariot awaits, Mrs. Bradford. It's a taxi."

"Mom!" Angie looked properly horrified. "I knew it! I knew it! You two . . . You lied to me. You were doing what he said . . . noodling around," she said, pointing to Josh.

"We were not. You're inebriated, Angie. Shame on you!"

"Joshua, go to your room."

"Why should I? No! I'm moving out and Angie is going to come and visit me. When I move to England, she's coming to visit me there, too. So, Pop, what do you have to say to that?"

"Talk to me when you're sober, and I will have plenty to say. These ladies need to go home right now. You need to go to bed, Joshua."

Josh looked over at Angie and said, "He only calls me Joshua when he's really mad. Come along, fair lady, I always see my dates home. Do you want me to stay with you until I find an apartment?"

"Sure," Angie said agreeably. "Mom can stay here. Win-win. Works for everybody. I think I'm going to be sick."

Eva fixed her angry gaze on Josh, and said, "Young man, I am holding you personally responsible for my daughter's condition. Do something!"

Josh stepped up to the plate for the second time that evening. "And I and I alone accept that responsibility." He offered up a second sweeping bow and fell over, toppling one of the kitchen chairs. "The meter is running," he said as Angie bolted for the kitchen door.

"Do something, Angus!" Eva hissed.

"It's your daughter who's . . . Well, she's . . ."

"Your son got my daughter drunk. Don't deny it."

From his position on the floor Josh said, "No, no, she got that way all by herself. She had so many ideas." A moment later he was sound asleep on the kitchen floor.

Angus shrugged. Eva did her best not to laugh.

Angie came back and looked down at Josh. "He's not . . . dead, is he?"

"I'm thinking tomorrow morning he might wish he was," Angus said.

Angie sat down on the floor next to Josh. "Oh, I had so many ideas. Josh liked all my ideas." She untangled herself and laid her head on Josh's stomach.

"I say we just leave them here," Eva said. "I'll let the taxi driver go. You get some blankets and pillows."

"Then what?" Angus asked.

"Do you want me to draw you a map, Angus? Do you want to make your son out to be a liar? We're going to canoodle."

"Oh!" Angus wondered if Eva picked up on the anxiety in his voice.

And then she was back in the kitchen, a wicked gleam in her eyes.

Chapter Five

The sun was just making its way to the horizon when Josh stirred on the kitchen floor. He felt like a ton of bricks was sitting on top of his chest. Somehow, he managed to crank open one eye. A nanosecond later, his other eye flew open. He gasped. The woman wrapped around his torso stirred and mumbled something he couldn't quite hear. Josh moved. Then the woman moved and rolled over onto the floor. She was awake in an instant, looking around as she tried to figure out where she was and why she was lying on a strange kitchen floor. A tortured groan escaped her lips.

Josh groaned in sync as he struggled to sit up. His eyes were as wild-looking as his hair, which was standing on end. Angie didn't look much better.

"Ah, did we . . . ? What I mean is . . . Do you remember?" he finished lamely.

Angie rubbed her temples in an attempt to ease the pounding in her head. "No, I don't think, and . . . No, I don't know," she said just as lamely.

"Why are we . . . ? We slept on the floor?" Josh asked this as though sleeping on the floor was one of the Seven Wonders of the World. "Why did we do that?" he asked as he got to his feet. He stretched out a long arm to pull Angie to her feet.

"Maybe because we were drunk?" It was a question and a statement.

Josh looked down at the floor to see the pillows and blankets. He cursed under his breath as he pointed them out to Angie. She looked away in embarrassment. "Are you sure we didn't . . . ?"

"I think I would remember *that,*" Josh said, walking over to the coffeepot. He thought his head was going to pound right off his neck. He filled the pot, measured coffee, and pressed a button. "Do you want some orange juice?"

"I didn't even brush my teeth. It feels like something is growing in my mouth," Angie said. "No on the orange juice. Oh, God, we left our cars at the Jade Pagoda. Now I have to walk there to get it. Damn. I look like someone who just . . ."

"Had a wild night of sex?" Josh asked.

"Stop saying that. We didn't . . . I'm almost . . . No, I'm sure we didn't. We never should have had that plum wine after drinking beer. This is all your fault, Josh. You said we couldn't insult Mr. Win Lee by refusing the complimentary wine."

"You guzzled half that carafe all by yourself. You even got sick. I did not get sick. I only pretended to drink the wine."

"Ha! My mother . . . Your father . . . They saw us. They covered us up. Where's my mother?"

"How should I know? You're her daughter, you should know where your mother is at all times. What kind of daughter are you, anyway?"

"The kind that doesn't know where her mother is. I bet your father . . . I bet he took unfair advantage of her with her new knee. My mother is naive and not the least bit worldly. Your father is a shark. Just like you." Oh, God, did she just say that?

"Are you accusing my father of attacking your mother? My father, who can barely walk, who just had a hip replacement? That father?" Damn, his head was pounding so bad he could hardly stand it. A shark! Damn.

"Ha! Your father's new hip and my mother's new knee are those *titanium* joint things. That probably makes them almost bionic. They can *walk*. If they can walk, they can do *other* things."

"My father would never . . ."

"Yeah, well, neither would my mother. Your father is a lot bigger than my little mother. She only weighs a hundred pounds. Your father must weigh two hundred. I rest my case. Oh, please give me some of that coffee before my head explodes. This kitchen hurts my eyes."

Josh poured coffee. "Do you always complain like this so early in the morning? What's wrong with this kitchen?" Josh asked, looking around the ancient kitchen.

"It's outdated for one thing, just like the store. I never saw a stove with legs. What the heck is that funky-looking round thing on top of your refrigerator? I don't see a dishwasher. Not that it's any of your business, but the only time I complain this early in the morning is when I'm hungover, which is almost never, and when my mother goes missing. Have you noticed we're fighting?"

"Everything works. We're not fighting, I'm discussing things and you're . . . Well, what you're doing is complaining."

Josh gulped from his coffee cup. Angie did the same. The word noodling came to Josh's mind. Wouldn't it be a hoot if his old man had more action going for him than he did? He started to laugh at the thought. He shared his thought with Angie, who, despite her pounding head, also started to laugh. Sometimes he was so damn witty he couldn't stand himself.

Behind the kitchen door Eva and Angus listened to their offsprings' mating call. At least that's what Eva told Angus it was. Angus just shook his head. "She's right about your kitchen, it's a disgrace. You need to get with the program, Angus."

Angus nudged the door open a sliver and let his gaze roam around the kitchen. "I like things I'm comfortable with, and I'm comfortable with this kitchen. Everything works just fine." Then, tongue in cheek, he said, "Your daughter doesn't really know anything about you, does she, Eva? You are not naive, and you're as worldly as they come, if last night was any sort of indicator. Does your daughter know how good you are at improvisation?"

Eva giggled. "That will be enough of that, Angus. What are they doing now?"

"My son is whispering in your daughter's ear. That could mean any number of things. I suggest we go back to our chairs and let them find us. Pretend to be asleep."

Twenty minutes later, Eva reared up from her chair. "I don't think it's going to happen, Angus. They aren't going to find us," she said, limping over to the doorway. They're gone. What time does your day lady come in? Do you think she can give me a ride home?"

"She's due right now. Of course she can take you home. Will you come back, or should I have her bring me to your house later on? Better yet, why don't I call a car service so we can have a driver at our disposal. Will that work for you, Eva?"

"Yes, I think it will. You have my cell phone number. Call me when your day gets under way."

* * *

Thirty minutes later Eva entered her own house. She stopped at the refrigerator for a bag of frozen peas, then made her way into the family room, where she settled herself in her favorite chair. She sighed with relief when the cold from the frozen peas seeped into her swollen knee. With the three Advil she'd just taken, she knew she would feel better in a little while. She leaned back and closed her eyes. Overhead she could hear the water gurgling in the pipes; Angie washing away the night's activities.

Soon after, Eva's eyes snapped open when she felt a presence near her chair. "Did you have anything to eat, dear?"

"No, but that's okay, I'm not hungry. I'll get a bagel or something in the food court later on. What are you going to do today, Mom?"

"Well, Angus said he was going to hire a driver and come over later. We're going to do our best to pitch in and help Josh with the store. I worry that Eagle's will go under. If that happens, Angus will be destroyed. Did Josh . . . Is he still planning on going to England after New Year's? Did he say?"

Angie perched herself on the arm of the

sofa and stared at her mother. "He's still going. Mom, the guy tried for ten years to get
Eagle's off the ground. I think I'd pack it in
after ten years myself. His father is a selfish
old man. You can tell him I said that, too.
You stayed there all night, didn't you?" Her
tone was so accusatory, Eva flinched.

Eva brushed at the hair falling over her
forehead and adjusted the bag of peas on
her knee. "I think I'm a little past the stage
where I have to account to you for my
whereabouts, Angie. Where I was or wasn't
last night has nothing to do with our current
situation. I'm sure you noticed I didn't say
anything to you about how you spent your
night or the condition you were in. Because,
my daughter, you are old enough to make
your own decisions, and you are account-
able for your actions. Now, run along so you
aren't late."

Angie bit down on her lower lip. She de-
bated presenting an argument but didn't
think she could possibly win any war of
words with her mother. "Mom, where are all
those cottage-industry magazines you sub-
scribe to?"

"In the basement in the cabinet over the
washing machine. Why?"

"I'm going to contact some of them. Everything for the most part is homemade. Small businesses like that have a hard time marketing their wares. I'm thinking . . . Now, this is just a thought . . . But maybe we can make this Christmas season a homemade, down-home Christmas. People love to buy things that are made by hand. If any of those little businesses have inventory, that will help us. What do you think?"

"I think it's a wonderful idea. I really do. I worry that vendors won't be able to get merchandise to you in time for the holidays. It might be too late, dear."

Angie stamped her foot. "No negative thinking, remember? Anyway, we won't know if we don't try. Josh wants to go off knowing he did the best he could. Failure isn't an option at this point." Angie pointed a finger at her mother and said, "Since you seem to have the inside track with Angus Eagle, it's your job to keep him out of our hair so we can make it happen. The minute he sticks his nose into this venture, I'm outta there, and I feel confident in saying Josh will flip him the bird and leave on the spot. Do you think you can convey all that to Mr. Eagle? While you're at it you should get him to work on that kitchen of his. In case, you know, you ever want to move in there."

A minute later, Eva could hear her daughter stomping her way to the basement. She made three trips carrying the boxes out to her car. One of the things she loved about her daughter was that she always followed through on things. If there was a way to make Eagle's Department Store soar, Angie was the one to make it happen.

The second Eva heard Angie drive off, she picked up the phone to call Angus. "I'm ready, Angus. Have your driver pick me up; we're going to take a trip. And, Angus, bring your check book. Where are we going? To the Amish country, where we're going to buy everything they have that's for sale. We're going to eat homemade bread, homemade soup and homemade pie for lunch. I'm excited, Angus. Almost as excited as I was last night. Like I said, I'm ready. I'll be waiting on the porch. I don't like to be kept waiting, Angus." A low, throaty, intimate laugh erupted when she heard Angus's reply.

* * *

Josh Eagle happened to be on the loading dock when Angie arrived. He was dressed in jeans, a UCLA sweatshirt, and battered high-top sneakers. *Toss your line in the pond and reel him in.* He looked good enough to make a girl's head spin. Not that hers was spinning. Well, maybe it was revolving just a tiny bit. "Hi," she said brightly, as he reached out to take the box of magazines from her. She went back out to her car to get the other two boxes and they headed to her shop.

"What are you going to do with these?" Josh asked when he set the last box on the counter in the gift wrap department. Angie explained. She liked the sudden twinkle she saw in Josh's eyes. "Do you think it will work?" His voice was beyond anxious-sounding.

"A homemade, down-home Christmas! Isn't that what Christmas is all about? I'm almost certain it will work. I really am. But we need a campaign to go with it. I think you might have to call an advertising agency to get it off the ground. We're just two people, Josh, we're going to need help. I'm determined that you are going to go out of here with a bang. Along with your father's

respect." Now it was her turn to sound anxious. "Are you having second thoughts
about leaving?"

"No, not at all," he lied with a straight face.
Suddenly the allure of the prestigious Harrods and going to England were losing their
appeal.

"I know this is none of my business, but
do you have an operating account to draw
from? Do I have to run everything by you, or
do you trust me to order things without your
approval? How do you want me to arrange
payment?"

"Yes, no, and just charge everything to the
store. I'll give you a corporate card. And,
yes, I trust you. I have phone calls to make
and several meetings with some of the old
staff. The discount people are here to start
moving all the merchandise. Alma Bennett
is in charge of all that. The minute everything is out of the store, an electrician is
coming in. And then the painters, who
promised to do their work at night. A clean-
ing crew will be right on their tails to clean
and polish the new floor. That's more or less
behind-the-scenes stuff. Our real challenge
is to get merchandise to fill the space. I'll
call an advertising agency at some point

this morning to get that going. You'll have to sit in on that meeting. How about lunch?"

"I'd love to have lunch with you. How about twelve thirty in the food court?"

"Works for me." His hands jammed into his jean pockets, Josh started to whistle as he made his way to the second floor. He could hardly wait for lunch.

"Are those stars I see in your eyes, Angie?" Bess asked.

"Nope. Just new contact lenses."

"Yeah, right. Okay, what's up? What do you want me to do?"

Angie quickly outlined her plans, then told Bess everything that had transpired since she'd seen her last.

"Wow! Can we do it all in time? What about the vendors? They promise everything and give you zip."

"I know, I know, so we're going to insist on penalty clauses. We're also not really going to count on them. We're going to make this a down-home Christmas and try . . . I said *try,* to get up and running with the cottage-industry merchandise. Today you and I are going to scour these books, call the little companies, and see what we can get here in time. We won't have to worry about gift wrapping today since the store is closed. Everything is on target with your husband and the decorations, right?"

"John is on it. He loves woodworking. He's made prototypes and is working off them. It will all be done in plenty of time. So tell me what's responsible for the sparks in your eyes. Is it Josh Eagle? *Wooeee,* you're blushing, Angie."

"I am not. It's . . It's really warm in here. Now, let's make some coffee and hit these magazines."

The morning passed quickly as the women consumed two pots of coffee while earmarking pages for further discussion. By noon, Angie's yellow legal pad was full of telephone numbers and notes on which merchandise she was interested in.

With one box of magazines to go, Angie washed her hands, fluffed up her hair, and checked her lipstick, ready to meet Josh for lunch. "Do you want me to bring you something for lunch, Bess?"

"No, I brought my lunch. You do remember how to flirt, don't you, Angie?"

Angie stuck out her tongue in Bess's general direction, but in the end she had to laugh. "Do I look okay?"

"You look good enough to go fishing. Remember what I told you about tossing your line in the pond. Play it cool, and he's all yours. That's assuming you want him. From where I'm sitting, the guy is one heck of a catch. Go already. It's not nice to keep the boss waiting."

"Jeez, he is my boss, isn't he? That's going to take some getting used to. Are you sure I look okay, Bess?"

"You look fine, now go. Just remember to smile a lot. Pretend you're interested in what he has to say. You don't always have to be a know-it-all."

On the way to the food court Angie wondered how many women were waiting in the wings for Josh Eagle. She just knew he went for the long-legged modeling types with their glossy smiles, sun-streaked hair and designer clothes. And, according to Bess, who was up on all things Josh Eagle, if any of them had a brain, they'd be dangerous. Angie sniffed. Bess didn't know everything even though she said she did.

Josh was waiting for her by the Philly Cheese Steak booth, which probably meant that's what he intended to eat for lunch. He was holding a twin to the legal pad she was carrying. Ah, a business lunch. She smiled.

Josh waved the yellow pad. "Guess this means we're going to work through our lunch. I had a pretty good morning. How about you?"

"Bess and I made some progress. I want to run it all by you before I make some calls this afternoon. I just want half a sandwich and a cup of coffee. And a brownie." She smiled. And smiled.

"Are you happy about something? You keep smiling. Is it anything you want to share?"

Angie made a mental note to slap Bess upon her return to the gift wrap shop. "Actually, I am. Happy, that is. I can see light at the end of the tunnel, believe it or not. How about you?"

"You look pretty when you smile. You should do it more often. But to answer your question, I certainly feel a lot more positive than I did yesterday morning."

Angie didn't know what else to do because her heart was beating so fast, so she smiled. And smiled. Then she smiled some more. *I'm still going to slap you, Bess.*

Chapter Six

It was midafternoon when Angie pushed herself away from her tiny desk where she'd been making call after call in the hopes of saving Eagle's Department Store from closing its doors.

"How about a nice, cold soda pop?" Bess asked as she peered into the minifridge in the alcove where the coffeepot was located. Angie nodded.

Bess pulled over a stool and sat down next to Angie. She looked pointedly at the canvas bag at Angie's feet. Poking at the colorful bag with her foot, she asked, "You haven't told Eva, have you? Or Josh?"

Angie bit down on her lower lip. "I meant to tell Mom. I had it all planned, and then she up and decided to have her knee done. I didn't want to upset her. I don't . . . What I mean is, I don't think I owe Josh an explanation. As soon as Mom is in high gear again, I'll tell her. She knew this was not a forever job for me. I agreed to help out when my aunt died, then things went south. It's time for me to do what I do best, and this isn't it. Besides, she has you, Bess. It will all work out." Her tone was so defensive, Bess winced.

"Did you sign the contract yet?" Bess asked.

The contract Bess was referring to was an employment contract between Angie and the Sunnyvale, California Board of Education for Angie to teach the third grade starting next year.

"I have three more weeks before I have to submit the contract. I can overnight it. I know, I know, I will tell my mother before the three weeks are up. Don't go getting your panties in a wad, Bess. I know what I'm doing."

Bess pushed her granny glasses farther up on her nose. "I don't think it's so much that you'll be leaving as where you're going. Why couldn't you take a job around here? Why do you have to go all the way to California?"

Angie jumped off her chair. "See! See! You

sound just like my mother. I'm thirty-five years old. It's time for me to do what I want. I stayed here after my dad died so Mom wouldn't be alone. I still live at home, for God's sake. What thirty-five-year-old do you know who still lives at home with their parents?"

"Josh Eagle," Bess said smartly. "I think he's thirty-seven, though."

"Well, he's leaving, too. I guess that makes us both late bloomers."

Bess mumbled something that sounded like, *"You just tossed your line in the pond, now you're going to let it sink to the bottom."* Angie ignored her and picked up the phone again to make another call.

Standing outside of both women's line of sight, Josh Eagle turned on his heel and left as silently as when he arrived. His shoulders were slumped, and he was dragging his feet.

Why should he care if Angie Bradford was leaving in January? He was leaving, too, so he wouldn't miss her. Would he?

The thought was so disturbing, Josh stopped in the middle of the main floor where all kinds of activity was going on. He felt like one of the mannequins as he watched the merchandise being wheeled out of the store on dollies.

The urge to throw his hands in the air and run as far and as fast as his sneakered feet would take him was so strong, Josh reached out to grasp the edge of one of the counters to hold himself in check.

Damn it to hell, he liked Angie Bradford. *Really* liked Angie Bradford. For some strange reason he suddenly felt like she'd betrayed him.

Josh made his way to his secret haven, the stairwell that led to the second floor. This was where he always went when things went sour with his father, or when he needed to get a handle on something. He sat down on the steps and looked at the hole in his sneaker over his big toe. He looked around at the gray stone walls that suddenly seemed as gloomy as his thoughts.

Josh knew what he should do, but did he have the guts to do it? For the first two years of his tenure at Eagle's, he'd spent a lot of time out here in the stairwell trying to decide if he should go toe to toe with his father. Out of respect, he'd never done that, and now here he was. He needed to go to Angie, tell her he'd overheard her conversation, and ask her point-blank what her intentions were. She'd probably tell him it was none of his business, and he'd have to agree with her. But . . . And there was always a but . . . He liked her, *really* liked her. That's exactly what he should do. No doubt about it. Oh, yeah. So what if she told him it was none of his business? He was a big boy, he could handle a put-down.

Before he could change his mind, Josh banged open the door leading to the main floor of the store, where he retraced his steps.

As soon as he hit the small entryway to the gift department, Josh called Angie's name. Bess took one look at his face and excused herself.

"What's up?" Angie looked up from the notes she was making on her pad.

"Why didn't you tell me you were planning on leaving?" His voice was so cold, so gruff-sounding, Angie felt her heart kick up a beat. She immediately swung into her defense mode, crossed her arms over her chest, and glared at the tall, good-looking man towering over her. "What?"

"You heard me. I came down here to talk to you, but you were talking to Bess and I didn't want to intrude so I waited . . ."

"And listened to a private conversation. That's pretty sneaky in my opinion. I don't think it's any of your business, Josh. Which brings me to my next question. Why do you care what I do or when I do it as long as it doesn't interfere with the store?"

Josh hated the stubborn look he was see-ing. He was all too familiar with that look. He'd seen it every time they met in court. He advanced a step and sat down on the stool Bess had vacated. He hooked his feet in the rungs and rocked back and forth. "I shouldn't care, but I do. I'm not sure why that is. I really didn't mean to eavesdrop. I'm sorry about that. And, you're right, Angie, what you do come January is none of my business. I guess I thought . . . When I told you about leaving, I guess I thought you should have told me about your plans, too. You really should tell your mother. Don't do what I did with my old man."

Somewhat mollified, Angie unfolded her arms and stared at the man sitting on the stool. She licked her lips. "I thought about telling you, but there was so much going on. I didn't want to add to your angst. I know I should have told my mother. If you were listening, then you know I didn't sign the contract yet. Maybe I'm dragging my feet. Maybe it's a mistake. Maybe a lot of things. For some reason I haven't been able to do that. I love the idea of going back to teaching. I love the kids. Working here was great, too, but Mom and I both knew it was temporary.

"You're leaving in January, so why should you care if I stay or go? For all either one of us knows, this little . . . plan we have might not work, and your father ends up having to close the store. It's all one big crapshoot, Josh."

"I like you!" Josh blurted. *Shit, did he just say that?* "I was hoping we could get to know each other better."

Angie's head bobbed up and down. She couldn't believe the words that popped out of her mouth. "I like you, too. I don't want to fight with you, Josh. I'm sick and tired of walking on eggshells. I do enough of that with my mother, and I'm sure you do the same thing with your father. Let's just get

through the next few months and make decisions later on."

"But you said you had to sign the contract
in three weeks."

Angie smiled and Josh's world tilted.
"There will be other contracts, other jobs.
I'm a good teacher. I've had other offers.
The California one was just to get me on an-
other coast. Truce?" she asked, holding out
her hand.

Josh grinned as he grasped her hand.
"Truce. How about dinner tonight?"

"Okay. You're going to come to my house,
ring the bell with flowers in hand, a real
date. Or is this business?"

"Nope, a real date. Flowers, eh? I think I
can handle that. Does seven thirty work for
you?"

"Yes, it works for me, but I was joking
about the flowers."

The conversation was over but Josh didn't
want to leave. "You should see what's going
on out there on the main floor. I'm glad my
father isn't here to see this. He hasn't called
me today. That's not like him."

Angie started to laugh and couldn't stop.
"My mother just called a little while ago.
Seems your father hired a driver and, as we

speak, the two of them are in the Amish country, where they are buying up all the quilts and whatever else the people are willing to sell. They rode from shop to shop in a buggy."

Josh sucked in his breath and for the life of him couldn't think of anything to say other than, "Uh-huh."

Eva settled herself in the town car, her legs extended. She flinched at how swollen and red her knee was. There was no doubt about it, she'd overdone it today. She could hardly wait to put the bag of crushed ice on her knee. They'd picked it up at a 7-Eleven store when they left the Amish country.

"How bad is the pain, Eva?" Angus asked, his voice full of concern.

"Probably as bad as yours. We're two old fools, Angus. At least I am. I didn't think this little trip through. I didn't realize we'd have to get in and out of the buggy so many times. I don't know what I thought. I'm sorry. Do you want some of my Advil?"

Angus held out his hand. He swallowed two of the tablets while Eva took three with the soda pop they'd also bought at the 7-Eleven.

"As soon as the ice and Advil kick in, we'll feel better. You have five weeks on me, Angus. I'm just eight days from surgery. Did you have trouble getting used to the pronged cane?" Eva asked, in the hopes that talking would take her mind off the pain in her knee.

Angus leaned back and closed his eyes. "Not at all. I had trouble with the walker. I felt like I was ninety years old. Tell me this damn trip was worth it, Eva. Just tell me that."

"It was worth it. Five hundred quilts! And all those jams and jellies. Even with all that *horse-trading* you did with the elders, I suspect we might have overpaid a little. The kids will have to mark them up considerably. Everyone wants a homemade quilt."

Angus opened his eyes, then reached for Eva's hand. "What's bothering you, Eva?"

Eva patted Angus's hand. "What makes you think something is bothering me?"

"Because I see something in your eyes. Sometimes if you talk about it, it helps a little. I'm a good listener, Eva."

"It's Angie. She thinks I don't know, but

she's planning on leaving in January just the way your son is leaving. I was looking for something, and for some reason I thought it might be in her book bag. I wasn't spying. There was a teaching contract that she hasn't signed as yet. For a school in Sunnyvale, California. If you want the whole ball of wax, I need to work. If the store closes, I don't know what I'll do. My Social Security isn't all that much. My house is paid off, but the taxes are now more than the mortgage payment was. Angie wasn't really taking a salary, just money as she needed it. We have to pay Bess a regular salary. I'm sure that by January, if the store closes, my knee will be okay. I'll just have to find a job where I can sit part of the time. I just wish I had known about the store's difficulties before I had the operation. I would have put it off. The worst-case scenario is I'll sell the house and move into one of those garden apartments. I don't think apartment living will be too bad. Most of those apartments come with a little terrace. I might even get a cat for my golden years." Eva wound down like a pricked balloon.

Angus digested this information as his

brain whirled and twirled. "You could move in with me, Eva."

"No, Angus, I cannot move in with you. Now, are you sorry you asked me what's wrong?"

"No, not at all. Good friends always share their problems. If there's a way for my pig-headed folly where the store is concerned can be corrected, Josh will do it. I have so many regrets, Eva. I don't think Josh is ever going to forgive me."

"You don't know that for sure, Angus. This is no time for negative thoughts. Parents are allowed to make mistakes. It's human and it's normal. You do your best at the time. However, once our children come of age, there's no more room for mistakes. At least that's how I look at it. In many ways we've both been lucky. Your son stayed with you the way Angie stayed with me. That has to mean something. We can't be selfish now. Do you agree?"

"Yes, I agree. Maybe our answer is to just close the store in January." He watched as Eva nodded her head. For some reason he felt disappointed.

Eva's eyes opened wide. "So, what you're saying is we're quitters. You and I. You said

if there was a way to turn things around,
Josh would find it."

"I did say that. I don't know if it can happen or not. I'm trying to convince myself
that Eagle's won't be closing its doors."

"Let's give them a chance, Angus. But
only from the sidelines. All we'll do is offer
encouragement and compliments. I think
we can do that."

Angus squeezed Eva's hand. "I think so,
too. How's the pain?"

"It's easing up. How's your pain?"

"I feel wonderful," Angus lied.

Bess covered her ears when Angie let out
a shriek that almost split her eardrums.
"What? What, Angie?"

But Angie was out the door calling Josh's
name as she ran through the ground floor of
the store. People turned to stare as they
tried to figure out why the young woman
was shrieking her lungs out. Josh appeared
out of nowhere. Like Bess, he shouted.
"What? What's wrong?"

"Wrong? Nothing's wrong. I have news.
Good news! Wonderful news!"

"Come with me, my dear," Josh said leading Angie to his private sanctuary in the stairwell. "This," he said, pointing to the steps as though they were His and Hers thrones, "is where I come to think and plan. Good place for good news, I'm thinking. What, what?" he all but shouted, his excitement palpable.

"Okay, okay," Angie said, sitting down on the second step from the bottom. She was aware Josh was holding her hand. She squeezed it. "I found this woolen mill in Portland, Oregon, that's going out of business. We can buy up their entire inventory. Their entire inventory, Josh! You can go online to see what I'm talking about. It's up to us to truck it here. The mill and the manufacturing end of it is all family-owned. The last surviving member of the family just sold out to a developer for big bucks. He was almost giddy that he could unload his warehouse in one swoop. All he wants to do is take his money and go. You need to call them right away and make an offer. They're expecting your call. Here's the number. The man's name is Samuel Eikenberry. Hurry, before he changes his mind, Josh."

"Stay right here. I have to go to the office for my cell phone. Wait for me. I want to make this deal in my . . . here on the steps. Will you wait?"

"Of course." A nanosecond later, Angie felt his lips brush hers.

"I promise to do better next time," Josh grinned.

"I'll hold you to it." *Oh, Bess, my line has a nibble*. Angie clapped her hands in glee at what had just transpired.

Twenty minutes later, Josh snapped the phone shut. His clenched fist shot in the air. "We have a deal and Mr. Eikenberry is going to truck it here at my expense. I snapped up the offer. The latest styles, the best of the best and all wool. He asked if I wanted the blankets, and I said yes."

Josh's excitement was contagious. "You can never have enough blankets."

Then she was being kissed like she'd never been kissed in her life. Her world rocked, righted itself, and then rocked again. "You didn't lie. You did do better. Wanna try for perfection?"

Josh was about to give her his definition of perfection when his cell phone rang. Thinking it might be Mr. Eikenberry, he answered it. His father's voice boomed over the wire. All he heard was five hundred

handmade quilts, tons of jams, jellies, pre-
serves and two thousand Amish cook-
books. He laid the phone on the step and
proceeded to show Angie his version of
perfection.

When the couple came up for air they
could hear Angus and Eva talking.

"I don't know what it is, Angus. It sounds
like two cats fighting with each other. Of
course, my hearing isn't what it used to be.
What does it sound like to you?"

"Like someone is in pain and is moaning
and groaning. Must be a bad connection."

Angie clapped her hands over her mouth
so she wouldn't laugh out loud. Josh
snapped the phone shut and reached for
her again.

I've got the fish on the line, Bess.

Chapter Seven

Eva and Angus rocked contentedly in the rockers in what would be the temporary day care center for Eagle's Department Store.

"Isn't it amazing, Angus, how this all came together in three weeks? Angie did a wonderful job with all the vibrant colors, the mobiles, and the colorful play tables and chairs. She got everything secondhand and just spruced it up. Speaking of my daughter, have you seen her?"

"You mean that harried, overworked young lady who is burning the candle at both ends? That daughter?"

"Yes, that one."

"She said she had to talk to Josh about an important matter. Something about Halloween items for this little center. I think I heard her say they were supposed to be delivered this morning and they didn't arrive.

We lost three weeks of revenue, Eva. That's how long the store has been closed," Angus said, changing the subject. "It was supposed to be two days, then five days, then a week. Three weeks!"

"I know that, Angus. When the store opens next week, you'll make it up." Eva's voice turned anxious when she said, "You didn't say anything to Josh, did you?"

"No. I think he's waiting for me to lambaste him. I know, I know. Not a word. He knows what he's doing. At least that's what he's telling me a dozen times a day."

"Then believe it," Eva snapped. "Where is that daughter of mine? Stay here, Angus, I'm going to see if I can find her."

Angus waved her off and continued to rock in the new chair he had come to love. He wondered what it would feel like to rock a baby. Eva said he was going to love the feeling. Eva seemed to be right about most things, he thought happily. In a short period of time he'd come to trust her judgment completely.

Eva walked out to the main section of the second floor. Her startled gaze took in two things instantaneously. Her daughter looked like she was frozen in time as she stared at

Josh Eagle and a tall woman who was kissing him. She blinked, and then pinched her
arm as she walked up to her daughter to
place a motherly hand on Angie's shoulder.
She could see tears in the corners of her
eyes. *This is not good, this is not good, this
is not good. A mind's eye picture in real time
will never go away.*

"I'm sure it's not what it looks like, Angie.
She's probably someone he used to know.
You young people tend to kiss hello, good-
bye, and everything in between. She probably just stopped in to see what's going on.
Everyone in town wants to see what's going
on. Come along, dear," Eva babbled.

Eva thought it was magical how her
daughter could talk without her lips moving.
"Really, Mom! How do you think she got in
here when all the doors are locked? She
called Josh 'darling' and was reminding him
that they had a date for the Harvest Ball on
Saturday. She pinched his cheek and was
so cutesy cute she made my hair stand on
end. Josh . . . Josh just smiled. He smiled,
Mom. You're right, let's get out of here."

Josh took that moment to look in their direction. He looked so guilty even Eva had a
hard time defending his actions.

Together, mother and daughter marched off, Josh calling their names. "Walk slower, Angie. I cannot run. And if you run, he'll know you're upset."

"Damn it, Mom, I *am* upset. I'm here busting my butt, working round the clock for that jerk so he can prove to his father that he knows what he's doing. We have a date on Saturday. Won't it be interesting to see how he wiggles out of it. I was starting to trust that jerk! Did you hear me, Mom?"

"Sweetie, I think the whole store can hear you."

"Guess what, Mom, I don't care! I'm going home. Don't worry, I'll be back at some point. If that Halloween stuff I ordered arrives, just unpack it. I'll see you later."

"Angie, I don't think going home . . ."

"Don't say it, Mom. Don't call me, either. I'm going to try and catch a few hours of sleep. I was here all night."

Eva, her heart heavy, watched her daughter as she made her way down the dim hallway that led to the Eagle's, loading dock. She looked behind her to see if Josh was anywhere in sight. He wasn't.

* * *

Angus had only to look at Eva's face to know something was wrong. "Do you want to tell me about it, or are you going to wear a hole in this new carpet?"

"Your son! He's a cad! He's out there on the floor kissing some long-legged woman who looks like she's been varnished, then shellacked. It seems he has a faulty memory. He has . . . I guess I should say, *had,* a date with Angie for Saturday evening, and that shellacked person stopped by to confirm her date with *your son* for the Harvest Ball on Saturday. I'm going home. You can have *your son* take you home. I don't know if I'll be back or not."

"Eva . . . wait!"

"Don't talk to me right now, Angus. Talk to that son of yours."

Angus heaved himself out of the rocker. He wondered how in a few short moments things could go from wonderful to terrible. He looked up to see the terrible end of things approaching at breakneck speed, a look of pure panic on his face. For some unexplained reason, the panicked expression on his son's face pleased Angus.

"Where's Angie, Dad? Did you see her? Is Eva here?"

"Is something wrong, son?" Angus asked.

"Hell yes, something is wrong. Angie caught—saw Vickie Summers kissing me. At least I think that's what she saw. Don't even ask me how Vickie got into the store. That woman can do anything she sets her mind to. I don't know how long Angie . . . What I mean is I don't know what she heard . . . She wanted . . . She thinks . . . I'm not doing it . . . She won't take no . . . Where the hell is Angie? I know her mother said something to you. You two are joined at the hip these days. What'd she say, Dad?"

A devil perched itself on Angus's shoulder. "You don't want to know, son. It will only upset you. You can't dangle two women on a string, Joshua. I think I told you that when you were sixteen, and girls were throwing themselves at you. You should have listened to me back then. Sit down, Joshua."

Josh recognized the iron command. In no way was it an invitation. He sat down in one of the rockers. "What? I think I'm a little old for a lesson on romance. Where did Angie go, Dad? She was pissed off, wasn't she?"

"No, son, she was hurt and humiliated. If the situation were reversed, how do you think you would feel?"

"Okay, okay, I get the point. Look, I didn't invite Vickie here. Like I said, I don't have a clue how she got into the store. I haven't seen her in . . . months. Actually, the last time I spoke to her was back in April. I did not invite her to the Harvest Ball. I didn't, Dad. That's the truth. Before I knew what was happening, she planted a lip-lock on me and I had a hell of a time pushing her away. That's when I saw Angie watching. If you know where Angie is, you better tell me, Dad, or I'm walking out of here and never coming back. I'm serious. She's my girl! I want to get to know her better. Hell, I think I want to marry her. I can't pull this off," he said, waving his arms about, "without her. Will you help me out already for God's sake?" Josh pleaded.

Lip-lock? It must be a new term for kissing. The devil on Angus's shoulder started a lively dance. Marriage. Maybe he'd get to rock in a chair with his very own grandchild. He just knew he was going to make a wonderful grandfather. Then he remembered the look on Eva's face and the way she'd said, *your son,* like he was the Devil incarnate.

Angus pulled his pipe out of his pocket and stuck it in his mouth. He chewed on the stem, his eyes on his son. "I'm too old to be offering advice. You're on your own, son!"

"That's it? I'm dying here, and you're telling me I'm on my own? What's wrong with this picture? Thanks for nothing, Dad."

Angus removed the pipe clenched between his teeth, and stared at it. "In my day, which was a lifetime ago, a fella would crawl on his knees, flowers in hand and the truth on his lips. If that didn't work, then the fella would throw a pebble at her bedroom window at night, and when she opened the window he'd sing her a song. Doesn't matter if the fella sounds like a frog. It's the thought that counts."

Josh was listening intently. "Yeah, yeah, what else would that fella do?"

Angus shrugged. "I never got beyond the singing part." He watched his son out of the corner of his eye and was pleased at what he was seeing.

"How far did you have to crawl?"

Angus wanted to laugh out loud, but he didn't. "Up the walkway, up the steps, across the porch, and into the foyer. She kicked me out. I got two holes in my trousers for my efforts."

Josh looked down at his jeans. They were

sturdy. *What's a few holes? I can always buy another pair.* "Thanks, Dad! I knew I could count on you. Take care of things, okay? I don't know when I'll be back."

Angus was so pleased with himself he made his way out to the loading dock, where he fired up his pipe and smoked contentedly. There was a lot to be said for experience.

Eva opened the front door. How quiet the house was. The first thing she saw was the brown envelope on the foyer table. It had enough stamps on it to go around the world at least three times. Eva's heart fluttered when she looked down at the address on the envelope. In a few minutes the mailman would be here to deliver the mail.

"Angie!"

"I'm up here, Mom. Do me a favor," she called down. "I see the mailman coming up the street. Give him the envelope on the table."

"Sure, honey." Eva picked up the envelope and slid it into the drawer of the table. The only way Angie could see the mailman was if she was sitting on the window seat in her room. Crying, from the way she sounded. Carrying out her charade, Eva opened the door a few moments later to accept the mail. She commented on the weather for a minute, then closed the door.

She called upstairs. "Angie, come down and talk to me. You know I can't do the stairs comfortably. Please."

Eva was right, she saw as Angie descended the stairs and stood next to her— her daughter had been crying. "How about a nice cup of hot tea? Tea always makes things better. At least that's what my mother always said." She wrapped her arm around her daughter's shoulder and led her into the kitchen.

"I don't want to talk about this, Mom."

As Eva bustled about the kitchen, she said, "Well, I for one can certainly understand that. Men are so callow. They don't have the same feelings women have. I guess that might be a good thing. I think I would be remiss as a mother if I didn't point out to you that there are two sides to everything. You should ask yourself how that young woman got into the store. If she came uninvited, then you can't blame Josh for that. Ask yourself if Josh acted like he

was enjoying the meeting. He looked kind
of stiff to me, like he didn't want her there,
but that's just this old lady's opinion. I didn't
see him return her kiss. He just stood there.
That's the way I saw it. You only heard the
young woman say they had a date for the
Harvest Ball. You didn't hear Josh agree,
now, did you?"

"Whose side are you on, Mom?" Angie
sniffed.

"The right side. I happen to think Josh is a
stand-up kind of guy. He didn't beat around
the bush the day he eavesdropped on you.
He fessed right up, didn't he? It's when
things fester that the problem gets out of
hand. In short, my dear, I think you saw
something you never should have seen.
Having said that, it probably meant nothing.
That's why you shouldn't have seen it—because you reacted without giving Josh a
chance to explain or defend his actions.
Now, drink your tea."

Angie picked at the fringe on the green-
checkered placemat. "So what you're saying is I should go back to the store and wait
for Josh to come to me and . . . explain
what I saw."

"See! Now you're getting it! Yes, in my

opinion, that's what you should do. If you don't, you'll always wonder what he would have said. You did tell me you really liked Josh. You told me you dream about him. He might be *the one,* Angie."

"She kissed him. You saw her. Kissing is . . . Kissing is . . ."

"Quite wonderful, depending on who is doing the kissing. I did not see Josh returning the kiss in question. There was no passion there that I could see. No reciprocity. That's about all I have to say, Angie. Think this all through, and don't throw away something on a jealous whim that could otherwise turn out to be wonderful."

The doorbell rang, cutting off whatever Angie's response was going to be.

"I'll get it, and then I'm going back to the store," Eva said. "Finish your tea. By the way, I won't be home for dinner this evening. Angus and I are going out for Japanese. He loves the knife show the chefs provide."

Outside, after Josh Eagle had run up to the Bradfords' front porch and rung the bell, he ran down the steps and out to the walkway, where he dropped to his knees. He sucked in his breath and proceeded to knee-walk his way to the Bradford front porch the moment the front door opened.

"Angie! Angie! Come quick! Hurry, dear!"

Thinking her mother fell or banged her knee, Angie barreled to the foyer. She almost screamed in relief when she saw that Eva was all right. She turned and looked where her mother was pointing. Her jaw dropped at what she was seeing. Josh waved. Angie, more or less, wiggled her index finger as she watched the man's progress. She could tell it was slow going for the tall man on his knees.

Eva tactfully withdrew and left by the kitchen door. She peeked around the corner of the house. He was still crawling. She laughed all the way to her car.

Angie walked out to the porch, her arms across her chest to ward off the October chill. By the time Josh reached the steps, Angie took pity on him and motioned for him to get up. "Do you mind telling me what you're doing?" There was a bit of frost in her tone that did not go unnoticed by Josh.

Josh struggled to his feet. "Angie, look, what you saw . . . It wasn't . . . It isn't what you think. Vickie is someone I used to know. And I didn't know her that well. I haven't seen or spoken to her since way back in April. She was looking for an escort to take her to the Harvest Ball. I have to assume I was a last resort because I never pretended to be anything other than a distant friend. She kisses everyone. I just found out that she bribed one of the workers with twenty bucks to let her into the store. If you hadn't turned tail and run, you would have heard me tell her I was seeing someone and had other plans for Saturday evening. So, are you okay with this? Please tell me you're okay with this so I don't have to do that singing thing under your window tonight." Josh wondered if he looked as exhausted as he felt. Would Angie take pity on him? Childishly, he crossed his fingers.

He was seeing someone and had other plans. That almost makes us a couple. It sounds like we are a couple. "I didn't know you could sing. Do you want a cup of tea or a beer? I can make some coffee."

"I'll take a beer and I can't sing. My father . . ."

"Offered you advice. Yeah, my mother stepped in and offered some, too. Okay, you're off the hook."

"Thank God! I'm going to have to guzzle

that beer and get back to the store. Are you staying home?"

"No. I just got . . . miffed and came home. I did . . . I think I did something I might come to regret. I reacted and I . . . I signed that damn contract and it went off in the mail. The mailman came a little while ago, and Mom gave it to him."

Josh looked at her as though she'd sprouted a second head. "You were that angry? Damn, now what are you going to do? Are you sorry you sent it off?"

"Yes. Yes, a hundred times yes. I was going to call tomorrow and explain that I wouldn't be accepting the position. I never did tell my mother."

"Get your coat. Maybe we can catch the mailman. Do you know in which direction he goes when he finishes up your street? Never mind, you go one way and I'll go the other. It's still early so he won't be returning to the post office. If I find him first, he won't give it to me, so I'll call you on your cell. If you find him first, call me and I'll meet up with you."

Thirty minutes later the couple sat down on Angie's front steps. "He said Mom never gave him any mail. That has to mean she knows and kept the envelope or hid it. Parents are so devious," Angie groused.

"Oh, I don't know, sometimes they're pretty smart. Your mother saved your butt by not mailing that contract. My father gave me some shitty advice, but here we are with a better understanding of what's going on." Josh reached for Angie's hand and squeezed it.

"I think your father and my mother are going to end up together. They get along so well. And, they're great company for one another. Tonight they're going out for Japanese food. I'm okay with it, are you?"

"Yeah, you bet. My father is a different man these days. He hasn't given me one moment of grief as the bills come in. I think it's all due to your mother." This last was said so shyly, Angie smiled.

Angie held up her hand palm out and high-fived Josh. "To our parents!"

"To our parents and to *us*."

A red ring of heat popped up on Angie's neck. Then it crept up to her cheeks. She didn't know what else to do, so she smiled.

Chapter Eight

On a cold, blustery November day, everything Eagle swung into high gear. Announcers on the local airwaves invited shoppers to soar with the Eagle and avail themselves of the hospitality that was being offered by the Eagle family to all the families the store had served in the last hundred years.

Flyers and giveaways were handed out at all the mall entrances and parking lot to entice people into the store. There were flyers for the day care unit, flyers for the knitting and cooking classes. Flyers for sale after sale on just about every item in the store.

When the doors opened at ten o'clock, Josh, attired in a power suit and tie, stood next to his father to welcome and greet old and new customers alike.

Standing on the sidelines, Eva and Angie sighed with relief as shoppers flooded the main floor. They watched for a while, amazed and delighted that all their hard work was paying off with cash register activity. "I think we did okay, Mom. Now, if the merchandise keeps flowing in, and no one screws up, we just might make it through the holiday season and, if we're lucky, pay the bills and maybe show a tiny profit. If we're lucky," she repeated.

"Honey, we agreed, no negative thoughts. I have to get back to the second floor. We have a good crew to help with the kids. I'll see you later."

Angie meandered over to the cosmetics counter. She was pleased to see the free Vera Wang samples going like hotcakes and being followed up by sales. She looked around and realized the salesgirl had been right. Too much variety and people can't decide, so they walk away. Her advice had been to go with three manufacturers, and it now looked like she was right.

Josh had taken the salesgirl's advice to heart and instructed the few new buyers he'd hired to do the same thing. It looked like the strategy was working throughout the store.

Angie was so pleased with the way things

were going, she gave herself a mental pat on the back as she walked the floor, hoping to hear comments or criticisms she could relay to Josh. She moved over closer to the door to better observe Josh and his father. How tired they both looked. But it seemed to her like a happy kind of tiredness.

Angie crossed her fingers that things would continue through the end of the year. Her eyes were everywhere as she continued to meander around, then made her way back to the front door, where she leaned up to whisper in Josh's ear. "Your father needs to get off his feet. Tell him to go up to the day care so he can sit down in one of the rockers. I can take his place if you like."

"I like. How's it going?"

"I think it's going very well. The big fishbowl for the nine o'clock drawing is almost filled. When school lets out, the kids will be here in droves in the hopes of winning the iPod. The safari department appears to be doing a brisk business. Cruise wear is beyond brisk. It's happening, Josh. How much longer are you going to do this meet and greet?"

"Not a minute longer. I want to check the stockroom. What's on your schedule?"

"I'm going to float around, check on Mom and your dad, that kind of thing. If Bess needs me in gift wrap, I'll help out. It's really working, Josh," she whispered.

"Because of you," Josh whispered in return. "When you're done, why don't you meet me in the stockroom?"

Angie wiggled her eyebrows. "That's one of the nicest invitations I've ever gotten. I'll be there. Wait for me."

Angie thought her heart would leap right out of her chest when she heard him say, "Forever if I have to."

Angie flew to the second floor. She skidded to a stop at the small desk to take in the scene in front of her. Angus and Eva rocking chubby babies, who were gurgling and cooing as Eva sang a lullaby. Angus looked so contented and peaceful, she felt a lump rise in her throat. Toddlers crawled through a maze of colored plastic tunnels, giggling and laughing. Infants in swings, their eyes following the mobiles overhead. Juice and cookies were being laid out on the play tables, after which it would be nap time. When she left the area her only thought was that the day care was going to net a profit. She couldn't wait to share her thoughts with Josh.

To the right and around the corner of the day care unit, a senior citizen was teaching six young mothers how to knit, her students paying rapt attention. The cooking class was all done via video and a large corkboard. The lesson today was how to bake a turkey for Thanksgiving. All was well there, too.

Now she could head for the stockroom. There was a bounce to her step that showed her excitement.

Angie opened a door that said NO ADMITTANCE and, underneath, EMPLOYEES ONLY. From far back in the room she could hear voices. Josh and a strange male voice. She didn't know why, but she tiptoed in the direction the voices were coming from. She peeked around a stack of sweater boxes. Bob McAllister, the general manager of Saks. What's he doing here in the stockroom? she wondered. As much as she wanted to spy and hear what was going on, she couldn't do it. "Josh!"

"Over here, Angie. Meet Bob McAllister."

Angie held out her hand. "Hello. We've met before. What's up?"

Josh laughed. "I just convinced Bob to take my job at Harrods. For obvious reasons, he doesn't want anyone to know until he can give his notice. That's why we had this meeting here in the stockroom."

Angie's head bobbed up and down. Josh wasn't leaving. He was staying. *Oh, thank you, God!*

"You guys did a hell of a job," Bob told her. "When Josh first told me his plan, I told him he could never pull it off. I'm happy to see I was wrong. If it means anything, you have the bulk of customers in the mall. Good prices, too. Great idea with only three choices per item. I've been trying to sell that idea to my people, but they won't buy into it. See you around, guys. Let's have a drink before I leave, Josh."

"You got it."

And then they were alone. Josh reached for Angie and she stepped into his arms. "I love you, Angie Bradford. We're a team. This store is in my blood the way it was in Dad's blood. When I saw him writing out all those checks I knew he was investing in me, Josh Eagle, his son, not Eagle's Department

Store. He finally moved beyond the store. These last few weeks he's turned into a real father."

"You should sneak up to the day care to see him rocking the babies. He looks so peaceful, so happy. Mom, too. I suspect they'll both make wonderful grandparents. We did good, Josh."

"We had a lot of help along the way. Eagle's is never going to be a Saks or a Neiman Marcus, and that's okay. We never aspired to be anything other than what we are—a family store where families come to buy merchandise because they trust us. Those families who shop at Eagle's grew up with us. We got off the track there for a little while, but we're back in business now. But, I can't do it without you, Angie. I'm not too proud to admit it, either. I want to marry you," he blurted.

Whoa. For the first time in her life, Angie was speechless. Because she couldn't make her tongue work, she simply nodded, her eyes glistening with happiness.

"If I kiss you, it's all over. You know that, right?"

Angie found her tongue. "Right."

"So . . . Want to help me open these boxes?"

"Sure."

The young couple worked in happy sync as salesperson after salesperson bounded into the store room to ask for more merchandise.

And before they knew it, the first announcement came over the loudspeaker that the drawing was about to be held for the winner of the iPod. They both ran out to the main floor just as Angus reached into the fishbowl to draw the winning number. "Annette Profit!" he said, holding up the winning entry. Annette Profit of Chez J's La Perfect Salon stepped up smartly and accepted the iPod. Angus hugged her and thanked her for shopping at Eagle's.

Five minutes later, when the last of the crowd disappeared, Josh locked the doors. The Eagles and the Bradfords walked back to the gift wrap department, where Angie handed out soft drinks.

"It was a hell of a day, son! I'm proud of you!"Angus beamed.

"No, Dad, you need to thank Angie and

Eva and all those people who worked the
floor. We aren't home free yet, but if we can
keep up the kind of momentum we had today, I think we might coast right into the
New Year in the black. By the way, I'm not
going to England and I asked Angie to
marry me."

"Wise man," Angus chuckled.

"Good choice," Eva said.

"It's time for us to leave," Angus said, getting to his feet. Eva followed him, leaving
Josh and Angie alone. They looked at one
another and then groaned because they
knew they had three or four more hours of
work before they could leave.

"I'm starved, Josh. Let's go out for a pizza
and a beer and come back. We can both
use a break. I haven't been outside all day.
We can walk to the pizza parlor and clear
the cobwebs."

Outside in the brisk air, Josh reached for
Angie's hand. "Are we officially engaged or
are we 'keeping company,' as Dad would
say? I'm not really up on all the protocol on
things like this. I never told anyone I loved
her, and I sure never asked anyone to marry

me before . . . Are you *ever* going to say something?"

"I'm thinking. I like being engaged. That pretty much makes it official. No one ever told me they loved me except my mom and dad. For sure no one ever asked me to marry him. I guess we're starting off even. I was a little disappointed in our parents' reaction."

Josh laughed. "My father can be a sly old fox sometimes. He told me if I didn't act quickly, you were going to move on. He sounded so convincing I figured he and Eva planned it all out, and I had better pay attention. I was never the first guy out of the gate."

Angie stepped aside as Josh opened the door of the pizza parlor. "At least you got out of the gate; I never did. Let's get the works on the pizza. I want one of those apple dumplings, too."

"Whatever you want, it's yours."

Angie could hardly wait to call Bess to tell her what she'd pulled in on her line. She laughed to herself as she imagined what Bess would say. *"You pulled in the Big Kahuna! Way to go, Angie."*

Chapter Nine

Two days before Christmas, Angie woke at four thirty AM, more tired than when she'd gone to bed. *Just let me get through today. And tomorrow,* she pleaded. *Don't let me fall asleep standing up*. If she could just sleep five more minutes. Just five. She'd settle for three, but she knew she had to get up even though it was still dark outside. It had been Josh's decision to open the store at seven and close at midnight. Then there were two hours of getting things ready for the next day, the trip home, and two hours' sleep. Still, she shouldn't complain, it was all working out perfectly.

Today was special, though. Bob McAllister had stopped by the gift wrap department late last night to whisper in her ear. It was her job to get to the store at six, open the doors and lead Josh to the food court, where all the general managers in the mall were holding their traditional private Christmas breakfast.

In the bathroom, bleary-eyed from lack of sleep, Angie looked out the window as she waited for the shower to start steaming. As she raised the window she screamed, and then screamed again. "Snow!" She stuck her neck out the window to see if she could see what kind of accumulation there was down below. Her heart fluttered. Snow was every merchant's nightmare. Especially during the last week of Christmas shopping.

It was the shortest shower in history. In less than ten minutes, Angie was showered, dressed, and tapping her foot impatiently as she waited for the coffee to run through the filter. "Snow!" The minute there was enough coffee in the pot, Angie poured, and then turned it off. She was out of the house a minute later and in her car. While it warmed up, she climbed back out to clear the snow off her windshield and back window. The little Honda was a marvel in snow and rain, so she had no worries about getting to the mall. She might even have a bit of an edge, traffic-wise, since it was just five o'clock. Another hour, and it would be a different story. As she made her way to Route 1, she listened to the local weather on the radio. Snow at Christmas was the kiss of death to every retailer. She wondered if Josh was up and had seen the snow. She wondered if she should call him, but she hated using a cell phone while she was driving. He would see it soon enough.

Twenty minutes later, when Angie blew into the mall on a strong gust of wind and swirling snow, Josh was waiting for her. The first words out of his mouth were, "This is going to kill us. The weatherman is saying six to eight inches. They're closing the schools. We need these last two shopping days like we need air to breathe. Damn! No one is here yet, so I made some coffee."

Josh reached for her hand. "I need to tell you again how grateful I am. I could never in a million years have pulled this off without your help."

"We'll find a way to make this work, Josh. It's the season of miracles. Come on, let's go get that coffee. Maybe we'll be able to think more clearly with some serious caffeine under our belts."

"There was no snow in the forecast. How'd this happen?" Josh demanded.

"It just happened, and we have to deal with it. Did you go home last night?"

"I went to the Best Western, got an hour's sleep, and took a shower. I snatched a clean shirt off one of the sale tables, and here I am. I don't know when I've ever been this tired." Josh reached for Angie's hand and squeezed it. "I wonder if the managers' breakfast is still on."

"Trust me, it's still on. It's a tradition. We're low on merchandise, Josh."

"I know. Your cottage people promised a delivery for early this morning. They were going to truck it in overnight. Then we have to unpack, log it all in. If it even gets here. I'm thinking I might have to blow off that breakfast."

Angie reared up and spilled her coffee in the process. "Absolutely not! That breakfast is part of the way things are done around here. We're going to follow the rules and hope for the best. C'mon, let's go check the loading dock. For all we know, we could have merchandise piled to the rafters just waiting for us to unpack."

There was no erasing the doom and

gloom Josh felt. "My father is going to pitch a fit. Somehow he's going to find a way to blame me for this snow. He knows how important these two days are. I know it. I feel it in my gut."

There was nothing for Angie to say, so she remained quiet. Somehow, though, she didn't think the elder Eagle would blame his only son for a snowstorm. At least she hoped not. And if he did, she knew she would have a few choice words for such an action.

Three miles away Angus Eagle was pacing back and forth in his old-fashioned kitchen, where Eva was calming mixing pancake batter.

"Calm down, Angus, you can't control the weather. Something else is bothering you. Don't deny it, Angus. You're pulling on your ear, and you only do that when something is bothering you. Do you want to talk about it?"

"Yes, I guess I do want to talk about it. I'm almost broke, Eva. If I had stayed on top of things these past years I wouldn't be in this mess. It's all my fault for being so pig-headed. I didn't want Josh to start the year off in debt. So I've paid for everything as the bills came in. My personal funds are just about depleted. I wanted . . . It was . . . I can't ask you to marry me when I have nothing to offer. I thought . . . If I sell this old house and you sell yours, we could buy a smaller house or a condo. I think we could manage nicely and, if we're careful, we can live out our lives without . . . without depending on the kids. It was my intention to give the store to the kids if they got married.

"Now, with this snow, we're going to lose more revenue. I'll have to tap into the remains of my portfolio. I'm not complaining, Eva, I just want you to know where I stand. Can you see yourself roughing it with this old man?"

"Oh, Angus, is that why you've been so cranky these past few weeks? I'm all right with everything. How nice and yet how silly of you to be worried about me. It's the Christmas season, so let's get ready for a miracle, and if that was a proposal, I accept. Now, sit down before you wear out what's left of this horrible linoleum. How many pancakes?"

"Four!" Angus said smartly. "I have an idea."

"Let's hear your idea, Big Popper," Eva said as she slid a stack of pancakes on a plate.

Angus burst out laughing. "Promise me you will never call me that in front of the kids. I don't think they'd . . . uh . . . understand."

Eva's eyes popped wide when Angus leaned across the table to share his idea. "Oh, Angus, can you make that happen? That will surely be the miracle we need." She pointed to the seven-inch television on the counter and said, "Now they're saying twelve inches of snow. Never mind those pancakes, Angus, I'll eat yours. Get on the phone and work some magic."

The traditional Managers' Holiday Breakfast was already in progress when Josh and Angie made their way to the food court. Croissants, coffee, and juice were being passed around as Bob McAllister, the president of the association, started to speak.

"We're going to make this short and sweet because we all have things to do to combat the weather none of us expected. As you all know, I'll be leaving the first of the year. I want to take a minute to thank all of you for your support over the years and to wish you all the best in the coming year. I'm turning the reins over to Josh Eagle, who I know will do the same fine job I've done in the past . . . That was a joke, people.

"Moving right along here, all of us sitting here today want to congratulate Josh Eagle and Eagle's Department Store. We've been rooting for you every step of the way. You had us all chewing our nails wondering if you could turn the store around, and you did. Each and every one of us is proud of you and wish you and Eagle's every success. Did I also say we're all slightly jealous? We are. Utilizing the cottage industry was a stroke of genius and I for one applaud you."

Josh flushed at the round of applause.

"Having said that, Abrams' Trophies in the west wing made this up for you," Bob said, holding up a small bronze plaque. "It says, 'TO EAGLE'S DEPARTMENT STORE: THE MOST INNOVATIVE STORE OF 2007.' There's a card to go with it that every store owner signed. Congratulations, Josh!"

Josh stood, walked to the front of the gathering, and reached for the plaque. "I

don't know what to say other than thank
you. Maybe someday I'll be able to tell all of
you what this means to me. Not right now,
though."

He looked to the back of the room to see
Angie waving her cell phone at him, an
ear-to-ear grin splitting her features. She
walked to the front of the room to hand the
phone to Josh, who listened, his jaw dropping almost to his chest.

"People! People, wait a minute! That was
my father. Maybe we aren't dead in the water after all. My dad called down to Edison
and Piscataway and asked all his friends
who have horse farms if they'd get their
wagons out and hitch them up and bring
them our way to transport shoppers. Eva
Bradford called all the radio stations to an-
nounce our wagon train shopping solution.
It's a plan, and it's under way. We're going
to lose a few early-morning hours, but my
suggestion is we all stay open around the
clock. Good luck, everybody."

Josh whirled around to hug Angie. "Now
where in the hell do you think my old man
came up with this idea? Oh, who cares!
Let's just hope it works."

"Oh, it's going to work. All people have to

do is get to the central points and leave the rest up to us. Your dad saved the day, Josh."

Josh's eyes misted over. "Yeah, he did, didn't he," he said softly.

"Mr. Eagle! Mr. Eagle! Annette Profit here. I have the salon in the east wing." She held out her hand and smiled. "I just want a minute to tell you my mother used to bring me to Eagle's when I was little. It was always such a special treat. Especially when it was time to go back to school. Your dad always stood at the door and gave each one of us kids a free box of crayons and a tablet. On the Fourth of July he'd give us a gift certificate for a free ice-cream cone. At Easter it was a chocolate egg, and at Christmas it was a silver bell to ring so Santa would know where we lived. They were wonderful memories. Eagle's was a tradition. I'm glad you were able to turn the store around. Good luck, Mr. Eagle."

Josh was so choked up he couldn't get his tongue to work. He reached out to hug the young woman and smiled. He finally managed to choke out the words, "I'll bring that tradition back next year if you promise to bring your kids."

"Count on it, Mr. Eagle."

Angie linked her arm with Josh's as they turned to go back to the store. "That was so nice. I vaguely remember Mom talking about it, but the store was too expensive for us to shop. Mom did that discount thing. If it wasn't on sale, we didn't buy it. It's all about goodwill and family."

"These last few months have certainly been an eye-opener," Josh said. "I learned things about my father I never knew, I found the love of my life, and I now know I can run this store."

Angie laughed. "I think I'm going to go back to the food court and find out if one of the vendors will be willing to honor hot chocolate vouchers for our customers. And those big fat sugar cookies for the kids. If Bess isn't busy, ask her to make up some vouchers and run them off. See if you can find someone to go over to the south wing where that huge candy store is. Buy up all the candy canes and hand them out at the door to the kids."

"Super idea! Where *do* you come up with these ideas? I think I'm going to be marrying a genius."

"I'm thinking you're right." Angie laughed

again and waved her hand as she headed back to the food court.

It was the noon hour when Josh flipped on the television in his office. As local television cameras caught the wagon train heading for the mall he watched the unfolding scene with his mouth hanging open. Even the anchor seemed to be beside himself, his words running together. Josh turned when he felt a hand on his shoulder.

"Dad! How'd you get here?"

"I came on the first wagon. Eva is down in gift wrap. What do you want me to do?"

The lump in Josh's throat was so big he thought he was going to choke to death. "What you do best, Dad. What you did for years and years. Stand by the door and hand out treats—we have candy canes and vouchers for hot chocolate and cookies at the food court. Bundle up, Dad."

"You remembered I used to do that?"

Josh felt shame river through him. "No, Dad. Some lady came up to me and told me how you used to do that. She told me it was an event for her when she was a kid. I'm going to do that again. Want a job?"

Angus swung his scarf around his neck. "Depends on how much the job pays," he said craftily.

"I was hoping you'd do it for free."

"Sounds about right to me. You got yourself a new employee, son. See you later," Angus said, picking up the stack of vouchers. "Where are the candy canes?"

"In a big barrel by the front door. The candy people just delivered them."

Josh leaned against the door when it closed behind his father. His eyes were so wet he knew in a second that tears were going to roll down his cheeks. *It's not a bad thing*, he told himself. He knuckled his eyes before he opened the door, knowing in his heart that he was blessed. Maybe all this that was happening was the miracle everyone talked about during the Christmas season.

By four o'clock the mall was so busy that people were bumping into each other. Camera crews, photographers, and reporters from all the local news channels contributed to the gala that seemed to be going on.

Everyone was being interviewed. Only smiles and camaraderie could be seen.

The food vendors worked at breakneck speed to prepare food to be given to the drivers of the wagon trains. The coffee shop was almost out of coffee they were brewing by the gallon. And, one reporter put it, everything was free.

The primary channels ran with the story on the six o'clock news, referring to the event—the wagon train, the freebies the mall was giving out, along with the camaraderie of the shoppers—as Marketing 101 at it's best. By the time the eleven o'clock news came on, they were calling the wagon train a phenomenon. Within seconds the story flashed around the world via the Internet.

It was midnight when Josh walked to the front door to relieve his father. When he saw Angus being interviewed by CBS News he stepped back to listen. He knew he was eavesdropping, but he didn't care. The interview would play out in real time instantaneously.

"Now, you listen to me, young fella. What you're seeing out there is not about money or the bottom line. This is about people coming together to help each other. Those farmers and their wagons aren't getting a penny for all their hard work. They've been out there bringing shoppers back and forth since early this morning. It's Christmas, son, a time when people help each other. Every merchant in this mall is my friend and my competitor. I want to help them as much as I want to help myself. But more important, we don't want to disappoint anyone and we want everyone to have a wonderful Christmas, especially the children.

"Mother Nature served us a hard blow today, but we all pitched in and did whatever we could to save the holiday. There aren't any shining stars here today. Everything is a group effort as you can see. You want a candy cane or a voucher for hot chocolate, young fella? It's time for my break now, so I'll be seeing you tomorrow. I don't want to be interviewed anymore."

And that was the end of that.

Josh grinned. "Guess you set them straight, huh?"

"Son, I didn't say anything but the truth. Now, if you don't mind, I'm heading upstairs to that rocking chair that has my name on it."

"Dad . . . I . . . I need . . ."

"No, you don't need to say anything. We need to talk more, son. Here!" Angus said, shoving a candy cane into his son's hand.

Eva wrapped an afghan around Angus's shoulders as he lowered himself gently into the padded rocking chair. A cup of hot chocolate found its way to his hand. "It's been a heck of a day, Big Popper. I just saw your interview on TV. You were wonderful." When he didn't answer Eva realized Angus was already sound asleep, so she removed the cup of hot chocolate and drank it herself. As she rocked silently, she realized she had never felt more peaceful, more happy than she was feeling at that precise moment. She reached over to pat the Big Popper's shoulder.

Life was wonderful.

Curled together with Josh in sleep in the gift wrap department, Angie stirred and bolted upright. "Josh, wake up! What about the horses?"

"What? What about the horses? What time is it?"

"They've been out there all day and night. That's cruel. It's six o'clock."

"No, no, no!" Josh said, sitting up. "Dad got the armory to donate the space. They've been rotating the horses. It's warm in there. This is no Mickey Mouse operation, you know. My old man covered all the bases. Relax. Damn, my mouth feels like Dad's pipe smells. Turn on the radio, Angie. I want to know how much snow is out there." He knew he was babbling but couldn't seem to stop.

"Eighteen inches," Angie said as she filled the coffeepot. "And it's still snowing."

"I'm going out to the main floor to check on things, and I want to see how my father's doing. I won't be long. Do you want me to get you anything from the food court?"

"A sticky bun would be nice, and a tooth-brush."

Josh laughed as he unfolded his tired bones. Satisfied that his father and Eva were sound asleep in the rockers, he made his way to his office, where he went online to check out the headline news. He was as-tounded to see that the mall had made the front page of just about every newspaper in the country.

The tiredness that seemed to have invaded Josh's body suddenly washed away. His step was light, his mood upbeat as he made his way out to the mall. He picked up two toothbrushes, some toothpaste, four oven-hot sticky buns and four cups of coffee.

Christmas Eve.

Josh realized he no longer cared if the bottom line at closing was red or black. All that mattered were his neighbors, his business associates, all the volunteers, and, of course his family. He thanked God for all the people who had come to his aid.

Singing "Jingle Bells" at the top of his lungs, Josh made his way to the second floor, where he handed out sticky buns and coffee to his father and Eva. He didn't miss a beat as he turned around and headed back downstairs to see the love of his life.

No doubt about it, Angie was the wind beneath his wings.

His mouth full of toothpaste in the small lavatory off the gift wrap department, Josh bellowed, "Angie, the cottage people came through. We have to unpack the merchandise. I guarantee we're going to be sold out before six tonight. We've been sending customers to other stores. All in the spirit of Christmas."

"I've been wrapping gifts for free. I hope you don't mind."

"Not one little bit," Josh said, biting into the still-warm sticky bun. "We better get our tails in gear, there are people waiting in line for their packages to be gift wrapped. It's just all so glorious. By the way, we made the front page of every newspaper in the country. We're even on the pop-up when you turn on the computer."

"That's great! Did they plow the parking lot?"

"They tried but gave up. It's still snowing, too. I have this suspicion we are going to be celebrating Christmas right here in the store."

Josh's suspicions turned out to be on the money.

The crowds at the mall started to thin out around four o'clock. By five there were just a few stragglers waiting to be picked up by one of the wagons.

At five thirty the loud speaker in the mall exploded into sound. "Promptly at six thirty, cocktails, compliments of Stephens' Liquors, will be served in the food court, followed by dinner, compliments of the vendors in the food court. One and all are invited to go caroling up and down the halls of the mall at eight o'clock. A silent midnight service will be held promptly at midnight. Sorry, folks," the tinny baritone said, "there will be no gift exchange because there's nothing left in the stores to exchange. Merry Christmas to one and all."

Holding hands, Josh and Angie walked to the front door of Eagle's, where Angus was operating the mechanism that would secure the store for the night. Josh thought he had never seen his father so happy.

"No more candy canes. Merry Christmas, son."

The pesky lump in his throat Josh thought was becoming permanent found its way to block his vocal cords once again. He wrapped his arms around his father and whispered. "Thanks for being my father. Merry Christmas, Dad."

Standing in front of the huge Christmas tree that dominated the middle of the floor was Eva, who held her arms out to her little family. "Merry Christmas!"

Together, the Eagles and Bradfords walked out to the food court to a chorus of "Merry Christmas! Merry Christmas!"

A High-Kicking Christmas

Marie Bostwick

Chapter One

The passenger car of the Amtrak Vermon-ter was warm, and the rhythmic thump of wheels on rails as soothing as a lullaby. When the station announcement came over the loudspeaker, Kendra Erickson was dead asleep.

"Maple Grove next station! All out for Maple Grove!"

"Lady." The conductor nudged Kendra gently, but she didn't stir so he grabbed her shoulder and gave it a good shake. "Hey! Lady, wake up! Aren't you supposed to be getting off at Maple Grove?"

"Hmmm?" Kendra opened her eyes briefly but shut them again. It took a moment be-fore the conductor's words registered in her mind. "Oh." She yawned. "Are we almost there?"

"Yup," the conductor replied. "In about

five minutes. You'd better get your gear together, lady. The train don't stop long in
Maple Grove."

Kendra took a peek out the window, but
all she saw were a lot of trees and a handful
of white frame houses, certainly nothing
that looked like a town. There was a good
foot of snow blanketing the ground, but the
day was bright and sunny. One of the residents of the little frame houses had hung
their washing out to dry. The line of bright
red, green, and blue shirts looked like the
row of flags that hung in front of the Wal-
dorf-Astoria Hotel. That was the only thing
in sight that reminded Kendra of New York
or, for that matter, civilization in general. She
looked at the conductor doubtfully. "We're
going to be in Maple Grove in five minutes?
Are you sure?"

The conductor nodded. "Now it's more
like four. C'mon, lady, I got a schedule to
keep. I'll get your suitcases off the rack and
you get your bags and the cat. You're the
only one getting off at Maple Grove and I
doubt there'll be anybody getting on; hardly
anybody ever does. There was some talk
about closing the station a couple years
ago, but it got a last-minute reprieve. I think

the governor's brother-in-law has a ski cabin or something up here. You know how that goes," he harrumphed. "Politicians."

While the conductor chattered on about the disappointing state of the political landscape, Kendra was more concerned about the physical landscape.

This couldn't be it, she thought to herself, but the conductor didn't look like he was in the mood to answer any more questions, so Kendra gathered up her pocketbook, her black tote, her Bloomingdale's shopping bag, and the hard plastic pet carrier in which her cat, Wendell, a rotund shorthair with tawny fur and white patches, was sleeping. She struggled to her feet, grabbed the wooden crutches she'd left propped against the back of the seat, wedged them under her arms, and started limping her way down the aisle of the lurching passenger car while trying to keep from dropping her pocketbook, the tote, the shopping bag, or Wendell, who had woken up and was meowing pathetically. "I know, Baby. I know," she murmured to the unhappy feline. "Just hang in there for a few more minutes. We'll be there soon."

The conductor groaned as he hefted

Kendra's oversized black suitcases and followed her toward the end of the car. "Sheesh! These things are heavy. You must be planning on staying for a while. You got family in Maple Grove?"

"No," she answered without offering more. Kendra wasn't interested in discussing her personal life with a stranger. Still, the conductor was carrying those big suitcases for her so she felt she ought to be polite, but what was it about people in the country? Why didn't they just mind their own business?

"Well, with that cast on your foot, I know you're not coming up for the skiing. What happened? Did you fall?"

"Yes," she answered, hoping to leave it at that, but the man looked her expectantly so she added, "I'm a dancer," as if that explained everything. The train was slowing, pulling into the station. Kendra readjusted her crutches and her baggage, eager to part company with the nosey conductor.

"Oh," he said thoughtfully as the train stopped.

The doors opened and let in a blast of frigid air that set Kendra's teeth chattering. Loaded down with luggage and Wendell, and still unused to walking on crutches, she stared nervously at the gap between the train and the platform, but the conductor hopped down first. He piled Kendra's bags on the ground, then reached up to help her down, making sure she had a firm grip on the crutches before releasing her arm.

"Thanks," she said sincerely.

"My pleasure." He tipped his hat, then stood for a moment, taking in all five foot nine inches of Kendra's willowy frame, his eyes traveling from the top of her black knitted hat, to her black cable knit sweater and black wool pants, to the tip of her trim black ankle boot, which looked incongruous beside the fat white cast.

It seemed he was about to ask another question, but just then the whistle blew so he scrambled back into the car and hollered, "All aboard!" even though there was no one besides Kendra standing on the platform. The conductor stood at the door staring curiously at Kendra as the train gathered speed and pulled away. Finally, he yelled a question over the rumble of the engine. "You're from New York City, aren't you?"

"Yes!" Kendra shouted.

The conductor nodded as if he'd expected as much, then, as the train moved down the track and out of shouting distance, he hollered, "Lady, what in the heck are you doing here?"

The train wheels squealed against the cold steel rails, a sound like fingernails on a blackboard magnified fifty times. Wendell yowled in terror. Kendra covered her ears and closed her eyes. When she opened them, the train was gone and she was left standing, shivering on a deserted train platform in Maple Grove, Vermont, with a traumatized cat and a small mountain of luggage piled at her feet.

Kendra looked around. "What in the heck am I doing here? Mister, that's a good question."

Just a week before, Kendra was doing what she'd done every fall and winter for the previous ten years, getting off the subway at Fiftieth Street on her way to Radio City Music Hall and her job as a Rockette.

It was a cloudy day in late October and there was a chill in the air. A man who was either late, rude, or both, pushed past

Kendra as she climbed the stairs to the street and carelessly smacked her shoulder with his briefcase. A seasoned New Yorker, Kendra would normally have responded to this intrusion of her personal space with an irritated *"Hey! Watch it!"* But today she didn't bother. She was tired, depressed, and just plain fed up, but it wasn't just the chill of impending winter that was getting her down.

Her agent had called the night before to tell her the news. Even though the director had given her a big smile at her callback, a smile that Kendra was certain meant she'd nailed the audition, she hadn't gotten the part. Kendra was heartbroken. It wasn't a big show, just a limited holiday run of a musical version of that old chestnut *Christmas In Connecticut,* but Kendra had thought that, after all these years, she was finally going to break into Broadway. But it wasn't to be. Stanley told her not to be discouraged.

"They loved you, Kendra. Really. The director told me so himself. He thought you were a knockout and the best dancer they'd auditioned by far, but your voice just wasn't strong enough."

That was always the problem. Kendra was

a terrific dancer, a decent actress, and had a sweet—some even said angelic—voice, but she just didn't have that "belt-it-to-the-balcony" style Broadway directors were looking for.

"Cheer up," Stanley said. "It could be worse. At least we've still got the Radio City gig."

Sure we do, Kendra thought bitterly, *the same gig I had for the eight years before I became your client, except now you're getting 15 percent.* But she knew it wasn't Stanley's fault. He'd gotten her the audition. She hadn't gotten the part . . . again. Kendra sighed.

"OK, Stanley. Thanks. Is there anything coming up?"

"Nothing's casting until after Christmas. But, hey," he said encouragingly, "you're gonna be too tired to audition anyway, right? You open in a couple weeks and then you've got four shows a day until January. Buck up, kid. There's always next year. Gotta run," he said and hung up.

There's always next year. That's what Kendra had been telling herself for a decade. As she walked down Sixth Avenue, Kendra stopped for a moment and looked up. There it was, Radio City Music Hall, one of the world's biggest indoor theaters, home of the Radio City Rockettes and the Christmas Spectacular.

As a shy nineteen-year-old, Kendra, fresh off the bus from Ohio, had auditioned for the world-famous Rockettes, known for their precision dance numbers and show-stopping "eye-high" kicks. When she learned she'd gotten the job she was thrilled! She'd been in New York for only three days and already someone was going to pay her to dance! Of course, the Rockettes only danced, and got paid, for a couple of months during the holidays. New York was one of the most expensive cities in the world, so she'd have to find other jobs, but that didn't bother her then. She was on her way.

She could still remember how nervous and excited she'd been at her first performance. It was a full house, more than six thousand people in the audience. Kendra stood backstage with the other girls, wearing her snowflake costume, a silken confection trimmed with white fur and encrusted with rhinestones. For a second she thought she was going to be sick. But when the curtain rose and the music started, she pasted a smile on her face and started tapping along with the other girls, matching her movements to theirs exactly. When it was time for the big finish, Kendra and the other thirty-five Rockettes formed a line and kicked in perfect time, looking for all the world like one dancer reflected in thirty-six mirrors. The audience went wild! Kendra had been dancing in front of audiences since she was five years old, but she'd never known that applause could be so loud and or so satisfying. It was the best moment of her life and, even now, Kendra still felt that tingle of excitement when the show went well. She truly loved performing.

However, by the end of that first run, after listening to jingle bells rung and carols sung four times a day, twice accidentally stepping in camel droppings left by the live nativity, and stumbling onto the subway at eleven every night on aching, blistered feet, Kendra was sick of Christmas.

Her mother had sent the box of ornaments Kendra had been collecting since she was a little girl, but Kendra didn't put up a tree. "I get plenty of that at work, Mom. One more 'Ho, Ho, Ho,' and I'll happily strangle Santa with a piece of tinsel garland, then start on the elves," Kendra joked when she called her parents in Ohio. And it was almost true; in performing the business of Christmas, Kendra somehow missed the celebration. That was all right, she reasoned. It would all be worth it in the end.

But that was a long time ago. In spite of her auspicious beginnings, it turned out New York had not been waiting for Kendra Erickson to take it by storm. She'd gone to countless auditions and endured countless rejections. She'd gotten a few small parts Off Broadway and done some modeling, but for the nine months of the year she wasn't working at Radio City, Kendra waited tables and worked retail, like thousands of other actresses waiting for a break. Those jobs by themselves wouldn't have been enough to live on, so Kendra counted on her annual gig as a Rockette to make ends meet, at least until Broadway came knocking.

Once, she'd come close, landing the ingénue role in a musical. It was a great part for her, with big dance numbers and a score that suited her voice perfectly, but three weeks into rehearsal, the leading man had come down with pneumonia, so they'd replaced him with Danny Jervis, a well-known New York actor. Kendra was thrilled to be making her Broadway debut with someone so famous, but when they were introduced Danny smiled, asked if she would excuse him, and went to find the director. The next thing she knew, she'd been fired. Danny was only five foot seven and he refused to work with an actress who was taller than he was. The show, and Kendra's understudy, got great reviews and, three years later, it was still running. That was when Kendra started to think that maybe it wasn't going to happen, maybe the big break would never come her way.

Her mother had said she should come home to Ohio. But why? So she could wait tables in Akron? Performing was what she loved and all she knew, so when fall came, she signed on for another season with the Rockettes, hoping that Stanley was right, that there was always next year and that, this time, it would be her year.

Kendra had a headache. The clatter of thirty-six pairs of tap shoes wasn't helping. Brenda, the cranky choreographer, was in a sour mood and kept shouting, "Get the lead out, ladies! We open in two weeks and you've got to get this number down!"

Kendra rolled her eyes. She could do this in her sleep, most of the girls could. The choreography changed very little from year to year. When it comes to Christmas, audiences like tradition. Eighty-year-old grandmothers wanted their granddaughters to see the toy soldier routine performed exactly the way they'd seen it when they were little girls, and since Grandma was paying as much as $250 for a VIP ticket in the high season, Radio City Music Hall was happy to oblige.

Like Kendra, many of the girls came back year after year. For the veterans, the challenge lay not in doing the steps but in keeping them fresh, and they worked at it. That's why they were hired year after year. Of course, there were always a few newcomers.

Kendra had befriended one of them though, as a rule, she preferred to keep her work life and personal life separate. But on the first day of rehearsals, when Brenda called lunch and the girls all left with friends to get something at one of the nearby restaurants,

Kendra noticed one rookie sitting by herself eating some yogurt.

"Is that all you're having? With all the dancing you're doing, you don't need to diet," Kendra said. "You could eat donuts every day and still burn it off."

The girl smiled shyly. "Oh, it's not that. It's just . . . Well, I won't get my first paycheck for a couple of weeks. I just moved here from Vermont and everything is so expensive! I haven't found an apartment yet, not one I can afford, and the hotel I'm staying in is costing me an arm and a leg!" The girl blushed. "Sorry. I didn't mean to bore you with the story of my life. I'll be fine when I get paid and settled somewhere."

Kendra remembered her first year in the city and how much she'd paid for her first closet-sized apartment. Thank heavens she'd found a nice place in Queens, small but sunny and right on the subway line. Her neighborhood was starting to become fashionable and the rents were bound to go up but, fortunately, Kendra still had two years to go on her lease.

Kendra felt sorry for the new girl. "Come on," she said, smiling. "Let me buy you lunch. There's a deli around the corner that makes a great pastrami on rye."

"You're sweet, but I couldn't," she replied, turning an even deeper shade of red.

"Sure you can." The girl still looked doubtful so Kendra said, "Look, you've got to eat something or you'll pass out and if that happens, Brenda will be in a worse mood and take it out on the rest of us."

The rookie laughed. "If you put it that way. Thanks a lot . . . What's your name?"

"Kendra Erickson."

"Nice to meet you. I'm Stacey Loomis."

Over lunch, Kendra shared valuable information with the newcomer: where to look for a cheap apartment, how to get half-price tickets for shows, and which restaurants served good, inexpensive meals. Stacey pulled a little notepad out of her pocketbook and wrote it all down.

When they walked back to the theater, Stacey went on and on about how nice Kendra was to help her. Since then, Stacey waited at the stage door for Kendra every morning before rehearsal, greeting her with a big smile and hug, as if sharing a pastrami sandwich and a Diet Coke had suddenly made them best friends for life. At first

Kendra thought it was sort of cute, but now it was starting to get on her nerves. This was New York, after all, not Grover's Corners, and in New York the rule was: keep your distance. When it came to Stacey, Kendra was starting to wish she'd done just that.

She had no way of knowing that her unintended, unwanted friendship with Stacey Loomis might just turn out to be the best Christmas gift she'd ever received.

Chapter Two

"Come on, ladies! Break's over!" Brenda snapped her fingers impatiently. The girls abandoned their water bottles and scurried into line. "We're going to do the reindeer number . . . again."

Everyone groaned. The girl next to Kendra muttered, "What's got into her today? We've already done it about fifty times."

"I heard that, Joanie!" Brenda snapped. "And unless you get it right, we'll do it fifty more times. Ready? Five, six, seven, eight!"

The music started and thirty-six dancers started tapping in time, trying their best to look like a line of magical, tap-dancing reindeer. They must have been doing a good job because while Brenda wasn't actually smiling (Kendra had never seen Brenda truly smile; the closest she came was a pained grimace she put on whenever photographers showed up to take publicity shots.), she kept nodding her head in time to the music, which was Brenda's way of saying she liked what she was seeing. But that didn't mean she didn't have suggestions.

"Stacey! You're smiling too wide, look in the mirror. Your smile should be the same as the girls on your left and right."

"Joanie! Snap your head on that turn. Give it some flair!"

"Kendra! Get with the program! You're not kicking high enough!"

Kendra had been nursing shin splints and her legs were killing her, but, with a regulation-sized Rockette smile pasted on her face, she kicked higher.

"Come on, Kendra! You're not trying!" Brenda stopped, nodding her head, and her already deafening voice raised a couple of decibels. "Eye-high kicks, Kendra! Eye-high! Get that leg up there!"

Clenching her teeth through the pain, Kendra kicked her leg as high as it would go. And that's when it happened. During the lunch break, someone must have spilled some water on the floor. Kendra slipped, her legs flying out from under her. As she landed she heard the sickening crunch of breaking bone and felt a searing pain that made her scream in agony.

Instantly, the music stopped and a ring of frightened, concerned faces surrounded Kendra. Brenda pushed her way through the crowd and got down on her knees. "Kendra, are you all right? What happened? Can you get up?"

The pain was awful and Kendra could barely speak but she managed to choke out a few words through her tears. "Call an ambulance. I broke my ankle."

Kendra sat on the edge of the examining table staring at her cast while the nurse read a list of instructions off a clipboard.

"Doctor says to take two of these every six hours for pain, but only if you need them. Try not to get the cast wet. Wrap it in a plastic bag while you're bathing. No showers. Try to keep weight off the foot. Make sure you use the crutches; don't try walking on the cast. Come in for another set of X-rays in a month, so we can make sure it's all healing properly, but it's a bad break so you'll probably need a cast for at least ten weeks. And, other than that, just try not to overdo it." The nurse looked up and smiled. "Any questions?"

Yes, Kendra thought, *plenty. What am I supposed to do while I'm waiting for it to heal? How am I supposed to pay my rent? Will I be able to dance once the cast is off? Does the hospital have any openings for a dancer with a broken ankle and no medical training?*

But instead she just shook her head and said, "No. Thanks."

By the time she left the emergency room, it was dark and it was raining. Kendra sighed. It would be next to impossible to find a cab in this weather. She'd have to take the subway, but the thought of descending the stairs on wobbly crutches was daunting. Kendra thought of herself as pretty tough, but she was about ready to burst into tears. This had been one of the worst days of her life.

"Kendra?" a voice called out. Kendra looked her to her right and saw Stacey leaning against the wall of the hospital, holding a coffee cup in one hand and a shopping bag in the other. "Are you all right?"

"Oh. Hi, Stacey. What are you doing here?"

Stacey tipped her head to the side and

smiled as if this was the silliest question she'd ever heard. "Waiting for you. I've been here for hours. I was starting to think you'd left through another door."

Kendra didn't quite understand. "Waiting for me? Why?"

"To help you get home, of course. I don't think we'll be able to get a cab, but between the two of us, I'm sure we can make it to the subway. Here. I brought you a mocha latte. It isn't all that hot anymore, but it should still taste good." She handed the cup to Kendra and then held up the shopping bag. "And after we get you home, I'm making dinner. The deli had some great-smelling chicken soup."

For a second, Kendra wondered what planet this girl had come from but, after taking a sip of the delicious, creamy mocha— the first thing she'd put in her stomach since breakfast—Kendra was so grateful she didn't care.

True to her word, Stacey escorted Kendra all the way back to her apartment in Queens and then made dinner while Kendra changed into her pajamas and robe. Stacey made a big Caesar salad to go with the soup and, after they'd eaten, pulled two cartons of Ben & Jerry's ice cream out of the freezer.

"Cherry Garcia or Phish Food?" Stacy asked.

"My favorites! How about some of each?"

"Why not?" Stacey scooped out two big bowls of ice cream and brought them to the table.

Kendra took a spoonful of Cherry Garcia and groaned with pleasure. "That is so good!"

"You know," Stacey said, "they make all this in Vermont, right near my home town. The factory isn't far from Maple Grove."

Kendra laughed. "You've got to be kidding. You're actually from a place called Maple Grove? Sounds like a town they'd invent for one of those Hallmark Hall of Fame specials, where all the houses have front porches and picket fences, and all the kids ride their bikes to the drugstore for strawberry phosphates after school."

Stacey smiled as she dug a fudge fish out of her ice cream. "Actually, you've got it just about right. Downtown Maple Grove is right off the cover of a New England travel guide—white clapboard houses, the town

green, and a church with a belfry and a big
steeple. It was a great place to grow up but
small, only six thousand people. In fact, it
doesn't even have a dance studio. My
mother had to drive a half hour each way,
three times a week so I could take dance
classes."

"Well, it must make her proud to know her
efforts paid off. Are your folks going to come
down from Vermont to see the show?"

The smile faded from Stacey's face. "My
dad was killed in a car accident when I was
nine and my mom died of cancer during my
junior year in high school."

Kendra was shocked. Stacey was only
nineteen, which meant she'd lost her mother
only a couple of years ago. "I'm so sorry,"
she said sincerely. "That must have been
terrible for you."

Stacey nodded. "It was. I missed my mom
so much. My brother moved home, and I
lived with him and his little girl until I finished
school. Andy is fifteen years older than me.
He's a minister. Fortunately, our church had
started looking for a new senior pastor just
before Mom passed and they were happy to
hire Andy. As sad as I was about losing my
mom, I felt like God was watching out for

me. After all I'd already been through, it would have been really hard to leave my town and my friends. And I think it was good for Andy, too. He really needed to make a fresh start."

"What do you mean?" Kendra asked. The casual way Stacey referred to God watching out for her, as if God actually had time to worry about her troubles, made Kendra a little uncomfortable. She wondered if Stacey's brother was one of those pulpit-banging preacher televangelists. Maybe he'd run afoul of the IRS and was hiding in Vermont.

"Andy's wife walked out on him and their little girl, Thea, about three years ago. Sharon just woke up one day and said she didn't feel like being a wife and mother anymore. Andy tried everything to get her to reconsider. They went to counseling and he even said he'd move to a different town if that would help, but Sharon was determined to leave. She moved to San Francisco, filed for divorce, and that was it. She's never tried to see Thea, which is so sad. Thea is eleven and she's such a sweetie."

"That's terrible!" She wondered how any mother could just leave her child and never look back. Kendra had two big dreams in her life: to act on Broadway and to fall in love and have a family. But now, with her thirtieth birthday just around the corner, she was starting to think she'd struck out on both counts.

"Yeah," Stacey agreed sadly, then lifted her hands in front of herself, like she was determined to push away any thoughts of gloom or self-pity. "But, listen to me going on and on! We should be talking about you. Tell me what the doctor said."

"Not much. I've eaten shellfish with more personality. He said to come back in a month for another X-ray and then wait another month for the cast to come off. After that, we'll know if I can dance again or not." Stacey clucked her tongue sympathetically. "Then he made a comment comparing dancer years to dog years and wondered if I should be thinking about retiring."

Stacey winced. "Ouch! Sounds like a great guy."

"Yeah, that's what I thought." Kendra tried to smile but couldn't manage it. She dropped her spoon and buried her face in her hands.

"Stacey, what am I going to do? Radio City will give me some compensation, but the medical bills will eat that up. I'd wait tables, but no one is going to hire me with this thing on my foot. The rent is due and my savings are gone; my new audition photos cleaned me out. If I can't pay, the landlord will toss me out like that"—she snapped her fingers—"he could get a lot more for this place now than when I signed."

Stacey looked around the little studio, admiring the sunny yellow walls and shining wood floors. "It's a darling apartment," she said wistfully. "Ten times better than any of the dumps I've looked at. I'll never be able to afford something this nice."

Kendra lowered her hands and looked at Stacey, thinking. "Yes, you can," she said slowly, her voice brightening. "You could sublet my apartment. It's a perfect solution! You'd have a nice place to live for a couple months, until you can find something more permanent, and I wouldn't lose my lease!"

"But," Stacey asked doubtfully, "where would you live? It's only one room. There isn't space for two of us."

Kendra bit her lower lip and considered the question. "I guess I'll have to leave New York until my foot heals. Maybe go back to Ohio." Kendra groaned. "Oh, anywhere but back home with my folks! I always promised myself I'd never do that. But," she sighed with resignation, "at the moment, I don't have a lot of other options."

"Not necessarily," Stacey said as she sprung up from her chair, bounded into the tiny kitchen, and started rummaging around the counters and through the empty shopping bags. "Where's my pocketbook?"

"Right over there." Kendra pointed to the coatrack by the door. "Why? What are you looking for?"

Stacey grinned and grabbed her bag. "My cell phone. I've got an idea!"

And before Kendra quite realized what was happening, it was all arranged. Stacey called her brother, who called a few more people, and the next thing Kendra knew, for a salary of two hundred dollars a week plus room and board, she'd been hired to direct and produce the thirty-fifth annual Christmas pageant of the First Community Church of Maple Grove, Vermont, which took place every year on the eve of Christmas Eve, December 23.

"But, I still don't get it," Kendra argued a week later, as Stacey was helping unload her luggage from the back of the taxi and carting it into Penn Station. "Why would they hire me sight unseen? I've never directed anything in my life."

"One, because you're a wonderful dancer and you've got ten years of professional experience. Two, because I vouched for you and that kind of thing counts for a lot in Maple Grove. Three, because Dr. Benton, the church organist who directed the show since before I was born, died last year and they need a replacement. And four, because you're willing to do it for a price they can afford to pay. You won't be getting rich, but you won't have to pay for food or rent, so it'll be enough to get by on until your foot heals and you can come back to New York."

"But, Stacey. Me? A director? I've never . . ."

"Oh, for heaven's sake, Kendra! It's a little community Christmas play, not Tennessee Williams! You'll do a great job. Have a little faith, will you?"

It was a Friday in late October. The fall foliage season was over but a surprise snowstorm brought winter in a little early that year, much to the joy of New England's tourist industry. Scores of New Yorkers were heading north for a weekend of skiing, sleighing, and sipping cocoa by the firesides of romantic country inns. That meant Kendra had to wait on line for twenty-five minutes before buying her ticket, which gave her barely enough time to make the train, but plenty of time to worry about what she was getting herself into.

"Here, you sit down and hold Wendell," Stacey said when they finally found an empty seat. "I'll put your luggage up on the rack. Do you want me to leave your tote bag down? Your sandwich and books are in there."

Kendra nodded distractedly. "These people I'm supposed to be staying with," she asked, "what makes you think they want a complete stranger living in their house?"

"Denny and Sugar? Don't be silly. They'll love having you. They're the sweetest old couple."

"Sure they are," Kendra said sarcastically. "They'd have to be. Denny and Sugar Sugarman? What kind of a name is that?"

Stacey grinned. "It's the perfect name for a maple syrup farmer. Denny's syrup is the best in the state."

Kendra rolled her eyes and made a retching sound. "See? That's what I'm talking about. I mean, how precious can you get? They can't be for real. How do I know you're not sending me off to live at the Bates Motel? It's probably all some ploy so you can have the apartment forever once I'm found murdered in the shower. Or maybe I'll be trampled to death, killed by a renegade moose."

Stacey shook her head. "You know, I'm amazed that some big-time director hasn't discovered you by now. Your potential as a full-time drama queen is nearly limitless. It's not too late for us to go back to the counter and buy a ticket to Akron."

Kendra made a face. "All right. All right. But if I hate it there, I'm going to remember who got me into this," she said darkly.

"You'll love it. Everyone loves Vermont! It's one of the most picturesque places on Earth. Beautiful scenery. Nice people. Lots of fresh air."

"Yeah, but what about the things that really matter? Can I get a decent bagel, the *Times,* HBO?" Kendra's concerned expression changed to panic as a new worry entered her mind. "What about my phone? Will I be able to get a cell signal?"

Outside the conductor shouted, "All aboard for the Vermonter! Last call! All aboard!"

"I've gotta run. I'm late for rehearsal." Stacey leaned down, gave Kendra a quick squeeze, and walked quickly to the door. "Have a great time and don't worry about anything," she called over her shoulder. "Send me a postcard when you get there! Bye!" Stacey stepped out of the car and started running down the platform toward the stairs.

Struggling to get up without knocking Wendell's cat carrier to the floor, Kendra lowered the window and shouted after her friend, "Postcard? Why do I have to send you a postcard? Stacey, that's not funny. I'm not kidding! Is there cell service in Maple Grove?"

Chapter Three

Fifteen minutes after the train pulled out of the Maple Grove depot, Kendra was still waiting for Denny and Sugar Sugarman to pick her up. She dug her cell phone out of her purse with the thought of calling them but then realized she didn't have their number. Not that it would have mattered if she did; when she flipped open her phone, the display screen read, NO SERVICE.

"I knew it," she grumbled to herself. "Stacey, if I ever get my hands on you . . ." It had started to snow again, fat flakes drifted lazily from the sky like stray thoughts.

If I wasn't about to freeze to death, Kendra thought, *I'd think they were pretty*. Clearly, she was going to have to buy some gloves and a heavier coat. She sat down on her suitcase and pulled her jacket closer around her body.

Finally, she heard the sound of a car pulling into the parking lot. Kendra grabbed her crutches, got to her feet, and started gathering her things. Behind her, a deep male voice asked, "Miss Erickson?"

Kendra looked up and saw a tall man, at least six foot three, approaching. His eyes were brown and so was his hair, but there were streaks of blonde in it, as if he spent a lot of time outdoors. His skin was tanned and Kendra noticed a shallow etching of crinkles at the corners of his eyes, a sign of someone who smiled often and laughed easily. He was wearing a sheepskin coat just like the one that the actor who'd played Curley to her Laurey had worn in the way Off Broadway production of *Oklahoma* she'd appeared in a couple of years back. In fact, the man approaching her looked a lot like her leading man . . . utterly gorgeous. But, Kendra was pretty sure that, unlike her Curley, this man was straight.

He bounded toward her, grabbed one of the bags, and lifted it as easily as if he was hefting her overnight bag instead of a 60-pound suitcase, and asked, "Have you been waiting long?"

Kendra reminded herself to breathe. "Denny?" she asked.

The man laughed. "Sorry, I should have introduced myself. I'm Andy Loomis. Stacey's brother. Nice to meet you." He extended his hand and Kendra shook it.

"Really?" Kendra asked with undisguised disappointment; if he wasn't a pastor, Kendra could definitely have gone for him, but there was no way she could picture herself being attracted to a man of the cloth. "You're a minister? Shouldn't you be wearing a black shirt and one of those white collars?" She blushed, embarrassed by her own bluntness and the look of amusement that crossed the young pastor's face.

"On Sundays I wear a black robe in the pulpit, my daughter calls it my party frock, but during the week I wear street clothes. Sorry you had to wait," he said, changing the subject. "I know you were expecting Denny and Sugar, but I wanted to meet you, too. The train's usually at least half an hour late, so I imagine they'll be here any minute."

Sure enough, it wasn't long before a bandy-legged man with a white beard and moustache and a smiling woman with bright blue eyes and high, pink cheekbones, rounded the corner of the depot—Denny and Sugar Sugarman. They reminded Kendra of the actors who played Santa and Mrs. Claus in the Christmas Spectacular, except they were shorter. When they saw Kendra and Andy waiting, they began trotting toward them.

"Were you waiting long?" Sugar asked, concerned, and then elbowed her husband. "I told Denny we should leave at three, but he kept tinkering in the garage."

"Gee, I'm sorry!" Denny said, puffing a little from exertion. "I was putting a new alternator in my old Toyota so Kendra can use it while she's here. Thought I had plenty of time; the train's usually at least a half hour late."

Introductions were made, handshakes exchanged, inquires made about Kendra's journey and whether she was tired, hungry or both. Five minutes later Kendra's luggage was loaded in the back of the Sugarmans's sport wagon.

"Denny, Sugar, I know you're anxious to get your guest settled in, but would you mind if I ran Kendra over to the church?" Andy asked. "Rehearsals start in a few days, so I imagine she'd like to see the stage and all. I can run Kendra out to your place later."

"That's fine. I dressed a nice roaster for supper," Sugar said. "Why don't you stay and eat with us? Bring Thea along. I just about finished that dress I was making for her. She can try it on tonight and I'll mark the hem."

"I'd love to, but we can't. It's parent-teacher conference night at school. Maybe next week."

"All right," Sugar said. "I'm holding you to it. Kendra, we'll see you later and don't worry about Wendell. I'll give him something to eat. Stacey told me you had a cat, so I saved the giblets for him." The Sugarmans waved as they drove off.

Kendra climbed into Andy's car. "They are so darling! Stacey said that people in Maple Grove are nice, but letting a perfect stranger move into your house. Giving her a car to drive. Even thinking to save the chicken scraps for her cat!" she said, amazement apparent in her voice. "It'd never happen in Manhattan, that's for sure."

"Well, Stacey's right," Andy said and put Kendra's crutches in the backseat. "Folks in

Maple Grove are nice." He paused before slamming the door. "Most of them, any-way."

Before they went to the church, Andy gave Kendra a quick tour of Maple Grove. It was exactly like Stacey had described it. The streets were straight, tree-lined and quaint, with white clapboard houses in tidy rows on either side. Some of the homes were tall and majestic, with high-pitched roofs traced with elegant dentil molding. Others were stubby and ramshackle, with oddly bumped-out rooms and uneven roof heights, as though they had been added onto again and again by homeowners who thought hiring architects was just a superfluous expense. But no matter the size, each dwelling looked like a home that had been welcoming visitors for hundreds of years. And, judging by the historical plaques hung by the front doors, it was true.

"That house was built in 1779," Kendra marveled. "And people are still living there? Amazing!"

"Oh, that's nothing," Andy replied. "Some of these date back to before Maple Grove was even a proper town. One has been in the hands of the same family ever since. See?" He pointed out the window to a small saltbox with a sloping ridgepole and windows of thick, bull's-eye glass. "That's Darla Benton's house. There has been a Benton living in that house since 1768."

"Benton? That name sounds familiar."

Andy nodded. "Maybe Stacey told you about him. Dr. Benton was our church organist, the man who wrote the script for the Christmas play and directed every show for the past thirty-five years. Of course, he wasn't a full-time organist. He taught English literature and music at the community college, too. His wife, Darla, still lives in the house." Andy cleared his throat.

"Actually, that's why I wanted you to come to the church today, so you can meet her. Darla belongs to the Quilting Bees, a group of ladies who get together every Friday and make quilts for missionaries, single mothers with new babies, elderly shut-ins, even the Red Cross. I thought it would be a good idea if she could meet you, get to know you personally."

Something about the too-smooth tone of his voice set off warning signals in Kendra's brain. With Big Apple bluntness, she said, "You're worried that the queen bee won't be happy about seeing a new face in the hive?"

"No," Andy assured her. "I'm sure you'll get on just fine, but Jake only passed this summer and this show was his baby—and Darla's. Of course, audiences were getting smaller every year, but Jake did the best he could." Andy glanced at Kendra as he turned the corner onto Main Street. "I'd just appreciate it if you could make her feel comfortable, let her know that you're going to put on a show Jake would have been proud of."

Andy gave her a sideways glance. "And, by the way, it might be better if you didn't mention you were a Rockette, not right off."

Kendra bristled. "Why shouldn't I? Your own sister's a Rockette. What wrong with that?"

"Nothing," he said calmly. "I'm thrilled for Stacey, it's a great opportunity for her, but this is a small town. Darla is old and set in her ways. On top of that, she's still grieving. Once she gets to know you, it'll be fine, but I'm worried that she might think a Rockette won't treat the show with the dignity she feels it deserves. From what Stacey told me, you're more than up to the job, but until Darla realizes that, too, I think we'd better just tread lightly. Darla Benton's opinion carries a lot of weight in this town; you'll want to start off on the right foot with her."

"Oh, I see how it is," Kendra nodded and her voice dripped sarcasm. "We've got to curry the favor of the old guard. See, that's why I never go to church. They're filled with hypocrites."

Andy smiled mischievously as he pulled into the church parking lot. "Is that so? Like I always say, 'Come on down, anyway. There's always room for one more.'"

"Well, I figured I'd start going," Kendra said grudgingly. "If I'm going to be paid by the church, then I guess it would look funny if I didn't show up on Sundays, but I'm not planning on enjoying it."

Andy laughed out loud. "That's the spirit!"

She knew he was making fun of her. Still, Kendra couldn't keep herself from smiling.

"Hello, ladies. How are you today?" Andy boomed cheerfully as he opened the door of the classroom. The whirring of sewing machines and snip-snip of scissors stopped as a dozen or so mostly older women looked up and returned the pastor's greeting. "This is Kendra Erickson, the young woman who will be directing the Christmas play. Kendra, these are the Quilting Bees."

Kendra nodded and smiled, hoping she looked more confident than she felt. "And this," Andy continued, approaching a woman who was hand-sewing long, basting stitches into a finished quilt top, "is Mrs. Darla Benton, the lady I was telling you about." The old woman was a striking contrast to the others, with their gray halos of short hair and plump, grandmotherly figures that made Kendra think of rising bread dough. Mrs. Benton was tall, almost angular and she carried herself proudly. Her eyes were gray-blue and glittering, her hair silver-white, worn in two long braids coiled around her head in a crown. Kendra's first instincts were right, Mrs. Benton was definitely the Queen Bee.

"It's nice to meet you," the older woman said, but her unsmiling expression made Kendra wonder if she was telling the truth.

She tried to remember what Andy had said about Mrs. Benton being a recent widow and all, but something about the appraising way she looked Kendra up and down, like she was trying to guess her weight or competence or both, set Kendra's teeth on edge.

"Nice to meet you, too," Kendra lied. "I understand that your late husband wrote and directed the play."

The older woman nodded. "For thirty-five years. Jake was a pillar of this church and, under his leadership, the annual Christmas play became the most important holiday tradition in Maple Grove. You've got some very big shoes to fill, Miss Erickson."

Kendra, not exactly sure how to respond to Mrs. Benton's speech, was thankful when Andy stepped in. "Yes, I've told her all about Jake and the wonderful job he did with the show for all those years. That's why I wanted to find someone really talented and experienced to direct the play. Kendra has been working in *professional* theater for ten years," Andy said importantly and then paused a moment before coming in with the clincher. "In New York City."

For the first time, the old lady's eyes flickered interest. "Really? Well, that is quite impressive. What plays have you been in, Miss Erickson?"

Andy shot Kendra a look and broke in. "Oh, she's worked all over—dance, musicals, modeling—you name it. She was in a show that was scheduled to run through December, but then she broke her ankle. Sad for Kendra, but lucky for the church. Otherwise, we could never have attracted someone with her experience, someone who could leap the bar that Jake set so high for all those years, someone who could do justice to his memory." Andy delivered the speech with a theatricality that made Kendra wonder if he shouldn't be the one directing the play.

Mrs. Benton, clearly moved by the pastor's regard for her late husband, and impressed that the church had gone to such lengths to find a suitable replacement, smiled. "That's fine. That sounds just fine. I'm sure Miss Erickson will do a wonderful job. Auditions are nearly two weeks off, but I'm sure you'll want to look over the script between now and then. That will give you time to get a sense of the piece, an appreciation for the language. My Jake taught English, you know," the widow said proudly. "I'll get the script to you right away."

That night, after an enormous chicken dinner that looked like a dress rehearsal for Thanksgiving, Kendra pushed herself back from the table and groaned. "Thanks, Sugar, that was incredible! Everything was delicious, the chicken, dressing, and those sweet potatoes—I could have eaten a mountain of them! In fact, I think I did. And I don't even usually like sweet potatoes."

"Kendra, you picked the right place to stay, that's certain," Denny said and got up to give his wife a kiss before starting to clear the dishes. "My Sugar is the best cook in town."

Sugar beamed. "The potatoes are an old family recipe with a little twist; we use maple syrup instead of brown sugar. Makes all the difference. Now, how about some dessert? I've got a nice apple crumble."

"Sounds great, Sugar, but I really couldn't eat another bite; besides, now that I'm not dancing every day, I've got to start watching what I eat." Kendra got to her feet. "Let me help you with the dishes."

"Nope!" Denny said, waving away her offer. "I do the dishes around here. Sugar cooks and I clean up, that's the way it is; besides, you've had a long day. You're probably tired."

It was true, though Kendra denied it. But, Denny insisted he didn't need any help, so, after thanking Sugar again for dinner, Kendra went to her room and got ready for bed.

The main floor guestroom had its own bath and was decorated simply, with a beautiful quilt in bright blues and yellows on the bed and several lovely watercolors, all scenes from Maple Grove, hanging on the walls. Both the quilt and the paintings, Kendra had learned, were Sugar's creations. She was really quite an artist.

After finally mastering the trick of lowering herself into the old-fashioned claw-foot tub while leaving her cast hanging over the side, Kendra settled back into the soothing hot water and thought about her first day in Maple Grove. It had been a long one and she was tired, but all in all, things were going better than she would have expected.

To begin with, the Sugarmans couldn't have made her feel more comfortable or welcomed. And, though she'd been concerned about the problems in presenting a play in a church, she'd realized that when the pulpit and altar were moved there would be plenty of room onstage. The lighting and sound systems were better than she'd hoped, and there was plenty of seating in the sanctuary. Whether she'd be able to fill those seats was another question, but now that she was here, Kendra was determined to put on a first-class production. Sure, Maple Grove was a million miles from New York, or might as well have been, but Kendra had always harbored a secret wish to direct and now she was getting her chance. It was really kind of exciting.

Maple Grove was starting to grow on her, too. True, the town was smaller than she'd envisioned, but it had a certain charm. She smiled to herself, remembering how Andy had asked if she wanted to get some coffee before they left town. She'd quickly said yes, that a mocha latte would really hit the spot. Andy pulled into the Dunkin' Donuts drive-thru and laughed at Kendra's baffled expression.

"Kendra, there's no Starbucks here. This is rural New England; there's a Dunkin'

Donuts about every two miles. In fact, that's how we measure distance. Maple Grove to Montpelier is twelve Dunkin' Donuts. If you want to go to Burlington, it's eight but in the opposite direction," he joked, and then told the voice on the other end of the intercom that he wanted two large mochas with extra whipped cream.

That was another unexpected surprise—Andy. Stacey had neglected to say how good-looking her brother was, and how nice. Kendra thought his ex-wife was crazy to have walked out on him, not to mention their little girl, Thea. Andy had driven by the park, where Thea was sledding with a bunch of other kids, so Kendra could meet her. She was a darling. Her eyes were deep brown like her dad's and she was tall like him, almost gangly, but her features were fine and her blonde hair was long and shining, bound in two thick braids that framed her face. She was shy at first, but when Andy told her that Kendra was a real Rockette, her eyes shone. Kendra promised to teach her how to do those famous Rockette kicks when Thea and Andy came to the Sugarmans's house for dinner, and the little girl clapped her hands with excitement.

Andy told Thea that they had to run, that he'd be home in half an hour to make dinner, and then kissed his daughter good-bye. Kendra sighed, remembering the sweet picture they'd made. It was too bad Andy was a minister, otherwise . . .

Enough of that, Kendra thought to herself. *The last thing you need to do is get worked up over some man with a child and a whole church full of Mrs. Bentons looking over his shoulder. You're here to work, get well, and get back to New York as quickly as possible—that's all!*

Getting out of the tub proved even more of a challenge than getting in, but she managed. Wendell sat on the edge of the tub, occasionally dipping a curious paw into the water until Kendra shooed him off, worried that he might accidentally fall in. After drying off and putting on her pajamas she climbed into bed, propped herself high on a pile of pillows, and switched on the bedside lamp. Wendell jumped up on the bed and curled up into a ball at her feet, purring loudly, sleeping off the effects of the saucer of cream that Sugar had given him for "dessert."

Kendra opened the script Mrs. Benton

had dropped off earlier and started reading—page one, then two, and on through page one hundred and nine—sinking slightly lower with each turn of the page until, by the end, she was lying flat on her back and staring up at the ceiling, thinking about all the things that had gone right that day, and knowing that none of it mattered because what she was holding in her hands was, without a doubt, the worst play on the face of the planet.

Chapter Four

When Andy and Thea came to dinner the following week, Sugar outdid herself, serving a fancy Beef Bourguignon with thick slices of crusty French bread to soak up the delicious sauce, and salad. In her first week at the Sugarman farm Kendra had already gained two pounds, so when the platters were passed, she took lots of salad but only a small portion of the heavenly smelling main course and ate it slowly, savoring every bite.

After dinner, Sugar suggested they go into the living room and make popcorn. She laughed when Kendra asked how they were going to do that since the microwave was in the kitchen.

"My goodness, Kendra! You really are a city girl. Haven't you ever made popcorn over the fire? Not even when you were a little girl?"

"I grew up in a condo." She shrugged, blushing a little when she noticed the amused expression on Andy's face. "No fireplace."

Everyone trooped into the living room and gathered around the enormous stone fireplace. Denny challenged Andy to a game of chess. The two men settled in at the game table and started setting up the board.

"Back in the 1760s, when the house was built, they did all the cooking in the fireplace," Sugar informed Kendra as she pulled a long-handled wire mesh basket out of the closet and poured some popping corn into it. "That's why it's so big, you could roast a pig in here. And that indentation in the back is a beehive oven. They baked all their bread there."

Sugar pulled a big ottoman up near the fire, indicating that Kendra should sit there, then handed her the popcorn basket. Wendell, still licking his face clean of the last of the table scraps that Sugar had given him, sauntered in to see what all the excitement was about.

"Now you just hold that over the fire,"

Sugar instructed, "not too close to the flame, and keep shaking it until it pops. There's bowls and salt right there. Make sure you use that oven mitt when you open the basket. It'll be hot. Thea, I'm going to run get your new dress and we'll mark up the hem." Sugar scurried off to her sewing room and Thea settled in next to Kendra on the ottoman.

"Keep shaking it hard," Thea advised seriously. "Otherwise it'll burn."

"Thanks."

"So, you've really never made popcorn in the fireplace?" Thea asked, disbelief apparent in her voice.

Kendra shook her head. "Nope. Just the microwave. Actually, that's not quite right. Once my mom and I made Jiffy Pop on the stove, you know, in one of those disposable pans with the aluminum top that blows up like a balloon when the corn pops. Sugar's right," Kendra smiled. "I'm just a city girl."

"Dad took me to New York at Christmas once; we went to the Empire State Building, and the Statue of Liberty, and to the Christmas show at Radio City. I wonder if I saw you?"

"Maybe," Kendra said. "We have a few

days on and then a few off, but there's a good chance I was dancing that day."

Thea sighed and put her elbow on her knee, resting her chin on her hand as she stared into the fireplace. "The city was so wonderful. I bet you miss it. Nothing exciting ever happens in Maple Grove."

"Not nearly as much as I thought I would," Kendra said, surprised to realize it was true. "In some ways, I'm finding there's as much to do here as in the city, it's just that they're different kinds of things." A single popcorn kernel popped, then another and another until the room was filled with the sound of tiny corn explosions and the enticing smell of fresh popcorn. Wendell, fascinated by the sight and sound of jumping, cracking corn kernels, sat erect and alert by Kendra's side. Pleased by her small accomplishment, Kendra smiled and shook the basket harder, determined not to let a single kernel burn.

Thea rolled her eyes, the picture of preteen boredom. "Yeah, like what?"

"All kinds of things. Sugar is teaching me how to quilt. I'm making a pillow for my mother for Christmas. My seams are a little wobbly and the triangles didn't come out exactly the same size, but it's fun. Denny has been telling me all about how to collect maple sap and boil it down into syrup; too bad I won't be here in the spring when it's time to tap the trees. Yesterday, I spent the whole afternoon poking around the shops on Main Street. It's fun because the stores are all so different, not a chain in sight. I bought a handmade sweater that would have cost me ten times more in Manhattan. Plus I've really enjoyed sitting by the fireside after dinner, just reading, writing, or working on my pillow. You know, I haven't watched television once since I've been here and I don't miss it at all." The popping had almost finished so Kendra picked up the oven mitt, opened the basket, and poured the popcorn into a big bowl.

"And you're wrong when you say that nothing exciting ever happens here," Kendra commented while Thea sprinkled salt over the fragrant popcorn. "The Christmas play is going to be the best ever! Are you coming to the auditions?"

Thea smiled a little. "Well, it's not like I really have a choice. I'm the preacher's kid. They always make me play Mary—because of my hair," she explained, taking hold of the end of a braid and showing it to Kendra.

"It's kind of silly if you think about it. Why would anybody think Mary was blonde? Mary was from Israel and just about everyone there has dark hair."

"Hey!" Denny piped up from across the room. "That popcorn smells good. Think you might bring a bowl over to your dad, Miss Thea? He's going to need something to console himself after I take his rook." Denny moved his knight, triumphantly took Andy's rook, and placed it with the other pieces he'd already captured. Thea poured half the popcorn into a second bowl and brought it to the game table.

"Don't give up, Dad," she said, patting her father's arm. "You can still win."

"You're right, sweetheart," Andy said, grabbing a handful of popcorn before returning his attention to the board. "There's always a first time."

Thea returned to the fireside and sampled the popcorn. "It's good," she said, taking some more, and then, her eyes asking Kendra's permission, she tossed a popcorn kernel to Wendell, who crunched it happily while Thea scratched him between the shoulder blades. "Nothing personal, Kendra," she said, returning to their earlier conversation, "but none of the kids wants to be in the play. The only ones who try out are the ones whose parents make them. Everybody at school thinks it's completely lame."

"Really?" asked Kendra. "Don't the kids in Maple Grove like performing? I heard there's a big theater club at the high school, and a jazz band, and a good dance team. I'd think they'd all want to be in the play."

Thea shook her head. "None of those kids will try out. Kendra, have you ever *seen* the church play? It's so old-fashioned! I mean, who talks like that? You'll get Tommy Skinner because his mother is the church treasurer, and a few kids whose parents are on the deacon board but that's about it. None of the dance team girls will try out. Why would they? There's no dancing in it."

Kendra smiled, leaned toward the little girl, and whispered, "There is now."

Thea's eyes grew wide. "Really? You're kidding! You re-wrote the play?"

"No," Kendra said. "I scrapped the play and wrote a whole new one."

"And it has dancing! Gosh, Kendra. Could I try out for one of those parts?"

"I don't see why not," she said and tossed a popcorn kernel deftly into her mouth.

"But," Thea said, her smile fading, "I don't know how to dance. I've always wanted to learn, but there's no school here. Aunt Stacey took lessons in Manchester, but I could never do that. Dad works all day and can't drive me."

"Well, I can teach you. I've already worked out the choreography in my mind and it won't be that hard. If you work hard and promise to come to every rehearsal . . ."

"Oh! I will! I promise!"

"Well, then I don't see why you can't be one of the dancers." Thea was so overjoyed by this news that Kendra thought she was going to jump up and yell, but Kendra put her hand on her shoulder and said, "Wait a minute! There's just one more thing. I need you to do me a favor."

Sarah Fenimore sat at a large desk, surrounded by papers. When Kendra entered, she peered over the tops of her glasses and asked, "May I help you?" in a voice that suggested Kendra must be lost.

"Are you Mrs. Fenimore? The music teacher?" The woman nodded and Kendra continued. "In that case, yes. I think you can help me. My name is Kendra Erickson. I'm going to be directing the Christmas play at First Community Church this year."

"Oh, yes!" the teacher said enthusiastically as she rose from her seat to greet Kendra. "Please, call me Sarah. I've heard all about you. Darla Benton told everyone at the library board meeting about the professional director they'd imported from New York. And little Thea Loomis has been going around pestering the other students, even the upperclassmen, to try out for the play. I saw her in the hall between classes yesterday, dogging the boys on the football team, trying to convince them they had dramatic potential." Sarah laughed as she took off her glasses and placed them on top of her head. "That's quite a little casting agent you have there."

Kendra grinned. "Thea and I have a deal, if she'll help me recruit a cast, I'll teach her to dance."

"Well, I think she's making some headway. I've heard quite a few of the kids ask each other if they were going to try out. If she can convince a few of the popular kids, like Charity Proctor and a few of the girls from the dance team, the rest will follow their lead. Is that why you're here? The dance team is practicing in the cafeteria. They meet after school on Tuesday and Thursday."

"Thanks. I'll go find them later but right now I'm here on a different recruiting mission. I came to talk with you."

"Me?"

"I know that in the past, the play had only an organist playing incidental music, but this year we're going to be doing something a little different. We're going to have several dance and choral numbers. I need a jazz combo, plus a few violinists and, most important, a musical director." Kendra flashed what she hoped was a winsome smile. "Interested?"

Sarah's eyebrows raised into twin arches of surprise. "Musical numbers? Dancing? You rewrote the play?" The shocked expression on Sarah's face made Kendra nervous. She decided not to repeat her earlier comment to Thea, the one about scrapping the old show entirely. "Does Darla know about this?"

"Well . . . not exactly," Kendra began uncomfortably. "I mean . . . not yet." She had a sinking feeling in her stomach. She'd been counting on Sarah and had lain awake half the night worrying what she would do about the music if she couldn't enlist the teacher's help. Clearly that wasn't going to happen and now Kendra was just worried that Sarah would run and tell Mrs. Benton about Kendra's plan to remake the late Dr. Benton's sacred cow of a play into a production people might actually go to see without the goads of duty, guilt, or physical force being employed.

"I don't blame you," Sarah said, shaking her head slowly. "When Darla finds out she's going to pitch a fit. If I were you, I'd try to keep that piece of news from her for as long as possible, at least until it's too late for her to do anything about it." Sarah's eyes glittered and she grinned. "But, that being said, count me in!"

Kendra was shocked. "Really?"

"Yes, indeed! It'll be worth it just so I don't have to sit through that play again. By this time, I can recite the lines myself—and they were pretty awful to begin with. Jake had a good idea; he was a talented man, but a better musician than writer. And to write a whole play in rhyming couplets? You'd have to be Dr. Seuss or Shakespeare to pull it off and Jake, God rest his soul, was neither. So!" She clapped her hands and rubbed them together eagerly. "When do we start?"

The thump of crutches hitting linoleum echoed through the corridor as Kendra walked to the cafeteria. *One musical director down*, she thought, *eight dancers to go.*

The driving beat of a Madonna song could be heard as Kendra approached. The door was heavy and she had a little trouble opening it without dropping a crutch. Inside, eight teenage girls were going through a peppy dance routine. *Not bad,* Kendra thought, *but the arms are sloppy and the girl on the end keeps stepping off on the wrong foot.*

When the music ended, the girls stopped at the same time, or nearly the same time, with their arms raised in stiff V's. Kendra clapped. The girls turned to look at her.

A familiar voice shouted "Kendra!" Thea ran up and threw her arms around her.

"Hey, Miss Thea! I didn't see you hiding in the corner."

"Sometimes I come and watch practice. Aren't they great?" she said wistfully and then lowered her voice to a whisper. "The tall one is Charity Proctor. She's the captain. I told her about the play but she says the team is too busy."

Charity walked over, flanked by the rest of the team.

"Nice job. It looked good," Kendra said and stuck out her hand to the dance captain. "I'm Kendra Erickson . . ."

"I know who you are," Charity said, not unkindly. "Thea told me all about you. It's nice that you'd like us to try out for the play, but the state dance team competition is the first weekend in December and we're not anywhere near ready. Thanks for thinking of us, Miss Erickson, but we just don't have time."

Kendra bit her lip. If she didn't have dancers, she didn't have a play. "Well," she said smoothly, "you're talented; I can see that, but you're right. You're not anywhere near ready for a state competition." Charity looked a little insulted, then worried. Kendra saw her opening. "You know, if you were willing to dance in the Christmas play, I'd be willing to help coach you. I could work with you every Saturday morning. I'd even arrange play rehearsal around your practice schedule. Mrs. Fenimore said Montpelier is your big rival. With my help, I think you could smoke them at state."

Charity appeared interested but doubtful. She glanced at the cast on Kendra's foot. "How are you supposed to coach us in dance when you can't even walk?"

"My teacher back in Ohio, Mrs. Hagen, taught me for nine years without ever getting out of her chair and I turned out to be a pretty good dancer," Kendra said nonchalantly. "Good enough to make my living doing it."

"Yeah!" Thea piped in helpfully. "Kendra's already given me two lessons. She tells me how it should look and what to do and I do it. She's a great teacher."

Charity considered this endorsement, and then looked at the girl to her right, who shrugged. "Could you excuse us a minute?"

The girls went into a huddle. When they broke, Charity walked up to Kendra and asked, "Were you really a Rockette?"

Kendra took her wallet out of her pocketbook and pulled out a picture of herself dressed in full snowflake regalia, posing under the marquee at Radio City.

Charity's eyes gleamed and she passed

the photo to the other girls, who *oooohed* and *aaaahed* over it before handing it back to their leader.

Charity smiled. "All right, Miss Erickson. It's a deal."

Chapter Five

The news that the popular Miss Proctor had decided to try out for the play had exactly the effect Sarah Fenimore predicted. At Sarah's suggestion, Kendra decided to hold auditions and the first few rehearsals in band room at the high school instead of at the church, partly for convenience but mostly to keep Mrs. Benton off their trail for as long as possible. When she entered the room that Friday the place was packed with laughing, shouting, flirting teenage boys and girls. Kendra was a little overwhelmed.

"There must be seventy kids here," Kendra said out of the side of her mouth when Sarah came up to greet her. She spied Thea sitting with a group of younger kids and winked at her. "Where did they all come from?"

"Sixty-one," Sarah replied. "I counted.

What did I tell you? Teenagers travel in packs. Where the queen goes, the drones will follow."

And it seemed to be true, at least in Charity's case. She was sitting in a chair, surrounded by a group of boys who were all jockeying for a spot nearer the pretty captain of the dance team. Charity waved when she saw Kendra, and Kendra returned the greeting, thinking how fortunate it was that, in spite of her obvious popularity, Charity seemed to be a very sweet and well-grounded girl, not spoiled at all. And she was really a very good dancer, as Kendra had seen during their first coaching session. On top of that Charity worked hard, listened, and had the respect of her teammates, qualities Kendra intended to capitalize on.

"Don't look so worried," Sarah laughed. "At least ten of the kids will be in the band. Another half dozen want to be stagehands or run lights. So that leaves a pool of about forty-five actors, dancers, and singers. How many parts do you have?"

"Thirty, but I can expand on that. Maybe split up some of the lines."

"You don't have to take them all," Sarah said. "It is an audition, after all."

Kendra shook her head. "No," she said firmly. "One way or another, I'll find parts for them all. I've experienced rejection too many times. I won't do that to them. If they're willing to take a chance on me, I'll do the same for them."

Sarah tilted her head to the side and gave Kendra an appraising look. "You know something? I think Andy Loomis picked the right lady for the job."

Kendra took a deep breath. "I hope you're right because between you and me, right now I'm shaking in my boots. How am I going to get them to settle down so we can get started?"

"Oh, that's easy," Sarah assured her. "Watch and learn." Sarah walked to the front of the room, stuck her two pinkie fingers in either side of her mouth, and emitted an ear-piercing whistle. Instantly, the room grew quiet. Sixty-one pairs of eyes focused on the band teacher.

"Hello, ladies and gentlemen. You are at the First Community Church Christmas play auditions. So if you thought these were the tryouts for the wrestling team, you need to go down to the gym," Sarah joked, getting a few chuckles in return. "Well, since you all seem to be in the right place, let's get started by introducing our director, Miss Kendra Erickson. Kendra?"

The kids applauded politely as Kendra moved to the front. She cleared her throat and began. "It's nice to see so many of you here today. Thank you for coming. Here's how we're going to do this. The band members will follow Mrs. Fenimore to the practice room and she'll give you your music. If you're here to work lights, sound, or props, please talk with me after the audition. For the rest of you, we're just going to read through some lines, have you sing a little, and we'll teach you a few dance steps. Very simple. This is just so I can get an idea of where you would best fit into the show, but I want you to know right now, that there will be a part for anyone who wants one and is willing to come to the necessary rehearsals. You can't all have a big part, but everyone will have at least one line." Kendra paused for a moment. "So, that's about it. Any questions?"

A large boy wearing a lettermen's jacket, sitting slumped in a chair near the back of the room, raised his hand. Kendra pointed to him.

"Miss Erickson, what's the play about? Because if it's anything like the old one, I think I'd rather go down to the gym and take my chances with the wrestling team."

The kids snickered and Kendra smiled in spite of herself.

"Sorry, I should have told you that before. The play is called *In the Workshop.* It's fairly short; I imagine it will run less than an hour. The action all takes place in Santa's workshop just before Christmas Eve. The basic idea is that the toys are having an argument about what is the most important part of Christmas and, naturally, each toy thinks it's all about them. They'll do various songs, dances, gymnastics, maybe even an ice-skating routine . . ."

"Inside the church?" someone shouted. "How can you do that?"

"It's not as hard as it sounds," Kendra answered. "They do it in the Radio City Music Hall Christmas show, where I worked for several years. You just need synthetic ice panels—works just as well as the real thing." An impressed murmur wove through the crowd. Kendra went on.

"So, toward the end, Santa Claus walks in. The toys are all a little embarrassed when he asks what they've been up to, suddenly thinking that Santa is certainly the most important part of Christmas. But the old man says, no, he isn't. Then he gathers the toys around and reads the Christmas story from the Gospel of Luke, or a shortened version of it. The toys realize their error and the show closes with everyone singing 'Oh, Holy Night' as the toys climb into Santa's sleigh. That's it."

For a minute, no one said anything, then a girl in the front raised her hand and asked, "So, there's no manger? No angels?" Kendra shook her head. "No shepherds dressed up in ratty bathrobes?"

"Nope," Kendra answered. "No bathrobes. You'll all have real costumes."

The boy in the lettermen's jacket shifted in his chair and said doubtfully, "Nothing personal, Miss, but singing, dancing toys? Santa? Sounds kind of lame to me."

"Well, I think it sounds like fun," Charity Proctor declared from the center of her gaggle of admirers. "If you don't want to be in it, Jason, you don't have to, but I'm staying."

The boy called Jason backpedaled. "I never said I didn't want to be in it," he protested. "I just said it better not be lame. That's all." Jason kept his seat.

Kendra looked around the room to see if anyone else had had second thoughts, but no one moved.

"All right, then!" she said, clapping her hands together. "Let's get started!"

Two and a half hours later, Kendra thanked everyone for their efforts and dismissed them, promising she'd have their parts posted by Monday afternoon. The kids shuffled out, laughing and talking amongst themselves.

Thea, already wearing her coat and backpack, ran up to Kendra and whispered, "How'd I do?"

"Great!" Kendra whispered back. "You can dance and act, and why didn't you tell me you have such a beautiful singing voice? You're a regular triple threat, Thea!"

Thea beamed. "So, what's my part?"

"Nice try," Kendra said with a laugh. "You'll just have to wait until Monday. Hey, do you need a ride home? If you'll wait a few minutes I can give you a lift."

"That's all right," Thea said as she shifted her pack to the other shoulder and headed toward the door. "Dad's picking me up. See you on Monday, Kendra!"

Kendra spent a few minutes going over her notes, concentrating on the kids who had seemed particularly promising. There were quite a few of them, so many that it was almost a problem, but a good one. Kendra was grateful to have a whole weekend in front of her with nothing to do but re-work the play and decide on casting. She gathered up her papers, put on her coat, and switched off the lights as she left.

"How'd it go?"

"Andy!" Kendra cried, startled. "My gosh! You scared me!"

"Sorry," he apologized, but not convincingly, grinning as he walked beside her, slowing his gait to match Kendra's cast-impaired pace.

"Are you looking for Thea?" Kendra asked, peering down the empty corridor, a little concerned. "She left a few minutes ago and said you were picking her up. I thought she was going to meet you at the front door."

"She did. She's waiting in the car."

"Oh," Kendra said. "Are you waiting for someone? I think everybody left."

"As a matter of fact, I *was* waiting for someone," Andy replied. "You. I wanted to see if I could take you out to dinner tonight." Seeing Kendra's hesitation, he added, "To thank you for being so nice to Thea, giving her dance lessons and everything. I can't tell you how much it means to her."

"You don't have to buy me dinner just for teaching Thea. I'm having as much fun as she is, maybe more; besides, I've got a ton of work to do this weekend," Kendra said, tipping her head toward the script and the note-stuffed bag that hung from her shoulder.

"But you've got to eat," Andy protested. "What were you planning on doing for dinner? Heating up a can of soup? I know Sugar won't be home to cook."

"How do you know that?" Kendra asked suspiciously.

Andy opened the front door, letting in a blast of frigid air as they exited the school and headed toward the parking lot.

"Small town. Friday is Denny and Sugar's bridge night." Andy smiled, his brown eyes sparking mischief and Kendra was reminded of how handsome he was. *Much too handsome to be a minister,* she thought, *that's the problem but . . . maybe . . .*

Andy saw her resolve weakening and seized his opportunity. "Come on. It'll just be for a couple of hours, then you can go home and get to work. I'm not taking no for an answer," he added, then bolted off toward his car, where Thea was waiting. Kendra started to argue, but he ignored her and called over his shoulder. "I'll pick you up at seven! Make sure you wear warm gloves and a hat!"

Warm gloves and a hat, Kendra thought as she watched Andy's car speed away with a waving Thea in the passenger seat, *Where are we dining, in an igloo?*

Much to Kendra's relief, they didn't have dinner in an igloo, but in a cute, candlelit Italian restaurant. Each table was covered with white butcher paper and supplied with a jar full of crayons. Happy to have found a distraction from the melting smile and piercing gaze that made her heart beat fast and her cheeks flush, Kendra put the crayons to good use while they waited for the food to arrive, drawing a whole family of rabbits.

Andy poured some more Chianti into Kendra's glass before taking another sip from his own and saying, "Those look very lifelike—in a Hanna-Barbera sort of way."

"Very funny," Kendra replied, keeping her eyes on the paper. "I'm a dancer, not an artist."

Andy lifted up his hands defensively. "I wasn't making fun of you. I think you're very talented. I can't even draw stick people. But you must have about ten rabbits there. Why so many?"

The real reason was that rabbits were all Kendra knew how to draw, but, engrossed in her work and feeling relaxed from the wine, she unthinkingly joked, "Well, you know what they say about rabbits and re-production . . ." She stopped midsentence and clapped her hand over her mouth, horrified by what she had almost said to a minister.

Andy smiled and shook his head. He reached out, wrapped one hand around her wrist and, with the other, took the crayon out from between her fingers. "Kendra, look at me." She did. "I really make you nervous, don't I? Are you always this tense on first dates?"

Kendra swallowed hard. "Is this a date?" she whispered, not certain what answer she wanted him to give.

"I sure hope so," Andy said in mock seriousness. "On a minister's salary, I can't afford to eat out like this unless it's for a very good reason. Is that what has you so flustered? Is it because I'm a pastor?"

Kendra nodded and blushed. "It's just . . . I . . . I never really talked to a minister before . . . And I certainly never went to dinner with one."

"I see," Andy said with an amused expression on his face. "Well, it's not like pastors are a different species, you know. I'm just a man, like any other man. The only difference is that I've been called to a very special job and lifestyle, one that I love, to do my best to guide and serve a church family. But, that doesn't mean I'm perfect, far from it, and it doesn't mean I grew up in a glass bubble. I know all about rabbits and reproduction." He leaned toward her, looked into her eyes, and whispered, "I have an eleven-year-old daughter, remember?"

Kendra put her hand in front of her mouth

to cover her smile. "OK. I guess I deserved that. It's just I don't know quite know how to act around you."

"Well," Andy suggested, "why don't you just act the way you normally would when you go out with someone for the first time. Act like yourself. Tell me about yourself."

Kendra took a sip from her wineglass. "What do you want to know?"

"Everything," Andy said.

Riding back to the Sugarman farm, Kendra thought about what a lovely evening it had been. She'd told Andy all about growing up in Ohio, and her dream of being a dancer, her disappointments in New York, and her anxieties about her future. In return, he'd told her about growing up in Vermont, his call to the ministry and how he'd tried to avoid it for so many years, afraid of the awesome responsibility it entailed, about falling in love with his wife and the heartbreak he'd known when she left, and about the joys and anxieties of raising a daughter alone. He was honest and vulnerable, gentle and strong all at once; before long Kendra forgot all about him being a minister and simply saw Andy as a man, one she was becoming more attracted to as the minutes passed.

But now that they were getting closer to the farm, the fact that she'd just been on a date with a minister was very much in the forefront of Kendra's mind. If this had been a normal date, it would certainly end with a good-night kiss, Kendra offering a cheek if she wasn't interested and her lips if she was, though she wouldn't let things go further than that, certainly not on a first date, and probably not for several more after that. Kendra had strong feelings about not rushing into things and because of that had only a couple of truly serious relationships in her life. But, if you were dating a minister, surely the usual rules of engagement didn't apply, did they?

Andy took a hard right off the road that led to the Sugarmans's home. Kendra was so deep in thought that she didn't even notice until they pulled up in front of a big red barn that said ROBBINS FARM in white letters. "What are we doing here?" she asked.

"Having dessert," he said simply, then seeing her confusion, he continued, "We're going for a moonlight sleigh ride. That's why

I told you to bring your hat and gloves. Hank Robbins gives rides to tourists and he said he'd take us, on the house. He'll be out in a minute to drive us to a camp in the high meadow where we'll have some hot chocolate around the campfire and look at the stars. On a clear night like this, there are a million of them, so close it looks like you could pick them out of the sky like you were picking up diamonds off a piece of black velvet. You'll love it!" Andy hopped out of the car and walked around to get Kendra's door.

Kendra smiled to herself, thinking what a thoughtful man Andy was. She couldn't believe he'd gone to all this trouble just for her. She was really kind of excited. For all the times Kendra had danced at Radio City, feigning enthusiasm over the thrill of 'dashing through the snow in a one-horse open sleigh,' she'd never actually experienced it for herself. *This is going to be fun,* she thought and grabbed her crutches.

But her excitement waned when she saw the heavy blanket of snow that lay between the car and the waiting sleigh parked fifty feet away.

"Andy," she protested when he opened

the car door, "this was a great idea, but I can't do it. I'll never be able to get through that snow on my crutches."

"I know that." And before Kendra could say anything else, he bent down and picked her up in his arms, carrying her as easily as if she'd been a child. Kendra squealed in delighted surprise and wrapped her arms around his neck.

"What are you grinning at?" Andy asked, grinning just as broadly.

"Nothing." Kendra giggled. "I just never expected a minister to be so romantic."

"Is that so?" His grin faded. He stopped and bent his head low, placing his lips on Kendra's for a long, tender moment as the wind picked up and whirled a veil of snow around them, two lovers kissing, protected as if behind a child's globe of glass, encased in their own perfect, snowy world on one perfect, snowy night in Vermont.

Chapter Six

Kendra stood at the cleanup sink in Denny's workshop washing her hands for the third time.

"You're going to rub the skin right off if you keep that up," Denny said without looking up from the enormous toy box he was building. Kendra had enlisted his help to build the set and Sugar's to design and paint the backdrop. Lacking the technical and artistic talent of her hosts, Kendra put herself in charge of painting flats. They'd been working overtime trying to get everything ready for the first rehearsal in the church.

"At this point, sacrificing a little skin would be a small price to pay for eradicating the smell of paint thinner." Kendra dried her hands on a nearby towel, lifted them up to her nose, and made a face. "Yech! No good.

I guess I'd better douse myself in perfume before going over to Andy's."

"Are you having dinner there?" Sugar asked from the corner of the workshop where she was busily sketching outlines onto the backdrop with a big charcoal pencil. Wendell had decided to join them and dozed in a ball at Sugar's feet, occasionally opening one eye and looking up at the backdrop as if to check on Sugar's progress. Kendra wondered how Wendell could sleep through all the noise; she had to yell to be heard over the steady ringing of Denny's hammer.

"Yes. I've got my doctor's appointment, then rehearsal, then Thea and Andy invited me over to help decorate their tree. Do you mind?" Kendra asked, hoping she hadn't upset Sugar's dinner plans.

"Goodness, no," Sugar said. "I was just curious. You and Andy have been seeing a lot of each other lately, haven't you?" Kendra nodded, wondering if she minded *that.* Maybe Sugar didn't approve of the pastor dating, but Sugar just smiled and said, "That's real nice. Andy deserves a little happiness and you won't find a better man on the face of the Earth."

Denny put down his hammer. "Hey, what about me?" he asked, pretending to be offended.

Sugar batted her eyes at her husband and gave him a smile that made it easy to see how she'd gotten her name. "Well, of course I meant except for you, honey. You're off the market and you're all mine."

"Darn right," Denny said as he picked up a nail and resumed his hammering.

Kendra waved at the lovebirds, then grabbed her keys and headed out the door.

Flipping through an ancient copy of YANKEE magazine while waiting her turn to see Dr. Cheney, Kendra considered Sugar's observation that she and Andy had been seeing a lot of each other. It was true. They had brunch every Sunday after church. As Kendra had told Andy, since the church was employing her, she felt obligated to attend. But she found she actually enjoyed the service, especially the singing. And there had been several other dinners since that first, a few with just Kendra and Andy, but most included Thea, who Kendra was completely crazy about. On Thanksgiving, they'd had dinner at the Sugarmans's and it had been great, just like they were a big family. Kendra smiled to herself, remembering how Andy and Denny had installed themselves in the Sugarmans's little-used TV room after dinner to "watch the game" and how, not ten minutes later, she'd walked in and found them both sound asleep.

Most recently, they'd all caravanned to Burlington with the dance team for the state competition. The girls did a great job and were thrilled with their second-place finish—five places higher than they'd finished the year before and two spots above their rivals from Montpelier. Kendra was so proud of them and, she admitted to herself, proud of the small part she'd played in helping them realize their goal.

Of course, she missed being able to dance herself and she was sick to death of hauling a cast around everywhere, but she found a great deal of satisfaction in working with the talented, eager young people of Maple Grove. The play was really coming along well. Certainly there were still glitches to be worked out; her biggest problem at the moment was costumes. She'd promised the kids they'd have real costumes, thinking she'd be able to borrow some from the community theater in the next county, but they needed all their costumes for their own holiday productions. Sugar had said she'd help, but there was no way she could sew forty-five costumes single-handedly, so Kendra had been combing the discount stores and thrift shops for inexpensive clothing; they weren't exactly what she hoped for but they would fit the bill.

But, even with the costume problem, things were going well in Maple Grove, almost too well.

Kendra sighed, tossed the magazine onto the table beside her, and looked at her watch impatiently. Why did doctors always tell you to be fifteen minutes early for your appointment and then leave you to cool your heels in the waiting room for forty-five? If the doctor didn't call her in soon, she'd have to reschedule; the director couldn't be late for rehearsal. Besides, there wasn't anything to do in a waiting room besides wait . . . and think. And that's what Kendra was trying to avoid.

Sugar had said Kendra wouldn't find a better man on the face of the Earth than Andy. Kendra was starting to think she might be right and the thought made her nervous. As the days and weeks passed, Maple Grove was starting to feel more and more like home and Andy Loomis was starting to look more and more like the man of her dreams. Kendra had to keep reminding herself that Maple Grove, Vermont, was just a temporary stopover on the road to her ultimate goal: Broadway. *Don't forget,* she said to herself, *you're just passing through.*

Just then, a door opened and a nurse wearing a light blue smock looked at Kendra. "Miss Erickson? The doctor will see you now."

"Dad!" Thea called out a warning. "Careful! You're too high up on the ladder."

"Thea, these cookies are really good," Kendra commented from her perch on a kitchen stool where she sat watching as Andy put the final touch on the Christmas tree. Giving into temptation, she took another cookie from the plate.

"Thanks," Thea said. "I thought we ought to have some cookies for our tree-decorating party. Sugar taught me how to make them. They're her special Maple Syrup Cut-outs."

Kendra smiled. "Maple syrup. I should have known."

"Dad!" Thea called again. "Move it a little more to the left. It looks all crooked."

"Well," Andy said in a slightly exasperated voice, "I can't move it further left without climbing up to the next rung. My arms are only so long."

Kendra got up from the stool. "Hang on. I'll steady the ladder while you position the star. The last thing we need around here is one more person with a broken leg." She gripped the ladder firmly with both hands while Andy positioned the silver star tree topper left, then right.

"By the way," Andy asked as he climbed higher, "how did your doctor appointment go?"

"All right," Kendra said distractedly, keeping her eyes upward as she watched Andy. "I got to hang out in the waiting room for a half hour, and another twenty in the exam room, and when he finally came with the X-rays he stood there staring at them and frowning for ten minutes before speaking to me, but everything's fine. The cast should come off just before the show opens."

"That's good news," Andy said as he shifted the star to the exact center, adding the perfect finishing touch to the beautifully decorated tree. "There! That should do it." Andy climbed down from the ladder, then plugged in the lights. All three emitted an involuntary gasp of amazement as they admired the magical effect that twelve strings of tiny white Christmas lights had upon their ornament-laden tree, breathing in the resiny scent of pine mixed with the sweet smell of maple and baking. They had been working for two solid hours and it was worth it; everything looked and smelled like Christmas.

"Good work, gang!" Andy said, and Kendra agreed.

"It really does look lovely," she said. "I'd almost forgotten how much fun it is to put up a tree. It's been ten years since I've done this. In fact, it's been about that long since I've even celebrated Christmas."

Thea was scandalized. "You're kidding! What are you talking about? You were a Rockette! You're *part* of Christmas. How can you say you didn't celebrate it?"

Kendra looked at Andy and smiled, wondering how she was going to explain this. He looked like he was wondering the same thing. "It sounds crazy, I know, Thea, but for all those years Christmas was my job. I worked Christmas; I didn't celebrate it. I was surrounded by Christmas every day of the week. I heard Christmas songs and danced to Christmas music four times a day. I had Christmas up to here," she said, holding her hand even with her brows. "By the time the actual day came around, I was a real Scrooge, ready to take the next person who wished me a 'Merry Christmas' and boil him in his own pudding and bury him with a stake of holly through his heart. Understand?"

Thea, looking a little disturbed by Kendra's gruesome and violent literary allusion, shook her head. Kendra tried again.

"Well, imagine if you worked in a chocolate factory and all they made was those Valentine heart boxes filled with candy. Let's say you made those every day of the year, day after day. By the time Valentine's Day came around, the last thing you'd want to do is open up a big heart-shaped box of chocolates and dig in. See what I mean?"

Thea nodded slowly. "I guess so. But, Christmas is still your job. I mean, you're getting paid to put on the Christmas play, but you just said how much you liked helping to put up the tree, anyway. So you're celebrating Christmas even though you're still working Christmas." She paused for a moment and bit her lower lip, thinking.

"I guess if I'd been working in a Valentine chocolate factory all year, the last thing I'd want to do on February 14th is eat Valentine's candy. But if someone I cared about gave me the chocolates, I'd be really happy. Maybe that's it. Maybe it's who you're with that makes it a celebration."

"Maybe," said Kendra.

Later, when Andy was walking her out to her car, Kendra said, "I'm completely in love with your daughter, you know that, don't you? She is perfectly adorable."

"Yeah? Well, what about me?" he asked as he opened the door of the Toyota.

"Hmmm," Kendra mused, pretending to think it over. "I guess you're all right, too." She placed her gloved hands on Andy's shoulders and stretched up to give him a long, slow good-night kiss. When their lips parted she sighed and said, "I love it that you're so tall."

Andy laughed. "Well, gee. Thanks. I try."

She thumped him playfully on his shoulder. "I'm not kidding," she said. "When you stand five foot nine, it's hard to find a man who you have to reach up to kiss. I like it. It makes me feel feminine."

"You are feminine," he replied, running a cold, bare fingertip along her jawline, then tipping up her chin before kissing her again. "You're also very, very tempting," he groaned. "I'd better go inside," he said, but made no move to do so.

Kendra tipped her head to one side, disappointment etched on her face. Still, she respected him for his self-control and, in a way, appreciated the compliment. Like her, Andy wasn't the sort who entered relationships lightly and that made their kisses, as well as their desires, all the more special. Even so, Kendra found him hard to resist. Kendra leaned forward for one more kiss, but saw a curtain move in the window of the house.

"I think someone is watching us," Kendra

whispered. Andy turned his head and spied his daughter's face in the window.

He sighed. "In that case, I guess I really will have to go in. But, I'll see you tomorrow at rehearsal. Sorry I haven't had a chance to drop by before, but I've been so busy working on next year's budget," he apologized. "Thea hasn't told me much about it but she says it's going to be a great show."

"She's right," Kendra said. "And she's going to be great in it, but don't worry about not coming to rehearsal before. I wouldn't have let you in, anyway. My rehearsals are closed to the public. The kids are under strict orders not to tell any outsiders about the plot. It's all a big secret. You're only getting to come because the director has a crush on you," she said, batting her lashes flirtatiously and laughing.

Andy's face became serious. "Do you really mean no one else has seen the play?" Kendra shook her head, wondering why he seemed so bothered. "Or even the script? Not even Darla Benton?"

"Especially not her," Kendra puffed contemptuously. "I've been trying to keep it under wraps so she wouldn't try to meddle with it. You asked me to steer clear of her and that's what I've done."

"I asked you to consider her feelings and win her over, not keep her completely out of the loop. Darla feels this show is a very important part of her husband's legacy and she's right. Would it have been so hard to do her the courtesy of consulting her, making her feel a part of the process?" Andy's words were scolding, but his voice was gentle. Even so, the troubled look on his face put Kendra on the defensive.

"Well, I was just doing what I thought was best. And besides, she can't do anything to get in our way now; the show opens in three more weeks," she said. Andy was silent. "Can she?"

Andy shrugged. "Good night, Kendra." He gave her a quick peck on the cheek and walked toward the house.

Chapter Seven

The next afternoon Kendra stormed out of the church, trying mightily to slam the door. She was frustrated in her efforts by a safety hinge, which made the door close very slowly. Kendra spun around and watched the door arc lazily toward the latch in its own sweet time, finally closing with a gentle thud. She let out an aggravated yelp, kicked a nearby rock, and sent it scuttling across the parking lot where it narrowly missed hitting the window of her car, or rather, Denny Sugarman's car.

She didn't even want to think about how close she had come to shattering a car window she couldn't afford to replace on her meager salary. Getting behind the wheel of the Toyota she gave the door a satisfying slam, hit the gas, and raced out of the church parking lot, throwing gravel and epithets behind.

"Andy Loomis! You and Darla Benton and her whole clique of quilt cronies—in fact, the entire town of Maple Grove, Vermont, can just kiss my backside! I should never have come here in a million years! You wouldn't know decent theater if it came in and bit you on the . . ." She continued in a similar vein, ranting aloud, releasing her impotent rage into the atmosphere, stepping on the gas pedal harder as her voice grew louder, completely oblivious to the thirty-five-mile-per-hour sign she'd just passed and the patrolman parked on the side of the road. That is, until she glanced into her rearview mirror and saw the blue flashing lights and heard the wail of a siren.

Kendra groaned. "Great! Just what I need, a visit from Maple Grove's version of Barney Fife." Her fury only slightly dampened by her situation, she pulled over and turned off the ignition.

When the policeman approached she rolled down her window and said, in what she hoped was an innocent-sounding voice, "Is there a problem, officer?"

The patrolman took a look at the forced

expression on Kendra's face and said, "Actually, ma'am, that's just what I was wondering."

There was a problem all right. When Kendra arrived at the church that day, a full hour before rehearsal, she'd been in a good mood, having pushed the uncomfortable conversation with Andy to the back of her mind and eager to see how the new scenery would look in the actual performance space. But when she walked into the sanctuary an angry Darla Benton, flanked by a full swarm of Quilting Bees, was waiting for her. Somehow, one of the Bees had gotten hold of her granddaughter's copy of the script, read it, and gone running off to report to Darla, who was clearly not happy.

Pinching a corner of the script between two fingers and holding it well away from her body, as though she was disposing of some filthy object, Darla glared at Kendra and barked, "Just what is it you think you're doing, Miss Erickson?"

For Andy's sake, Kendra tried to be civil, but it wasn't easy. Who did this old biddy think she was, anyway? Kendra felt her jaw tighten and the color rise in her face. "Going to work, Mrs. Benton," she said through clenched teeth. "What are you doing?"

Darla put one hand on her hip, striking a stubborn stance. "I am here to make sure you don't *defile* this church, my late husband's memory, and even Christmas itself by presenting this . . . this *trash* in this church, that's what!"

More than a month in Maple Grove had softened but not completely sweetened Kendra's city-girl temper. Infuriated, her inner New Yorker rose to the surface. She shot back with both barrels. "Listen, lady! My play may not be Shakespeare, but at least it's entertaining! Which is a heck of a lot more than I can say for the mind-numbing, archaic, bad imitation of Greek tragedy you expected me to work with!"

"How dare you speak to me in that tone!" Darla retorted, her shock nearly equal to her fury. Behind her, the Quilting Bees buzzed in shocked agreement. Certainly none of them had ever dared to speak to Darla Benton that way. "My husband's play has been a tradition in this church! A *tradition,* I tell you! Bringing the beauty, mystery, and solemnity of the nativity to generations of young people in this community, for thirty-five years!"

"Yeah! And boring them for at least twenty-five! You should thank your lucky stars I came along or you wouldn't even have a play! The only kids that were willing to be in it were the ones whose parents forced them. They wouldn't even show up for auditions until I rewrote it! And how dare *you* criticize a show you haven't even seen!" Kendra shouted, her voice rising even higher.

Mrs. Benton increased her volume in line with Kendra's. "I don't have to see it! I've read it! Might I remind you that this is a church, Miss Erickson, not a house of burlesque! This is supposed to be a sacred play, yet you've reduced it to a trivial, mercenary, music hall farce, filled with silly dancing dolls and parading elves, reducing the birth of our Lord to a mere postscript in your little salute to Santa!" Mrs. Benton was shouting. "I don't know what Andy Loomis thought he was trying to pull by hiring you, Miss Erickson. I've done some checking and you're no more a Broadway actress than I am! You're nothing but a chorus girl! A Rockette! Parading around in those skimpy little costumes—all feathers and rhinestones and makeup an inch thick! No decent woman would let herself appear in public like that!"

"Is that so?" Kendra shouted back, her face a bare six inches from Mrs. Benton's, standing toe to toe with the matriarch of Maple Grove. "I guess you must be forgetting that your pastor's own sister is a Rockette! Are you saying that's she's indecent, too?"

Mrs. Benton narrowed her eyes and leaned in. "As my grandmother always used to say, 'If the shoe fits'! And another thing . . ."

"Ladies!" Andy boomed in his sternest, most reverberating voice. "That will be quite enough of that!"

Kendra, startled by Andy's interruption, and Darla, embarrassed at being caught declaring her pastor's own sister indecent, were silent. Kendra's chest was still heaving as if she'd been running, and anger-induced adrenalin was still pumping through her veins.

Unsmiling, Andy turned to the group of scandalized Quilting Bees, who'd been watching the altercation with wide-eyed fascination, and said in a calm but commanding voice, "Ladies, go back to the sewing room and carry on with your work. Not you, Darla. Take a seat in the lobby. I'll be with you in a few minutes. Kendra," he said, raising his eyebrows, "I'll see you in my office. Right now."

Andy had barely closed the door when Kendra started in. "All right! All right! I shouldn't have yelled at the old lady, but did you hear what she was saying about me? And about Stacey, too! What was I supposed to do, stand there and take it?"

Andy, looking suddenly tired, let out a deep sigh and rubbed his hands over his face. "I heard, but that isn't the point. Darla didn't mean any of that; she was speaking in anger. She felt slighted, pushed aside; you utterly excluded her. What's worse, you insulted her husband, whom she still misses so badly that it feels like half her heart has been torn in two. And you did it in public."

Kendra was seething. "I can't believe you're taking her side."

"I'm not taking anyone's side. Right now, I'm talking about you, not Darla. 'Bad imitation of a Greek tragedy'? 'Mind-numbing'? How could you say that to her?"

"See, you are taking her side!"

Andy took a deep breath, trying and failing to maintain his pastoral neutrality. "You know what your problem is, Kendra? You just don't listen!"

"And what's that supposed to mean?" Kendra asked, raising her voice a notch.

"It means," Andy said, glaring at her, "that I read Thea's copy of the play and Darla has a point—you've made the nativity a post-script. Jesus, Mary, and Joseph aren't even bit players in your drama! Kendra, they *are* the drama! They are the story of Christmas!"

Kendra rolled her eyes. "Oh, please! You didn't read the play. Darla came in here whining and you took her word for it! If not, you'd know that is exactly the message of the piece, that the nativity is the most important part of Christmas. That's why I have Santa read the Bible version at the end . . ."

"Yes," Andy interrupted, "a very truncated version. It's like you threw it in as an after-thought, just to keep the church folks off your back."

"Oh, come on, Andy! I'm just trying to keep things entertaining. That's what you hired me for. Everybody has heard that story a million times already."

"Have you?" Andy asked. "I mean, have

you *heard* it? Really heard it? I don't think so. Not lately at least. Because if you had, you'd be anxious to tell the story, you'd use that brilliant, creative mind of yours and your many, many talents to make people see that old story, the most wonderful story ever, with new eyes! Instead, you've settled for just entertaining." Andy shook his head and he looked almost sad. "You're doing it again, Kendra."

"What do you mean?"

"You're not celebrating Christmas, you're working it."

Kendra grabbed her purse off the table where she'd flung it when she came in and started for the door. "That's enough! I don't have to stand here and listen to any more."

Andy blocked her way. "Oh, yes, you do," he said firmly. "You've got to apologize to Mrs. Benton and you've got to figure out a compromise that everyone can live with. If you don't, there will be no play."

Kendra's eyes were blazing. "You'd do that? You'd do that to all these kids, after they've worked so hard? To your own daughter? What kind of father are you?" But before he could answer she shouted, "Well, I'm just glad I found out before it was too late! And to think I was actually considering giving up my dreams and not going back to New York. I must have been out of my mind!"

". . . and then I stomped out and got in my car and drove off going—how many miles an hour over the speed limit did you say I was going, officer?" Kendra asked sheepishly.

"Thirty-eight."

"Right. So, that's the problem," Kendra said, a little chagrinned now after hearing how the whole episode must sound to a stranger. "What do you think I should do?"

The patrolman tore a ticket off his pad and handed it to Kendra without saying anything. It read:

1. Drive to Mrs. Benton's <u>without exceeding the speed limit</u> and apologize.
2. Work out a compromise everyone can live with.
3. Make up with Reverend Loomis.

The policeman tucked the ticket pad back into the front pocket of his uniform and then tipped his hat to Kendra. "You have a nice day now, Miss. Drive carefully."

He walked back to his patrol car, climbed in, and drove off, waving to Kendra as he passed. Kendra looked at the ticket she held in her hand and thought, *Number one and two? I don't know. Maybe. Number three? Over my dead body!*

Kendra drove around aimlessly for the longest time, thinking about her run-in with Mrs. Benton, replaying the encounter in her mind. She was still absolutely furious at Andy for having had the gall to suggest that the whole thing had been her fault, and vowed never to forgive him, while silently congratulating herself for having found out what kind of a man he was before letting things go any further.

But, when it came to Mrs. Benton, she wasn't exactly proud of her behavior. The old lady shouldn't have been so mean to her. But, after all, anyone who expects to receive forgiveness must be willing to give it. *Where did I hear that concept?* she asked herself and then flinched when she remembered that it had come from a sermon Andy gave two weeks previously.

Well, she thought, rising to her own defense, *just because he can preach a good sermon it doesn't mean he's always right. If anything, it makes him that much more despicable! He's a minister, after all, he should know better than to act the way he did!*

Satisfied that her behavior in the matter of Andy had been entirely justified, she turned her mind back to Darla Benton. No, she finally concluded, no matter how she looked at it, she owed the old woman an apology. By the time she finally made the decision to drive to Darla's house, it was already dark. She was half-hoping the old lady wouldn't be home but when she pulled up to the house, the lights were blazing. There was nothing for Kendra to do but swallow her pride and ring the doorbell.

"Yes?" Mrs. Benton seemed a little befuddled when she answered, as if surprised that anyone would come visiting at that hour, but when she saw Kendra standing on the stoop, she quickly regained her composure. "Oh. It's you, Miss Erickson." Mrs. Benton paused.

"May I come in?" Kendra asked.

Kendra stood shivering on the stoop while Darla considered the request. For a minute Kendra thought the answer might be "no," but finally Mrs. Benton said, "Yes. Yes, of course." She opened the door wide enough for Kendra to pass. Somewhat stiffly, she offered to take Kendra's coat, then showed her into the music room.

Kendra sat in a red velvet wing chair near the fire. "This is the warmest room in the house," Mrs. Benton said. "These old antiques can be drafty."

"It's a lovely home," Kendra said sincerely as she glanced around the room, admiring the gleaming wood of the grandfather clock in the corner and the rich reds and blues of the Persian rug beneath her feet. Most stunning of all were the quilts. There was a wooden rack in the corner, displaying a row of truly exquisite quilts in rich colors and complicated patterns. Kendra had only just begun to learn the art of quilting, but even her unskilled eyes recognized the amazing quality of the intricate, tiny stitching in each quilt. These were quilts that wouldn't have been out of place in a museum. The room smelled of lemon oil and beeswax and age. *It's like living in an antique shop,* Kendra thought before saying, "Reverend Loomis said you've lived here all your life."

"Well, my husband, Jake, did. This is the house he was born in and when we married, just after the war, it became my home, too. Most everything you see here—the furniture, the portraits, even the accessories— were passed down through Jake's family. Except the quilts. Those are mine."

"They're absolutely lovely."

Darla nodded her head in humble acknowledgment of the compliment. "It's something I've always loved doing. The quilts I make with the Bees are different; we have to keep the patterns simple because our quilters come with different skill levels and we rely on whatever fabrics are donated, so the end result isn't always what we might hope. But, quilting has been my hobby since I was a girl. I made these when I was first married—trying to put a little of myself into the house, I suppose, and it worked. This is my home. There has been a Benton living in this house since it was built more than two hundred years ago." She sighed as she looked around at the room. Kendra saw a tear forming in the corner of the older woman's eye, but Darla wiped it

away with the back of her hand before going on.

"I don't know who will live here after I've
gone. One of the greatest sorrows of my life
is that Jake and I weren't able to have children. We decided to leave the house and
contents to the church. At least it will do
some good that way, but it seems so
strange to think of everything being sold off
piecemeal, all our memories broken apart
and sitting in the homes of people who
know nothing of the stories and heritage behind them."

*No wonder she's so adamant about keep-
ing the play just the way it's always been,*
Kendra thought, feeling even more ashamed
of her own insensitivity than she had when
the officer handed her the "ticket." Kendra
felt genuinely sorry for Mrs. Benton, but she
knew that saying so would only embarrass
the proud woman, so instead she said,
"Well, it really is a lovely room. And the organ," she asked, pointing to the beautiful
mahogany instrument that stood against
the far wall, "was that your husband's, too?"

"Yes," Mrs. Benton said as she rose from
her chair and walked to the organ, running
her hand lovingly across the gleaming wood.

Kendra followed her. "Jake played it every night after work. I can't play a note myself, so I suppose I should donate it to the church, but I just can't bring myself to part with it."

"I can understand that."

Mrs. Benton picked up a sheaf of papers and music that was sitting on top of the organ. Much of the music was handwritten and Kendra suspected that it had been sitting there since Jake Benton's passing.

"Jake was a gifted musician, but he was an even more gifted composer. Many of the pieces he played before church services were his own compositions." Mrs. Benton handed the stack of music to Kendra, who began leafing through them. Each composition—with titles like "Adoration," "Sacred," and "Rejoice!"—was written in pencil, littered with erasure marks, corrections, and notations, in a sharp, angular hand. Kendra had the sense that the composer was excited about his ideas and in a great hurry to commit them to paper while the melodies rang clear in his mind.

At the bottom of the pile was a thicker, more complicated-looking work, titled "The

Miracle." Kendra's brow furrowed as she examined it. "What's this?"

"Oh," Mrs. Benton said, "that was a piece he finished just before he died. It was his first orchestral composition. See?" She pointed to the second line. "That's the horn part and down here is where the flutes come in. He was very excited about it. It's such a shame that he never got to hear it played."

Kendra felt her throat tighten. She started coughing fitfully and couldn't seem to stop. Mrs. Benton started slapping her on the back and asked in a concerned voice, "Are you all right, Miss Erickson? Shall I get you a glass of water?"

Through tearing eyes Kendra choked out, "Yes. Please."

Mrs. Benton scurried off to the kitchen, leaving a coughing Kendra alone. By the time she returned with the water, Kendra's fit had subsided but she gratefully accepted the glass and drained it.

"Thank you. That's much better," Kendra said before coming to the point of her visit. "Mrs. Benton, I'm sure you know why I came over tonight and I just want to tell you,

I'm very sorry for the way I acted today. It was completely out of line."

"Well," the older woman admitted grudgingly, "I guess we both said things we shouldn't have. I'm sorry, too, but that still doesn't mean I'm happy about this play, Miss Erickson."

Kendra nodded. "Yes, I understand that. But I have some changes in mind that will turn this year's Christmas play into something we can both be proud of. All I ask is that you give me a little time."

"Well, I don't know . . ."

"Just a week, Mrs. Benton, that's all I'm asking. Come to rehearsal in one week and if you don't like what you see, we'll scrap the whole thing. I promise."

Mrs. Benton narrowed her eyes, thinking. "All right," she said finally. "I'll give it a week, but if I don't like what I see after that, I'm holding you to your promise. One week."

Kendra smiled, inwardly admiring the old lady's stubborn streak. She stuck out her hand to seal the bargain. "Fair enough, Mrs. Benton. One week."

*   *   *

Mrs. Benton offered to walk Kendra to her car, to make sure she didn't slip on the icy sidewalk, but Kendra assured her it was unnecessary. They said good-bye and after Mrs. Benton closed the door, Kendra hurried down the walkway as quickly as her broken ankle would allow and climbed into the now-freezing Toyota.

Just before turning on the ignition, Kendra reached into her pocketbook and pulled out a folded stack of handwritten sheet music. She opened the music and smiled.

"'The Miracle,'" she said aloud and then looked up. "Jake Benton, wherever you are, I hope you weren't kidding when you picked this title because if ever I needed a miracle, it's now."

Chapter Eight

The second she left Mrs. Benton's, Kendra raced over to Sarah Fenimore's house.

Sarah answered the door in her robe and slippers, but was happy to see Kendra and invited her into the kitchen for a cup of tea. Kendra sat on a stool while Sarah put on the kettle and searched the cupboards for a box of lavender-chamomile tea.

"I wondered what happened to you," Sarah said. "When I showed up for rehearsal the kids were all just milling around and you were nowhere to be seen."

Kendra clapped her hand onto her forehead. "Oh, my gosh! The kids! Between Darla Benton's insults and the tongue-lashing I got from Andy Loomis, I completely forgot about rehearsal! They must have thought I'd deserted them or something. How could I have been so stupid?"

"Don't worry. It all worked out. Andy filled me in on the day's events, well, at least the problem with Darla." The kettle started to whistle. Sarah poured steaming water over the teabags and handed a cup to Kendra. "He didn't mention anything about a problem between the two of you. What's going on?"

"Nothing. I don't want to talk about it," Kendra said sharply, holding up her hand like a cop stopping traffic and then taking a sip of the fragrant brew. "Except to say this! Andy Loomis is the most judgmental, holier-than-thou, infuriating man on the face of the Earth and if I never see him again it will be too soon!"

Sarah raised her eyebrows and smiled. "But you don't want to talk about it?"

"No." Kendra frowned as she drank her tea. "So how were the kids?"

"Fine. I just told them you weren't feeling well and would be back tomorrow. We ran through the musical numbers. They sounded pretty good; they'll be ready to open in three weeks' time."

"Yeah," Kendra said slowly, then opened her pocketbook, pulled out the pilfered sheet music and handed it to Sarah. "I wouldn't be quite so sure about that if I were you. We've got to make some changes to the show. If we don't, Darla Benton is going to shut us down in a week. It won't be easy, but we've got to do it, Sarah. There's no other way."

"What!" Sarah gasped, her eyes wide as she flipped through the pages of music. "You want to switch the music now? Are you kidding? The kids have those songs down and . . ."

Kendra held up her hand. "Not switch the music, add to it. I want you to keep everything you already have, we're going to put this in too."

"But where?" Sarah shook her head. "We already have music in every scene and this piece is long. I don't know where it will fit."

"I'm going to put it in the second act." Kendra got up from the stool, put on her coat, and hung her pocketbook on her shoulder.

"Second act?" Sarah asked in confusion. "Kendra, we don't have a second act!"

"I know," Kendra said, and then leaned down to slurp up the last of her tea. "But, we will," she said as she walked to the door. "Just as soon as I write it."

*   *   *

For Kendra, the week that followed ran entirely on fast-forward.

At rehearsal the next day, a bleary-eyed Kendra greeted her cast by handing out the new lines she'd stayed up half the night to write. Initially the kids were a little wary, but when Kendra explained the situation to them, they stepped up to the challenge like troupers, enduring an extended rehearsal schedule conducted in an atmosphere of complete chaos.

A second act required not only second roles for all the actors, new music for the orchestra, and songs for the singers, but additional props, augmented lighting, and a completely new set. Denny and Sugar were lifesavers, spending every spare moment building and painting the set. Denny even enlisted a few of his fishing buddies to help.

"It took a little doing, it being ice fishing season and all . . . ," Denny reported with a smile when Kendra asked where he'd managed to find three new stagehands. "But the ice has been a little thin and I told Marty that, what with that twenty pounds he's put on, he'd have more chance of swimming with the fish than catching any this year, so

he said he'd help. And Rob and Jim"—he
shrugged—"they just go wherever Marty
does."

Though it meant that the actors had to
shout their lines to be heard over the constant banging of hammers and the whine of
skill saws, Kendra was grateful for the help.
Besides, she said to herself, *it certainly is
helping the kids learn to project their voices.
Last week, I practically had to stand next to
Kerry Phillips to hear her line, now she's so
loud I can hear her in the rafters.*

Which was a good thing, given what happened on Wednesday. The sound board
blew a fuse, sending up a shower of sparks
that looked like the Fourth of July had come
early, and terrifying poor Tommy Frank,
Kendra's-fifteen-year old sound technician.

"I didn't do anything, Miss Erickson! Honest! Just plugged it in like always and—
kablooey!"

"I know, Tommy. Don't worry about it,"
Kendra said, rubbing her eyes and silently
wishing that Rob and Jim would stop hammering just long enough for her headache
to fade. "It's not your fault. Go up into the
office and ask Reverend Loomis if you can
use the phone. Call Ace Theatrical in Bur-

lington and see if they can't get us a new board, or at least a new fuse." Kendra sighed, wondering how they were going to do the play without a sound system, but there wasn't anything else she could do about it now, so she decided to worry about the problems she could solve, or at least the ones she hoped she could. And at that moment, her biggest problem was costumes.

In spite of her promise on the day of auditions, Kendra had no choice but to resurrect the ratty bathrobes and burlap tunics that she found in a closet of the choir room, the leftover costumes that had probably been used in every Maple Grove church Christmas pageant since the beginning of time.

In fact, Kendra thought, wrinkling her nose as she held up a sweat- and makeup-stained strip of formerly cream-colored cloth that was probably meant to cover a shepherd's head, *these look old and ragged enough to have seen use at the original nativity scene.*

But Kendra had no choice. There simply wasn't time to make new costumes for the second act. Even the first-act costumes were nothing to write home about. When Kendra remembered how glamorous she'd felt in the glittering, gilded costumes she'd worn in her days at Radio City, how the audiences had gasped with pleasure and surprise when they caught sight of thirty-six Rockettes dressed in matching bejeweled creations, and how her cast was going to have to take the stage in a motley collection of worn-out clothing, and discount store and thrift store finds, Kendra felt just awful. She'd promised the kids real costumes and they deserved them—they'd all worked so hard—but she was running out of time. She and Sugar devoted every moment they could to sewing new costumes, or trying to embellish the old ones with bits of fancy trim, but it would have taken a whole army of seamstresses to get the job done.

As it was, Kendra just prayed the audience had the imagination to see the characters dressed as she'd imagined them in her mind, a line of Raggedy Ann dolls in matching red pinafores instead of last year's dance team skirts, a regiment of toy soldiers in full military regalia instead of the school's old band uniforms that were two sizes too big, and a delicate music box ice skater in a glittering costume of snow-white silk encrusted with rhinestones instead of someone's older sister's cast-off ballet tutu held together with safety pins. Kendra sighed when she thought about how different the show looked in her mind than it did in reality, but she couldn't do more than she was already doing.

She worked morning, noon, and night— and sometimes through the night—busier, as Sugar said, than a cranberry farmer at Thanksgiving. Too busy even to see or speak to Andy Loomis if he'd dropped by or called, which he hadn't.

Well, Kendra thought testily, *fine with me. If he's too stubborn to admit he was wrong, then I'm better off without him. Besides, the only thing that matters is the show. I'll get these kids ready for Mrs. Benton by the end of the week if it's the last thing I do!*

Mrs. Benton sat stony-faced with her arms crossed over her chest and she stayed like that for the entire first act, not tapping her feet or cracking a smile, not for even the toy soldier song, or the lumbering teddy bear dance, or the jumping jack clown. Sitting in a center pew in the darkened church next to her, Kendra kept shifting her eyes sideways to see if she could gauge the older woman's reaction, but Kendra might as well have been sneaking peeks at a statue. When the stagehands pulled out the synthetic ice rink for Danielle Inman's music box ice skater number, Kendra thought she saw Mrs. Benton's eyes flicker with interest, but it was so dark that she couldn't tell for certain.

When the Raggedy Ann number finished, Mrs. Benton leaned toward Kendra and said in a scandalized voice, "Those skirts are much too short." But that was her only comment.

Kendra, who had been taking notes to give to the actors after the run-through, nodded and scribbled, "Costume note: Raggedy skirts too short" on her clipboard, to at least appear as if she was taking the older woman's advice. But in her heart, she was sure it was an exercise in futility, that Mrs. Benton had made up her mind before she even walked in the door, and that the minute the lights were turned up she would march into Andy Loomis's office and demand that he close the show. And Kendra would have no choice but to comply. That was the deal she'd made.

Come on, Kendra said to herself, *don't be*

such a pessimist. She hasn't seen the second act yet. If that doesn't get to her, nothing will. But in spite of her attempts at optimism, Kendra nibbled nervously on her fingernails as the stagehands quickly changed the scenery for the nativity set, following her instructions to run through the whole play without taking an intermission. And, when everything was ready and Sarah Fenimore tapped her baton against the conductor's podium to get the musicians' attention, then lifted her arms to guide the orchestra through the first tender strains of Jake Benton's musical opus, Kendra held her breath, waiting for Mrs. Benton's reaction.

But, as far as Kendra could see, Mrs. Benton was unmoved. Thinking that perhaps she didn't realize it was her husband's music that was being played, Kendra leaned over and whispered, "It's lovely, isn't it? I hope you'll forgive me for borrowing Mr. Benton's score, but I wanted to surprise you."

Keeping her eyes fixed on the stage, Mrs. Benton said nothing. Her only response was a short, sharp nod as Charity Proctor stepped forward.

Jake Benton's score didn't come with lyrics, so Kendra had taken another look at his original script with the rhyming couplet lines she had thrown aside on her first night in Maple Grove. As a spoken play, the lines had seemed stilted and hopelessly old-fashioned, but with a little adaptation and some help from Jake Benton's haunting score, Kendra transformed the old lines into lovely lyrics.

In her clear, slightly reedy soprano, Charity, who was playing the part of Mary, sang of her wonder and awe as she contemplated the miracle that was about to occur. In Kendra's mind, it was the most moving song in the whole show. She glanced to her right, hoping to see some kind of reaction from Mrs. Benton, and saw the older woman's lips tighten into a thin line. Kendra's heart sank.

She hates it, Kendra thought, and slumped down in the pew, fighting back tears. *It was all for nothing. And the kids, putting all that work into a show that no one will ever see. How am I going to tell them it's all over?*

The last bars of the closing number, "O Holy Night," faded and someone brought up the house lights. Quickly rubbing her eyes on the back of her sleeve so no one would see she'd been crying, Kendra got to her feet and faced the kids, who were all standing onstage, waiting for her reaction.

"Great job," she said in a tired voice. "Take a break and then I'll give you a few notes, but for a first run-through, it was terrific. Really."

The kids dispersed, talking and laughing as they left the stage to get drinks of water or sat down to rest their feet. Kendra felt a sharp poke in the back of her shoulder. "Come with me, Miss Erickson," Mrs. Benton commanded in a hoarse voice.

Resigned to her fate, Kendra followed Mrs. Benton up the center aisle of the sanctuary, into the foyer, and to Andy's office. Mrs. Benton rapped sharply on the door and, barely waiting for Andy's invitation to come in, barged in with Kendra trailing behind.

Andy was sitting at his desk, his hand resting on an open Bible. "Well, ladies," he said, looking at his visitors expectantly, "how did it go? Darla, what did you think?"

Kendra opened her mouth to speak, but Mrs. Benton beat her to it. "Andy," she said in a firm voice, "that was without a doubt

the very best Christmas play I've ever seen."
And then, without warning, the stony expression Kendra had mistaken for disap-
proval dissolved and Darla Benton burst
into tears. "Jake would have been so proud!"

Andy grinned and, without speaking,
reached out and pulled some tissues out of
a box that sat on the corner of his desk and
handed them to Mrs. Benton.

"It was just lovely," Darla wailed, blowing
her nose loudly as Kendra looked on
aghast, not quite able to take in this sudden
turn of events. "Please, Miss Erickson, forgive me for ever doubting your ability or
your vision. It's not only entertaining, it com-
municates the real message of Christmas.
You took Jake's words and music and
turned them into something more beautiful
and moving than he could ever have imagined! How can I ever thank you?"

"Oh," Kendra said weakly, "there's no
need, Mrs. Benton . . ."

"Call me Darla," the older woman said,
still weeping.

"Darla," Kendra replied awkwardly, "there's
really no need to thank me. I was just doing
my job."

"No, no," she insisted, patting Kendra affectionately on the shoulder. "I must find some way to make amends. From now on, I'm going to help you. I'm going to be your assistant director!"

And Kendra, wondering how she was going to explain to her new best friend, Darla, that she wasn't sure she wanted a cantankerous, bossy woman of solid Yankee stock helping her, murmured a flustered, "Oh, well, it's very kind of you to want to help but . . ."

"Don't mention it. It's the least I can do after all the trouble I've caused you!" Darla grinned and clapped her hands together, obviously excited about her new, self-appointed position. "I must run! I've got to call the Bees and tell them all about the show. I'll see you at rehearsal tomorrow, Kendra. Good-bye!" Waving her farewells, Darla scurried out of the office, leaving a stunned Kendra in her wake.

"Well, it looks like everything turned out for the best," Andy said, smiling as he came around the desk and stood near Kendra. "I was sure it would. I'm so happy for you." He reached out as if to take Kendra's hand but she pulled back before he could touch her.

"Happy for me?" Kendra shouted, her

eyes wide and incredulous. "I've just been saddled with a crabby, eighty-year-old assistant director who has no experience in theater and who, if she has her way, will probably have all my dancers wearing long sleeves and granny skirts, and you're happy for me? You've got to be kidding!"

"Kendra, I know that Darla's not exactly your idea of a perfect assistant, but she means well and it's only for a couple of weeks. The important thing is that the show can go on. Come on," he said in a teasing tone, "isn't it time we made up? I know you were mad at me, but now that everything has worked out, I'd think the least you could do is admit you were wrong. Why don't I take you out to dinner so you can apologize to me?" Andy grinned broadly, pleased with his own joke, but Kendra was having none of it.

"*I* was wrong? You're saying *I* was wrong?" Kendra barked. "If anyone in this room deserves an apology, it's me!"

Andy's smile faded. "Calm down, Kendra. I was just kidding, but you have to admit, if you would have listened to me in the first place, none of this would have happened."

"Hey, buddy!" Kendra said in the same

demanding tone and volume she would have used to hail a New York cabbie, poking her finger into Andy's chest. "None of this is my fault. If you had supported me from the start, I wouldn't be in this mess! I'd have been able to concentrate on making the show as good as it could have been, getting the kids some proper costumes and sets instead of having to waste my time adding in a second act that never needed to be there in the first place!"

Andy had clearly had enough. His eyes sparked with anger and irritation. "I read the show, Kendra. It was entertaining, sure, but it was weak. It didn't have any heart or message. If what Darla is saying is true, then you've given it that by adding your second act and I think you ought to be enough of a grown-up to realize it! Why can't you ever admit that you're wrong?"

"That's because I'm not wrong!" Kendra said, wagging her finger in Andy's face. "Not about this, anyway but believe me, I can admit when I've made a mistake. It was a mistake to come to Maple Grove and it sure as heck was a mistake to ever let you kiss me! Don't worry," Kendra growled, "that's one mistake I'll never make again. As soon as the show closes, I'll be on the first train out of here and back to New York."

Composing her face into a mask of wounded pride, Kendra pulled herself up tall on her crutches and limped her way to the door. "Now, if you'll excuse me," she said coldly, "I have a show to put on."

Chapter Nine

Kendra knew Charlotte Sawyer because her son, Taylor, played trumpet in the orchestra, but when Charlotte entered the exam room wearing a white lab coat, Kendra was surprised to see her.

"Hi, Charlotte. I didn't know you worked with Dr. Cheney. Are you one of his nurses?"

"No," Charlotte answered, pulling a strange-looking instrument with a small circular saw blade on it out of a drawer, "I'm an orthopedic technician. I'm the person who gets to take your cast off. Dr. Cheney will be in after."

Kendra waited anxiously on the examining table while Charlotte took some other instruments out of the drawer including a large and somewhat medieval-looking pair of pliers and a gauze mask that she placed over her mouth and nose.

"So!" Charlotte said brightly as she pulled a rolling stool up to the examining table and peered at Kendra's cast. "Today's the big day! Are you ready?"

"Yes," Kendra said. "I can hardly believe it, but everything is ready. At least, I think it is. Wait until you hear Taylor's trumpet solo! Of course, I'm sure you've heard him practicing at home, but it's different with the orchestra. You'll be so proud! Really, all the kids have done a magnificent job. I think people will really enjoy the performance.

"And." Kendra laughed. "Even if they're not theater fans, they've got to love the intermission. Darla Benton and the Quilting Bees have been baking up a storm. I don't think there's a bag of chocolate chips left in all of Maple Grove. The money they make from the bake sale will be donated to the local food bank. Not only that but they contacted the fire department to collect toys at the door, talked their husbands and sons into helping with the sets, helped me finish the alterations and hand-sewing of the costumes, and completely taken over ticket sales!" Kendra shook her head in amazement.

"Darla Benton has turned out to be a godsend. If I'd had any idea that having her for an assistant meant I'd also be getting twenty tireless volunteers, I'd have signed her up first thing! It's just remarkable how she's been able to get—"

"Kendra," Charlotte interrupted, the twinkle in her eyes indicating that a smile was hidden behind the gauze mask. "I'm glad the show is going so well, but when I said 'big day,' I was talking about getting your cast off. It's been over two months; by this time, most people are counting the minutes until they're freed from the plaster prison, and yet all you can talk about is the show." Charlotte laughed. "Taylor told me you are a terrific director and I can see he wasn't exaggerating. He's had so much fun with this."

"That makes two of us. I've loved seeing it all come together and especially working with the kids. Honestly, I've been so absorbed in the show that I've hardly had time to think about my foot. Of course," Kendra nodded toward the grimy, once-white cast, "it will be nice to have this thing off in time for opening night. I've got a pair of new high heels I'm just dying to wear."

"Not too high, I hope," Charlotte cautioned. "It was a bad break, Kendra. You're better, but you can't expect everything to work exactly like it did before your fall. That's why Dr. Cheney will be coming in when I've finished, to explain what you can and can't do from this point on."

Kendra shrugged, "Oh, sure, I know. I didn't expect to be tap dancing in four-inch stilettos the first day. It will take a little time before I'm back to my old self. In the meantime, I'll stick to sensible shoes, nothing over two inches, I promise." Kendra held up her hand in a teasing Girl Scout pledge.

Charlotte nodded approvingly. "In that case, I think we're ready to get this show on the road," she said. She pressed a button to start the saw and pushed it gently but firmly onto the surface of the cast, raising a storm cloud of shredded fiber and pulverized plaster under the blade.

Two hours later, Kendra, minus the cast and wearing a new pair of blue pumps with a sensible 1½-inch stacked heel, sat parked in front of the church, so absorbed in her thoughts that she'd forgotten to turn off the engine.

I'm sorry, Kendra, but you've got to face

facts. You're not going to be able to dance again. Not like you used to. Not ever.

Dr. Cheney's words kept replaying themselves in her mind, but she couldn't quite bring herself to believe them.

Something in Charlotte Sawyer's gentle admonition had made Kendra feel uncomfortable, but it wasn't until Dr. Cheney entered the exam room, followed by a dark-haired, serious-looking man who was also dressed in a lab coat, that she'd realized something was definitely wrong.

It didn't take Dr. Cheney long to get to the point.

"Kendra," he said, gesturing toward the other man, "permit me to introduce Dr. Wilson Slepian. Dr. Slepian is the head of orthopedics at the hospital. He works with all kinds of patients, but he specializes in athletic orthopedics, working with world-class athletes and dancers like yourself, people who perform at the very highest physical levels."

The dark-haired physician nodded gravely at Kendra. Dr. Cheney went on.

"I've been consulting with Dr. Slepian on your case. We've spent a lot of time looking at your X-rays, the set you brought from

New York as well as the ones we took last month and today, and we are in agreement."

Dr. Slepian cleared his throat and took over. "Miss Erickson, the bones in your ankle have healed nicely and you should have no trouble at all resuming normal activities." For a moment, Kendra felt a surge of relief. "But," he continued, raising a cautionary finger, "Dr. Cheney has told me about your work. As a dancer, giving as many as four very strenuous performances a day and spending countless hours in rehearsal, you've put tremendous strain on your ankles. This break was devastating, but you've been experiencing considerable pain for some time, haven't you?"

"Every professional dancer deals with pain," Kendra protested. "It's part of the job. You just learn to ignore it."

The doctor nodded. "Yes, and in your case you've done a heroic job of doing that—a little too heroic, I'm afraid. The X-rays show literally dozens of small stress fractures. Of course, we'd expect to see some of that in a professional dancer but not to this extent. You're a tall woman but the bones in your ankles are quite small. If your performance schedule wasn't so demanding, it wouldn't be as much of an issue, but you simply can't go on like you have been. Your age is against you as well. You've been pushing your body to the limits of endurance for years. This break made everything worse. You're simply not going to be able to regain your old strength and flexibility—"

Kendra interrupted, not wanting to hear what he was going to say next. "But, what about physical therapy? I'm willing to work hard . . . exercise, therapies, whatever you want. I've just got to keep dancing," she said pleadingly before her voice dropped to a whisper. "It's the only thing I know how to do."

Dr. Cheney smiled a little sadly. "I know that's what you think, but it's just not true, Kendra. Everyone in town is talking about you and the show. Clearly, you've got all kind of talents besides dancing. You'll see." He patted her on the shoulder, but Kendra was having none of it. She shook off his sympathetic gesture and got to her feet.

"I can't listen to this right now. I won't," she said in a voice that would have been rude if her tone hadn't so thinly masked the tears she was keeping back. "I have to go." She grabbed her purse and pushed past the doctors, refusing to let her eyes meet theirs.

She opened the door to leave and as she did, Dr. Cheney said in a voice that was firm yet kind, "I'm sorry, Kendra, but you've got to face facts. You're not going to be able to dance again. Not like you used to. Not ever."

The words echoed in Kendra's mind as she sat in the idling Toyota. She gripped the steering wheel with both hands and stared into space, not seeing or hearing anything, her mind completely focused on one thought: *What am I going to do? If I can't dance, then what am I going to do?*

"Kendra? Kendra!" Mrs. Benton's tap-tapping on the window increased in frequency and volume as the moments passed and Kendra didn't respond, finally reaching an insistent crescendo that broke through Kendra's reverie. "Are you all right?" Darla asked urgently when Kendra finally rolled down the window.

"Oh. Hi, Darla. Yes. I'm fine."

"I saw you drive in fifteen minutes ago and you've just been sitting here all this time. Are you sure you're all right?" Mrs. Benton asked, a look of almost maternal suspicion on her face.

Kendra nodded, speaking in a more definite tone. "Yes. Really. I was just thinking about something." Kendra opened the car door and stepped out.

"Well, look at that! You're actually wearing shoes! And walking!" Darla exclaimed, clearly impressed by her first sight of Kendra without crutches. "I can see that everything must have gone well at the doctor's."

"Yes. Just great."

"Well, at least there's some good news around here," Mrs. Benton replied, pressing her lips into a worried line.

"What do you mean?" Kendra asked. "Is there a problem?"

Mrs. Benton nodded. "There is," she said, "and her name is Charity Proctor."

Chapter Ten

Charity had a bad case of laryngitis; she could barely speak, let alone sing.

All Kendra's worries about her foot and her future were pushed into the background as she tried to tackle the immediate problem. In little more than an hour, the empty pews would be filled with eager audience members and Kendra had a mute Mary on her hands.

"I can still do the Raggedy Ann dance," Charity whispered hoarsely, "but I just can't sing. I'm sorry, Kendra. I let you down."

Kendra put her arm around the downcast teenager. "Don't be silly, Charity. You couldn't help it. Don't worry. We'll find a solution. After all, the show must go on," Kendra said with more confidence than she felt. "You just run get into your makeup and let us worry about this." Charity nodded silently and left.

Kendra turned to Darla. "Well, I guess we'd better go find ourselves a Mary," she said and started walking briskly down the hallway.

"Where are you going?" Darla asked, grabbing Kendra by the elbow.

"To the girls' dressing room," Kendra answered, a little perplexed as to why Darla was clutching at her arm, "to see if any of them can take Charity's part."

"Oh, you don't want to go in there," Darla insisted. "It's a mess! Costumes all over the place—a complete pigsty! I'll run get the girls and bring them to you."

"Well, it's not like I've never seen a messy dressing room," Kendra said and pulled her arm out of Darla's grip. "I used to share a dressing room with thirty-six Rockettes, remember?" Kendra started walking away but Darla dogged her heels, insisting that she'd be happy to round up the girls herself.

Just then, Sarah Fenimore appeared, carrying a stack of sheet music, and almost bumping into Kendra as she turned the corner. "Where are you going?" she demanded.

"To the girls' dressing room," Kendra said

in an exasperated voice, "to try to find a replacement for Charity Proctor. She's lost her
voice and can't sing."

Sarah's eyes grew wide. "You're kidding!
She was fine last night."

"Well, she's not today. I've got sixty minutes to find an understudy, so if you'll excuse me"—Kendra tried to continue on her
way, but Sarah blocked the path. Sarah
kept staring over Kendra's shoulder, and
Kendra got the definite feeling that Mrs.
Benton was standing behind her, making
signals. Kendra spun around on her heel to
face Darla, who had her hand held to her
throat and wore an expression of practiced
innocence.

"What the heck is going on here? Will you
two let me go and talk to the girls, for gosh
sakes! We're running out of time!"

Darla's eyes were as big as saucers and
she kept opening and closing her mouth, as
though she, too, had suddenly become
mute. Sarah took Kendra gently by the elbow and started propelling her up the corridor, away from the dressing room.

"Kendra, I'm the musical director; let me
handle this. Darla," she said calmly, "would

you get Thea Loomis and ask her to meet me onstage?"

"Right away," Darla said and scurried off.

"Thea?" Kendra asked. "Are you sure? She's so much younger than the others. I was thinking Tammy Nichols could do it."

Sarah shook her head. "Tammy's good, but then who would play the part of the angel? You'd have to find an understudy for your understudy. Trust me, Thea has a very pretty voice and I've had my eye on her. She just worships the ground Charity walks on; she's been watching her every move during rehearsal. I'll bet you anything she already knows the song and all of Charity's lines; and besides, she's so tall she's probably the only one who'll fit into Charity's costume. Thea's our best bet on short notice."

Kendra bit her lower lip and thought a minute. "All right. If you're sure."

"I'm sure," Sarah replied. "Now, haven't you got something to do besides stand around here and worry?"

"Gosh, yes," Kendra said and rubbed her eyes wearily. "I've got to go over the light cues with Tommy. He's still getting confused with this new board. And the Quilting Bees need the cashbox for the concessions, and nobody can find the shepherds' staffs, and Denny and I still have to do a sound check."

"Well, then what are you doing standing here talking to me? You go and do your job and let me do mine."

Kendra nodded and murmured, "You're right, you're right. I'll keep out of your way. Sarah," she said before walking away, "thanks. For everything. If it weren't for you, we'd never have been able to pull this off."

"We still haven't pulled it off." Sarah grinned and glanced at her wristwatch. "We've got fifty-four minutes until curtain. Still plenty of time for disaster to strike."

"Gee, thanks for reminding me." Kendra smiled wryly.

"By the way," Sarah said, raising her eyebrows and looking at Kendra's feet, "nice shoes! I see everything went well at Dr. Cheney's."

"Oh. Yes. Just great."

She told herself that later, when the kids had taken their bows and the curtain had closed, she could go back home, climb into bed, and cry into Wendell's fur while she tried to figure out what to do next, but right now she had a job to do. And at least for the next few hours, that was all she was going to let herself think about.

By the time Kendra finished dealing with all the other last-minute problems, there was barely ten minutes left to do a sound check. Denny had volunteered to run sound and stood behind the board, adjusting the levels while Kendra counted off into the microphones.

"Once more, Kendra. I think number three has a little too much bass."

Kendra spoke directly into the third microphone. "Check. One, two, three. Check."

Darla Benton, out of breath and disheveled-looking with several strands of her white hair falling in her face, came hustling onto the stage. "Kendra, the show is supposed to start in eight minutes and the vestibule is overflowing! You've got to let me open the doors. The ushers can't hold them back much longer!"

Kendra felt her stomach lurch in a pang of stage fright more intense than anything she'd ever experienced. For a second she thought she was going to be sick. "But," she protested, swallowing back a wave of nausea, "we're not ready yet. There's too much bass on the number three microphone."

"That's all right," Denny called from the back of the room. "I think we've got it now. Don't worry, Kendra. I'll make sure everybody can hear."

Kendra looked at Darla. "But what about Thea? Is she ready? And I want to talk to the kids before they go on. I have a pep talk all prepared."

"Thea's fine. The kids are in the choir room and ready to go." Darla looked at her watch. "There isn't time for a pep talk, Kendra; and besides, they don't need it. You've done a wonderful job with them. They're as ready as they'll ever be." Darla smiled and patted Kendra on the arm. "It's time, Kendra. The show must go on."

Kendra took a deep breath. "All right. Let them in."

Chapter Eleven

The church was full to bursting. It was the eve of Christmas Eve and the pressure that accompanies the festive season was beginning to ease. The halls had been decked, the cookies baked, the presents purchased or made, wrapped and shipped; and if they hadn't been—well, it was too late to do anything about it now. Christmas was upon them and the good people of Maple Grove were ready to begin their celebrations here as they had every year for the past thirty-five—by heaving a collective sigh of relief and, sitting next to family, friends, and neighbors in the darkened sanctuary-turned-theater of the First Community Church of Maple Grove, letting themselves be reminded how this Christmas business, this holiday, which was so often obscured by buying and busyness, came to be in the first place. And, because Maple Grove was a small town and word of the new director and new play traveled fast, this year they'd turned out in record numbers.

Each pew was designed to hold eight people, but thanks to the efforts of Darla and the Quilting Bees, who kept moving among the crowd, insisting that people squeeze together and toddlers sit on their parents' laps, they'd managed to stuff ten bodies into almost every row. But there still wasn't enough room.

Someone suggested they place a line of folding chairs on the end of each aisle, so Kendra and a few of the Bees went to the storage closet to get the chairs. Andy stood inside the big closet, lifting chairs off the storage racks and putting them into the hands of the waiting Quilting Bees. Kendra was the last in line and by the time she realized that Andy was in charge of chair distribution, it was too late for her to turn back.

"Thank you," she said stiffly when Andy handed her two folding chairs.

"You're welcome." He was silent for a moment and his brow was furrowed, as if trying to think what he should say next. It was the first time Kendra recalled seeing him without a smile on his face.

"Kendra, I know you're still angry with me, but I want you to know something. If I had to do it again, I'd still want you." His eyes, deep brown and fixed on Kendra's face, were sad, and Kendra felt a pang of guilt in knowing that she was the reason. "To direct the show, I mean . . ." His cheeks reddened and he stumbled over his words as he realized how his previous sentence could be interpreted. "I'd still want you to direct the show. I . . . I . . . Anyway, good luck. Or break a leg. Or whatever it is they say on opening night."

He stuck out his hand and Kendra took it, touched by his flustered sentiment. "Andy, I . . ."

"Kendra!" Denny came running into the closet, huffing and out of breath. "There you are! The orchestra is in the pit. Sarah is at the podium. And the audience is getting restless. Everyone is waiting for you. Come on!"

Torn, Kendra looked at Andy, then Denny, then back to Andy. "Andy," she said apologetically, "I have to go."

"I know. Get going; I'll be right behind you.

By the way," he said with a sad little smile, "nice shoes."

Denny escorted Kendra to the front pew, to the place Darla had been saving for her. Several members of the audience, mostly parents of cast members, applauded her entrance. Kendra smiled shyly, acknowledging their good wishes, a little surprised to realize how many of the faces were familiar to her.

When Kendra sat down, Sarah turned around and raised her eyebrows, asking silent permission to proceed. Kendra nodded. Sarah tapped her baton against the podium and the orchestra sat up straight with their instruments at the ready. The house lights dimmed and the orchestra launched into the overture, a medley of the tunes that would be sung that night. Kendra felt her stomach lurch again and she told herself to calm down.

Good heavens, you've been through dozens of opening nights in front of audiences ten times the size of this one, what in the world are you so nervous about? But she already knew the answer. This was *her* show, her vision, and how people responded to it would reflect on her personally. And while she would never in a million years have planned on coming to Maple Grove, Vermont, for anything other than a ski weekend, somehow, this place and these people had become very important to her. Their opinions mattered to her far, far more than she had realized.

Well, she thought as the overture came to a close, *it's too late to change anything now. They're either going to love it or hate it. I'll just have to wait for the verdict.*

Kendra sat back in her seat and watched as the curtain parted to reveal the darkened Santa's workshop set with a single, white-hot spotlight focused tightly on a lone Raggedy Ann doll sitting propped up center stage. The orchestra began playing a slow, melodious version of "Santa Claus Is Coming To Town" that masked the muffled shuffling of feet as the actors moved to their places in the dark. And when everyone was on their mark, the tight spot of light that encircled the doll spread to the rest of the stage and slowly warmed to reveal a scene that made the audience gasp with surprise and delight—Kendra along with them.

In place of the thrift store finds with tacky trimmings and quickly altered hand-me-

downs, the whole cast was attired in sparkling, brand-new costumes! Instead of brown
sweat suits topped off by headbands with
fuzzy ears glued on, the teddy bears wore
complete furry bear outfits in shades of
brown, black, and cream. The jack-in-the-
box had on satin pajamas and a matching
hat with jingling bells. And, most charming
of all, the Raggedy Anns came skipping out
wearing red mop wigs and adorable red,
white, and pink patchwork pinafores, blan-
ket-stitched with black yarn that gave each
costume a theatrically homemade feel.

The audience broke into spontaneous applause that continued as the rest of the toys
trooped in. Kendra leaned over and whispered into Darla's ear, "I know you're behind
this! How did you do it?"

"It wasn't me; it was the Bees. Of course."
She grinned. "I might have given them a few
ideas, but they did most of the work. I was
too busy being your assistant, and keeping
you from finding out, to help with much of
the sewing. You sure gave me a scare tonight. I thought I was going to have to tackle
you to keep you out of that dressing room!"
Darla squeezed Kendra's hand and leaned
closer to make herself heard over the ap-

plause. "When I heard what you'd done with Jake's music it was the nicest surprise I've ever had. I just wanted to do something nice for you, too."

Kendra shook her head, still not believing what she was seeing. "Darla, I can't thank you enough. Everything looks just beautiful! Better than I could ever have imagined."

"Wait just a minute. You haven't seen anything yet!" Darla grinned as she nodded toward the stage.

With the audience still clapping, Danielle Inman entered, elegant and graceful in her music box ice-skater dress of cream silk and trimmed with fur that seemed strangely familiar to Kendra. Kendra's mouth fell open in shock when she realized that Danielle was wearing one of the old Rockette snowflake costumes! And right behind her, marching in unison, came a column of toy soldiers, dressed in blue trousers and tall hats that Kendra also recognized as coming from the Rockettes' costume shop.

"How did you . . . ?" Kendra was too aghast to even finish the sentence.

"That was Andy's doing."

"Andy's?"

"Yes," Darla reported proudly. "He knew

you were upset that the costumes looked so shoddy, so he called up his sister Stacey and asked her to see if the Rockettes would loan us some costumes. They couldn't do that, but it turned out they were getting rid of some things that had worn out. Andy paid to have them shipped up here."

"Andy did that?"

"He did. Do you like them?"

Swallowing hard, Kendra whispered hoarsely, "Yes, I do. I just love them!"

So did the audience. Responding to their enthusiasm, the kids gave a stellar performance.

Every joke was met with laughter, every song with prolonged applause. But when the apple-cheeked Raggedy Anns came forward to do their dance, starting with the floppy, rag-doll steps that Kendra had taught the girls, then forming a line, and culminating in a series of stunning eye-high kicks performed with a precision that would have done any Rockette proud, the audience went wild! They jumped to their feet and Kendra jumped with them, applauding until her hands were red and stinging as the cast stepped forward to take bow after bow. Kendra was so proud of them.

When the curtain closed, Kendra was mobbed. She saw Andy at the back of the room, but the crowd was so thick that she couldn't get to him. Kendra wanted to talk with him, but it would have to wait until after the final curtain. For the moment at least, the kids were her first concern.

Moving away from the crowd of well-wishers, she climbed onto the stage and exited through the curtain. She wanted to congratulate the kids on making a great beginning while reminding them to stay focused for the second act. Most important, she wanted to find Thea. Undoubtedly, the little girl would be nervous and badly in need of encouragement.

Kendra found Thea backstage, sitting on a stool and biting her fingernails while one of the older girls, Megan Perry, tried to wipe off her Raggedy Ann makeup.

"For heaven's sake, Thea!" Megan told her. "Quit fidgeting! We've got to hurry!"

Smiling calmly, Kendra took some tissues from a nearby box. "That's all right, Megan. Why don't you go and get ready. I'll help Thea." Megan left and Kendra knelt down and the tissued off the makeup from Thea's frightened little face.

"Are you scared?"

Thea nodded mutely. "Well, I can understand that, but you don't need to be. You
know the song and you know all the lines.
You're going to a great job!"

"Oh, it's not that," Thea said quietly. "I'm
not afraid of forgetting anything."

"Then what are you worried about?"

"Do you remember when we first met and
I told you that I didn't like having to play
Mary every year? Well, it's different this
time. Before, the play seemed so silly; I
knew Mary wouldn't have talked like that.
But now, with the music and everything, it
just seems so *real*. So much more important. I know I'll remember the words, but I
want them to seem real to everyone, the
way they do to me." Thea lay her hand on
her heart and said earnestly, "I want the
people who are watching to know that
Christmas is more than just presents and
trees and watching the church pageant. I
want them to know that Christmas really is
a miracle! Do you know what I mean?"

The truth was, Kendra didn't. And she
didn't know what to tell the little girl or even
how to help calm her nerves. She thought
about her first day in Maple Grove, when

she told Andy that churches were full of hypocrites, people who showed up on Sundays just to keep up appearances, and she'd meant it. And that was the only reason she'd started going to Sunday services, just to keep up appearances. But after a while she'd been surprised to find that she actually enjoyed going to church. Most of the people she'd met there seemed so genuine, not perfect, certainly, but sincere. In the last few weeks she'd started to sense that there was something more to all church business, something worth seeking out, even though she wasn't quite sure how to go about it. So, kneeling on the floor of the dressing room, she suggested they venture onto the ground on which Kendra had secretly, skeptically, and for the first time since she'd been Thea's age, begun to tentatively tread: she suggested they pray. Thea quickly agreed.

Kendra knew that many of the people in the church prayed out loud, but she didn't feel comfortable with that, so she and Thea, sitting in a corner of the dressing area, simply bowed their heads and prayed in silence and unity.

God, Kendra began, *I don't know exactly*

what it is Thea needs right now, but I do know that, as young as she is, she has caught hold of a desire that is bigger than anything I've ever attempted or imagined. She wants to use her talent to draw attention to you, not herself. The selflessness and depth of this little girl leaves me speechless—except for this. Help her. Use her to help at least one person here understand Christmas and you the way she does. Amen.

And it happened just that way.

When the lights dimmed for the second act, a single violin began playing the first, plaintive strains of Jake Benton's score, filling the room with a sense of lonely expectation, of a world waiting for something or someone that would bring a hope they'd long heard of, but whose existence they'd secretly begun to doubt. Kendra felt Darla sitting stiffly next to her, emotion and anticipation stretching her tight as a bowstring. She squeezed Darla's hand reassuringly. And, indeed, the audience itself seemed to pick up on that sense of anticipation, their still, almost reverent expectation standing in stark contrast to the buoyant mood that had pervaded the first act. For the first time that evening, Kendra was aware that she was in a church, not a theater.

As the music faded, a wide spotlight focused on a platform to the right of the stage where Santa Claus sat, with several of the toys that had appeared in the first act at his feet. The jolly old fellow opened a thick book and urged them to listen closely while he explained what was truly the most important part of Christmas. Then the light dimmed on Santa and his listeners, and the curtain parted to reveal a group of shepherds, standing around a fire and warming their hands.

The scenes unfolded one after another, telling the old story that Kendra and the rest of the audience had heard for as long as they could remember, but somehow— whether because of Jake Benton's music or the sincerity of the actors, or the influence of some divine, invisible presence—the old story seemed new, at least to Kendra. And when little Thea Loomis stepped forward to sing in a clear, sweet soprano that radiated faith and purity, it was as if Kendra was hearing the song for the very first time.

Why I, a virgin, meek and low,
Should be so favored, I cannot know
Why God selected this mean place,
To meet his children face-to-face,
Why the King of All should come to Earth,
Choose humble stable for his birth,
I cannot know
But one thing is sure, my heart cries out,
And Angels affirm with joyous shout,
It's a Miracle!
It's a Miracle!

And all at once Kendra believed it. And in believing, all the anxiety and brokenness that had been plaguing her for the last weeks, months, and years—broken ankle, broken future, broken relationships—seemed out of focus in contrast to a greater reality: there was a plan for everything and in that plan was room for miracles.

A lightness of spirit, a deep sense of belonging settled over her, as though she had come home after a long journey. She felt so wonderful that she wanted to tell someone and the someone she wanted to tell was Andy.

When the final bow had been taken, and the curtain had closed, Kendra peered over the heads of the crowd of congratulants that hemmed her in on every side and looked to the back of the church where Andy had been sitting. All she saw was an empty chair.

Chapter Twelve

There had been an emergency.

Right after Thea's song, Andy's vibrating pager had gone off, informing him that a member of the church, Sharon Castillo, had been in a car accident. He was not among the proud families surrounding the cast members, who had streamed into the lobby after taking off their makeup and costumes. But when Denny explained to Thea that Andy had gone to the hospital, Thea understood.

"He wanted me to tell you that he thought you were absolutely wonderful and he was very, very proud of you. And," Denny said, pulling a bouquet of pink sweetheart roses out from behind his back, "he asked me to give you these."

Thea buried her nose in the blossoms.

"They're so beautiful! I've never gotten flowers before!"

Kendra put her arm around the little girl. "Well, after what I saw tonight, I'm sure these will be the first of many."

"Kendra's right," Sugar added. "You were just wonderful tonight, honey."

"Thanks. But what about Mrs. Castillo? I know her son, Matt. He's in my social studies class. Is she going to be all right?"

Denny shot Sugar and Kendra a look. "I know. Matt was in the car, too, but it sounds like he's fine. He had a few scrapes and a broken collarbone, but that's all. As far as his mom . . . Well, we'll have to wait and see. But, listen," Denny said, bending down to Thea's level and looking into her worried eyes, "your dad is going to take good care of Matt and his mother, and we'll say a prayer for them. All right?"

Thea nodded dutifully but her eyes were still serious.

Sugar smiled. "Come on now, Thea. Cheer up. This is your big night! I've got a chocolate cake back at the house. What do you say we go cut into it and celebrate your debut? Your dad will be late so you're going to stay overnight with us."

"Really?" Thea asked, brightening. "Can I sleep in Kendra's room?"

"Sure," Sugar said. "We can put the rollaway in there. That is, if Kendra doesn't mind."

"Not at all. I'd love to have a roommate. And you know what, I'll even let Wendell sleep on your bed. I'm sure he'd be happy to curl up at the feet of a star!"

"The star of Maple Grove? Puh-leeze." Thea rolled her eyes, but her cheeks flushed as pink as her flowers and, preteen worldliness aside, Kendra knew she was flattered.

Thea was sound asleep on the rollaway, breathing deeply while Wendell, who had wedged himself into the comfortable crook of her arm, purred loudly. Between the two of them, it was no wonder Kendra couldn't sleep, but the noise wasn't the only reason she was still awake as the first cold light of dawn began swelling over the horizon. She hadn't closed her eyes all night.

She kept thinking about the play, about the new understanding that had enveloped her as Thea sang, the sense of acceptance that wrapped itself around her like an embrace and stayed with her after Thea's song, after Sarah Fenimore reverently lowered her arms to silence the final notes of the orchestra, and after the audience signaled their approval by a tremendous burst of applause.

Kendra's happiness was only compounded by the joy she felt as she had watched the cast taking their bows. She was so proud of them. She had taken curtain calls of her own, but now she was a member of the throng of admirers rather than the object of their admiration—yet Kendra had never known a deeper satisfaction.

And when Thea had stepped forward to acknowledge the applause with a shallow curtsey, then looked over at Kendra and silently mouthed the words, "I love you," Kendra thought her heart would burst.

"I love you, too!" Kendra had said and her eyes filmed over with tears of joy. It was true. She loved Thea, and Denny, and Sugar, and Sarah, and even Darla Benton. She loved all of Maple Grove and, more than that, she loved Andy Loomis. She knew it. Yes, there were apologies to be made, wrongs to be righted, forgiveness to be granted, but somehow it would all work out. After what seemed like a lifetime of slumber, Kendra found herself awake and alive in a world of new beginnings, a world of miracles.

She couldn't wait anymore. As quietly as possible, she slid out from between the sheets and pulled on a pair of jeans and a chunky turtleneck sweater. Wendell, wondering if breakfast was about to be served, opened one accusing eye and stretched out his front paws as Kendra tiptoed past the rollaway. When Kendra looked at him sternly and put a warning finger to her lips, he burrowed closer to Thea and went back to sleep.

Kendra closed the bedroom door softly behind her before padding down the hallway into the kitchen. She pulled on a coat over her sweater, and then sat down to put on her shoes.

"Oh, it's you. I thought I heard something." Kendra looked up, surprised to see Sugar, yawning and bleary-eyed, coming down the stairs in her bathrobe and slippers. "What time is it?"

"A little after five," Kendra said sheepishly. Sugar squinted to see the kitchen clock and then raised her eyebrows. "Very little. Seems kind of early to be going for a walk, doesn't it?"

"Well . . . I . . . uh . . ." Kendra stammered, trying to think up a plausible explanation. For a moment, she considered saying she'd left her cell phone at the church and had to go get it, but her phone hadn't worked since she'd arrived in Maple Grove, so it seemed unlikely that Sugar would be convinced of the urgency of her predawn expedition.

"You going to find Andy?"

Kendra bit her lip and nodded.

"Well, it's about time. You've got to be one of the two most stubborn women on the face of the Earth, me being the second. When Denny and I were dating, I came this close to losing him over an argument almost as stupid as the one you started with Andy. I was beginning to wonder if you'd ever wake up and smell the coffee." Sugar smiled and yawned again before turning around to trudge back up the stairs. "There's a joke in there somewhere, but I'm too tired to find it. I'm going back to bed. Good luck, honey."

"Thanks, Sugar." As Kendra bent down to finish tying her laces she realized that Sugar's words had opened a chink in her armor. She'd started a fight for heaven knows what reason, probably because she'd been rejected so often that she'd decided to push Andy away before it could happen again. She'd had plenty of time, during the long, sleepless night, to review her behavior during the last couple of weeks and she didn't like what she saw. More than that, she realized that for all her huffing and puffing about wanting to get back to New York as soon possible it wasn't true anymore, if it ever had been. All her protestations were just another kind of playacting, a performance she'd staged for herself so life wouldn't seem so empty when she left. But the truth was, Maple Grove had gotten under her skin from the first day, and Andy most of all. Lying in her bed, her thoughts illuminated by the shaft of moonlight that spilled across the spangle of quilted stars that covered her, Kendra tried to imagine going back to New York, to her old life, and never seeing Andy again. She couldn't.

But what if it was too late? Andy was a man of God, but he was still a man. Surely there had to be a limit to his patience and willingness to forgive. Kendra prayed she hadn't brought him to the end of it. But it was Christmas Eve, she remembered. Maybe her cause would be helped by a little holiday magic? There was only one way to find out.

As she stepped out onto the front porch, the dark December air was so frigid it made her gasp, but not as forcefully as she did when she looked up and saw Andy coming up the front walkway toward the house.

"Going somewhere?" he asked.

Without thinking, Kendra answered, "Yes. To find you," and instantly regretted her outburst.

During the long night, she'd worked out a whole speech in her mind, one that would surely bring him back into her arms. But the sight of him, striding toward her through the gray dawn light, made her forget everything except her love for him. Looking at the amused, slightly perplexed grin on his face made her feel suddenly foolish. He'd probably been up all night and come straight from the hospital to collect his daughter; the last thing he'd want right now would be to find Kendra at the door, ready to throw herself at him. She could have kicked herself for being so transparent.

His smile spread slowly, like honey poured

from a jar. "Is that so? That's funny. I was coming to find you."

"You were?" she asked weakly. "So early?"

He nodded and mounted the steps to the porch, reaching for her, pulling her so close she could feel his warm breath on her cheek, smell the leather on his sheepskin coat, the same one he'd been wearing that first day they'd met on the train platform, feel his muscles straining against his sleeves as he wrapped his arms close around her, enfolding her in a protecting circle of warmth against the chill morning air.

"I couldn't wait anymore. When I saw you last night with your leg out of the cast, I realized that you'll be leaving soon and going back to New York. Unless," he whispered, "I can convince you to stay. The second I knew Sharon and Matt were going to be all right, I left the hospital and came over here. Well, not directly here. First, I went to Mark Overstreet's house and woke him up."

Kendra's eyes grew wide. "Mark Overstreet? Whose daughter, Melissa, is on the dance team and played one of the rag dolls? The one who owns the jewelry store on Main Street?" Her heart was beating so loud in her ears that she doubted her hearing.

"Not just the jewelry store. Mark owns half the commercial property in town. He showed me something last month, when we were still seeing each other, and I thought it was perfect for you. But I was afraid to give it to you, afraid that I might be rushing things and I'd scare you off. After that, you were so mad at me I figured there was no point. But when I saw you standing there last night . . . Well, Christmas isn't until tomorrow but I decided to take the chance before it's too late." Andy loosened his grip on Kendra's waist, reached into his coat pocket, pulled out a small green velvet box tied with a red ribbon, and put it in Kendra's hand.

"Andy . . . I . . . I don't know what to say." Kendra's mind was racing, half-thrilled, half-terrified as she stared at the little box.

"Don't say anything. Just open it."

Kendra swallowed hard, pulled a stray end of the red ribbon, and then slowly lifted the hinged lid of the green velvet box. "A key? You got Mark Overstreet out of bed so you could give me a key?"

Andy grinned and nodded vigorously. "It

opens the door of a storefront on Main Street. It used to be a gym. It has wood floors and one wall is mirrored. There's a little back office, and a big dressing area and bathroom. It's perfect for a dance studio!" Andy exclaimed. "Mark said he'd rent it to you for one hundred and fifty dollars a month."

"One hundred and fifty? Really?" Kendra asked, her disappointment temporarily overcome by her surprise. "He could probably rent it for four times that much."

"Probably, but Mark only has one daughter and she's got him wrapped around her little finger. Melissa wants a dance studio here in town and since you helped the team take a trophy at the state finals, she wants you to be the teacher. And after the success of the play," he said, his eyes crinkling up at the corners, "I'm sure every mother in town, and probably in the county, will feel the same way. They'll be lined up around the block waiting to enroll their children in Kendra's School of Dance."

He looked into her eyes, searching for a response, but Kendra was too overwhelmed to know what to say. "Kendra," he continued, his eyes becoming more serious, "I know this isn't New York; Maple Grove is a world away from the bright lights of Broadway. And I know you've only been here for a couple of months, but in that short time, an awful lot of people in this town have come to care for you.

"I was so proud of you tonight, Kendra. You took a terrible script and a bunch of kids that didn't want anything to do with the play before they met you, and you created something magical! Think about it, Kendra. You belong here. This town needs you. And I—"

His words were interrupted by the crackle of rubber tires on gravel. Kendra was blinded by the sharp glare of headlights as a battered blue sedan, spattered with road salt and belching a cloud of noxious-looking exhaust, pulled into the driveway.

"Who could be coming to visit at this hour?" she asked, stepping out of Andy's embrace and straining her eyes to see who had climbed out of the car and was striding up the driveway, cursing under his breath. "Stanley?" she called in disbelief, then turned to Andy. "It's my agent from New York, Stanley Kahn."

"Oh," Andy said, less than thrilled by the

interruption. Kendra walked to the edge of the porch. Andy stepped behind her.

"Stanley, what are you doing here?"

"Believe me, I've been asking myself the same thing all the way from New York," he grumbled, and kicked snow off his Italian leather shoes before mounting the steps to the porch, not even bothering to introduce himself to Andy. "I've been calling you for days. Don't you ever answer your phone?"

"There's no cell service here," Kendra said.

"Yeah, that's what this girl told me but I couldn't bring myself to believe it. What kind of Podunk town doesn't have a cell tower? Then I tried calling the number of the place she said you were staying, but nobody ever answered. Haven't people in Crabapple Cove ever heard of voice mail?"

"Maple Grove," Kendra corrected him. "And the Sugarmans don't like voice mail. Denny says that anybody who really wants to find him will call back."

The agent rolled his eyes and held his hands open, as if praying for patience. "Yeah? Well, I did call back—about thirty times. Never mind." He waved his hand wearily. "I kept calling you—no answer. I went to your apartment and banged on the door—no answer. I finally went over to Radio City to see if anybody knew what happened to you and I met this girl, this Stacey, who said you'd gone to the frozen North until your leg healed. Which," he said, glancing at Kendra's two functioning feet, "it clearly has. That's good news."

"Actually," he said with a self-satisfied smirk as he pulled a sheaf of papers out of his pocket, "it's just the beginning of the good news. That's why I rented a car and drove all night to find you. Look at the junk heap they gave me to drive," he griped. "With the holidays it was the only thing they had left on the lot. Anyway, four days ago, Trevor Danielson called asking about you . . ."

"Trevor Danielson!" Kendra squealed. "*The* Trevor Danielson? He called you about me?"

"That's the one," Stanley reported. "Director of *Suspended Animations* and the biggest collector of Tony awards on Broadway. He saw you in that audition for the national tour last spring and remembered you. He's putting up a new show and insists that you are perfect for the second lead. He doesn't even want to audition other actresses! Rehearsals start the day after Christmas. We've got to have a signed contract in his hand by five o'clock tonight or they'll have to start looking for someone else. That's what made me haul my cookies all the way up here."

Kendra's hand flew to her throat and she laughed out loud. "Stanley, you've got to be kidding."

"I never kid about money."

"But, Stanley," Kendra said, her brow furrowing, "I don't know if I can do it. The doctor said I shouldn't dance again, not like I did before."

Stanley snorted. "And you're going to take the advice of some quack who got his medical degree at Moose U? When we get to New York we'll go to Columbia Presbyterian and see what a *real* doctor has to say. Anyway, it doesn't matter. This isn't a big dance part. He wanted you because of your acting and your look. All you'll have to do is a little soft shoe while the chorus boys prance around and make you look pretty. Nothing to it. This is it, kid. The day we've been waiting for." He took a pen from the breast pocket of his jacket and held it out to Kendra. "All you gotta do now is sign the contract, come back to New York with me, and get ready to be famous."

Still stunned, Kendra reached toward the pen. She opened her fingers and stared at the key still clutched in her fist. Stanley was right, it was her big break, her Broadway dream come true, but looking at the key in her hand, breathing in the morning stillness unknown on the bustling boulevards of Manhattan, thinking of Thea, of Denny and Sugar and all the people she'd come to care for in Maple Grove, and turning to gaze into the loving warmth of Andy's deep brown eyes, Kendra realized her dreams no longer began and ended with the applause of strangers. She wanted more and she wanted it for always.

Though they'd known each other such a short time, when Andy handed her the jewelry box Kendra's heart had raced. A part of her was frightened at the idea of commitment and all it would mean for someone like her, someone who so recently had taken that first satisfying sip of the quenching waters of faith, to become the pastor's wife. It was a daunting prospect. But for just a moment, she'd dared to hope there was an engagement ring in the velvet box and when she'd found the key instead, disappointment had flooded her breast.

Kendra curled her fingers around the key.

What if I this is all I ever get, this key? I love Maple Grove. I love the town and the people and I love the teaching those kids, helping them dream dreams of their own. But, none of it will mean anything if I don't have Andy. The only key I really want is the key to his heart. But we've known each other such a short time. What if I give up my big chance only to have it all blow up in my face? How can I know for sure?

In that moment, Thea's face appeared in her memory, singing the faith and hope of a young girl who did not entirely understand how she'd come to find herself so far away from home, or exactly how all that she'd prayed and dreamed for would come to pass, but who believed entirely in the goodness of God and the possibility of miracles. Some decisions had to be made on faith alone.

"Kendra, what are you waiting for?" Stanley growled impatiently and thrust the pen toward her. "Come on! Sign this thing already so we can get out of here and go home."

Kendra took a deep breath. "I can't do it, Stanley," she said and looked to Andy. "I already am home."

After Stanley drove away in a choking cloud of expletives and exhaust, Kendra returned to Andy's embrace, snuggling as close to him as possible. "So what was it you were saying, before we were so rudely interrupted?"

"I was saying that you belong here, that the town needs you. And I need you, too, Kendra. I love you." He lowered his mouth to hers, their lips meeting in a kiss that banished all uncertainty from Kendra's mind and heart. She had spoken the truth; she really was home.

"Oh, good. You two finally made up," Sugar said cheerfully as she opened the front door and saw Kendra and Andy locked in an embrace. "Why don't you come in the house and have some breakfast? Everybody was awake, anyway, so I mixed up some waffle batter and Denny is stoking up the fire. Thea just got up and was asking what happened to you, Andy. She wants to know if she can open one of her presents a day early. I told her she'd have to ask you, but it is Christmas Eve. I don't see the harm in it."

"You're right. It won't hurt to open just one. Tell her we'll be right in," Andy said without taking his eyes from Kendra's face. Sugar closed the door.

"But first it's your turn," Andy said. "You have to open your gift."

Kendra smiled. "But you already gave me a gift," she said, holding up the key. "After breakfast, can we drive over to Main Street and check it out?"

Andy reached into the pocket of Kendra's jacket and fished out the jewelry box. "That was just the first half of your present. You have to finish opening it."

Kendra's hands were trembling as she opened the box for the second time. She gently pried loose the box's bottom and found a perfect round circlet of gold capped with a sparkling, solitary diamond hidden beneath the velvet.

"Oh, Andy!" Kendra's hand covered her mouth and her eyes filled with tears.

"I didn't want to put too much pressure on you, so I decided not to give you the ring until I was sure you wanted to stay in Maple

Grove. I know you've always dreamed of making it big on Broadway . . ."

"No, Andy Loomis. Not anymore. This is my new dream. You're my dream, for better or worse, for now and forever. I just didn't know until today that miracles really do come true."

Author's Note

Dear Reading Friend,

Thank you for taking time to join me on a holiday jaunt to the village of Maple Grove. I hope you found as much pleasure in the reading as I did in the writing.

While researching this story, I learned a lot about Vermont and especially about one of the state's most famous exports—Vermont maple syrup. I never realized there were so many ways to use this delectable ingredient in cooking. It was some of the most delicious research I've ever done and, believe me, pancakes are just the beginning!

I'd love to share some of my favorite maple syrup recipes with you, including Sugar Sugarman's Maple Syrup Cutouts and two other bonus recipes that are sure make your holidays just a little sweeter. To get these free recipes just send a request to:

Marie Bostwick
PO Box 488
Thomaston, CT 06787

Or, if you want to save yourself a stamp, you can visit my website, *www.mariebostwick .com,* and send a request on the contact form. While you're there, you can check information on my other releases, including my newest book, *On Wings of the Morning*, plus appearances, contests, and the like.

Please note that recipes will be sent only by U.S. mail, so make sure you include your name and address with your request. You don't need send postage; this is my Christmas gift to you.

Thanks again for stopping by to visit Maple Grove.

May your holidays be filled with comfort and joy.

Blessings,

Marie

Suzanna's Stockings

Cathy Lamb

To my sisters,
Cindy Ann Everts and
Dr. Karen Suzanne Straight.
And to the sisters of my heart,
Sheri Hallwyler and Nancy S.

Chapter One

I didn't look dead.

At least, not yet.

But I didn't look too good, either.

I watched a nurse in purple scrubs flutter about my bed. I was glad to see that she had gray hair, all plaited into tiny braids, and that she was not some young thing with a skinny waist, sleek hair, and perky boobs.

No, if I was going to be surrounded by blipping and bleeping machines, IV poles, and rails around my mattress in a darkened hospital room, I wanted someone experienced poking and prodding at me.

She examined a chart, made some notations, checked the machines, my pulse, my forehead, then, for a second, she stood, examining my pale, pasty face, half-hidden by an oxygen mask, her expression tired and sad.

I glanced at her nameplate. Adanna. She shook her head, sighed, then left the room, shutting the door quietly behind her.

I continued watching myself. Myself wasn't moving in the hospital bed. Myself was hardly breathing.

My hair was splayed out on the pillow, blah and boring. I hardly made a mound at all under the thin hospital blankets. Was there a body? Or was my head attached to my neck and that was that?

I hadn't realized how skinny I'd gotten.

Yuck.

But I had been busy. My gift shop business was struggling and I had almost no money. The Pooles were headed for disaster and I didn't know how to help them, Carly had a secret, Patricia seemed downright . . . *scared,* our beach town's very character was at risk, Ronna was deteriorating, Jack Benson was wreaking havoc in my life and in my nether regions, and I was engaged to someone else.

Most of all, I was trying to be happy.

Yes. Trying hard. And I was almost there.

Sort of. Not really.

Actually, the happy part hadn't been working.

I sat down on the hospital bed next to myself and picked up one of my hands. Limp. Cool. Deadlike, my nails chipped and ragged, my hands cracked with dryness.

Cold Oregon winters on the coast, especially here at Canyon Beach, can do that to you. Perhaps I'd get the first manicure of my life when I left here.

My face, white like a toilet, and so very still, appeared to be almost caving in on itself. Sheesh. Maybe I'd get my first facial, too.

At that moment all the machines in the room started ringing and zinging, a light flashed, an alarm blared. I scrambled off the bed so the doctors and nurses charging into the room could get to the me lying there in bed with an oxygen mask.

They hollered orders at each other and a huge light was swung over my body. Tools whipped from one hand to another, a machine was rolled in and liquid stuff dropped into my IV.

"We're losing her!" a doctor shouted. "She's crashing, people!"

That seemed to be code for run around and yell at each other in a controlled fashion until patient is pulled away from the tunnel of death.

After long minutes everyone suddenly froze and waited. A machine blipped. Relieved laughter floated through the room.

Adanna leaned over me and said, "Hang in there, Ms. Everts. You're in a coma but you keep fighting, girl. Keep fighting."

"I'm over here," I tootled from my place by the window, but none of them turned from studying the me not moving in the bed. "Yoo-hoo. I can heaaaaaar you."

No response.

"*Yadaloohoo* . . . . My glorious self is over here." I waved my arms.

No one moved. One of the doctors with a ponytail squeezed the hand of the me in bed.

Everyone left except Adanna.

All this, I tell you, in a calm and measured tone.

But I was not feeling calm and measured.

No, I was half a step away from panic-fueled hysteria. A second away from screeching like a banshee having a hot flash. A millimeter away from digging a hole in the ground with my teeth and hiding my head.

Surely I was hallucinating.

But no, I thought, as I continued to watch myself lying inert and deadlike in that hospital bed.

This was no hallucination.

I was alive. Clearly. Because I could see myself in that hospital bed from where I stood.

And, it appeared, I was in a coma.

Now, how 'bout that?

Two women, both the same woman, both me, one watching the other.

I started screaming.

Adanna didn't even notice.

Chapter Two

A tapping sound woke me up. I saw myself still lying on the bed with the tubes and oxygen mask, my eyes closed. The me that was slumped in a chair saw Magdalena Hernandez dancing around my darkened hospital room, her red hair flying out behind her, her black velvet coat swirling about like a bell. Her high heels, also black, tapped around the room.

At forty-five years old, she was tall and willowy and earthy and I'm sure every man in town secretly lusted after her. She has the most enormous greenhouse and sells orchids. She's single and told me she planned on staying single because, "Men are like leeches. They suck the life right out of you."

I watched her dance around the hospital room, little silver sparkles flying from her hands to the floor, like glitter, catching the

light of the moon. I figured my brain synapses were popping because there is no
way sparkles could fly from fingers, as sane
people know.

My eyes were drawn to the floor. Silver
sparkles everywhere. They reminded me of
the glittery glass art I used to love to create.
A familiar feeling of raw loss rattled through
me, but I batted it back down.

Magdalena started singing, low and
sweet, in words I couldn't understand, her
head thrown back, her curls curling in and
around themselves.

She touched the forehead of the me in the
bed with one finger and left.

"I'm trying to stop cheating on him," Carly
whispered to the me lying in the hospital
bed, not moving. "Can you believe it? Your
sister is a cheater. Me. A cheater with a cap-
ital *C*."

Ah, so that was the secret. As usual, Carly
and I had gotten right down to business.
Only I had not expected this particular adul-
terous business and I could not respond in
any way.

"I'm the president of the PTA at school.

Our Girl Scout troop sold the most cookies this year," she said, her voice a harsh whisper. "One minute I'm running the meeting for the school carnival and the next I'm walking along a lake with *him,* drinking white wine, and talking about the Swiss Alps, like I'm not a hard-core mommy. Like I'm a woman. I don't even drink wine and I've never been to Switzerland."

She wrapped her arms around her waist and banged her head against the mattress. "I wanted to tell you, but I knew you wouldn't approve. I'm only telling you now because I have to tell someone and you're the only one who won't tell anyone."

I chuckled from my place by the window, only semihysterically.

"I met him at Magdalena's when I was helping out that one day in July. We talked about orchids, then gardening, and pretty soon we're meeting to see a garden near Bankston together. Harmless, right? I think I fell in love with him over a bag of fertilizer, Suzanna. I fell in love with him over a bag of shit."

She groaned, wiped the tears from her red face.

"You keep asking me what's wrong, Suzanna, well, this is it. And you're it, too," she hastened to add. "You being in a coma is terrible. Terrible! And Christmas is almost here!" She patted my hands, folded neatly on my chest like I was already in a coffin. "I try not to see him, try not to call him, but I do, I do! I don't want to be in love with him, but it's hard! He's so nice, he asks me how I am and he really *listens*. I could recite Roman history in a monotone and he would listen to me with rapt attention. He makes me laugh, he tells me I'm beautiful.

"I wish I felt guilty, Suzanna." Carly banged her head again. "And that's the problem! I don't feel guilty. Paul doesn't even see me as a person. He sees me as a mother. As his wife. The words 'his wife' should be capitalized. I'm his cook and a servant. I've become blank to him. I'm like a sheet of paper with no writing on it. I'm a dishcloth. I'm mayonnaise to him. He doesn't even realize I have feelings and dreams and that I feel this desperate despair."

I took a peek at my wisp of a body in the bed. I sure understood desperate despair.

"Paul comes home from work and says hello and pats my butt and then talks to the kids. We have dinner together and he talks *at me,* not with me, *at me.* I'm supposed to be fascinated with screws and hammers and saws that he's selling at the hardware store." She hit the mattress with her fist. "He can't even tell that I'm so sick of hearing about tools I would rather swallow a screwdriver than hear about them one more time. Then he goes out and works on his car with Chloe or Scotty. He comes in an hour later, watches TV, asks me to bring him some ice cream and goes to bed.

"Suzanna, this has been going on for twelve years. Can you believe it? No one should get married at twenty. No one. That should be illegal." She leaned back in her chair, her head tipped up to the ceiling. "We have sex every other Saturday night. 10:00. On the dot. Right after we watch a movie. Like clockwork. I don't even orgasm. I don't even think he knows what an orgasm is. He's on me, he's off me."

My heart hurt. I loved my sister. I loved my brother-in-law. And what a barren marriage it was for Carly.

"Paul thinks everything is great, Suzanna. He doesn't see that I'm dead inside. Oh!" She clapped both hands over her mouth. "I'm sorry, Suzanna! Wrong words, but you're not dead, I know you'll be okay." She patted me again.

"I never thought I'd be cheating on my husband, Suzanna. Ever. But I'm so lonely. I'm so tired. And I'm so tired of being lonely."

She pounded her feet on the floor. "Help me, Suzanna. What should I do?"

Hell if I knew. My body was in a coma. What should *I* do?

The beeps and bleeping on the machines started up again and the doctors and nurses flew back in, barking orders and spewing alarming things like, "She's going . . . Blood pressure's down . . . heart rate erratic."

Two male nurses had to manhandle Carly out the door because she kept screaming my name, her eyes wild. "I love you, Suzanna! Don't die! Don't die!"

The next day two ladies came to visit me.

"Hairy balls," one whispered, "Oh, hairy balls!" She grasped my right hand, peering at my very still face from about two inches away. One lone tear trickled its way down and splattered on my oxygen mask.

"Damnation and hell's bells!" the other

one whispered back. She grabbed my left hand and put her face right next to her sister's. Three faces, inches apart.

Then Evie Chamberlain and Dawn Cardolino, who lived in their childhood Victorian-style home overlooking the ocean, both burst into tears.

"Now you wake up, Suzanna Everts! Do you hear me! You wake up!" Evie shouted, giving my left shoulder a little shove with her hand.

"This is nonsense," Dawn added. "Nonsense! You've had your rest, now you open up your eyes, girl, you open up those chocolate-brown eyes." As if what her sister did wasn't enough, Dawn grasped both my shoulders and gave me a little jiggle. "Come on now, girl, come on come on come on."

Evie pushed my knees up and down. Dawn clapped my hands together. Evie massaged my head with her hands.

"What are you doing?" Dawn asked.

"I'm massaging her brain. I'm communicating with her brain cells. I'm awakening her synapses."

"I see," Dawn said, crossing her arms in annoyance.

I knew Dawn was ticked because she hadn't thought of that.

Dawn grabbed my feet and massaged them.

"What on Earth and Jupiter and Pluto are *you* doing?" Evie asked, still massaging my brain.

"The feet are the heart of the body. Every part of the foot connects to the body. I'm massaging the part of her foot that is her brain."

"She doesn't have a brain in her foot!"

"I know that, Evie! But this part of her foot"—she stabbed her nails into the center of my arch—"this here is where the brain connects, that's why I'm rubbing it!" She gave my foot a shake.

"Oh, pshaw!"

"Pshaw yourself!"

During their rigorous rubbing, Evie said, "We're watching the shop for ya, darlin', now don't ya worry. Sales at The Red Lantern are about as bad as before but don't ya worry."

"In fact, darlin'," Dawn added, "sales still suck, honey, oh, they suck. But maybe we'll get some more customers this week. Only five weeks before Christmas, ya know, people will be out shopping, that's for sure, but our sales—"

"Suck, suck," Evie said.

I shook my head from where I stood at the foot of the bed. Like I needed to be told that now. I knew sales were horrible. I knew my little gift shop was not doing well. But, gee. What could I do from the comfort of a coma?

"Everyone on the street has sucky sales, but we think the world of ya and we'll stick at the shop forever, dear," Evie said.

"Forever!" Dawn shouted.

"Except on Square Dance Night," Evie declared. "I swear, it's the only time all week I get to see Ed Surbanks. You remember my Ed Surbanks?"

Oh, did I. I heard about Evie's unrequited love all the time.

"I also call him Ed Sugarbanks and Ed Sugarflanks, Ed Sugarbottom, Sugar pistol, Sugarmissile, if you can remember all that, darlin'."

"Righto, we can't keep it open on Square Dance Night or on Bunco Evening with the girls, either," Dawn said. "So sorry. And we can't keep it open when we have Erotic

Book Club Group. But of course you already know that, doll."

"And, if I ever get laid by my Mr. Sugarhands, I'll probably have to come in later in the morning, Suzanna, but I'll let ya know. Haven't had sex in years so if I get lucky I have to take the opportunity when it arrives."

"I don't think she understands that part, Evie. She doesn't seem to like sex."

Evie nodded, then whispered, across my comatose body to her sister, "Nope. Always workin', always worryin', not playin' much. And that fiancé. Man, he is the type that would have sex with his long johns on."

"Shush now, shush. She might hear you."

"I hope she does. That fiancé of hers has the sexual attraction of a squished tomato. Toe. Mae. Toe."

"Darned if you're not right. He has the magnetism of a bunion."

"The orgasmic ability of a slithering snake."

"The penile heat of a viper."

One of my machines blipped and both sisters spun around, then bent at the waist and peered at the lights.

"Hairy balls," Dawn whispered.

"Damnation," Evie echoed.

In unison they both shook their heads. In unison they sniffled. Evie used a pink Kleenex in her purse, then handed it to Dawn to use.

After a few minutes of silence, they adjusted their red leather pants, zipped up their red leather jackets, and tucked their red motorcycle helmets under their arms.

Then those two spirited sisters, aged 72 and 73, left my hospital room for their motorcycles and their ride back to their Victorian.

I missed them already.

And I was sorry to hear that sales sucked. That sucked.

My fiancé came in later.

Trenton Maycomber is about three inches taller than me, which makes him rather short. I am five foot three inches. He says he's five feet eight inches. I always let that go.

He has brown hair, not a lot of it, which bothers him, but he brushes it very carefully each morning. I think he's handsome.

We met about two years ago at a conference in town, called, "Controlling Your Life." We started chatting, mostly about comput-

ers, which is his field. He asked me to dinner and we started dating. We always split
the cost, or I paid for our dates, because I
believe in being independent from men.
Well, mostly I paid for things, especially
since we got engaged last year, because I
will be living in Trenton's house after we get
married. He says he's paying our mortgage
now, so I pay for our activities. Which seems
fair.

And when it doesn't, I ignore it.

We like to do the same things: Read.
Work. Live quiet lives. Trenton likes things
organized and structured and predictable. I
like things calm and ordered, with zero upheaval, as I had enough of that in the chaos
of my childhood.

He built his home last year on a hill above
the town. He calls it a "postmodern reflec-
tion of the twenty-first century with a nod
toward Asia and a slice of New York."

He has minimal furniture, all steel, and has
nothing on any surface at anytime. He likes
it that way. He makes his bed, he tells me,
the second he gets up. He likes his towels
folded a certain way and after I leave the
bathroom, he sneaks in there to check to
make sure they're done right. The jars are

lined up in order in his refrigerator as are the goods in the cabinets. The spices are arranged alphabetically.

When he invited me for dinner at his house recently he showed me how to load his dishwasher so all the dishes are washed equally. I told him that was a little extreme, but he pointed out to me that when we're married, and living together, we need to accommodate each other's needs without resentment.

He likes to live by a schedule, as I do.

This coma has really blown my schedule.

Trenton stood about five feet away from the me in bed. I ached for him. Although we're not very affectionate with each other now, we're saving that part for marriage, he's my fiancé, and I knew he would be devastated by my coma. I wrung my hands and waited for him to kiss me, to hold me, to rock me back and forth while he smothered a scream. I waited for him to collapse to the ground. I waited for him to cry.

I waited and waited and nothing happened.

Trenton stared down at me, then sighed. A spasm of anger crossed his features, but I dismissed it. He wasn't really angry at me.

When men get scared, they get mad, all women know that.

Then he swore, rolled his eyes.

I watched him, hardly daring to breathe.

He spun on his heel and left.

"Trenton," I said, my voice crackling, but he didn't hear me. "Trenton."

The ticking of my machines became blaringly loud, every tick sounding like a hammer hit.

I swallowed hard.

Chapter Three

Patricia Goodling came after Trenton. I was later to find that behind closed doors, secret lives lurk, although it had not occurred to me that there were any secret lives lurking behind Patricia's doors.

Patricia is about fifty, but looks close to seventy, with graying hair and protruding eyes behind glasses the size of the moon. The stern and serious expression on her face is as rigid as a picket fence.

I call her Canyon Beach's One-Woman Moral Police Force. Three times she's been to the Canyon Beach City Council to complain about pedestrians crossing against our one light (civil disobedience), motorcycle noise (disturbing the peace and harassment of the elderly), and raucous teenagers (lawbreakers) who she thinks should be confined to the south side of town (for the benefit of society at large).

She has a group of gals over to her little yellow home right outside town every day of the week, so they can all study the Bible and pray together. Everyone needs prayer, she tells me, glaring over the top of her glasses. You, too, Suzanna.

She comes in my store often and I make it a point to compliment her about something. Her sweater. Her brooch. Her hair. We chat about little things—the foggy weather on the beach, her beloved cats who used to be humans, she's sure, gardening. She buys a plate or a bowl or a cup to "complete her set," and then leaves, her large bottom twitching on the way out the door.

On some basic level, I'd have to admit we clicked. She's prissy and uptight, and I'm reserved and like things orderly. She dresses like an old-fashioned matron. I dress plainly. She has let her hair go gray, I pin my uncontrollable blond curls up in a ball, and wear glasses.

I sensed in Patricia a person who is basically alone. I am, basically, alone, too.

But in Patricia I had always sensed something else. If I was pressed to say what it was, I would say it was fear.

But that didn't seem right. What did Patricia have to fear?

That morning I watched as Patricia peered down at my pale, oxygen-masked face. I jumped when she made loud choking sounds, both hands flying to her face. She took long, deep breaths.

"I will compose myself I will compose myself I will compose myself," she breathed. She blinked rapidly, then pulled her little suit jacket over her ample hips. "Ohhhh!" Her picket-fence face melted into tears. "This is dreadful, Suzanna. Dreadful." Her hands shook. Her lumpy body trembled.

"Please get well. Please! You're the only person I can talk to. You understand why I treasure my brooches. You understand how cats offer comfort in this depraved and lawless world. You and I, we're the same. We have *real* conversations about everything." She whimpered a bit, then abruptly cleared her throat. "Well, I can't talk to you about the . . . *the business*." She said the word "business" hardly any louder than the sound of a spider's burp.

"No, no one wants to hear about that!"

She blew her nose quite close to my ear. "No one! I don't even want to hear about it myself any more than I have to. One must do what one has to do."

She fanned herself with her hand, then lowered herself into a chair. "Heavens, but I'm so ashamed, Suzanna. So ashamed. But if I quit what would happen to Elizabeth? *What would happen to Elizabeth?* That thought scares me no end."

I had no idea. I didn't know who Elizabeth was. I didn't know what business she was talking about. I didn't know why Patricia was so upset.

Being in a coma is baffling.

She fussed around a bit in her bottomless pink handbag and found a book, her hands trembling. It was a historical romance novel, the couple on the front in a passionate clutch. "I am going to bring you a little love and lust, Suzanna. This is *The Bodice Ripper*. It's one of my favorites. I hardly ever read this type of . . . *trash* . . . but I think we both need a wee break from life, don't you?"

She read for quite awhile, her words rushing during the good parts. It was quite graphic, and hearing prim and proper Patricia using words like "lustful" and "heaving breasts" and "moist," "savage," "dancing tongue," was really, well, it ripped my bodice.

He sat beside my bed, exhausted and drawn, as if he hadn't slept in a week. Which he hadn't, from what I could see.

Now and then he would get up and stalk right past the coherent me and glare out the window of the hospital toward the ocean, then stalk back to my comatose self and stare at my face, my hands, the machines. He never touched me.

Jack Benson was about six foot six inches tall, and lean, with shoulders the size of Montana. He had a scar near the corner of his left eye and another little scar on his chin. There was a white bandage across his forehead and I wondered what happened.

He was a real man—rough and rangy. But it wasn't something I thought about. At least not too much. And when I did, I made myself stop thinking about it. Immediately. Without dwelling on that five o'clock shadow or the glimpse of black chest hair I'd seen.

I did not think about how his low and rum-bling voice was a tad sexy. I did not dwell on how he looked in his jeans because I am engaged and in love with Trenton. I did not dwell on his smile.

He sure as heck wasn't smiling as he stared at the me in my hospital bed.

My comatose self didn't smile, either.

I reminded myself that Jack Benson would be the end of my gift shop (The Red Lantern), the end of a huge area of natural beauty, and that he had confused and confounded me before my coma to the point where I couldn't even think. It was as if he'd taken my whole life in his two huge hands, shaken it up, twirled it around, and left me gasping.

Jack stayed for hours. The sun was up when he arrived, down when he left. On his exhausted, angular face I saw this: pain. This utter, broken, life-sucking pain.

My heart clenched again, so quick, so harsh, I thought I'd scream. I covered my mouth when it bubbled up. Silly me. I had learned that no one could hear me.

Not even Jack Benson.

*   *   *

Ronna Lavey shuffled in, by herself, as usual. She wore a beige raincoat, her mousey brown hair wet from the rain.

Ronna was sweating. Dark circles ringed her eyes and her face was the color of glue, like mine. She was nervous, her hands trembling. Twice she got up and paced around the room, shaking her hands like she was trying to wring them out.

She finally settled in a chair by my bed, her whole body vibrating, and wiped her forehead with the back of her hand.

Within seconds she was up again, darting to the little bathroom attached to my room. I heard her vomiting in the toilet, then I heard the water running.

She stumbled out of the bathroom, her face sweaty and wet from the water she'd tossed on it. She leaned against the wall, swallowing hard. A second passed, then she whipped into the bathroom again and threw up her insides.

She sank into the chair by my bed like a rubber doll.

I had met Ronna when she rear-ended my car. It was foggy that day, the beach socked in. I have a very, very old, dented car, and didn't care about another dent.

Ronna cried she felt so bad. Cried when she apologized. Cried when I told her not to worry about it. She was sweating then, too, her body shaky.

"My insurance will pay you," she'd insisted.

I waved my hand. "Don't worry about it—"

"I will worry. I'll do what's right."

Her eyes were red and swollen, her face tight.

"My car has twenty dents already."

"I'm paying to have it fixed," she insisted.

And she had. I didn't know her well, she'd moved to Canyon Beach only the previous month and had kept to herself. Ronna gave me her car, took mine, had it fixed, and drove back two days later when we traded cars again.

She'd had my entire bumper replaced, knocked the dents out of my trunk, replaced a broken headlight, and cleaned it. Way too much.

I put my hand on her shoulder, then reached down and hugged her. She didn't feel me, of course, as I am like a ghost wandering around, but I felt better doing it.

I surmised she had the flu and that's why she was shaking.

She dropped her head on my bed, her wet hair dampening the sheets.

David Poole almost sliced off his entire right leg while working on a log cutter for Weston Family Mills.

By the time the paramedics reached him, the blood had poured out of his body like a waterfall. The reason he hadn't lost all of it was because his coworkers had wrapped a belt around his leg to use as a tourniquet. They had placed their bare hands against his gaping wound to keep the life from draining out of him.

He had been life-flighted to the hospital and had flat-lined twice, his heart checking out. They stabilized him in the hospital, dumped almost a full body's worth of blood into him, operated, sewed up his leg.

Days later, when he was coherent, the doctors told David about his future: He might still lose the leg. He was at risk for infection. He might never walk. If he did, it would probably be very, very painful.

Other operations, physical therapy for sure, were all in the works.

It was a tremendously bad day.

And things got worse from there.

Weston Family Mills paid for the initial medical bills. Two weeks into the medical adventure they pronounced, through some nasty legal letters, that David's personal insurance through the company had to pay for the rest.

But the company plan wasn't very good. In fact, it paid only a minimal amount of David's expenses. Then Weston Family Mills closed and the employees were told it was belly-up bankrupt. The fat-cat execs told David Poole not to bother hiring an attorney because, sadly, there weren't any "funds" left. The factory was then auctioned off and all of the higher-up mucky-mucks took off.

The Pooles believed them.

They sold off both cars, their camper trailer, and David's prized vintage motorcycle. Lorrallee told me privately that they'd had to use all their retirement funds. David received a small amount of disability through the government, but nowhere near what they needed to live on, to say nothing of paying the mounting medical bills. Lorrallee couldn't work because David needed almost constant help. And one tiny detail: the Pooles have five kids, aged two to ten.

People in town gave them cash but the Pooles gave it back, saying others were worse off than them. Next, many of us helped with food. But David Poole didn't want "charity food," either, so we had taken to dropping off the food on their back porch in the middle of the night.

We knew that Lorrallee would be the one to pick it up, not David, and that Lorrallee would take it to feed the kids.

David's face, as usual, was gray and sickly when Lorrallee wheeled him into my hospital room.

I got all teary. I had met the Pooles through Carly and Paul. They were so busy, had so many of their own catastrophic troubles, but here they were to see the comatose me lying flat in bed like a white pancake.

Lorrallee kissed me on both cheeks, David patted my legs.

"You get well soon, honey," Lorrallee said.

"Suzanna," David said, his voice still strong. "I know you can hear me, so hear this: You're gonna get better, I know it. I want to see you dancing at the Christmas party at the lodge, ya hear? Dancing. I know you don't like to dance but this year ya gotta break out. Freak out. Groove. Dance til you drop. You and what's-his-prissy-name."

"Shhh," Lorrallee said, tapping her husband's shoulder none too lightly. "Shhh."

"Well, I don't like him," David said. "He's not right for her. The man's a priss."

"A priss?" Lorrallee was intrigued.

"Yes. The man's a priss. Always so dressed up. Everything so precise and clean. He won't even look me in the eye because he can't handle someone in a wheelchair. Remember that time we saw him in town and you said hello? He ignored me, as if I wasn't even there. Wheelchair equals: I'm invisible. Another time he patted me on the head like I was a dog after he was forced into an introduction. Idiot."

"I really don't think she needs to hear this right now, David, she's got an oxygen mask over her face and she's not moving, you old grump."

"Hey, any male who is that into his clothes and spends two years designing a house that resembles a spaceship on drugs from

Japan, then doesn't put any furniture in it, according to his housekeeper, who is not allowed *ever* in an upstairs bedroom, which I think means he's hiding something—a male like that is not a real male. He doesn't have the right stuff in his pants. The goodies that make the testosterone run, you know what I mean? Your priss has problems, Suzanna. When you wake up you go out and find yourself a real man, not a priss."

They hung around for a few more minutes, arguing over Trenton and what was in his pants, my engagement to a pantless man, my choice of a prissy man and his smooth hair, then patted me again and left.

Chapter Four

I woke up in a chair by the window later that night. I suppose even people wandering around outside of their bodies need rest. As I was still reeling over my ghostly state and battling raw panic almost every second I got a wee bit tired.

These were, in no particular order, my most pressing worries: Was I going to live or die? If my body in the bed died, did I die, too? Were there others like me floating around and about? Was this floating about permanent?

And, oh, yes. One small and tiny question: how in hell had I gotten into a coma in the first place? I couldn't remember a darn thing.

*   *   *

About twenty-five more people visited me in the hospital. Most of them cried. Almost all of them held my hand or hugged me.

I couldn't believe it.

I had felt so alone for most of my life.

Clearly, I had been wrong.

I was not alone.

Magdalena whirled in at dawn the following day, her heels tapping. "It's time for you to go, Suzanna," she whispered into the golden light, arms outstretched, those weird silver sparkles fluttering down. "Leave the hospital. Listen. Learn. Find out what you need to know about the people in your life. Then hope for the best, Suzanna. Hope that you'll live."

She waltzed on out, her black velvet coat a swinging bell.

Leave the hospital? Leave my body? What if my floating-about body wanted my other body to be one and the same again and couldn't because I was out gallivanting around?

As if in answer to my question, the machines monitoring my precarious life started beeping and ringing and a whole crew of doctors and nurses stampeded in like their hair was on fire. It did not take a genius to know that I probably didn't have a lot of time left here on Earth.

I was still scared, though, and hesitated. I am not an impulsive person. I don't make bold moves. I like to stand back from life. Think things through. Slowly.

But this time, with a doctor straddling my body trying to get my heart rate rearin' again, I started to get all philosophical about my life.

I thought of the years as a child I'd spent hiding with Carly, waiting for our father's rage to subside as he hurled chairs across the room. I thought of all the times Carly and I had clutched each other in fear when our parents left for days at a time or my father got out the belt to whip my mother.

I thought of all the seventy-hour weeks I'd worked to escape that life and those treacherous memories and the dreams I'd smothered along the way. I thought of my glass art, how I'd shut down and given up.

Had I ever had fun? Did I know how to have fun? My life was one very weak heartbeat away from being over. Had I ever really *lived?*

I waited until the doctors and nurses revived my limp body again, the machines settled down, and the monitors indicated that, yes, I was still with the program. I gave myself a kiss on the cheek. And then I left.

I strolled right through that hospital. No one glanced my way, no one saw me. I passed by a mirror in the hall and there was no me. None. I sped right through the glass EXIT doors, no need to open them. I was invisible and ghostlike in my movements.

I laughed.

Although it was late November, the day was bright and sunny, the seagulls out in full force, when I strolled out of the hospital and onto Deauville Drive, the main street of town. Our downtown core, where my shop is located, is rather dull and a little tacky so therefore is not very successful in attracting tourists even though it's one block off the beach.

No one saw me when I did a jerky little jig, no one heard me when I warbled out a Pointer Sisters' song.

But that day everyone saw Dee Cahill drive her black sports car straight through the show windows of BryDee's Fine Furniture, which she and her husband, Bryan, own.

Dee Cahill hit her brakes smack in front of the store. She was driving too fast, her car swerving, and her brakes squealed. I smelled burning rubber. She then backed up at a 90-degree angle and maneuvered her car up and over the sidewalk directly across from their store. For a second she paused, and all was still except for one cawing seagull.

Then she revved the engine a couple of times, the sound splitting the air in half, and that slick sports car went flying across Deauville Drive, leaped over the curb, and smashed straight through the windows.

The glass cracked in a million different directions, wood chips from the frame of the store splintering and flying off.

The noise was deafening, not unlike a bomb.

With glass from around the edges of the showroom windows still shattering onto the sidewalk, and half a dining room table on top of her hood, Dee Cahill backed her car up again, onto the sidewalk across the street from the store.

She paused, like before, as if aiming, the seagull squawked, and then she hit the accelerator, wheels spinning, and peeled across the street.

This time her car torpedoed ten feet farther into the store, the explosive noises continuing as she rammed her way into bedroom sets and armoires. I heard someone screaming.

As if the second hit wasn't good enough, she backed up a third time, this time with a two-legged chair on the hood, zoomed across the street, and plunged her car almost all the way through the store.

When the din dimmed, I heard the screaming again.

I sprinted toward the store, carefully skirting around the back of the car to make sure Dee wasn't backing up yet again, then, I'm not kidding here, I stepped (literally) through the front door of the store, which was the only thing that wasn't smashed to smithereens.

The sports car was fully inside the store. Half a coffee table and part of a lamp wobbled on the hood. I bent down to make sure no one was stuck under the wheels. Thankfully, no one was there.

The screaming was coming from Bryan, who was in front of the car, his arms outstretched in his own defense. "Stop, stop, Dee! What the hell!"

Dee, sitting in the front seat of her car, her hair and makeup perfect, as always, was belting out an operetta.

These were the words: "You put your pee pee in the wrong place, wrong place, wrong place, and now you're going to fry. Fry fry fryyyyy . . ." She hit a high C, long and piercing.

"You're insane, Dee!" Bryan raved at her. "Insane!"

"I'm not insane, you—" And then she let out a stream of swear words, still in operetta, her face composed. She flung one arm out the window of her car for musical emphasis, then gunned the engine again, and her car inched forward.

Poor Bryan's face was white and shocked. He is such a gentle, unassuming man. He had come to see me twice at the hospital. With stores near each other, we often chatted, although never when Dee was around. Dee has a jealous streak wider than the Pacific Ocean.

"Dee! What are you doing? *What are you doing?*"

"You pissant!" She left the operetta behind. "You want someone else? Fine by me! She can have you! I wonder how she'll like dating a man who has a squished penis!"

Dee inched the car forward, cackling. I screamed at Bryan to leap on the roof of the car. He didn't hear me, but leap he did.

Dee cackled again, in triumph, then hit another high C note, and I realized that's what she'd wanted all along. She reversed out of BryDee's Fine Furniture, Bryan clinging to the window wipers and begging her to stop. The sports car glided to the street, then Dee slammed the gears into DRIVE and zigzagged down Deauville, fire engines and police cars following her in hot pursuit.

I hurried after Dee's car, which wasn't going very fast, as did about twenty other people.

She didn't have far to go. She veered left and hung a right, with Bryan still clinging on to the windshield wipers for dear life. I saw her turn into the driveway of a brown and white home down the street.

Oh, no no no no, I thought. Oh, no no no no. The home was neat and tidy, the lawn trimmed, the paint new, the bushes well rounded, every leaf where it was supposed to be.

Dee rammed the front of her sports car into the garage. Even from where I was near the corner of the block, I heard the reverberating bang and wood splitting. I continued running and watched Bryan scramble off the top of the car and leap for the porch.

Carly stumbled out the front door wearing jeans and a white T-shirt, her blond hair in a ponytail. I breathed a sigh of relief, knowing Chloe and Scotty were at school.

Dee scooted out of her car, slammed the door, and yelled, at the top of her voice, "He's yours, Carly, you sick slut. You scheming witch, you loathsome, depraved husband stealer."

Then, she stared straight up at the sky, flung out her arms, her red nails manicured, and let out still another operatic high C.

She ended with this long peal, "You aaarrrree a sllluuuttttttt . . ."

I watched the police surround the house and car, heard them ordering Dee to put her hands up, don't move, and get on the ground. Then Dee Cahill was face-down on

Carly's driveway, handcuffs clicking around her wrists.

She never stopped singing.

I glanced up at Carly on the porch.

This was not good. Not good at all.

Carly and Bryan?

No. It absolutely, positively couldn't be true.

Could it?

Dee Cahill was charged with assault, criminal mischief, and reckless driving. Bail was set at $250,000.

And, gee, I forgot this one. She was also charged with attempted murder. In Oregon, that's an automatic ninety months' sentence.

Dee would not like wearing an orange jumpsuit.

Unlike many people who came to see me at the hospital, including Jack Benson who came every day for most of the day, Trenton had come to see me only once in the last week. I decided to go and see him.

I tried to stamp down the anger and the

hurt that flared up in me. I reminded myself that different people show grief in different ways and that Trenton wasn't good with changes to his schedule, that he wasn't emotional, that he didn't like conflict, avoided distressing situations, etc.

I understood that. I try not to get emotional, either. I don't like conflict, and distressing situations are, at their essence, distressing, so I avoid them, too.

Our relationship had not been built on passion and romance and fluff. That gets you into trouble, we both agreed. Marriages should be built on solid friendships and values. We have common interests and lifestyles, and intellectual conversation. We agreed not to have sex before we were married so the passion could wait.

I would probably find Trenton holed up at home, exhausted and depressed, and would feel terribly guilty for maligning him.

He was home when I arrived.

I slipped in through the front door and took a deep breath.

How hard this must be for him! How heartbreaking. Me, his fiancée in a coma. He doesn't know if I'll live or not, or if there are permanent injuries. He finally finds someone, it had been years since he'd had a girl-friend, and now . . . this.

I heard his muffled voice in his office. I pic-tured him sobbing out his feelings to his mother over the phone and I felt worse. I peeked in.

Trenton was on the phone.

Laughing.

Trenton was laughing.

Chapter Five

Don't ask me what precisely made me jump into Jack Benson's pickup when I saw him leaving The Red Lantern with a box.

Perhaps it was Trenton's laughter.

Or, perhaps it was Trenton's call to his lawyer where he'd yelled and screamed, "Fix the damn problem, Chad, that's why I'm paying you! Find the loophole!"

Or, perhaps it was a call he took from someone else, which ended like this, "I'll be coming into some money soon and I'll pay you then, so shove off."

Or, perhaps it was the phone conversation I'd overheard with his sister, Alyssa, who was one of the kindest people I'd ever met.

"Alyssa, you're closest to Mom and Dad, you help them," Trenton whined. "I'm twenty minutes away. You're only ten minutes away. You can help them a lot easier than I can . . . Hey, you don't work. I know you have four kids, Alyssa, but *you don't work.* You're home. You have time to take Mom and Dad to their doctors' appointments and to give Dad his insulin shots, and check on Mom. I don't. I know the doctor said Mom's heart is bad. He's been saying that for years. What does he know?

"Hey, Alyssa, no. Did you hear me? *No.* I know it's your fifteenth anniversary and you want a weekend away but I don't have time to play nursemaid to Mom and Dad. I won't come. Hey, hire someone to stay with them. Mom and Dad don't have the money? Then pay for it. I'll pay you half. What do you mean I didn't pay you half the last time? *How much* are you saying I owe you? Give me a break, Alyssa. It's not that much."

I was also sickened by what I saw in his spare bedroom. Trenton had told me he stored computer equipment in there, because his business is buying and selling computers, and he locked it for security reasons. What I saw in there was not computer equipment.

But the real ringer was when I glimpsed the documents that Trenton was holding in his hand, a slight smile on his features. Formal documents with my signature at the bottom.

I felt sick.

My mind reeling, I headed back to town, intending to check on my shop, The Red Lantern, which I'd named after a store my great-great-greatgrandmother had owned in Durango, Colorado. Her mother had been a pioneer and had had a red lantern with her on the journey, hence the name.

Instead, I jumped into Jack's truck, which was parked in front of The Red Lantern.

Seconds later, he placed a red box from my shop between us and I knew he'd made another purchase from my store. He bought items from The Red Lantern all the time. At first I had been flattered. And grateful. Then it clicked and I was ticked. He bought things to help my business, which I could handle by myself without his help.

I wondered for a millisecond if Jack would have liked the glass art I created years ago, then locked that thought away real tight.

Jack drove out of town, his face bleak.

I first met Jack Benson when he came into The Red Lantern five weeks ago. The bell above the door rang, but I ignored it because my hands were full of reindeer wood carvings that seventy-five-year-old Tran Hanovan made.

The sun had finally peeked through the clouds over the ocean and the rays slanted through the windows. When I turned around, Jack was staring at me.

I pushed my glasses back on my nose and stared back.

Even then I found him intimidating. Probably because he towers over me, is unreadable, and definitely seems a little rough and tough.

"Hello," he said after lonnnng seconds.

I smiled. "Hello. Can I help you?" Inside my heart was tripping over itself a wee bit. Surely because of all the hard work I'd done decorating The Red Lantern for Christmas.

"Yes. I'm . . ." He lost his train of thought, started again. "I'm . . . uh . . . looking for . . ." He paused, took a quick glance around the room, then stared at me for a few long, heart-stopping moments. "I'm looking for . . . uh, plates and mugs. Yes, plates. And mugs. That's what I need."

"Ah, well, I have those." I handed him some hand-painted plates made from clay.

Our fingers brushed, I felt this whiz shoot right up my arm, and I let go of the plate too soon. It shattered on the floor. We cleaned it up together and knocked heads twice.

"I'll pay you for the plate," he'd said in a don't-argue-with-me tone. "And I'll take you to lunch. My treat. Unless you're married?"

"I'm . . ." His eyes were so green, and light, and piercing. I couldn't get my thoughts together. "I'm . . ." What was I? "I'm . . ." Oh, yes. *That*. "I'm engaged."

He nodded. "That's no surprise."

I laughed. Tucked a stray curl firmly back in my bun.

"To whom?"

"I'm sorry?"

"To whom are you engaged?"

There was something about him that sizzled. I couldn't think.

"His name?"

What was his name? *Him*. "Trenton! Trenton Maycomber."

"Trenton's a lucky man."

"I don't know about that." I smiled. I couldn't help myself.

Jack blinked. There was a silence between us again.

"You must be excited, then."

I loved his hair. Black and thick.

"Are you?" he asked.

And his cheekbones. They were angled slants down his face and they tapered right down to his mouth and that mouth . . .

He smiled, his teeth white, his eyes, for a split second, softening.

"Am I what?" I asked him, dazed.

"Are you excited to be getting married?"

"No." I shook my head. My stomach clenched, and I started again. "I mean, yes. Definitely."

"When's the date?"

He had such a nice smile . . . "Hmmmm?"

"When's the date?"

I gathered myself together. *Breathe!* "We haven't set a date."

"No?"

"Uh. No."

"Why not?"

"Because . . ." He was huge! So tall. And why did his voice have to be so low? "Because, because . . ." I blushed. He laughed. I let my gaze wander away.

"Yes?"

"Because we haven't." My tone was a little snappish. Truth was, Trenton didn't want to set a date yet, though we'd been engaged for a year. He said he wanted to be sure I totally understood him.

"Ah."

"Ah, what?" I was coming to my senses. "What does 'ah' mean?"

"Ah . . . I think I'll buy the plates now. I'll take"—his eyes skittered around the nearly empty shop—"I'll take fifteen plates and fifteen mugs."

My mouth dropped in surprise. I snapped it shut.

I rang them up, his eyes intent on me and my blushing face. He insisted on paying for the broken one, too.

"Thank you," I said.

"Thank *you*." He smiled, winked, and left.

I leaned heavily against the counter and fanned myself with my hand.

The next day Jack Benson came back and stayed for three hours, chatting and helping me unload boxes of Christmas gifts. I told him it wasn't necessary, he insisted it was. I told him I was sure he had better things to do, he insisted he didn't. I said I could pay him, he insisted I not.

I found out he had four brothers and all of

them lived in Oregon. His parents lived in Portland. Both parents had between four and six siblings, they all lived in Oregon, and they all had kids. In Oregon.

"Big family," I said.

"Huge, meddling, noisy, nosy, off-their-rockers family."

I caught him studying me often. I am not as plain as a pear but I'm not a babe, either. Carly is always after me to stop slamming my curls back in a tight bun. *"You hide your beauty, Suzanna. Stop hiding."* Evie and Dawn say I am deliberately frumpy and have eyes like chocolate and should show off my "spellbinding" figure. But I don't. I like to blend in. Spending lots of time on one's face and hair is shallow and silly, anyhow.

It is. Silly and shallow, I reassured myself, patting my hair.

The next day Jack dropped in again. Every day for ten days. Each time he bought several items. A music box with Santa's elves on it for a sister-in-law. Pillows with embroidered scenes of Christmas trees for nieces. Elegant gold and white linens for an aunt.

He would ask me to lunch, I would say no.

He would go and get lunch and we'd eat amidst the merchandise.

"Why are you here?" I asked him, laughing. "Don't you want to do guy things like fish or hunt?"

"I'm here because of you." His green eyes stayed right on me, until I busied myself with the cash register. "If you won't come to lunch with me, I'll hang out with you here."

"Well, that's ridiculous. I'm not that entertaining."

He chuckled. "Yes, Suzanna, you are."

Our conversations got more and more personal, although I blew over my childhood until Jack asked me about a photograph on the wall of my office. It was of me and Grandma Tilly and Carly.

"Who are these people?"

I was surprised he'd asked. Trenton never had. He knew our parents were dead, that I'd been raised by Grandma Tilly, and that was that.

"My parents died when I was twelve and Carly was ten. We went to live with Grandma Tilly."

"I'm sorry." He reached over and stroked my hair, so gently, then left his hand on my shoulder. I didn't move. Couldn't move.

"Thank you," I managed to rasp out. I then busied myself with a box of ceramic Santa Clauses. My sales had to be good this Christmas or Santa might as well pack me up in his red sack and toss me out.

"What happened?" Jack asked, taking the box from me and doing it himself. "I'm sorry. I shouldn't ask that."

"Don't worry. It was a long time ago."

I straightened up. My past didn't bother me. I could talk about it. I had overcome it, dealt with it. Sure I had. I had never talked about it with anyone but Carly and Tilly, but I could talk about it without feeling like my guts were being shredded. Right?

I lost myself in Jack's green eyes and felt part of my insides start to splinter. "Our parents were both hard drinkers, although my mother was a sweet drunk. At least to us."

"And your father?" Jack froze.

My eyes dropped for a fraction of a second to his mouth. He had a full lower lip and grooves from nose to mouth that were so kissable.

But only if I was interested in kissing him, I told myself, which I'm not. At all.

"Let's say he wasn't as sweet as my mother when drinking. They died together when our father rolled his car driving the wrong way on the freeway."

Jack flinched. "I'm sorry, Suzanna."

"We grew up in Montana. I was a nervous, withdrawn child, embarrassed about my parents and my home, which was almost always a chaotic wreck." I smiled at Jack, but in truth, I hardly saw him. All I could see was a home in constant upheaval, all I could smell were beer and whiskey, all I could hear were the screaming and fighting or the dead silence that meant my parents had passed out.

"My first memory is the day of my third birthday. My mother made a cake for me. My father pushed my mother's face into it during a fight. The candles had been lit at the time."

I heard his quick intake of breath.

"One time I saw my mother stab a knitting needle at my father's eye from about one foot away. To this day, I cannot hold a knitting needle."

I tried to smile and be brave. I felt my smile wobble. I felt sick. Jack ran a hand over my shoulders. At first I stilled at his touch, then I relaxed as his warmth seeped through.

"I remember my father coming home with

an expensive car one night. We were evicted the next day for not being able to pay the rent. We lived in that car for two weeks. Within three months, it was towed away. We were living in an uncle's garage by then, along with the rakes and shovels and a rat we named Georgetta.

"We went to bed at odd hours, ate sporadically, and attended school with unbrushed hair and dirty clothes until I was in third grade and a little girl made fun of me.

"She told me I was a 'garbage girl,' those were her words, garbage girl. The sad thing was, I had actually found the clothes Carly and I were wearing in a black trash bag by a Dumpster that someone had tossed. I had been thrilled with my find and so had Carly.

"I stuck our clothes in the washing machine in town, dumped in a bunch of soap and dried them. I learned my lesson that day. No one ever made fun again of the way we were dressed or our hair."

The rest of my life, I had made sure I was neat and proper. I had done nothing to call attention to myself, though. Nothing flashy. I had wanted to disappear during much of my childhood. It didn't take a shrink to know that that complex had carried into adult-hood.

"You can't possibly want to hear more of this." I laughed self-consciously and tried to move away, but Jack put a hand on my back.

"I do. I want to hear everything."

I fluttered about a bit more, then I told him.

"When the police came to our house at 2:00 in the morning, we knew something was wrong and told them to call Grandma Tilly. She came from her home in northern Montana and wrapped us in her arms. Grandma Tilly was a long-haul trucker. She was completely different from her daughter and said she thought that Mary Beth got her wild side from her own mother. 'It's a gene thing, honey,' she'd told us. 'Every other generation screws up.' She told us our parents had been killed.

"When she adopted us, she bought the small trucking company she worked for and stayed in town. She started with three trucks and by the time Carly and I left for college, she had thirty. She married ten years ago and moved to Florida. She met her husband at a convention. He owned a long-haul trucking company, too. They merged their companies and now spend most of their time on cruises."

I smiled at him but my smile dimmed quickly.

"Carly grew up wanting a family of her own. She wanted a kind man who was always predictable and reliable. She found that in Paul."

"And you? What did you want?"

I thought about that. "Quiet. Order. Predictability. That's what I wanted then. That's what I want now."

"Have you found it?"

His green eyes blazed into mine. I thought of a few recurrent flashbacks when my parents chased each other around the house wielding various tools, like fireplace pokers and kitchen knives, during their fights; the way my dad drove his car after a few hits of tequila, and several choice incidents when my parents were arrested for one thing or another. "Yes. Sort of. Most of the time." And then the truth, "I'm trying."

He nodded at me, then picked me up in his arms, sat down on a chair, and pulled me onto his lap. "Keep trying, Suzanna."

I sunk into his warmth, his arms, his solid chest, my forehead on his neck. He smelled

like the forest and mint and musk, his jawline rough with an incoming beard.

Exhausted by the truth, I could hardly
move. And then I realized I was pressed
tight against Jack Benson. I tried to scramble off his lap.

He held me fast. "Where are you going?"

"I'm going off your lap!" I pushed my
glasses back up and kept scrambling.

"Why? What's wrong with my lap?" I could
tell he was amused.

"I'm not supposed to be on it, that's
what's wrong!"

"Says who?" he drawled, using one hand
to cup the side of my face.

Now that did it. "I'm engaged, Jack. Engaged. I can't be sitting on another man's
lap." I struggled again and he released me,
standing up in front of me before I could
bolt down the aisle.

He stared down at the floor for a second.
"I apologize. I shouldn't have hugged you,"
he said. "Or put you on my lap."

"Well, yes, no, yes . . ." I was completely
flustered.

"I'm sure your fiancé wouldn't have liked
it."

"Yes! No! No, I don't think he would."

Would he? Trenton would protest, wouldn't he?

"I'm sorry for hugging you on my lap."

"I . . ." I caught his eye and I knew. Jack Benson wasn't sorry at all. Not a bit.

He smiled at me, slow and sexy and easy and open.

I could barely breathe.

Chapter Six

Two days later Jack Benson told me he had bought a house overlooking the ocean on the north end. I knew exactly which one it was. It was a Craftsman style with a wraparound porch. I'd always loved it. I imagined you could see almost to the edge of the ocean in that house, plus the entire town.

"So you're moving here? I thought you said you were here temporarily because of some business or other. You've been vague about that, you know." I smiled at him, couldn't help it.

"I'm staying for awhile," he said, grinning back at me. "I'm looking forward to Christmas at the beach." My heart tripped. My face got hot. My body tingled.

Jack Benson laughed.

* * *

It was Dawn and Evie who broke my dreamy bubble a couple days later.

Jack was making a mess of me. Before he'd strutted into my life everything was in order. I had a plan for my life and my life was on that plan. *I was engaged, engaged, engaged*.

But I started doubting the plan. I huffed and puffed at myself. I was simply projecting my fears of marriage onto Jack and it meant nothing. He was an attractive man to whom I meant nothing. There was no problem here, none.

I listened with half an ear to Evie and Dawn as they discussed their latest seniors' cruise to the Bahamas. They had instigated Streaking Saturday and ran around with a bunch of other old people naked at midnight. The captain protested and a ninety-year-old man whacked him with his cane.

"He's building, you know," Evie said, her voice soft. She slung an arm around my shoulders.

"Who's building?" I came out of my reverie.

"Jack Benson is. He's building a shopping center. Right down the road at the end of Deauville Drive, honey."

I froze. Jack Benson was here to build a *shopping center?*

"I don't understand," I said, shoving my glasses back up my nose. "I didn't know any of this."

"Apparently the negotiations have been going on for awhile, sweetie. But you know how we don't get involved in town business. Too boring. A mind-numbing waste of time and brain cells. And me and Dawn, we live dangerously. We can't waste a minute! Not a minute!"

A shopping center. I was sunk. My business couldn't survive that.

"But now the people at Canyon Beach can protest!" Evie raised her hands above her head, fists clenched. "We can picket! We can yell and scream! Me and Dawn can ride our motorcycles through town with the horns blaring and yell, 'Down with Mr. Hot, down with Mr. Hot!' "

That got me. "What? Down with who?"

Evie was a wee bit deflated. "Well, dear, we're on your side, of course, but we call Jack Benson 'Mr. Hot.' "

Mr. Hot. Sheesh. I pushed both hands through my hair and leaned against a cabinet. Gall. My heart squeezed tight. Jack wasn't interested in me, or in being friends. He was building a shopping center and probably wanted to be on friendly terms with me—and everyone else—so we wouldn't fight him in city hall.

I was sick with humiliation. And hurt. How blitheringly stupid could I have been? He probably used that smile on all the women.

I was an idiot.

"How could you?" I asked him when he strolled in after I had closed that evening. Evie and Dawn had left to get ready for Erotic Book Club Group and I was setting up a Christmas tree. "How could you? You never told me you're a builder, that you're here to build a shopping center. You're going to ruin the town, put me out of business, and destroy a beautiful piece of land that isn't far from the beach . . ."

I went on and on and Jack stood there, the rain pelting the windows.

When I stopped for breath, Jack said—so quietly, so low, so soothingly I could have cried—"I'm not going to ruin the town, Suzanna. The shopping center will blend in with the Old West style you all already have here, it won't be visible from the ocean, and it won't block anyone's view."

"But what about the field you're building in? What about the trees? The wildlife?" I shoved a star on top of the tree.

"We're cutting down as few trees as possible. We're not taking a huge space of land. There's plenty of room here for wildlife."

"But what about my business, Jack? You'll put me out of business with a shopping center . . ."

For a flash, I saw pain in his eyes, then they shuttered right up again and became hard. "That's not my intention."

"But it'll happen."

"You have a great business here already, you're established."

"I'm not established!" I shrieked, dropping a box of ornaments. "I'm barely making ends meet! Evie and Dawn work for almost nothing because they like being here." I was filled with the worst sinking sensation. I had trusted him. Had hardly known the man but I trusted him. I didn't trust anyone except Carly and Paul. "The only reason you've been in here is because you don't want me to put up a fight, right? You've probably been going door to door here making friends with everyone, offering assurances, hoping to smooth everything for your stupid development!"

Burning, stupid tears sprang to my eyes.

"No," Jack said, taking steps closer to me. "That's not how it is."

"Yes!" I cried. "That's how it is! I feel like such an idiot. I actually thought you were a nice guy!" *Yes, I did, Mr. Hot!*

"I've been here because I wanted to be." His eyes sparked in anger. "Because I wanted . . ." He stopped, and for once that confident visage slipped. "I wanted to be with you."

"Shut up, Jack! Just shut up!"

"No. I won't. I will not shut up." Jack stood inches from me, but I stood my ground.

"This has been in the works for months. I came here to Canyon Beach to build this shopping center. My crew is coming in spring. I don't actually need your approval. I would like it, but I don't need it. I'm building it."

"How can you say that? We're a town. You can't stroll in like some cowboy and build. There's a process to go through."

"I've been through it. Your mayor, your council, they've all approved the plan. Yes, the citizens here can weigh in now and, yes, some of them will protest. Most won't, Suzanna. Your town needs this shopping center. It will attract more people to Canyon Beach, more business for you . . ."

I was so hurt I felt like I would split in two. "You lied to me."

"I never lied."

"You lied to me by not telling me the truth about who you are and why you're here." *And you made a mess out of me for nothing!*

I am engaged! And damn happy about it!

"I wanted to know you, Suzanna." I could see every eyelash framing those bright eyes. I sensed his anger and frustration, too. "Ever since the first day I walked into The Red Lantern and the sun was shining on your hair, and you smiled right at me, your voice, Suzanna . . ."

I swallowed hard. I had been told I have a sexy, low voice. No kidding.

"You are the only woman I know who makes everyone feel special. I've seen you with Patricia and how she comes in un-happy and walks out smiling. I've seen you with the Pooles, how you joke with David. Yesterday, I saw you talking outside with a woman who was practically hunched over.

You hugged her. You're an amazing person, Suzanna."

He exhaled, the top of his high cheek-bones a little red. "We never stop talking when we're together, did you notice that, Suzanna?"

I had.

"We have the same sense of humor."

I'd noticed that, too.

"We agree, most of the time, but not all the time, and we can disagree without getting in a fight."

Sheesh. That, too.

"You're funny, Suzanna, and so damn smart."

No comment.

"I wanted to get to know you. I knew this was going to be a problem between us, but I was hoping we'd get past it."

"I'm not past it. I'm not getting past it." I had trusted him. I didn't even trust Trenton. That revelation hit me like a hammer to the face.

"I was honest with you, Jack. You weren't honest with me." I took a deep breath and told my tears not to spill over my cheeks and embarrass me. I really didn't need Jack to know how hurt I was. "Get out."

"No. I'm not leaving. We're going to work this out."

"There's nothing to work out." My voice sounded cracked and bitchy and I pushed him away from me.

"I can't believe we're fighting. I don't want to fight with you, Suzanna."

"I am not going to fight *with* you, Jack. I'm going to fight *against* you."

Definitely. I was going to fight him as soon as my heart stopped banging against my chest, as soon as my body stopped trembling.

Jack tipped his head down toward mine and pulled me tight up against him. I saw deep into his green eyes, I saw the slash of his cheekbones, that darkening shadow around his jaw. We were way too close.

I couldn't kiss him, couldn't kiss him, couldn't kiss him, I told myself. When Jack cupped my cheek and brought me within millimeters of his mouth and we were both breathing heavily and I felt this lust running through me like a surfer on a wave and his eyes dropped to my mouth, I whipped myself right out of his arms.

"I'm not doing this, Jack," I whispered. My

body screamed at me. It had really wanted to kiss Jack.

"You won't do what, Suzanna?" He caught my arm and yanked me back to his chest. "You won't? You can't? Why don't you admit it, Suzanna? Why don't you admit *us?* Why don't you admit what's going on?"

That's when I said the words that made Jack Benson look like he was going to blow his stack. "Don't, Jack, please. I'm engaged. I'm engaged to . . ." Damn, what was his name? His name was . . . now I had it! "Trenton."

"Trenton." The name fell off Jack's lips like Trenton was ant vomit. "Engagements are broken all the time, Suzanna."

"Not mine," I told him, but I felt weak and terrible and my words were shaky. "Not mine."

"You've made a mistake, Suzanna. I met him, I know."

That was true. Trenton and Jack had met. Comparing the two had made me think of a *Tyrannosaurus rex* and a grasshopper. The grasshopper would be Trenton.

They had not gotten along. Trenton had been supercilious and condescending. Jack had not been forthcoming about what occupation he was in, so Trenton has assumed he was one of the men from the city working on the street outside and had even suggested that Jack get back to work.

Jack had laughed at Trenton, and Trenton flushed bright red. Without hardly saying a word, Jack had made Trenton appear little and stupid.

"I haven't made a mistake."

"Let me tell you something, Suzanna. I can guess at why you're attracted to Trenton. You had a horrendous childhood and a lot of loss. He represents stability to you, maybe reliability, but you're not going to be happy."

"I will."

"You won't be. Not with him."

I shuddered, tried not to notice that Jack smelled like the ocean and sand and sunshine and fresh air. "I will be." Wouldn't I?

"I will never hurt you, Suzanna," he whispered. "I won't hurt your business and I won't hurt you."

"Please leave, Jack," I said, my heart feeling like it was being shredded. "Please."

At first I could tell he wanted to argue but we were in a really dangerous, lusty place and he knew it. He stood within six inches of me, his green eyes locked with mine. He leaned in and kissed my cheek. And left.

I sagged into a chair, then kicked away five stuffed Santas. Ho, Ho, Ho.

Jack had been right about the negotiations with city hall. They were all for it. Progress. Growth. Improvements to Canyon Beach. More money for taxes.

And, to be honest, Jack's plan for the shopping center was brilliant. People loved it. He was keeping with the genteel, Old West style we had made vague attempts at. The center would have wooden boardwalks with benches, a huge central square with grass and a gazebo, several fountains, benches galore, and old-fashioned lamp-posts complete with flower baskets.

Along with a handful of other people, I fought against it, I protested, I spoke at two meetings.

I lost.

After both meetings, Jack tried to talk to me, but I hustled into my car and escaped.

He forced me to interact with him, though, by coming to The Red Lantern and buying things. Kites. Christmas ornaments. Ceramic Santas.

He would ask questions, I would answer monosyllabically. He would chat, take his time. I would ring up the sale, and he would come back the next day and we would repeat the whole scenario again.

And I felt terribly, horribly guilty and kept telling myself I was engaged, engaged, engaged.

And happy to be engaged.

Engaged.

Chapter Seven

I slipped right through Carly's front door and found her lying spread-eagled on her bed, the covers over the top of her head, crying her eyes out. Her Christmas tree was up in the corner of the family room. Kid-made ornaments hung at odd angles.

The house was dark, the kids at school. I noticed that the garage door Dee had rammed was already fixed. I lay on the bed next to her, patting her back. It made me feel better to pat, even though it offered her nothing. She snuffled and sniffled.

I heard the front door open and shut, then Paul's footsteps.

Paul was built like a rectangle with a head. He had spent ten years in the Air Force and owned Paul's Hardware Store. He had lived in Canyon Beach his whole life. He had a square jaw, square shoulders and looked people square in the eye.

"My God, Paul," Carly cried, fighting with the covers as she scrambled to sit up in bed. Her blond hair, the same color as mine, was sticking up all over her head, her eyes red and swollen.

Paul paused in the doorway but didn't speak. He wrestled down two suitcases from the top shelf of their closet.

"No, Paul!" Carly tumbled off the bed and clutched her husband's muscled forearms. "Don't leave, please, I'm begging you."

As if she was nothing more than a gnat, he pulled himself away from her and dumped both suitcases on the bed, his rigid expression not changing.

"Paul!" Carly's voice was harsh and high-pitched. "I told you that I didn't have an affair with Bryan Cahill! And I haven't! There is nothing going on! Call him yourself!"

Paul opened dresser drawer after drawer, extracting his perfectly folded shirts, folded underwear and balled socks while Carly begged and pleaded.

He tucked them neatly into the suitcases, then grabbed sweaters and two pairs of ironed jeans.

"I'm calling him myself!" Carly shrieked, her hands shaking. She picked up the phone. "Bryan? Bryan if you're there, pick up! Pick up! Are you there?" Her voice became more shrewish. I saw her face crumble as she slammed down the phone. "Why don't you believe me, Paul? You're taking the word of a woman who crashed . . ." She stopped for a moment as her voice cracked. "Who crashed through the front window of her furniture store in her sports car and then drove her husband on the top of her hood to our house—over what I'm telling you!"

Paul ignored her. He snapped the tops of the suitcases closed.

"You're leaving?" Carly screamed, then blocked his path. "After fifteen years of marriage? Out you go? Without even talking about this? What about Scotty and Chloe? It's almost Christmas!"

Paul swung the suitcases off the bed and pushed past Carly, his back ramrod straight. He ignored my sister, who was crying hysterically, clutching at his arm.

He opened the front door, but she threw her body against it and slammed it shut. He opened it again, she did the same thing, her body heaving with sobs. He dropped both suitcases, picked up my sister, threw her over his shoulder, headed back to the bedroom and tossed her on the bed.

Carly was speechless. Paul had never laid a hand on her or the kids.

"Good-bye, Carly," Paul said.

As if she sensed the finality, Carly gave up. "Fine then, leave! I don't even care, you asshole!" Her body shook. "You big, huge, screwdriver-loving asshole!"

From my invisible place in the front row of the courthouse, I watched as Dee Cahill was released from jail three days after her driving adventure. Bryan paid bail. A reporter was there because Dee was a very popular and expensive interior designer on the coast, in addition to owning BryDee's Fine Furniture.

After Dee was sprung back into the free world, she and Bryan drove straight to a "restful place," where Dee was invited to say yes to drugs so she could sleep and cool off. Apparently, she hardly woke up for four days.

Bryan Cahill took off. No one knew where he went.

* * *

The next day I hitched a ride out to Magdalena's house with one of her neighbors, a mom with six kids. The van was ear-splittingly noisy and one kid threw up his soda pop. The mom cried.

Magdalena's house is about a half mile from the beach in a grove of trees. I was sure I saw her in her greenhouse, but when I arrived she wasn't there.

I waited, then took a little nap on her porch under a sprig of hanging mistletoe. When I woke up, I saw silver sparkles all around me, the same type I'd seen in the hospital. They were also on the porch and a trail of sparkles led to the greenhouse, but there was no Magdalena.

Jack and I sat with the comatose me for most of the next day. After a week he was no longer wearing his bandage. I saw the cut and about 12 stitches on his forehead. He would have another scar, no doubt.

The nurses flittered in and out, smiled at Jack. He was polite but not chatty.

"Is Suzanna your wife?" a nurse asked who I had not seen before.

Jack closed his eyes briefly. "No."

"Your sister?"

He shook his head. "She's my fiancée-to-be."

"Ah." The nurse appeared a tad confused, probably because of Trenton. "I'm sorry, sir."

"Thank you."

She tried to make conversation, but he didn't respond much and, after checking all my vitals, she left. A tear slipped down Jack's cheek. He did not bother to wipe it away. I tried to wipe it away. It didn't work.

My body in the bed appeared to be shrinking. I was pasty. I would use the word "lifeless" but I prefer not to. Would I live? Would I die?

And, would someone please tell me how I had gotten into a coma in the first place? That teeny, tiny detail was gone.

I shuddered. Fear. How I hate it.

I went to Trenton's house again. He was home, yelling at his lawyer. "It is not illegal, Chad. It's a business, it's a choice. Don't talk to me about crossing state lines . . ." Still yelling, he took a key off his key ring and yanked open the door to the spare bedroom. He grabbed pieces of his collection off the shelf and hugged them close, stroking and rocking them.

He hung up on his attorney and took another call. "I told you, I'll get the money," he screamed. "It's coming! From where? None of your business."

He hung up.

His cell phone rang again.

"Not now, Alyssa. Deal with it," he told his sister, shutting his cell phone.

He hugged his arms close around his collection. Gall. Weird. So very, very weird.

I learned about Patricia's "business" the next morning after I hiked along the beach for miles, picking up shells as I went. I was hoping to find wisdom in the waves, but that hadn't worked.

Patricia's yellow house sat under an arch of trees at the end of a winding lane off by itself. As usual, there were about seven cars in front of her home. I noticed a man in a blue sedan down the street, but didn't think anything of it.

Another Bible study, I figured, slipping through her door.

The pink entry opened to a living room with mauve-colored carpet. A pink- and white-flowered couch matched two chairs. The chairs matched the curtains. The curtains matched the runner on the dining room table. A Christmas tree, decorated entirely in pink with pink lights glowed from a corner.

I heard talking upstairs, so I headed on up. There was a bedroom to the right, obviously Patricia's, decorated in mauve with pink flowers everywhere. To me, it was a pink nightmare.

Another bedroom was painted yellow with a white bedspread and white furniture. Posters of horses covered each wall. It was a teenager's room, but it felt empty.

The end of the hallway opened up to a huge room, with blue walls, windows on both sides, and lace curtains. Christmas music lent a festive air as did a collection of carved snowmen on a table.

On each of eight separate tables was a phone, stacks of files, paper, pens.

In front of each phone was a woman. Two of them probably weighed a hefty three hundred pounds. One was skinny and the height of a giant. Another was plump with some real skin problems. She wore a sweatshirt that said, I DON'T BITE. Another was skeletal with stringy hair and tattoos up her left arm, and two women clocked in at about seventy, one with gray hair, one with white hair like messy cotton. The last one had a nose ring and pink spiked hair.

The two hefty women thumbed through decorating books. The skinny one wrote a letter on orange stationery to her Grandma Ethel. The plump lady was scrapbooking, using photos of what appeared to be her children. She was using stencils to cut out "Mikey's first trip to the zoo! He loved the pandas!" and "Our Family's Beach Trip!"

The nose-ringed one knitted a baby sweater, the cottonhaired one needle-pointed, the gray-haired woman put wart-remover medicine on her foot, and the tattooed lady studied a *Science Journal.*

All of the women were talking on the phone.

Nothing wrong with that, you say?

Here's what they were saying:

* * *

"Tell me more . . . Describe it . . . What would you want me to do . . . ? I'm naked on my bed . . . Are you yet? Yes, I can feel you, I can feel it . . . huge . . . too much . . . Don't stop now, big guy . . . Don't stop now . . . I'm not done, no, I'm never done, bring it on . . . You're sooooo good . . ."

Now you would think that after seeing myself in a coma in a hospital bed that I would not be able to be shocked.

That would be wrong.

Canyon Beach's One-Woman Moral Police Force was running a phone-sex ring.

That's right. One of those places where men call up and think they're conversing with gorgeous women about all their perverted desires.

I glanced around the room. The skeletal woman shoved an entire pastry in her mouth at once, then made groaning sounds to her caller.

The woman with the nose ring knitting the baby sweater murmured, "You're bad, you're soooooo bad," into the phone.

The scrapbooker held up a photo of a baby and kissed it. She set down the phone quietly on the table and used her scissors to cut a couple more shapes out real quickly, then snatched the phone back up again. She panted into it. Moaned twice. Dropped the phone, cut a couple more shapes. Moaned again.

One of the three-hundred pounders, unable to fit her enormous stomach under the table, covered the phone with her hand, belched, then started murmuring sexy things again. The skinny-giant woman next to her laughed like a hyena, as did the woman with gray hair, who thumped her red cane in appreciation. All three women covered the phones with their hands so their callers wouldn't hear their laughter.

And then there was Patricia. She was over in the corner working on a computer, answering calls in a deep and seductive voice, putting the callers on hold, assuring them that their favorite girl, "Candy," or "Bam Bam" or "Sharona" was definitely in and could take their call. She took their credit card numbers, assured the callers that the girls were hot today, *so hot,* and funneled the calls through.

It about busted my bodice again.

* * *

I slept in my hospital room that night. My comatose self had another incident of near death but those brilliant doctors and nurses saved me again. Adanna breathed a sigh of relief, lifting all her braids off her neck with one hand and fanning herself with the other.

"Stick with us, Suzanna," she whispered to me after the others left. "Stick with us."

Trenton did not come to see me. Jack stayed at the hospital all night, his face grave, with visits from the Pooles, Evie and Dawn, Ronna, Carly, and Paul.

Carly and Paul glared at each other over my body. One time Carly threw a cotton ball at Paul's face.

Chapter Eight

The next afternoon, with my body now stabilized, I went home. There was order there and organization. Everything has its place and everything was in its place. Nice and neat.

I thought it would bring me a sense of calm.

I was wrong.

All of my walls are white. I have a little wooden table to eat on. My couch and chairs are beige and hold beige pillows. My bed has a beige bedspread. My dresser and armoire are battered but they work.

My kitchen is white and clean, nothing on the counters. I have virtually no personal items like frames and plants because I like things . . . neat.

My house looked unlived in, I thought as I went from room to room. Like no one was ever home. "But I live here," I said out loud. "I live here."

My words echoed off my white walls, then ricocheted in my body. "I live here!"

Nothing.

I hustled across my white deck to my workshop, trying to lose the unsettled, bleak feeling that followed me.

My workshop was actually a fifty-year-old three-car garage. I had unloaded all my glass-making paraphernalia and my glass sculptures and designs in it the day I moved, and locked the door.

The air inside was as still as a mausoleum. My "glory hole," a steel drum that heats glass to 2,400 degrees until it's like thick honey, sat in a corner, unused. Cylinders of colored glass in blue and green filled boxes on shelves. Poles to blow through to make my glass designs, giant tweezers, and other tools had gathered a thick layer of dust.

Years ago I had loved creating glass art. I had lived for it, actually. In college, a room-mate took me to an art studio near campus and I had watched her professor twirling molten glass to make bowls with undulating edges and asymmetric vases and organic art sculptures. Flowing beauty that came from nothing but a chunk of glass. I was hooked.

Creating glass art was blazing hot and intense and creative and a constant surprise, as the colors reacted differently each time to each other. As I worked, my childhood went away, the ugliness was lost, the chaos in my head dulled to a faint whisper.

Over the years I made four-foot-tall glass art sculptures and glass murals. I attached free-flowing glass flowerlike sculptures in bright, cheering colors to one another and hung them on walls. I had a garden series where I made iridescent glass balls, glass water lilies, and glass plates for hanging on fences.

I didn't sell much of my art. Too shy to promote myself, I sold to individuals only, barely squeaking by financially. I rented space in a warehouse in a run-down part of Portland, lived in the upstairs loft, and worked about twelve hours a day. I dated some, not much. I was dead broke, but I was content.

Then I met Kelton McKenna, an accountant, who had an office nearby. He was sophisticated and well traveled. He eventually told me that my glass art was a "nice hobby" but a waste of my time financially. He never "got art," anyhow, he said. "Art is a snobby person's useless toy." As I was already insecure about my art, he convinced me there really wasn't a market for my "fancy-schmancy bowls and vases and stuff" that he couldn't even recognize. My glass work took up our evenings and our weekends, and I needed to make some real money if we were going to have a future together and be a family and have some kids.

With happy visions of a bunch of kids and a husband clouding my thinking, I'd nodded my head and dropped my dreams. I got a job in an art gallery and worked four nights a week as a waitress in a high-end restaurant. There was no time for glass making anymore. Then Kelton wanted a boat. I paid half. Within a month of getting said boat, he took off with a twenty-two-year-old girl he'd met online.

I should say I was devastated by his betrayal, but I wasn't. I was devastated that the family life I had envisioned was gone, but not that he had taken off for bluer oceans. I hired a lawyer and got my money back. He had to sell the boat. The twenty-two-year-old left him.

I moved to Canyon Beach to be near Carly, Paul, and the kids and because I thought the ocean might bring me peace. I put a down payment on my home with what little savings I had and with the rest I rented space on Deauville Drive and opened The Red Lantern.

That was five years ago, and I hadn't opened the door to my "workshop" since. I had settled in to selling other people's arts and crafts.

I clicked the tweezers together, and up rose a little puff of dust. I ran my hand over the glory hole. I picked up a stick of glass, tapping it on my open palm, the weight of it calming, smooth.

I took off my glasses. I had really blown it.

I thought of the oxygen mask over my face in the hospital, my body lifeless. I had suffocated my own dreams. I had smothered what I loved doing. I had played it safe.

And I had lost. I had lost my soul, I had lost what had made me tick.

I had lost me.

* * *

I woke up in my own bed with tears on my face. I ate my cereal, the same bran cereal I had eaten every day for years. I made toast and used strawberry jelly, the same jelly I'd eaten for years. I made a cup of coffee, using the same ground stuff I'd drunk for years. I cleaned up and made sure nothing was on my white counters.

I changed my clothes. The clothes I had been wearing, the hospital garb, instantly became visible so I hid them under the couch. The clothes I put on, a beige sweater with a white-collared shirt beneath it, a pair of beige slacks, and a pair of outdoor boots became invisible.

I brushed out my blond curls, then put them back up in a bun. I faced the mirror.

Nothing.

Jack Benson strode into The Red Lantern later that morning. He nodded at Dawn and Evie. He bought three paintings. He spent over a thousand dollars and was in and out in five minutes.

Evie and Dawn grinned and did a little square dance together. "Mr. Hot is hot," Dawn crowed.

"Burning hot for our Suzanna!" Evie echoed.

I shook my head.

I couldn't find Jack, so I strolled over to Ronna Lavey's house and did not like what I saw.

She was reading a legal file about three inches thick. On the inside of the folder she had taped a photograph of a family.

Her hands shook as she flipped through the pages. At the back of the file were several newspaper articles. I read through them quickly.

Ron and Shaylee Schilling had a little girl named Sarah. Sarah had a terrible disease. The insurance company refused to pay for her treatment for myriad inexcusable reasons.

The Schillings hired an attorney.

The newspaper detailed how the attorney for the family had a secret drug habit, had missed deadlines, missed court dates, lost documents, and wrote rambling, inaccurate briefs. To top it off, the lawyer had dragged her briefcase into a bar with all necessary documents the family had provided to prove that the insurance company had been negligent—none of which had been photocopied—and had lost the briefcase.

The family sold everything for the treatment—their cars, their home, their possessions, then went through their retirement accounts and an inheritance from an aunt. The girl got the treatment and survived. The case was high profile and the insurance company almost went out of business.

But the family was screwed. They lost everything.

And the drugged-out lawyer?

The drugged-out lawyer was Ronna.

When Ronna was done reading, she carefully placed the file next to her on the couch and picked up a little pamphlet. It was a "How To Commit Suicide" pamphlet.

Ronna Lavey read it earnestly, dabbing at her sweating forehead, her breathing shallow, her body twitching now and then. When she was done, she lay face-down on her rug.

I sure as heck needed to get out of my coma.

*   *   *

I headed over to Lorrallee and David Poole's house the next day. Lorrallee was hunched over a pile of bills on her table, her head in her hands. After fifteen minutes of pounding numbers into her calculator, and a few curse words, she hurled the calculator across the room, kicked a chair away from the table, and leaned her forehead against the wall. She banged it twice.

I glanced over her shoulder. The medical bills for David were hideously high. Their household bills were overdue. The water department was threatening to shut off the water. The electric department was threatening to shut off the heat. The telephone company was threatening to shut off their phone.

The worst letter was from the bank. The word FORECLOSURE stood out in red. Pay or else.

I was furious. David almost loses his leg at the timber factory, he can't work, and the Pooles go broke?

What was that all about?

"It's going to be a crappy Christmas," Lorrallee whispered. "Ho Ho Ho, we are broke."

* * *

Jack yanked open the French doors of his home and stomped out onto the deck, his expression grim and tight. He glared out across the stormy ocean. The waves rollicked and rolled as the rain came down in sheets, first one way, then the other.

Jack slammed a fist against the railing and swore.

About five minutes later he stomped back into his house, not caring about the water dripping from his clothes. He yanked his cell phone out of his pocket. "Andrew, we're not building here in Canyon Beach. No, I'm not kidding. Scratch everything. We'll start over somewhere else." Then he flipped the phone shut.

"Come on, Suzanna," he whispered, his voice tortured. "You can do this. Wake up, honey."

I was in my hospital room checking on my comatose self when Trenton sauntered in, his hair brushed down, his white shirt perfectly ironed.

"No change?" he asked Adanna.

"No." She pushed her gray braids behind her back, watching Trenton closely.

"Do you think she'll wake up?"

"I don't know." She paused, fiddled with her Christmas wreath pin. "You're her fiancé, aren't you?"

"Yes, um . . . Well, yes, and no."

I raised my eyebrows. Yes and no?

"I am her fiancé but not if . . . not if she doesn't wake up . . . I mean, I can't be held to that if she's not talking and walking." He laughed nervously. "I can't marry someone who can't walk or talk. Or, you know . . ." He winked at Adanna.

Adanna stared back at him, her face grave and disgusted. I would say she was gravely disgusted.

"I can't put my life on hold forever for this, can I?"

Adanna crossed her arms over her chest, arched an eyebrow.

"I'm pretty young still. Only forty. I mean, Suzanna's great and all but life is for the living, right?"

"Last time I checked Suzanna was still alive. Do you see that?" She pointed at a machine. "That means her heart's still beating. Do you see that?" She pointed to another machine. "That means her brain's still working."

Trenton went on as if he hadn't heard her. I was used to that, I realized. If Trenton didn't want to talk about something, he changed the subject. "Suzanna would understand how I feel about all of this. We're both practical people. She would want me to get on with my life. She wouldn't want me coming and staying all day every day."

"You've hardly been here, young man."

"I work, you know . . . I have things going on, things I have to attend to. It's not like she can see me or hear me or anything so what good is it if I'm around?" He made a snorting sound in his nose. A sound that meant, *"Hey, you stupid lady. Don't you get it?"*

Adanna glared. "I would hardly want you to be inconvenienced."

"I already have been." He rolled his eyes. "I've taken out a chunk of my day to be here." He wiped his nose. "Somebody should wash her hair. It's greasy. It's gross."

His cell phone rang and he flicked it open, leaving without saying good-bye to Adanna. "Hey, man, what's shaking?"

I watched Adanna checking the machines and the IV lines, fluffing my pillow, re-straightening my blanket. Then she bent down and whispered in my ear, "Ms. Everts, when you wake up the first thing you need to do is break up with that little shit."

I nodded my head from where I stood by the window. No kidding. That was at the very top of my to-do list.

But first I had to shred those papers.

Why? Because Trenton was in charge of my life. He had not only insisted that we draw up a prenuptial agreement, we had drawn up wills. Everything of mine went to him and vice versa in the event of either death. Trenton had said, "Suzanna, you don't have anywhere near as much as I do, but I don't resent that." We also signed affidavits giving each other control over medical care/end-of-life decisions, etc.

That was a bad, bad move on my part.

Trenton Maycomber, after all I'd learned about him, could end up being my plug-puller.

Chapter Nine

Evie, Dawn, Ed Surbanks, and another gentleman friend all came to see me before Square Dancing Night in their full regalia, the ladies' ruffled skirts flaring out two feet on each side. They danced for my comatose body, the music on high. When they left, the ladies curtsied to me, the men bowed.

I visited the Pooles the next night. David Poole was in such wracking pain that Lorrallee and their oldest two children had to haul him out of bed and into his wheelchair so that Lorrallee could rush him to the hospital.

"Don't cry, Lorrallee," David said, his face lined with agony, his voice weak. "Honey, you're bustin' my heart."

Lorrallee sniffled, whimpering sobs escaping her mouth. "I'm trying not to cry, David, quit nagging at me. You're always nagging."

"I nag?" David gritted his teeth as another wave of pain hit. "As soon as I get home I'm making you a banner that says QUEEN OF THE NAGS."

"I don't nag that much."

"Yes you do."

"No I don't." Lorrallee raised her hand to slap his shoulder, then thought better of it. David grabbed her hand.

"Remember when we were seventeen and we ran through your dad's cornfields naked?"

Lorrallee laughed through her tears and nodded.

"Your old man would have shot me straight through the heart if he'd known what we were doing."

"He probably would not have liked that the first time we made love was in his tractor, either. That wasn't very comfortable."

"Baby, you were hot. You're still hot. You're as hot as you were when we were skinny-dipping in the creek and dancing in our birthday suits in my grandpa's barn."

"The risks we took, David. My father

would have sent me off to a convent if he knew. Plain and simple." A light turned red. Lorrallee lifted David's hand to her mouth and kissed each knuckle. "You were worth the risk of a convent."

"Thank you. I don't think you would have been a very good nun. You're too lusty."

Lorrallee snorted.

"Yep, the sisterhood would have been a problem for you, sweetie. We're going to have fun soon again, Lor, I promise you. Except for the sex-in-the-tractor part. That's not gonna work. Neither will you see me running naked through a cornfield."

"Good. That would frighten the cows to death. Poor cows."

David was in the hospital for five days fighting an infection.

When he got home, the water had been turned off.

"All righty, everyone," Evie yelled over the crowd of people milling about The Red Lantern several nights later. "Thank you all for coming!"

A space had been cleared in the middle. Three wooden tables were pushed together and around the tables sat Dawn, my sister Carly, who looked wan and exhausted, and her kids, Scotty and Chloe, Lorrallee and two of her daughters, who all looked wan and exhausted, Dee Cahill, who looked wan and exhausted, Ronna Lavey who had shuffled in, head down, who also looked wan and exhausted, Patricia Goodling who looked prim and prissy, along with several of her "business" employees, and about fifteen other people from town.

"Now, we're all concerned about Suzanna, of course, and that darn girl being in a coma," said Evie. "I know there's a ton of flowers in her room and when she wakes up she's going to think she's died and heaven's a florist shop. Me and Dawn thought it would be groovy cool if we could make her something that would last, a gift that could warm her skinny bones."

I watched in amazement as Evie explained her idea. Everyone agreed it was a "groovy cool" idea. I saw Ronna snatch up scissors. I saw Dee Cahill discussing the design with Evie. I saw Patricia pick up a needle and thread.

And once they all had their jobs figured out I watched as they tentatively started chatting with each other, then laughing. Within an hour the noise in The Red Lantern was deafening.

I sat down in the middle of the floor and bawled my eyes out.

The next day I dropped by Patricia's house for a little amusement. I noticed the man in the blue sedan again and thought it quite odd.

I entered Patricia's house and went up the stairs. All of the women were there. Scrapbook Momma was on a new page. The skinny-giant woman had problems with flatulence, so I quickly moved away.

The gray-haired woman was repainting her cane purple while moaning on the phone. Several women hummed along with the Christmas music.

From what I could tell, Patricia had a very profitable business going on. The phones did not stop ringing. Patricia would call out, "Brandy . . . Nicoletta . . . Boom Boom, your client is waiting for you . . ."

And one of the ladies would pick up the phone and feign surprise and delight at her caller. "Of course I remember you! One of my best afternoons ever! That was so sexy! Are you ready? What shall we play today?"

I scooted past the panting, moaning women, and saw that Patricia was writing in a pretty blue journal. She barely stopped writing to answer the calls.

When I left, the man in the blue sedan was still there and I realized he was watching Patricia's house.

It sent a snaking shiver down my spine, it did.

Carly was making me nervous. She hustled the kids off to school the next morning, then rushed to her bedroom. She wriggled into black slacks, black heels, a low-cut burgundy-colored sweater, and added gold bangles to her wrist and neck. She brushed on makeup and spritzed on perfume.

We left her house and zoomed to the hospital where she cried over my deathly still body for about an hour. Next we drove to the city and pulled into an underground garage. Carly talked to herself as she drove, saying she hated Paul, she didn't care that he had left, he was bad in bed, and he was an overly large, stupid, donkey-ass, vomitous freak.

We took the elevator up to the sixteenth floor of a modern high-rise apartment.

A tall, hip young man opened the door when she knocked. He smiled at Carly and kissed her on the neck.

I did not go inside.

Almost every night I was drawn back to The Red Lantern. Inside, til almost midnight, people worked. Each night more people came.

They brought dinner and desserts and cookies.

They cut fabric, they sewed, they shared a bit about their lives.

And laughed.

That group laughed. All the time.

I even saw Ronna crack a smile.

"I've lived here for ten years," said Cy Miller, the owner of one of the grocery stores. "What took us so long to get together like this?"

* * *

The eviction notice was hammered up on the Pooles' front door the next day. David tried to reach it from his wheelchair. He struggled to stand, and I could tell every bone in his body felt like it was splitting.

He folded it, slipped it into his shirt, collapsed back into his chair.

One of the kids bopped out of the house and climbed into his lap and gave him a big kiss. The desperate expression on David's worry-lined face was replaced by a smile. As soon as the child bounded off, the raw desperation crept back.

Gall. I had to wake up. Soon. Somebody had to help them keep their home.

When Carly came to see the comatose me two nights later at the hospital she'd dyed her hair red.

She put her head on my stomach and cried, begging me to wake up, that I was her best friend, she couldn't live without me. I patted her back again.

"I don't even know who I am anymore, Suzanna. I don't even know how to think on my own, what I like and don't like, what I believe. It's like I've been hammered into submission by domestic motherhood."

She lowered her voice to a whisper. "But Marty . . . that's his name—he's made me *feel* again. Like I'm someone. I want to make love to him so bad, my body's thrumming. *Thrumming.* I need to feel again. Like a woman, *like me*. The other me that was me before I married, does that make sense?"

Yes, it made sense, dear sister, it made sense.

"But Paul left me! He left! And I . . ." she hiccupped through her crying jag. "I should be glad but I miss him. I begged him not to leave even though he forced me to be a mashed, moronic mommy! I can't sleep at night and I can't imagine living without the bionic dimwit, but I hate him, too."

She cried her way through washing and brushing my hair, filing my nails, giving me a pedicure. She kissed my cheek before she left, her tears on my cheeks.

What a mess. What a terrible mess.

A week later, when Bryan Cahill came back to Canyon Beach, the skies above the ocean burst open and flooded us in rain. The wind whipped up the waves and everyone hunkered down.

In the afternoon Paul entered BryDee's Fine Furniture, pulled his arm back, and belted Bryan in the face, breaking his nose.

Paul was restrained by four contractors who were there to assess the damage caused by Dee's little vehicle excursion. I heard a neighbor tell Carly later at her house that had Paul not been held back, she was sure he would have killed Bryan.

"He was like a fire-breathing beast, Carly. I thought he was going to hammer poor Bryan Cahill to the ground. I've never seen Paul do anything like this before. Ever. And I've known him since he brought his collection of plastic army tanks for show-and-tell in kindergarten!"

Bryan was taken to the emergency room, Paul went back to his hardware store.

When a policeman went to Paul's Hardware, Paul told him that Bryan was cheating with his wife. The policeman rolled his eyes, patted him on the back, declined to cite him, and left after buying a new power saw.

Paul was amiable and friendly to his customers and did a brisk business that day, as usual.

Paul came to see me the next day at the hospital, at 2:00, which is when he always comes. He sat by my bedside and held my hand. I noticed the knuckles on one hand were scraped. "Sugar, you gotta wake up. Everything's falling apart. I need you to help me with your sister. I don't even know where to start."

And then he laid that big head of his in the open palm of my hand and cried his eyes out.

When he was done crying, he read poetry. Robert Frost made him cry again.

I went to Patricia's because I was worried about the man in the blue sedan.

He was still lurking. Still watching, like a slug in a rug. He had binoculars.

I worried all the way up Patricia's stairs, but I cracked up when I heard Scrapbook Momma murmur, "That would be slinky, so slinky and warm." And when the skinny woman who could stuff an entire pastry in her mouth moaned, "Bring it on. I can take it! I have my fire-resistant space suit on," I laughed again.

Patricia was scribbling in a journal on her desk when I arrived. After about ten minutes, she closed the book, adjusted the pearl buttons on her Mrs. Claus sweater, waved good-bye to the moaning and groaning ladies, and left. I followed her.

We listened to a steamy romance novel on tape all the way in to the city. Patricia fanned herself during the good parts.

We stopped at a place called Castin's Care Home. It was a brick building with beautifully landscaped grounds. The receptionist greeted Patricia, and we proceeded down a bright corridor.

I peeked into the rooms of each resident as we passed. They were clean, neat, and individually decorated. One had a whale theme, another had a collection of dolls, one had posters of sports heroes.

A nurse was brushing the hair of a young woman in a wheelchair in a sunlit common room. A group of kids with walkers and wheelchairs sang carols nearby. The young woman's head lolled to the side, her tongue partway out of her mouth.

Patricia greeted the nurse, then hugged the young woman. "Sweetheart," Patricia murmured, smiling. The young woman did not respond, her eyes rolling back and forth. "I love you. Mommy's here. Mommy's here."

We stayed all day. By the time we left, after Patricia had finished brushing her daughter's hair, doing simple exercises with her, reading and listening to music, not to mention chatting to her almost-nonresponsive daughter, we left. I was exhausted.

Patricia squared her shoulders and visibly lifted her chin after she dressed her daughter in her pajamas and put her to bed. She thanked the staff, then stopped by the front desk and wrote an enormous check. Patricia glanced back at her daughter's room, decorated with horse posters. I did not miss the aching, guilty, worried expression.

It was dusk by the time we drove back to Canyon Beach. Patricia mumbled to herself, "I have no choice I have no choice I have no choice." I berated myself the whole way. I had been too quick to judge Patricia, both as the prissy person I had thought her to be and also as the phone-sex business owner.

Too quick.

I was ashamed.

When we got back to Canyon Beach, the same sedan was parked down the street from Patricia's house with the same man inside. He peered at Patricia through his binoculars.

Chapter Ten

Days later, I stopped at the end of Deauville Drive where Jack was going to build his shopping center. The last time I was here, my body had not been stuck in a coma. I had seen Jack in a tank top, jeans, and work boots standing with other men. They were studying blueprints.

My heart had thumped and twittered and rolled over in my chest.

I had tried as hard as I could to think of Trenton, but my thoughts kept skittering back to Jack in his tank top.

The next day when Jack stopped by The Red Lantern, I couldn't get those naked shoulders and muscled arms out of my mind.

"How about going with me to Trudy's Desserts for some chocolate pie?" he asked, his smile teasing.

"No, still no," I said. I busied myself with the orchid plants Magdalena had brought me to sell. He was standing way too close. "Back up, Jack."

"Why?"

"Because . . . because . . ." I stuttered, "You know why."

"I know I like the smell of you."

"The smell of me?" I had to laugh.

"You smell like roses and cinnamon tea and the beach. Want to go to the beach?"

"My, aren't you poetic. Let's see, you know how to bring in tractors, flatten a piece of land, build a shopping center on top of it, and"—I paused, with great drama—"you sound pretty."

He chuckled. "Here's a real poem for you, Suzanna. "My longing for lunch is tearing me down, how 'bout lifting me up and getting rid of that frown?"

"Funnier still," I said, moving another pot of orchids. He reached around me and grabbed my hands.

"Dessert, Suzanna, that's all I'm asking. It'll take an hour. I'll bring you right back."

"No." I faced him, my hands on his chest so he wouldn't try any tricky business.

"How about a drive down the coast?"

I shook my head.

"No? A weekend trip to Carmel?"

I laughed.

"Why no?" His eyes teased me, but I did not miss that steely determination.

"Because it's not right."

"Why are you not seeing what's here? What's between us?"

"There's nothing here," I said. But I knew there was. He knew that I knew. I gave up. "Jack . . . You and I . . ."

"You and I what?"

There's no future with you, I wanted to say. I would have to be brave to be with you and I'm not. I would have to take a gargantuan risk and bust out of my ordered life and bungee jump into the unknown. I would have to dare. I couldn't.

"You and I are not a 'you and I.'"

"No. We are a 'we,'" he said, grinning. "You're fighting it." He put his hands on my waist, I moved them away. He laced his fingers between mine, I pulled them away.

"I want to cook you lasagna and light candles and eat out on my deck together. I want to grab a blanket and lie down on the sand and name the stars. I want to go to the mountains and ski with you." He cupped my face. "Look at me."

I couldn't.

He tipped my face up. "I'm not giving up on you. I won't give up on you."

"I can't ski."

"I'll teach you."

I took off my glasses. "You don't get it. I don't want you to teach me anything. I want things to be how they were before you barged into my life. You have done nothing but mess me up, mess my business up. I can't have you in my life anymore."

I did not miss the bitter hurt that crossed Jack's eyes. "You can't have me in your life?"

"Yes. No. Yes. I'm not a toy. I'm not someone you play with and then—"

"And then what?" He was furious.

"And then leave. Please, Jack, go."

He swallowed hard, then hugged me close. "I'm a smart man, Suzanna. Once I had you I would never leave you," he whispered in my ear. My body shuddered and I knew he felt it.

He did leave that night and I saw him again, at his house, and . . . and . . . What happened? *What happened?* I wracked my very tired brain. I couldn't remember. Nothing. I couldn't remember what happened next.

Jack and I sat and watched my body all night at the hospital. My body did not have a good night and the medical personnel were in and out almost constantly. Words like "critical" and "should have woken up by now" were tossed about.

"Jack," a doctor said to him. "You can't go on like this. You need to sleep."

"I can't sleep," he said, his face gray around the edges. "I see Suzanna when I do. I see her all night. As soon as I close my eyes. I can hear her voice. It's like I can feel her nearby. It's like she's with me."

The doctor nodded. "She's got so many people coming in and out. She obviously has a lot of friends. I wished I'd known her before this happened."

Jack rubbed his temples. "I wish I'd known her my whole life."

"People, we have a problem," the doctor with the ponytail said the next morning.

"What is it now?" Adanna asked, rolling her eyes. "Don't tell me it's the weasely fiancé again."

I heard a general groan.

"It is."

"So what's new?" a young male doctor asked. His hair was in a ponytail, too. "Does he want us to snuff her out with a pillow or give her cyanide to drink this time?"

There was a general grumbling.

"The fiancé"—the doctor checked his notes—"Trenton Maycomber, is making a lot of noise about letting Ms. Everts die. Our position is that she can still recover, still regain all her faculties at this point."

"Damn straight she can," Adanna said. "I have a feeling about this one. She's gonna pull through."

There were a few nods.

"Let's hope so. However, in the meantime, continue to stress to the fiancé that Suzanna will get better and no action is necessary at this time. He does, however, have those documents, signed by Suzanna, that I talked to you about before. They're lethal and can be used in court against our position."

"And if he pushes for us to pull the plug?" a nurse asked.

"We push back at the skinny rodent," Adanna said. "Shove him back in his hole."

When everyone left Adanna whispered to me, "Honey, we can hold this off for awhile, but not forever. You're gonna have to come back to the land of the living."

Sure I was. And as soon as I did, I would destroy those papers Trenton had.

Things were not better with Carly and Paul. On Tuesday morning Paul went by the house to borrow the lawnmower for his rental house.

"How are you, Carly?" Paul asked. His square chin was up, his square shoulders back, and he looked her square in the eyes.

"I'm wonderful. Lovely," Carly said, her sarcasm thick. She was in her robe in her kitchen, her mascara smeared under her eyes. "My sister's in a coma and my husband has moved out."

"You brought it on yourself, Carly."

"No, you brought it on us." She got up to put bread in the toaster. "You don't want to take any responsibility, though."

"*I* brought this on?" For the first time, I was seeing Paul's temper. "How did I do that?"

"How?" Carly crossed her arms in front of her chest and glared at him through a sheen of furious tears. "By treating me like I was nothing, like I wasn't even a person. By not showing any emotions, any feelings toward me. You haven't seen me in years, *really* seen me. You've ignored or blocked out that I was unhappy married to you and you didn't do anything about it! Didn't you realize that I was dying! I was dying of loneliness married to you, Paul!"

I saw the utter shock in Paul's eyes.

"I don't . . . How can you say that . . . ? What are you talking about . . . What . . . How . . . ?" He was completely flustered. "You cheated on me with Bryan, Carly. I can't forgive you."

"*You can't forgive me?* I never cheated on you with Bryan, ask him yourself, you unemotional, cold robot. But here's a news flash for you, Paul, *I can't forgive you!*"

I saw Paul's Adam's apple move up and down his throat. "You can't forgive me?"

"No, I can't. Get out, Paul. Good-bye. Go find some other woman and take her out to dinner and give her flowers and then as soon as you're married to her, start ignoring her, like she's wallpaper, like she's a couch, like she's cat litter, and we'll see how long the next woman stays with you. Adios, schmuck."

She dumped coffee beans in the grinder and flicked it on. She left it on for a long time.

When it was finally off, Paul spoke, his voice ragged. "For months, Carly, you've disappeared for hours at a time. Hours. I knew something was going on. You bought new clothes. New bras, even, and under-wear." Paul's face flushed, as if even saying those words was embarrassing. "You got your hair cut. You lost weight. You started going to the gym and you started wearing a different color of lipstick. Red lipstick. You forgot to make Beef Stroganoff on the sec-ond Friday of the month and you didn't want to go with me to Bargain Night at the movies. You hugged the kids more and sang little songs around the house. You bought bubble bath and all these scented lotions."

He coughed, spread out his hands. "You were happier, Carly. You laughed more. You smiled more. But you didn't kiss me when I came home from work and you didn't hug me when we made love."

I saw a pulse leaping in his left temple. "You made love differently, too, Carly."

"Good!" Carly said, tossing a handful of spilled coffee beans so hard into the sink they bounced back out. "Good! Although I'm surprised you noticed! You always, always had to have control over sex, Paul, and I'm sick of it! You're in charge of everything here—the money, the decisions, the food, the kids' schedules, even the sex. And that's all it was for me. Sex. S.E.X. Most of the time, you treated having sex with me as one more thing you had to check off your schedule. *Fuck the wife.* Done."

She swiped at the tears streaming down her cheeks. "And, if she doesn't have an orgasm for ten years, who cares? *Who cares?* Not you."

She grabbed a cookbook from the counter and hurled it at his head. Then she grabbed up another one. And another. He caught each of them with one hand, his face white.

"You haven't . . ." he foundered. "You haven't . . ."

"Can't say it, can you?" Carly yelled. "You can't say orgasm. O. R. G. A. S. M. It's too embarrassing for you, isn't it? You can't even talk about it, much less spend time giving me one! Do you know what it's like to have sex with someone for ten years and not have an orgasm?" Carly lapsed into laughter. "You don't, do you? It's always fine for you. The sex is efficient and clean, that's all you want, P-P-Paul," she stuttered, choking on her own sobs. "That's all you want."

Paul didn't move, his face white and stricken. If Carly had morphed into a purple witch it would have shocked him less.

"Leave, Paul. Go! Take your prized possessions—your lawnmower and your power tools—and stick them up your tight butt."

Paul didn't move. "It's called," he whispered, then cleared his throat. "It's called making love, Carly, that's what it's called. Making love."

"No, you uptight Air Force freak. We didn't make love. You had sex on top of me, rolled over and went to sleep. Then I stayed up until about two o'clock in the morning, my body so frustrated I couldn't sleep. And I heard you snoring. Snoring, while I wondered what it would be like to have sex with a man who made me orgasm!

"Why did I even ask you not to leave weeks ago?" She threw her arms up in the air. "Why did I do that?" she wailed. "I'm getting used to this! Now I'm free. Now I can have sex with a man and have an orgasm. In fact, I can have sex with many men! Me! Carly. I can have an orgasm! Call me Mrs. Orgasm. Mrs. O.R.G.A.S.M. That's who I am."

She picked up a stool and threw it across the room at Paul. He stepped to the side. "Plus, maybe next time, *you mean husband,* I'll have sex with someone who cares about me, who really asks me how I am, who can see if I'm happy or miserable. Then I'll call it making love."

Paul didn't move. "Why didn't you tell me this before, Carly? Why didn't you?"

Carly opened her mouth. Shut it. Opened it again. "Why didn't you notice? *Why didn't you notice me for even a second?* I hate you, Paul!"

"You hate me, Carly? You hate us? We have a family. We have a home here at the beach and at the mountains. We have a business. We have friends and a church. We have history together. You have never had to work outside this home. I've never asked you to, I never will. My only goal has been to support you and provide for this family. I have been loyal and faithful to you our whole marriage and you have always been free to do what you want."

Carly blinked, her face still.

I could tell Paul's iron control was snapping. "When you wanted a garden, I dug the beds for you. When you wanted a trellis out back and a deck, I built those, too. When you wanted to go to the Canadian Rockies, I planned the trip. When you wanted room for your sewing and craft projects, I cleaned out my home office, painted the room pink, and built you a long table and shelving. When you wanted that six-thousand-dollar sewing machine, I bought it for you."

Paul squared his shoulders, but he looked utterly defeated. "I'm not good in the emotions department, Carly, you knew that when you married me. I'm not good at expressing myself. I tried to show you I loved you by what I did for you. It wasn't enough, though, was it?" Paul blinked rapidly. "I don't hate you. I would never hate you. I know there's someone else in your life, I've known it for months. I thought it was Bryan. It's not. I want to kill whoever it is. You may hate me, honey, but I hate him with every breath and bone in my body. I hope that one day he goes through even a fraction of the hell I've gone through." Paul stopped, inhaled. "You're my best friend, Carly, and I still love you. I always will."

He left, but I saw what Carly couldn't: hopeless, raw, open pain.

The type of pain you think will kill you.

Chapter Eleven

I found Bryan Cahill lying on a partly smashed table in his own furniture store about midnight several nights later. The white bandages on his nose shined in the dark.

He had not turned on a single light so only the moonlight glowed through the windows. The darkness did not hide the almost-total destruction.

He didn't move and for a moment I thought he was dead. When he came to see me after Dee had deposited him on Carly's driveway, he had grabbed my pasty-white hand and cried without making a sound.

I sat on the floor and watched Bryan staring at the ceiling. I ached for him. A smashed store. A wife facing criminal charges. A broken nose. Financial ruin upcoming to defend said wife in court. And a friend of his in a coma.

A Christmas wreath lay smashed on the floor.

We stayed like that for a long time. Tears flowed from his eyes, down his cheeks, and onto the partly broken table. He didn't make a sound.

After an hour, the table collapsed beneath Bryan's weight and he tumbled to the floor.

Bryan Cahill didn't even bother to get up until the sun was high in the sky.

I gave Carly her privacy when she kissed Marty in a park in Portland at dusk as the snow floated down. The light posts around the perimeter of the park were wound with red and green lights, with a giant Christmas tree in the center, almost tall enough to reach Santa's flying sled.

To everyone else, they were another in-love couple. To me, they were a disaster.

Marty smiled when he kissed Carly's forehead, her cheeks, and pulled her close. He murmured something and kissed her again. It was one of those long and involved types of kisses and if you're a participant it can almost melt your toes it's so hot.

Carly ended the kiss and when she pulled away, and gazed into Marty's smoldering, smiling eyes, I knew she'd made a decision.

Carly and Jack sat on either side of me in my hospital bed the next night. It was difficult to say who was more run-down, more ragged. They sat in a thick silence, lost in their own corrosive thoughts.

My machines started to blip and bleep and they both startled. It was a false alarm, I wasn't on the stairway to heaven yet, and after the doctors had checked on me and left the room, my visitors settled back into their black misery.

At 9:00 Carly said, "Let's go to The Red Lantern and help out with Suzanna's project, Jack. If I sit here for another minute I think I'll go straight loony."

"I'm already there." I noticed the dark circles under his eyes, the lines in his face deeper now.

"When did you fall in love with her?"

I didn't think he was going to answer at

first. "I fell in love with her the day I met her at The Red Lantern."

"She's beautiful," Carly said, sniffling.

"She's beyond beautiful."

Paul made a mistake that evening.

He took a swing at Jack.

Carly and Jack and I took a shortcut through town to The Red Lantern. When we arrived, Paul was there.

His face hardened into a boiling fury as soon as he saw Jack open the door for Carly.

"No, no Paul!" Carly yelled. "Stop!"

But it was too late. The calm and con-trolled Paul had lost his calm and control. Again. "Is this the boyfriend, Carly? Please let me introduce myself."

Paul pulled back his muscled arm, aimed right for Jack, and swung. I was stunned by the swiftness of the punch, stunned further that Jack hadn't been hit.

Jack ducked, then ducked again when Paul took another swing. "Hey, buddy," Jack said, his voice calm, "I've been patient here, and I understand what you're going through, but if you try to hit me again, you will land on your ass."

"Don't threaten me," Paul said, panting. "Stay away from my wife!" And then Paul's arm swung in an arc toward Jack's head. Jack sidestepped first, then smashed his own fist into Paul's jaw.

Paul landed on his ass.

He scrambled back up and went straight for Jack. Jack sidestepped once again, and pummeled Paul in the chin. I heard something snap. Paul crumpled to the floor.

Now, this is not what usually happens during these group potlucks at The Red Lantern. Usually there are a whole bunch of men and women sitting around chatting— about gardening, their dogs' puppies, their teenagers' piercings—as they work. They laugh a lot, and Ed Surbanks, Evie's Mr. Sugarbottom, makes a Baked Alaska dessert once a week, complete with piles of meringue, and sets it on fire for effect.

It's peaceful.

Jack bent over to Paul, extended his hand, and helped him up. "Paul, I'm not after your wife." He bent down close and whispered in his ear. "I am, however, after your sister-in-law. And when she wakes up

I'm not going to give her a moment's peace until she dumps Trenton and marries me, so you and I gotta get along. We're gonna be brothers-in-law for fifty years so we don't have a choice. Got that?"

Paul touched a hand to his chin, which was already impressively swollen. "You're not Carly's boyfriend?" The words came out muffled. Paul spat out a tooth.

Jack shook his head. "Wouldn't think of it. All I can think about is Suzanna."

Paul's eyes darkened. I knew he was upset about me. I had seen him earlier that day, 2:00. He'd read poetry. Maya Angelou. He'd cried again. "I miss Suzanna."

"Me, too," Jack said. "Me, too."

Trenton insisted on switching his table twice at Crane's Toasty Fish. The first one was too noisy. The second was too close to the kitchen.

I watched as he settled himself down, and opened up a menu.

Dianna, the waitress, did not bother to hide her disdain. "Hello, Trenton, what can I get you tonight that you can complain about?"

Trenton did not acknowledge the waitress. "The salmon dish, tell your chef not to over-cook it like last time or I'll have to send it back again. Garlic potatoes, no chives, ex-tra cheese. Don't bring me the sourdough, I want the French bread. You should have memorized that by now. House salad, make sure you put the Italian dressing on the side—got that?—on the side." He closed the menu. "Scotch on the rocks, too. More water."

Above his head, Dianna stuck out her tongue.

Trenton flipped open his newspaper, dis-missing her.

Before Dianna served Trenton's food she spit on each dish.

He left her a dollar tip. The complaint he wrote on the bill: "Water not served quick enough. This is basic. Get it together."

After that he went and got his back waxed and a manicure. His back-wax person and the manicurist seemed to hate him, too.

I'd had no idea.

"You tried to run me over with your car, Dee," Bryan Cahill said, flipping a pancake on the griddle in their modern kitchen. I sat on a stool at the bar. I noticed there was not a single bit of Christmas décor anywhere in the house. The Cahills were not expecting Santa, obviously.

Call me a voyeur, but I couldn't help it. I cared for Bryan and I wanted to know how a couple worked it out when one crashed a car through a jointly owned furniture store.

Dee's hair was ripped back in a ponytail, her roots a gray streak. It appeared that she hadn't showered in days. Her nails were bitten down to the quick and huge owl glasses perched on the tip of her nose.

"You smashed our furniture store, you pinned me against the wall. You humiliated yourself and us." Bryan flipped another pancake. I was struck by his tone. He wasn't angry, wasn't condescending or accusatory.

He was factual.

Which was, of course, worse. No emotions usually equals: I don't care enough about you anymore to feel anything.

And I could tell that Dee knew what that tone meant, too. Her hands shook.

"I have tried to reassure you so often, Dee. I have told you a million times I think you're beautiful, that you were the only woman I loved, that I never needed, or wanted, anyone else. Ever. I have done everything to keep your jealousy at bay and to help you get rid of your insecurities."

He flipped three pancakes onto a plate and handed the plate to her.

Dee's face was plastered in fear. Bryan's was calm.

She didn't eat, her eyes locked on his.

"Dee," Bryan started, his voice soft.

"No, Bryan, please." Dee's whole body shook, her trembling hands reaching for his.

He pulled away.

"I can't do this anymore, Dee."

She made a strangled sound in her throat. "Bry, please, I'm sorry. I'm so sorry. I lost it—"

"That was your excuse before, too, Dee," Bryan said. "You 'lost it.' It was your excuse when you hired a private eye to trail me around town for six months. She didn't find anything, did she?" He stabbed his fork into his own pancakes. "What on Earth made you think I was having an affair with Carly?"

"Because Dianna heard Paul talking to Johnny, saying he thought Carly was having an affair. She heard it when she was serving them at Crane's Toasty Fish."

Dianna gossiped madly about everyone in town. Johnny was Paul's best friend. They'd been best friends since kindergarten when they'd crashed their tricycles into each other head-on. Both had needed stitches in their heads and had the scars to remember their eventful meeting.

"And you took Dianna's word for it?" Bryan took a deep breath. "You've got to be kidding. Even if Carly was having an affair, which I doubt very much, why did you assume she was having it with me? No, don't answer that. Here's the truth, Dee: I didn't have an affair with Carly or with Randall's wife down the street or with Suzanna Everts or with the college student who serves me coffee. I have never cheated on you, Dee. I have never even thought of cheating."

Dee bent her head. Defeated.

"I want you to be happy, Dee."

Dee wailed, then clamped a hand over her mouth.

"And I want to be happy, too."

Dee reached for his hands again but he pulled away. Her face fell.

"No, Bry . . . Please."

"I can't be happy with you, Dee. I'm sorry."

She got off the stool and tried to hug him. He sidestepped.

"Dee, honey, I know you have the best set of lawyers and I hope they can get you off with the judge. If they can't, I hope a jury shows you mercy, I really do." He bent his head. "I don't want anything from you. You were the one with money when I married you and I had nothing so I'll take nothing out of it. The house is yours, and the business can be sold off to help pay your legal bills." He cleared his throat as Dee alternately sobbed and gasped for breath.

"I'm sorry, honey," he said and then kissed her on the forehead. She clung to him, but he forcibly removed her hands. She chased him down the hall, pulling on him, but it didn't do any good, despite her pleading. He opened the front door and she stumbled out after him. He climbed in his car and locked the doors. For a few long, horrible seconds Dee held on to the door handle as he drove away, her voice scratched and broken.

He drove slowly, so she wouldn't get hurt, but eventually Dee was forced to let go. She lay face-down in the dirt and, at last, was still.

* * *

I went by The Red Lantern the next day.

There were two customers in the store at the time but they didn't buy anything.

"Oh, Mr. Benson!" Evie called out when Jack strode in.

I sucked in my breath. Huge and unsmiling, his black hair swept around by the wind, he nodded a greeting at Dawn and Evie.

The ladies watched Jack whirl around the displays buying about five-hundred-dollars' worth of merchandise. Dawn and Evie wrapped up his items in red boxes.

He was in and out in five minutes.

"Our Suzanna has got herself a suitor, doesn't she?" Dawn asked Evie.

She and Evie laughed, then did the tango together through the aisles.

I had to chuckle myself. Stuck in a coma and clinging to life but I finally had me a suitor.

A suitor. I liked the sound of that.

Ronna Lavey wasn't sweating or shaking as much. Vomit was rare. She'd even taken a shower and washed her hair. The dark circles under her eyes that mimicked miniature black balloons were clearing a bit. I could only surmise that her withdrawal symptoms were improving.

She ventured out into the town after visiting me at the hospital. People she'd met at my shop said hello, chatted with her.

She seemed surprised by their greetings, their smiles. But pleased.

Then she went back to her house, shut the door, pulled out the file in her briefcase, with the photograph of the Schilling family, and started hitting it with her bare hand.

Chapter Twelve

On Friday Patricia handed out the women's paychecks. They all smiled to themselves before tucking the money carefully into their sensible handbags. They grabbed their sensible brown raincoats, rain hats, and canes, and Mandy lowered herself into her motorized scooter. They all agreed to meet at Lizzy's Café down the street for a celebratory dinner and marion berry pie. The pie was on sale for a dollar a slice, with dinner, a holiday special, which they thought was a splendid deal.

Patricia again did not notice the man in the car down the street from her home. He watched the women through binoculars all the way down the street.

Creepy. So creepy.

* * *

I checked in on Paul at Paul's Hardware about 8:00 that night. He was in the back room working, one dim light on over his head.

On top of a file cabinet was a photo of Carly.

With one finger, he traced the outline of her smiling face, then made a low sound in his throat, like an animal fighting for its life.

He set down the frame, then picked up one can of paint after another and heaved them across the room. The cans smashed against the far wall, the paint spurting onto the cement floor.

When he'd destroyed about seven cans of paint, Paul took a deep breath, then ran his finger over the outline of Carly's face again.

He slept on the couch in his office that night with the frame on his chest.

Home sweet home.

Carly, on the other hand, was more lovely than I'd seen her in years.

She redecorated her home. She had all the furniture, including their bed, hauled over to Paul's rented house on the other side of town. I knew she'd always hated it.

She bought new furniture through Bryan, who handled things online. A red couch, a flowered chair, a blue chaise, and a new four-poster bed with a wrought iron frame. She bought a country-style table for the family room, which she painted red, and the six chairs she painted yellow, blue, or green.

She had the outside of the house painted blue, with white trim and a red door and erected an eight foot tall blow-up reindeer on her lawn.

Then Carly went shopping.

Whew. Did that sister of mine shop.

I saw Dee Cahill leaving the pharmacy and I jumped into her black sports car. She had not had it fixed. The damage was impressive.

We drove to a medical office building in a town north of us. Dee was wearing none-too-clean jeans and a droopy sweatshirt, which was a far cry from her usual sequined tank tops, leather skirts, and high heels. Her hair fell lank and dirty to her shoulders.

We waited in a pleasant, if boring, reception area for about five minutes.

"Mrs. Cahill, so nice to meet you." A woman, about five feet tall, came out of an office, extending her hand. Dee shook it, unsmiling. Defeated. Hopeless. We went into the office.

By the end of the counseling session, I was an emotional wreck.

I found out that Dee's mother had dropped her off at kindergarten one morning and never came back. Her father, who lived in another state and whom she'd seen only twice, came and got her. When Dee was six, he deserted her and her stepmother because he found someone younger. The stepmother died of cancer two years later. Her father came and got her when Dee's school realized the second-grader was living alone. After two weeks, he dropped her off at her mom's apartment for a weekend visit, his daddy duties forever over.

Dee soon learned that when Mom said, "I'm tired of mommying," it was Dee's cue. She'd be dumped off at one relative's place or another. She did not live well.

"Cockroaches, that's what I remember," Dee told the counselor. "And mice. And rats. Rats the size of small raccoons. And all of this black on our walls. I know now it was mold, but I didn't know it as a child."

She went out on her own at sixteen, became promiscuous on her quest for love, got pregnant, gave up the baby for adoption, got pregnant again at seventeen, did the same thing.

She missed her babies every single day of her life.

Had she told her husband about her childhood?

"Oh, no," Dee said, "oh, no."

She couldn't? Why?

"I'm so ashamed. I'm ashamed of myself. My life. My mistakes. I'm so dirty. I'm a dirty person."

Had she told her husband about the babies?

"No. Not that, either. I can hardly speak about my daughters without . . ." she cried. "Without . . ." She tried again. "Without crying. God, my heart hurts. Do you think I'm having a heart attack?"

No, no she wasn't, the counselor said.

"Making money allows me to buy clothes and jewelry and cars. I didn't want anyone to know who I really am. They're my cover.

They're my lie." She plucked at her sagging sweatshirt. "It was my lie. Now I don't care."

Bryan was the only kind and decent and loving man she'd ever known, Dee said, and she had been constantly, obsessively scared that he would abandon her, too. She tore the tissue in her hands into little pieces. She loved him but she'd crashed her sports car right through the window of their furniture store, stopping only inches away from dividing him in half.

"My worst fear is here. Bryan's gone."

I hung my head. I had judged Dee with such harshness, had never tried to get beneath her chilly exterior. Never.

Who else had I done that to?

I had problems, too. Specifically, my fiancé, Trenton. Yes, the one who screamed at his lawyer, stiffed waitresses, owned a shaky business, thought he had money coming to him "soon," (because of my impending death) and had a very odd collection for a man—all of which I'd known nothing about.

Back at the hospital, Trenton was once

again stating his case for my timely demise. "I've said this before and I'll say it again because I don't think you people understand the gravity of this situation," Trenton said to two doctors and Adanna. "I think we should let Suzanna die naturally. She's not going to wake up and this is torturous for her and for everyone else."

"There's no call for that yet," Adanna snapped. She waved her pointer finger at him, as if in accusation. "None. This lady's gonna wake up. She is. You watch."

"I think there's a possibility of it, too, Mr. Maycomber," said the male ponytailed doctor.

"Give me a lousy break. Be real," Trenton said, pointing at me as if the people in the room would have difficulty locating me. "She's dying. She may well be suffering or awake in there and we don't even know it. I'm not going to stand by and let her live in this nightmare."

"This isn't a nightmare," Adanna insisted. "It's not at all. She's comfortable. We take outstanding care of all of our patients—"

"Mr. Maycomber, we've been over this with you before and I must say I'm curious as to why you want to give up so easily," the ponytailed doctor said.

Trenton threw his hands in the air. "You make me sound like I want her to die! I don't want that at all, but I'm simply not one of these people who believes in miracles. Suzanna's not coming out of this."

"How do you know?" the older doctor asked, tapping his pen against his open palm. "You're not a doctor. She's not brain-dead. We've seen other people come out of comas before with the same signs she has."

Trenton looked exasperated. Frustrated with these imbeciles. He glared at the doctors and nurse as if they were silly children, then waved his hand in the air dismissively, like they were buzzing flies. "Remember the papers I showed you. *I'm* in charge of her health care. I will ultimately make decisions about her future."

"It's our responsibility to make the best decisions we can about our patients' health care, Mr. Maycomber, and we will continue to do so, taking into account their designated beneficiaries' motives," the older doctor told him, his eyes narrowed.

"You're accusing me, Doctor, of not having her best interest at heart. I can take legal action against you for that, and perhaps I will." He wagged a pointed finger. "As to the rest of the medical mumbo jumbo here . . . *Whatever.*"

"No," said Adanna. "It's not 'whatever.' If you want to get on with your life, Mr. Maycomber, please do."

Trenton blinked at Adanna, tilting his head, as if he was really only seeing her for the first time. He does that to people, I realized. Acknowledges them on his own terms. Deigns to talk to them when he wishes. Controls conversations at all times. How clear life was from a coma!

"My lawyers will address this with you," said Trenton. "I'm not going to allow Suzanna to live like this any longer."

He slammed out the door.

"I'll call the lawyers for the hospital," the ponytailed doctor said. "We're going to have a fight on our hands."

The fight began and it got ugly. Jack was so furious he about popped a vein when Adanna told him what Trenton had said. Jack had attorney friends in high places and he offered up those attorneys to the hospital for free. They were a small hospital and they took him up on it. Jack's attorneys went on attack and began to bury Trenton in paper. They began with insisting that Trenton wanted me to die so he could inherit my estate.

Like I said, it was ugly.

But for all the hoopla about Trenton trying to yank my plugs, and the ominous and threatening legal calls whirling back and forth, it really didn't matter.

I knew, from the way I felt (not so good) and the way I seemed to be sinking into myself in that hospital bed (even worse) that I was dying.

Yep, I was on my way out.

In town the next day, I was sure I saw Magdalena leaving The Red Lantern. I hustled toward her as fast as a rapidly weakening person could. She rounded a corner into an alley.

I reached the alley.

She was gone.

But all around me were silver sparkles.

Two days later, I watched as about twenty-five people crammed into my hospital room including Jack Benson, Patricia, the Pooles, Ronna Lavey, Carly and Paul and the kids, and Bryan and Dee Cahill. Carly and Paul snuck looks at each other, Bryan avoided Dee, but Dee couldn't stop staring at him.

They had finished the project and they laid it over my deathly still body.

I studied the intricate, beautiful quilt on myself from the foot of the bed. It was huge, covering the whole bed and falling over the sides. Each square was its own story, with lots of reds and greens to celebrate Christmas. In the center of the quilt was a huge gold lamé stocking.

"It's Suzanna's stocking," Patricia said, clasping her plump hands together.

What can a dying woman say?

I loved it.

The Pooles were evicted from their home. Their minister let them live in his home while he was on a missionary trip to Mongolia for the year.

Although grateful, it offered little peace to Lorrallee or David Poole. They had no home. They had no security and, worse, they had been forced to accept charity. It darn near did David Poole in.

"A man supports his family," David told Lorrallee that night, his face gray. "I am no man."

Paul was reading Emily Dickinson to me, his eyes misty with tears as usual, when Carly entered my hospital room, her red hair setting off her lovely blue eyes, her black sweater snug, her beige pants outlining her new figure.

They were not happy to see each other.

"I'm leaving," Carly said. She gave me a kiss. "I'll come back in an hour."

"No, I'm leaving," Paul said, snapping the poetry book shut.

"Well, maybe you should leave. After all, you're good at that, aren't you?"

"I believe that's your talent, Carly."

"I've called an attorney, you overgrown ro-bot."

"Overgrown robot?" Paul's words came out in stacatto. "Why did you choose someone else, Carly? Why?"

"I chose someone else, Paul, because you weren't choosing me. Your back was to me, and to our marriage, for years. I was lonely. I was alone. All the time. I didn't sleep with him and I don't give a damn if you believe me. I kissed him, I hugged him, he held me. I needed it."

The silence was screaming loud.

"Are you in love with him?"

Carly didn't answer at first. "No." She held her chin up and I knew she was telling the truth. "I'm not."

Paul's head dropped to his chest for a second, then he left.

"I'm still in love with you," Carly whimpered. "I'm still in love with you, overgrown robot."

Ronna shuffled in and set up a miniature Christmas tree. She covered it with hand-carved wood ornaments and a gold star. The Pooles came and Lorrallee hung twinkling red and green lights around my window and the frame of the bathroom door.

Carly's kids made homemade ornaments and she strung them from the ceiling. Evie and Dawn came in, massaged my brain and feet, and hung up a red stocking.

Merry Christmas, you comatose lady, you.

Chapter Thirteen

I felt like I was suffocating.

My breath wasn't coming normally. My floating-around body seemed weaker to me, slower, more plodding.

I did not want to die.

My hospital room was jammed with tense, crying, worried people 'round the clock.

Jack and I stayed at the hospital the whole next day, with him holding the hand of the comatose me the whole time. I felt weak and empty.

I had never been a raving beauty, especially while lying on that hospital bed with the tubes and oxygen mask and machines beeping and blipping all around, but today I compared myself to runny white pudding.

The doctors and nurses were in and out,

none of them wearing their happy faces, so to speak.

"She's not maintaining," they said gently to everyone there around 1:00 in the morning. I noticed that Jack had white hairs running through his black hair. "Her systems are shutting down . . . breathing labored . . . vital signs declining . . ."

Carly was crying, Paul's face frozen in grief. Evie and Dawn alternately clutched each other and peered at my face from two inches away.

"Yoo-hoo, Suzanna," Dawn called. "Yoo-hoo!"

Patricia sat on a chair muttering to herself, "I won't cry I won't cry I won't cry," and wiping her eyes.

Dee and Bryan Cahill, looking utterly defeated, had each collapsed in a chair. Lorrallee leaned against a wall, one hand on David's shoulder. Adanna stood by my bedside. Ronna had darted in, for once not trembling and sweating and, upon hearing my grim prognosis, had sunk to the ground.

Trenton was not there but he did call. Adanna answered.

"Yes, Trenton, this is Adanna. You don't remember me? I am your fiancée's nurse.

We've met on the *very* few times you've been here. The *very* few. You finally remember me? That's right. Yes, I'm the fat one with all the braids. Isn't that special that you remember those things? What can I do for you?

"Yes, I know you contacted a lawyer so you can ensure that your fiancée dies so you are not further inconvenienced. What? Dear me. I apologize then for my language. Silly me. How is she doing? She's not well. You would be here except that you're in sunny San Francisco? Ahh. Well, that makes sense, then. Of course you needed a vacation. Such a toll all of this has taken on you.

"Is she dying? Who can say? Her vital signs are poor. Yes, poor. No, not as opposed to rich. I'm sorry. I wasn't prepared for a joke right now, Trenton. I'm usually not when our patients are in critical condition. Forgive me for not laughing."

Adanna rolled her eyes, then said, "Yes, Jack Benson is here. I disagree with you. Jack Benson does have a right to be here. Everyone has told me that Jack and Suzanna are close friends. I will be happy to let you speak to him. I'm sure you want to thank Jack for all the time he's spent with

Suzanna and how he's helped manage her care." She handed Jack the phone.

"Jack Benson," Jack said into the phone, his voice low and furious. He listened for a second.

"Listen, you weak, pathetic pissant. I am at the hospital and I will stay at the hospital as long as I damn well choose. Trenton, you have been here only three times. You criticize the nurses, order the doctors to cease medical care so Suzanna will die, call an attorney, and infuriate everyone you come in contact with here. And, yes, Trenton, I am well aware of her will. I will have that will declared null and void if it is the last thing I do with my life.

"When Suzanna gets out of her coma my greatest hope is she will see what a miserable loser you are. I cannot imagine why someone as warm and funny and smart as Suzanna became engaged to you in the first place." Jack had a few more choice words for Trenton, which I will not remention, and hung up the phone.

Everyone clapped. The Christmas lights twinkled.

* * *

In a movie, a person in a coma suddenly wakes up amidst friends and family, perfectly lucid, saying quixotic or amusing things and dropping pearls of wisdom.

It doesn't happen like that in real life.

And it didn't happen here. About 3:00 in the morning, everyone had left except Carly and Jack.

Carly cried, her head near my hip, her hand wrapped around mine.

Jack held my other hand to his heart, stroking my hair back, careful not to jiggle the oxygen mask.

I stood by Jack and felt myself being sucked toward a swirling darkness.

It was not an unpleasant darkness but I could hardly keep my eyes open, and I experienced a deep-seated weakness I'd never felt before, as if fatigue was a living, breathing thing and commandeering my body inch by inch.

"Keep fighting, Suzanna," Jack said, his voice rippling, low and intense. "You can do this, honey. I'm right here. It's Jack, and I'm right here."

I struggled to open my eyes. I saw Jack move the oxygen mask and kiss the comatose me, right on the lips, lingering there for long, long seconds. He kissed my forehead, my cheeks.

Startled, I put my fingers to my face. I could feel Jack's kisses. I could feel the warmth of his lips, the roughness of his jaw.

"I love you," Jack said, his voice ragged and broken. "Always, honey."

As I felt the fatigue enter my bones, the darkness shut out all light. I said, "I love you, Jack. Merry Christmas."

And then I let go, the pull too strong. Hello, Heaven, I thought. Hello, Heaven.

Apparently, though, it was not my time to stand outside those golden gates. I opened my eyes and saw the clock hanging across the bed—4:00 in the morning and dark as death outside my window. To the left of my bed I saw the flashing machines and all the apparatus that was plugged into various parts of my body. The IV stand was to my right and over my face was an oxygen mask.

I took a breath.

I was not dead.

Not dead at all.

I felt the stocking quilt under my hands.

Joy, and a profound, mind-numbing relief flooded me. I was still with the program. Still with the living. Still breathing.

As a bonus, my wandering self was inside my comatose self. Only I was no longer comatose.

Life is sweet.

So sweet.

I felt a weight on my side and saw Carly's head on the bed. She was asleep, her red hair splayed over the mattress, her face splotched from crying.

I saw Jack by the window, his hands gripping the back of a chair as if he couldn't hold his tall, lean body up by himself for a second longer, his shoulders hunched way down.

I pulled the oxygen mask from my face. "Jack," I said, but my voice was only a wee whisper.

"Jack," I said again, but no good.

"Jack," I croaked a third time.

This time Jack Benson heard me. Our eyes locked. I smiled. Slow and easy.

Yum. So, so yum.

Jack Benson would be a delicious Christmas present.

* * *

The doctors and nurses swarmed over me like worker bees, buzzing and whirring, talking medical talk and checking vital signs.

I kept my eyes on Jack and Carly. Carly cried and Jack kept turning his back to wipe away tears.

I wanted to talk, but I couldn't get that ole voice of mine to work again and soon exhaustion overcame me and I allowed that black oblivion in.

When I woke up, it was 11:00, the sun streaming in through the windows, outlining Jack's figure as he sat hunched in the chair by my bed.

"Jack," I whispered, my voice hoarse from the tube that had lived down my throat for weeks. I held out a hand.

"Suz . . ." He couldn't talk, swallowed hard. "Suzanna." He grabbed my hands with both of his. "How do you feel?"

I thought about saying, "I feel good and you look yummy," but figured he would think that I had lost my brain so I settled for a profound, "Good."

He searched my face, his green eyes wandering over every inch of it. "Do you . . . do you remember what happened?"

I nodded. Yes, yes. Now I remembered.

I remembered running from his home at top speed. I remembered throwing myself in my car and driving, with Jack following me in his truck. I remembered careening around a curve and my car crashing . . .

Jack had placed an order for six birdhouses and asked me to deliver them to his home. "I like birds," he'd said to me over the phone, in explanation.

He was not supposed to be home. In fact, he'd told me he would be in Portland on business. When I arrived, he opened the door, smiled cheerily, and told me his business meeting in Portland had been cancelled, and wasn't that great?

He grabbed the other birdhouses from my trunk and asked me in for lunch. I was worried about being alone with Jack. It was a dangerous situation and I knew it.

But I glimpsed the ocean peeking through the trees, the sun unusually bright and cheery for a late-November day, and I took a dare, for once, and said yes.

He had lunch ready, catered by one of Canyon Beach's best chefs. There were clams in a butter and garlic sauce for appetizers, a delectable pasta, several salads, bubbling champagne, rich chocolates. Wild-flowers in a vase. He lit the candles when I sat down.

"Beautiful," I'd said, shaking a little in my seat. I knew I was in trouble. Amazing food. Candles. Chocolates. Giant he-man with shoulders the size of Montana sitting across the table from me.

"Thank you. You deserve it."

I bent my head. I deserved it? No man had ever done this for me. "I don't."

"You do. You're a champagne-and-choco-lates kind of woman, Suzanna. You deserve candles and flowers."

I was at a loss as to what to say, so I picked up my fork and stabbed a clam. That the clam practically melted in my mouth made the tears run down my face. I pushed the tears away with the tips of my fingers and stabbed another clam. Same response.

"It's that bad, is it?" Jack asked.

I glanced up. It had been almost five weeks since I'd met Jack and I knew him better than I knew anyone besides Carly. I knew Jack knew how I was feeling. He reached across the table and wiped a tear off my face, then licked it off his finger.

Now that about undid me so I cried more.

Too many years of loneliness, I figured, too many sterile years of coldness in my life. And now there was warmth. And light. And a promise of enduring joy.

I stopped stabbing clams as guilt wracked every cell in my traitorous body.

"We'll fix your engagement," he said, smiling.

"Fix it?" That made me chuckle, semihysterically.

"Yes, fix it. He's not right for you, you know that."

"And you are?" But I knew he was. I had been fighting it, but I knew. It's that gut-level response you have to some people. They're completely right. Right for you. Right for your life. Right to love.

"Yes. I am." He tipped my chin up. "You're it for me, Suzanna. I don't have to look any further than right now. I can see us, together. How we are now, how we'll be in twenty years, in fifty years. I love the vision. I love you."

He reached for the rubber band holding the bun in my hair.

"Plus, you are the sexiest woman I have ever met and I can't wait til I can take your hair out of that . . . that . . ."

"Bun," I snuffled, my heart about to burst. "It's a bun."

"Right." He pulled out the rubber band and my blond curls fell all over my shoulders and halfway down my back.

"It's probably tangly," I snuffled again, distraught. I was an immoral ant. I was having lunch with one man, engaged to another.

He ran his hands through it, then pulled me close. "No more buns, Suzanna. They aren't you. Let's find you. I want you to find you again."

That Jack had known I'd lost myself, that he wanted to help me find *me* again was my undoing, even more than being an inch away from kissing his delectable mouth and bounding into a wonderful naked romp with him.

I gave a little strangled cry and ran for the door.

When Jack called out for me to stop, to wait, to talk, I threw myself in my car, blinked away the tears that fogged my vision and drove. And then I'd crashed.

I looked at Carly's kids' homemade ornaments strung from the ceiling.

"I never should have run from you, Jack," I whispered from my hospital bed, my voice hoarse.

His face paled.

"You saw my car crash?"

"Yes."

"What happened?"

"You missed a curve and hit several trees."

There was more. I could tell by the trauma I saw in his green eyes.

"And then what happened?"

Jack stared at the ceiling for a second, as if he couldn't speak of it.

"What happened, Jack?"

"Your car landed upside down in the river." His voice was ragged, his face losing some color.

I could hardly conceive of it. "In the river?" Sheesh. What had I been thinking? The river was miles from Jack's house. "How did I get out of the car? Did I climb out?"

Jack shook his head. "No. You were unconscious."

"Then how?" Then it dawned on me. I am so slow. "You pulled me out of my car underneath the water."

He nodded. "You weren't breathing. I did

CPR. I called an ambulance on my cell. You started breathing again by the time the paramedics were scrambling down the hill, and we brought you here. Your concussion was severe, obviously."

"Ah! That's why you had a bandage on your head."

"How did you know that?" he asked, confused.

"Uh. Uh . . . I think a nurse told me. Adanna, maybe."

"Hmmm." He shook his head, his brow knitted a bit.

So how do you thank someone for saving your life? For diving into a river raging with winter rains, pulling you out of your car, and performing CPR until you were breathing like a human again? Now that's a tough one.

"I love you, Jack." I smiled at him, then pulled his head down to mine, and planted a big kiss on his mouth. I did not miss the utter surprise or the raw passion in his eyes. His tears mixed with mine.

"You're so yummy," I told him.

Chapter Fourteen

Patricia came immediately to the hospital. She brought me a steamy romance novel. I told her that she was being watched by a man in a blue sedan in front of her house.

All the blood left her face. "I'll bet it's Mad Michael. He's always threatened to come and visit us in his spaceship!" She ran off to call the police.

Mad Michael, aka Steven Baker, was arrested in Patricia's mauve living room wearing a sexy space suit.

Inside the car, they found a matching space suit and voice recordings of Mad Michael's celestial conversations with Bam Bam.

But no weapons. Mad Michael explained that he felt a hypersonic cosmic connection with Bam Bam and only wanted to live out one of their space-galaxy fantasies.

Bam Bam went to see him at the jail. Teresa, aka Bam Bam, the skeletally skinny woman, showed Mad Michael how she could stuff an entire pastry in her mouth.

Mad Michael said he would never bother Bam Bam again.

Dee came by and brought me a poinsettia in a red lantern. I thought that was very clever. We skittered around the surface stuff for awhile, then I said, "How are you, Dee?"

That broke the flood walls. All her recent adventures came pouring out.

"How's Bryan?"

"I don't know, Suzanna," she said, her voice catching. "I don't know. He won't talk to me. I can't blame him. He had to leap onto the hood of my car so I wouldn't bisect him."

I tried to make light of it. "So, are you headed for a little jail time?"

"Probably," Dee said, her face resigned, accepting. "And I deserve it."

Bryan came about an hour after Dee. He hugged me, told me he was delighted I was awake. We talked about me for awhile then I said, "I heard that Dee drove you to Carly's."

Bryan rubbed his haggard face with his hands. He'd lost weight. He'd aged about ten years. Ten bad years.

"Do you miss her?"

Silence. And then, "I do. I miss her every minute. There's something addictive about Dee. Something exciting and passionate and compelling. She's so into me, into us. She's real and complicated and crazy. I'm not happy without her. I could do without all the drama but I can't do without her. I can't envision a 'me' without a Dee. Do you know what I mean?"

I sure did. "What do you know about her childhood, Bryan?"

"Nothing. She won't talk about it."

"Ask her again."

Bryan Cahill nodded at me. "Okay. I will."

Bryan asked, Dee told him.

And Dee and Bryan began a long series of counseling sessions.

She never used her car as a torpedo again.

* * *

Trenton came to see me three days after I woke up, charging into the hospital room with an "I've been so worried" expression on his skinny white face.

Jack stood up when Trenton flew in, his eyes narrowing. Jack's attorneys had already drawn up new papers that I had signed, so I was no longer legally tied to Trenton in any way.

"Darling!" Trenton proclaimed, leaning down to kiss my cheek, deliberately ignoring Jack. "I got the message that you were awake but I was on a business trip and absolutely couldn't get away."

I couldn't even look at the little weasel and kept my eyes fixed on the far wall. I did feel a blast of hurt. I had been engaged to this man. I had been dating him. I had spent countless hours of my life with him. And he had not been here for me during my coma.

"Darling!"

I stared straight ahead, saying nothing.

"Dammit," Trenton whined, his hands going to his head. "What happened? I heard she had woken up from her coma. Can't she talk?"

Jack said nothing.

"Damn and crap!" A wave of anger swept

over Trenton's weak features. "She's mentally whacked out, isn't she? Her brain's sizzled. Will she always be like this?"

Jack raised his eyebrows at Trenton. I could feel Jack's fury emanating from him like a hurricane.

Trenton whipped around on his heel and drove a frustrated hand through his hair. "Damn! Now what'll I do?" he muttered. I could see his mind whirling. What are my responsibilities to a woman who can't talk? Can I walk out now? Should I wait twenty minutes? "I knew we should have pulled the plug."

He spun around to face me again. "Suzanna!" he shouted.

I kept staring.

"She's a vegetable, isn't she?" He blew his nose on a Kleenex. "I'm engaged to a vegetable. I can't do this, I can't. I'm not going to put my life on hold for one more day. She's not my responsibility . . ."

He rolled his eyes at Jack, as if he wanted to bond with him over my mental state, then leaned over me like a vulture. "Suzanna!" he yelled. "Can you hear me? Make a sign, wiggle your fingers! Suzanna!"

Well, that was an invitation if I'd ever heard

one. I stuck the middle fingers up on both hands.

Jack chuckled.

"Thank Gawd!" Trenton said, sighing, not getting it. "Can . . . You . . . Talk?" he asked, enunciating each word, his voice booming.

"Yes. I. Can. Talk."

"Excellent! Premierly excellent! Well! I've been so worried about you, so . . ." He paused, unsure of himself, realizing immediately I'd heard what he'd said about my being "whacked out."

"It was *awful* having you in that coma, wondering if you'd ever come out of it, if you would die, what I would do next. It's been so stressful for me, Suzanna, I'm wiped out. This has been a terrible, horrendous experience for me."

"Yes, horrendous, Trenton."

"These last few weeks, I've been here for you, Suzanna. I've practically lived at this hospital. *Lived here.* And you know I hate hospitals. There are so many germs here. This has been a sacrifice for me, but you're worth it. It's simply ironic that when you woke up, I wasn't here."

"Ironic? That's your word for it, then?"

Trenton wasn't stupid. He sensed my

anger. He stood as tall as possible and said, "Mr. Benson, thank you for your time. I understand you stood in for me with Suzanna on the odd days I couldn't be here. If you could leave me and my fiancée alone, I think we need some time to talk." Trenton's tone and manner were dismissive and pompous.

"I will not be leaving you alone with Suzanna," Jack said, his green eyes steady. "Ever."

"Excuse me?" Trenton raised his chin. Jack towered over him. "I'm sure I didn't hear you clearly. I asked you to leave. Now."

"I'm not leaving."

"You are. Suzanna and I are engaged. I appreciate your help when she had her little accident, that was good of you, and your help these past few days, but it's unnecessary for you to stay any further."

"It is quite necessary."

I held up my hand. I had decided that Trenton did not deserve too much fluff or politeness from me. "Trenton, I've changed my mind."

"You have? About what, sweetie?" He picked up my hand, stroked it, raised an eyebrow at Jack as if to say, *See here, buddy, she's mine.* I used my other hand to pry away Trenton's grip.

"About us."

"About us? Why? What do you mean?" Trenton asked, his tone patronizing. "You've had a bad accident, you're probably tired. Things are confusing to you now but everything will become clear. You and I are engaged to be married."

"We were engaged. We are no longer."

"What?" Trenton smiled down at me, trying to be the indulgent fiancé who is dealing with an addled woman who doesn't know her own mind. "You've had a bad hit in the head, sweetie, but we'll get past it. Now, now, you rest. Relax. Lay back. I'll handle everything. These doctors and nurses, especially one called Adanna—what kind of a name is that, anyhow? They've been difficult. Impossible, really. But I took charge and will continue to do so."

"Trenton, I'm breaking up with you for many reasons. Let me be brief. I know you are not in the computer business. Your business can gently be called a pyramid scheme. I believe, however, the proper term is 'fraud.' It's illegal and immoral." I did not tell him that I had told the authorities and they were already gathering evidence via wiretaps and surveillance.

"I think you're cheap, especially with a waitress named Dianna, who, by the way, hates your guts and spits in your food because you tip so bad. As for your parents, Trenton, your behavior toward them is unforgivable. Alyssa is a saint. Your sister, you selfish snake, has four kids, and she is caring for your parents. She is, *at least,* three times busier than you. You owe her money. Pay her."

Trenton made a gurgling sound in his throat, his face pasty. "You're imagining things, you've had a concussion and you've never been rational when upset, you've had problems with impulsive behavior and you must calm down, breathe deeply—"

"I am breathing deeply and this is what I know: Although I am sure you're terribly disappointed, you will not be coming in to any money from me, Trenton, via my will, as you can see I'm not dead, although you certainly put forth your best efforts to end my life."

He blushed a lovely shade of red and purple, then coughed as if his throat was closing up on him. "Suzanna, I have no idea who has been spreading these lies. Perhaps it's you, Mr. Benson? How dare you! Lying to my fiancée to gain the upper hand. You haven't won here, Benson!"

"Jack has nothing to do with it. All of it is true. Admit it, Trenton, or I might have to open my mouth and tell Jack about the collection of girls' dolls you have in the spare room that you stroke obsessively. I believe there are forty-three of them at last count? Now, please, tell me why a grown man is collecting dolls?"

"They're pretty . . ." he protested and then caught himself. "How did you know? Suzanna, how did you know all this?"

"Because I was a ghost for the last few weeks and I've been flying around town spying on people. You were one of the most entertaining."

Trenton chuckled nervously, then stared straight into my eyes. His chuckle stopped abruptly.

"You've been spying on me, then." He tried to sound indignant. "You have cameras in my house, don't you? You've had a private eye watching me."

"No, no, and no."

"Then how . . . How do you know?"

"I told you. I was a ghost. Good-bye, Trenton. Go back to your pyramid scheme and your dolls."

There was some fussing on his part, some protests.

Then Jack took a step closer to him and said, "Good-bye, Trenton. Out you go."

"You can't tell me what to do," Trenton said, his voice weak.

"I can." Jack took three steps closer to Trenton. Trenton skedaddled on out.

Over the next few days, my room was almost constantly mobbed with people from town.

I have to stop myself there.

I shouldn't call them "people from town."

I should call them friends.

Me. Suzanna Everts.

I had friends.

Chapter Fifteen

Many days later Jack took me home. My refrigerator was packed with scrumptious food from friends and my elaborate stocking quilt hung on a wall. The outside of my house had been covered in white twinkling lights.

"I'm almost glad I was in a coma," I said later to Jack as we sat on the couch together, my hand entwined in his. He had a warm, warm hand.

"You are? Please. Tell me you're kidding."

"No, I'm not. I wasn't living before this, Jack. I was surviving. I was functioning. I was getting things done. Everything was ordered and organized, because I needed that, but I was afraid to find myself and be me. I was dying while I was still alive."

I knew that sounded ridiculous but I also knew he understood.

"You look really alive to me now, love." He reached out a hand to curl my hair around his finger.

Waking up from a coma and almost instantly telling Jack I loved him had been a bit startling to the poor man. I tried to explain myself but whaddya say? Something wise, I told myself. Something meaningful and deep. So I said: "I biffed it, Jack. I biffed us."

He had smiled, the lines crinkling in the corners of his eyes. "No, you didn't—"

"I did. I was stuck in my little life and you came out of nowhere and you were . . .". How to describe him? "Christmas and chocolates and sun all wrapped up. We fit together. Plus you're unbearably gorgeous and loyal and so very true. You hit me like a bulldozer, Jack."

He chuckled, deep and low. "I saw what I wanted, which was you. Beautiful, beautiful Suzanna." He shook his head, in confusion. "I swear, Suzanna, when you were in your coma, I could feel you sometimes around me, hear you. I could almost see you."

What to say to that? "It was probably because you were here so much. You've got to be exhausted, you hardly slept."

I saw confusion cloud his eyes again and hurried to cover myself. "Adanna and the doctors, they told me, you were here. A lot. All the time." I coughed.

"I wanted to be with you. Where else would I be?"

I smiled at that and tears squished out of my eyes, which he kissed away.

"I'll take it that, yes, you'll go out to lunch with me now?"

I laughed. "That would be a yes, Jack, a definite yes."

I scooted closer to him on the couch and kissed him, softly at first, then gathered my courage and kissed him again, and again. I straddled him and kissed his neck and chest and worked my way down.

Yes, it was a night where I felt very, very alive. Alive with Mr. Yum.

We went to get a Christmas tree together and spent the day decorating it. We strung lights in my house and I put out every single Christmas knickknack I could possibly find.

I was ready for Santa.

*   *   *

The next morning I grabbed the box of bran cereal, the strawberry jelly, and the bread that I'd been eating for years. Out they went to the garbage. I made apple pancakes and hash browns.

I dared myself to enter a salon in town. The seventeen-year-old hair stylist, Gigi, cracked her gum the whole time she worked. She had black spiky hair with a purple streak running through it and wore an orange plaid miniskirt.

"You're gonna be majorly improved when I'm done with ya, Suzanna, not nearly so old-womanish. Ya gotta play up those blond looks, those puffy lips, those brown eyes. You been hidin' in a cave or something?"

I laughed. "Yeah, I think I have been. Cut away, Gigi. This cavewoman needs a make-over."

After Gigi whacked off about six inches of hair, highlighted it, and spritzed something on it to make my blond curls even curlier, I grabbed Carly and she taught me the fine art of shopping.

* * *

I met Jack at a restaurant in town for dinner wearing my new contact lenses. He was already seated at a small table by the fireplace. The lights were low, red candles flickered at every table, and a huge Christmas tree in the corner twinkled with colored lights.

He didn't notice me as I headed toward the table. In fact, I watched him look around me toward the front door, waiting for me to appear.

He was wearing a blue jacket and white shirt and was so rawly male I could hardly breathe.

Jack raised his wineglass to his mouth about the same time that I stood in front of him in my new black dress with little sparkly straps.

His wineglass clattered to the table.

The next morning I made French toast with vanilla and powdered sugar. I did not miss my bran.

* * *

I knew who to go to for help with the
Pooles.

I found Ronna Lavey at home, alone, as
usual, rattling around. I handed her the thick
folder I had gotten from the Pooles including the details of the accident and David
Poole's medical records.

She opened the file, then slammed it shut
tight.

"I'm not qualified," she said. "Not qualified."

Her hands shook around the teacup she
was holding. She put it down and it wobbled in the saucer. Tea spilled out.

I grabbed her hand across the table. "You
can, Ronna."

"No."

"Ronna." I grabbed her shoulders. "I know
about the Schilling case."

She let out a pathetic moan.

"Listen to me. You're not that person anymore. You have punished yourself enough."

"No, I haven't. I'll never be able to let go.
Never. They hired me to represent them,
and I did a miserable job. Worse than miserable. Because of me, they went bankrupt
over their daughter's illness. The insurance
company won and they should have paid

the Schillings's medical bills. I was too drugged out and strung out to see what was right in front of my face. They lost their house, Suzanna. The Schillings sold their home to pay for Sarah's medical care. They live in an apartment now in a scary area of town."

So what do you say to a person who has really screwed things up? "You screwed up, Ronna. There's no question. But you can't let what happened make you feel like diving off a cliff."

"I can. I am. I probably will."

"No, you can't. Listen to me, Ronna." I picked up the folder and whacked her over the head with it. "You listen to me right now because the Pooles need help and I don't want to watch you wallowing in your own endless self-misery for a minute longer when they've got a problem. You do know they've been evicted from their home?"

"I can't do a trial again—"

I whacked her over the head again. "You can. You are. You will."

And then I opened the folder and read to her aloud the injury that David Poole had suffered. I told her about the company going bankrupt and closing down and telling David he was on his own.

Ronna pulled her feet up and wrapped her arms around her legs. "I can't do this," she rasped.

I handed her the file. "Here's your opportunity to de-screw things for David."

She banged her head against her arms a few times, then, without lifting her head, held up a trembly hand for the file.

For the next five days Ronna Lavey didn't leave her home. Law books and notebooks and case studies were stacked up and opened all around her. Her concentration was fierce, her focus unwavering. She lived off soda pop and popcorn. There was one light on over her head, day and night.

Her home was as still as a grave, which is not a good parallel, given my recent coma. On the fifth night I let myself in.

"I got 'em," she told me, cackling a bit. "Holy hell, Suzanna, do I got 'em."

Next I took a little side trip to Paul's Hardware Store. I bought paint.

Lots of paint.
And a few odds and ends.

When I was done a few days later, I invited Jack over for dinner. I had transformed my tiny house. The family room and kitchen were butter yellow, the tiny dining room a light blue with flowing, hand-painted leaves lining the new chair rail, and the hallway leading up the stairs was a mocha color. I had ripped down my old boring curtains and put up new ones with bright colors that popped off the walls. I bought plants, slipcovers in reds and plaids and florals for all my furniture, and new throw rugs. I painted old furniture white.

Finally, I dug around dust-covered boxes in my workshop and found my glass art. I put a group of blue and yellow three-foot-tall curving vases on my dining room table. I hung some of my red and gold glass flowerlike pieces along one whole wall. I lined up three giant bowls with curving edges on my white coffee table. I placed giant glass balls in purple and green and red out in my garden.

When Jack came in the door, flowers and

wine in hand, he kissed me, then froze, his eyes on my art.

He didn't speak for many long minutes as he wandered around my home, studying the color-blasted glass plates I'd hung on my stairwell wall and the small glass balls I'd hung near my windows.

"Your talent floors me, Suzanna. It's incredible," he said, sincerity ringing every note.

"New hair. New clothes. New house," he muttered into my mouth while kissing me. He carried me up the stairs to my bedroom. "New you."

I daresay he liked my light pink walls and the gold and white glass art piece I'd made that was sitting on the dresser, but we didn't really have time to discuss them much.

It was time to fix Carly and Paul. The whole event was simple, really. They would be my prisoners.

I set up a table in my workshop, covered it with a crisp white tablecloth, china, silver, red candles and a poinsettia. I bought their favorite take-out Chinese food.

I asked both of them, separately, to come

to the workshop to see my new designs and have dinner with me. Carly arrived first and I made an excuse to go back to the house, then Paul arrived, and I locked them in.

Carly shrieked at me from inside but Paul didn't say a word.

"I'll be back in two hours, you two. Now why don't you both admit you're still crazy about each other and work this out! Paul can stop hitting people over quilts, Carly can stop crying over her overgrown robot and we'll all be happy. And, by the way, Paul, have you ever told Carly you cry when you read poetry?"

Silence.

Carly told me later what happened.

When Carly was done shrieking, she whipped around to Paul, expecting a fight.

"You look beautiful, Carly," Paul said. "So beautiful."

Stunned by the brokenness in his eyes, the humbleness, she didn't say anything at first, then muttered, "Really? Do you think so?"

"Yes, really. More beautiful than ever."

"Thank you. And you—"

Paul shook his head. "Don't bother. I know I look like shit."

Carly laughed. Paul never, ever swears. And he did look like shit.

"And I like"—he reached out, then dropped his hand—"I love your hair."

"You do? I thought . . . I always thought you thought redheads were too flashy or too sexy . . ."

"I love your hair any way you have it, Carly. Any way at all." Paul was so beaten, Carly told me later she wanted to kiss him. Right there. "And I like the furniture you bought for the house."

"But it's red and yellow and bright and there's tons of flowers everywhere!" Carly giggled.

"Who said I didn't like flowers?"

"You told me you liked beige and brown furniture, so that's what I bought."

"But you always wanted to have flowers and color?" Paul was confounded.

"Yes. Always."

He gave up, let all his emotions hang out. "Then why didn't you?"

"Because I thought you would be happier if we had guy sorts of furniture. Beige. Boring. Leather."

"Carly," he started, then stopped as he got choked up. "It's your house. You do with it what you want. I don't care about stuff like that, honey, not at all. I care about you."

Carly felt a good cry coming on. "But what about . . . What do you think about my new clothes?" Carly was not going to give up the cool clothes.

Paul's eyes raked her up and down. She thought he looked sexy checking her out. "Your new clothes are driving me crazy, Carly."

"But do you like them?" She grinned.

"Yes. I do. And I have made love to you in my mind one hundred times these last weeks. You have always been everything to me, sweetheart. Everything. From the day we first met. And now you're gone." He swiped a huge hand over his tearing eyes. "When I wake up in the morning, alone, I think I'm going to die and when I go to bed at night, alone, I think I'm going to die."

"Paul . . . I'm sorry . . . I'm not . . . He's not . . . I'll never see him again . . . It's over . . . Can you forgive me? God, please, Paul."

"Honey, you have nothing to be sorry for. Nothing. Carly, I have thought about us every minute we've been apart. I have been a lousy husband. I took you for granted. I'm not asking you, I'm begging you, let me try again. I will not fail you. I will fix this, fix myself, fix our lives."

Carly got up and hugged him but the tears were different this time.

"And Carly . . ." Paul tipped her chin up, not bothering to hide his own tears. "Honey, I know you're not a couch. Or wallpaper. Or cat litter. I came from nothing, Carly, you know that. My world was gray and sad before I met you. You brought light into my life. You are my light. You have always been my light and I love you."

I went back to the workshop in two hours and peeked through the cracks of the door.

Whew! I quietly unlocked the door and snuck back to the house. The table was bearing up well under the weight of two naked, happy people.

The next day I wandered outside and into my workshop. I ran my finger over the glory hole, the shelves, my poles and tools for glass making. I saw a stack of boring blue bowls I'd made years ago.

I tossed one bowl onto the floor and listened to it shatter. By the time five bowls had smashed I knew exactly what I would do.

Chapter Sixteen

It took many attempts for me to shape my glass Christmas stockings into works of glass art. The molten glass was heated in my glory hole to 2,400 degrees until it was the consistency of honey. Using a long steel rod, giant tweezers, and tools, I later shaped it into stockings.

I worked from early in the morning until about 7:00 at night. In the end, I had twelve colorful Christmas stockings, each made of glass in various reds, greens, and purples. All of them had gold leaf running through them so they sparkled. I loaded them up in my car and drove to the city the next day. I hoped to sell them to several stores. The first store bought all of them. The next day I was called to refill the order. The owner wanted twenty-four.

I called them Suzanna's Stockings.

Days later a photographer for the state newspaper stopped by and took photos of me, my stockings, and my workshop. Must have been a slow news day. The newspaper ran the story and I was buried in orders.

Evie and Dawn handled phone and Internet orders even though Evie called the Internet "the Devil's computer" every time it did something wrong to "curse her." They both wore Santa hats.

I was in high gear making stockings. But I didn't work around the clock.

That would have been impossible. When I was with Jack the only heat I thought of was the heat that burned molten hot between the two of us.

"Sales of Suzanna's Stockings don't suck," Evie told me, smiling.

"Nope, they don't suck," Dawn added, putting on her motorcycle helmet.

"Remember we have to leave early tomorrow, Suzanna. It's Erotic Book Club Group Night."

"I remember," I laughed. "Go be erotic."

* * *

For breakfast I made us a cheese and ham omelet and Jack made sweet rolls. "Say no to bran," I muttered.

"What?" Jack asked.

"Nothing." I kissed him. Life was yummy.

"I'm not building the shopping center, Suzanna," Jack said.

We were outside on his deck one evening watching the waves froth in the distance, the sun slipping below the horizon. He had wrapped little white Christmas lights around the rails of the deck. I was definitely in the Christmas spirit.

"I know," I said, then caught myself.

"How do you know?"

"Well . . ." What to say? I was a ghost and flitting around town and sleeping in your bed and listening to your conversations, so I know? "You haven't been talking about it, so I assumed you were, at least, putting it off."

He nodded. "I'm not putting it off. I'm not building it altogether."

"You should build it, Jack."

"No. It's not what I want to do."

He hauled me onto his lap and cuddled

me in close. For such a he-man, he was surprisingly affectionate.

"You should build it, Jack. The Old West plans are beautiful and it will bring new life to Canyon Beach. We need it."

"The town will live without it. I'm thinking about retiring."

"Retiring?" I laughed. Jack might grumble, but he loved his work. I had seen him, in my human form, pour over blueprints and plans and contracts. He would not be happy without his work.

"Yeah, then I could stay home and hang out with you all day. I've waited my whole life for you, Suzanna, and now you're here and I don't like being apart."

"You're not retiring, Jack. Listen to me." I put my forehead on his. "I have a little surprise for you."

He kissed me for a bit so the surprise got sidetracked. I pulled away.

"Want to know my surprise?"

"Does it involve you being naked?"

I laughed. "No."

"Does it involve you being in the red Mrs. Claus negligee I bought you yesterday?"

I laughed again. "That's a no."

"Does it involve you lying down in front of

the Christmas tree with only a giant red bow tied around your waist?"

"Nope."

"Then let's put the surprise off." He kissed my neck, pulled me up tight to his chest.

"Jack, I told you that the sales for my glass stockings have taken off?"

He kissed my mouth, my cheeks.

"I'm working from home from now on and will sell directly to stores and through the Internet. My business is still going to be called The Red Lantern, but the shopping center won't compete with me."

He kissed my neck.

"Are you listening?"

"Yes. You taste good."

"Lovely. Build the shopping center, Jack."

"I'll think about it."

We didn't think too much after that.

Jack asked me to marry him one night while we were on the beach, after the Christmas party at the lodge where we danced for hours. David Poole told me I really grooved well.

There were six million stars in the sky shining brighter than ever, the moon was up, the breeze was cool, and Jack got down on one knee, just like in those cheesy old movies, and proposed.

I laughed and cried and made this little snorting sound I was embarrassed about, but then he kissed me and that was that.

"One more thing. Suzanna."

"Yes?" I couldn't help it. I glanced at my ring. Good heavens.

"Kids?"

He was worried, I could tell. He loved me, would marry me either way, but I knew what he wanted.

"Many. You?"

He picked me up and twirled me around and later we splashed in the water.

Just like in those cheesy old movies.

Dee's attempted murder and assault charges were dropped. Bryan refused to cooperate and didn't want charges pressed. No one had actually been hurt. The property that was damaged belonged to both of them. The district attorney gave up.

Dee would never have to wear an orange jumpsuit again. We became great friends.

* * *

I went to visit Magdalena Hernandez in her enormous greenhouse. She had decorated it for Christmas with five different Christmas trees. One had seashells and stars, another was adorned with miniature plates and mugs, another was sprayed silver, the fourth held tiny birdhouses, and the fifth had a Western theme with cowboy hats and boots.

"Merry Christmas, Magdalena. Do you have a minute?" I asked.

Her red hair was braided with red and green ribbons. She twirled and smiled. "Have you considered building yourself a greenhouse?"

I caught myself. "Uh. No." Not at all. "I wanted to talk to you about one night when I was in the hospital . . ."

"Greenhouses let you escape from this life. They wrap you in warmth, hug you with color, loll you to peace." I followed her down an aisle, both sides lush with plants.

"Yes. And yours is so beautiful, Magdalena. Anyhow, one night in the hospital, when I was in the coma, I thought I woke up and saw you . . . well, dancing in my room.

And you were tossing something out of your hands. I thought I saw silver sparkles."

"Flowers can grow year-round in green-houses. Plants, shrubs, tiny trees. Plus, in a greenhouse you can pursue your art. For me, it's creating mosaic designs or using malleable branches to form rose trellises."

"You're so artistic, I've always admired that, now this is going to sound silly—"

"Nothing is silly, Suzanna." She picked up a purple orchid, let the soft leaves caress her face. "Except disbelieving what one doesn't understand."

I closed my mouth. I was going to say, "I don't understand."

"Sometimes we have to believe even though logic says not to. We have to trust. Would you like to take this orchid with you?"

She handed me the pot. The orchid and I were eye to eye.

"Magdalena," I tried again, "when I was in the coma . . . I was not in a coma . . . too, I could see everyone, I watched people in town—"

She patted my hand. Smiled. "Of course you did, dear." Then she winked at me. I noticed she had lots of silvery sparkles on her black coat. "Merry Christmas, Suzanna."

Epilogue

One Year Later

My Life As A Phone Sex Operator was a best-seller for forty-three weeks on *The New York Times best-seller list.* When the book came out, Patricia Goodling became an overnight media star.

The crush of media attention swamped Canyon Beach. Reporters came from near and far and there sat Patricia, prim and proper, in her button-up blouses and little-old-lady sweaters, her gray hair unruly, her plump body lumpy.

The reporters took photos of her employees, too. The very large ones, the very skinny ones, the older ladies with gray and white cotton hair, the nose-ring one, and the scrapbooking mother.

Not a soft, pliant, willing sex kitten among them. The talk shows loved them. The phone sex companies hyperventilated, their sales crashing.

But during all of the hoopla for the book, Patricia took care to tell everyone why someone might be driven to create a highly lucrative business like this. In her case, it was because she needed care for her disabled child and appropriate care was appallingly expensive. She detailed, quite clearly, on talk and radio shows, and in her book, the nightmare that parents of disabled children faced—emotionally, physically, and financially. She lived in dire fear that she would not have enough money saved to provide for her daughter.

In the end, she brought an enormous amount of publicity to a subject that was dear to her heart, people sat up and listened, and state policies were changed.

Many of us from Canyon Beach were in court when Ronna Lavey delivered her fiery and articulate closing argument as David Poole's attorney.

Part of what she said: "Mr. Poole and his

wife of twenty-five years, Lorrallee, and their five children, were evicted from the home they owned because they were not able to make their mortgage payments. *Evicted!* Why were they not able to make the payments? Because David's leg was almost sliced off by a timber-cutting machine at Weston Family Mills, and the company abandoned them.

"Before they lost their home, their water, phone, and electricity were cut off. Why was that? It was because they, the owners of Weston Family Mills"—she pointed to the defense table—"pretended they had no money. They lied to David. They deceived him. David made the mistake of believing them. He had worked for them for twenty-five years and trusted the company. Let me tell you again about David's injury and the machine that did it. Let me tell you again about the safeguards not in place."

Ronna was graphic about the injury, the fountains of blood, the shredded muscles, the screaming, and what could have prevented the tragedy that day. Then she showed the jury photographs of his injured leg. By the end of her speech, the jury mem-

bers appeared rather green, sick, and royally pissed off.

"David's life was ruined. He did not receive the medical care he needed and
ended up in a wheelchair. A wheelchair. A
forty-five-year old man who is in so much
pain, he can hardly get up. Here's the good
news though, folks: with medical care,
David can get better. He'll walk again. He
may never be without pain. But he won't be
in such mind-numbing agony that he can't
hold his children in his lap. He won't hurt so
bad he can't shoot hoops with his kids. He
won't be in such grinding pain he can't fish.
David Poole wants to hold Lorrallee's hand
and walk on the beach. Please give him that
chance."

The jury was out for thirty-one minutes.

They jury foreman glared at the defense
attorneys for a full, blistering thirty seconds
before delivering the verdict.

David was awarded three million dollars
for his injuries and fifteen million dollars for
punitive damages.

The verdict hit the front page of the newspaper. Weston Family Mills decided not to
appeal because of the lousy publicity and
forked up the money to the Pooles.

The Pooles bought themselves a rambling house overlooking the beach, funded the kids' college-education funds and their retirement, then donated the rest of the money for the town's first recreation center, complete with a pool, basketball courts, and classrooms for crafts and dance classes. It was named after Ronna Lavey and the Pooles managed it. David Poole received the medical care he needed. He and Lorrallee watch the sunset together every night on the sand.

Ronna took her cut and wrote a check for two and a half million dollars to the Schilling family.

"They deserved more," Ronna told me. "They deserved better counsel. But at least I have a measure of peace now. Maybe that's all any of us should expect, or wish, out of this life. A little peace."

She opened a small law practice in town. She didn't charge much and seemed perfectly content.

Ronna Lavey attended Narcotics Anonymous meetings and never touched the stuff again.

* * *

As for me, it is another very Merry Christmas this year. I even catch myself singing Christmas carols at odd moments.

To complete the cheesy movie scene, Jack and I were married at his house, on his deck overlooking the ocean, at dusk, with our family and friends, seven months ago. All Jack's brothers and their families showed up as did his lovely parents and all their siblings and all their children and grandchildren. The house was mobbed.

I wore a slinky white dress with wildflowers embroidered in a curving line from my bodice to my hem, sewn by one of Patricia's ladies.

Jack wore a black tux and darned if that man didn't take my breath away. Before I slithered into my wedding dress, we snuck past our guests and met in the closet in the guest room and had a good kiss. I daresay he liked my bridal panties.

My glass art business has taken off, and I am currently buried in orders for the holidays. I am not only making glass stockings, but glass ornaments, vases, organic art, giant decorative plates, curving bird baths, and glass murals. My work has been featured in several magazines and newspapers. Jack says people call me The Glass Lady.

Since Jack loves to fish, I have made him a glass fish mural for his office for Christmas. He'll love it.

Jack built the mall, exactly as the plans detailed, and it is beautiful, with wide boardwalks, outdoor art and a grassy square surrounded by benches. It has become a destination point for many people visiting from the city and for all of us here in town. It is currently decorated with a huge herd of reindeer made from sticks and wrapped in white lights.

Jack and I use the square's gazebo to play Mr. and Mrs. Santa to all of the kids in town every Saturday afternoon. He makes for a sexy Santa, I tell him.

We are not yet pregnant but that is at the top of the list of our New Year's Resolutions. We're thinking four kids, or maybe five. Maybe a half dozen. Jack says he wants enough to fill Santa's sleigh. "Ho, ho, ho, let's have a bunch of little elves, Mrs. Claus," he told me last night.

I have found that wearing my red Mrs. Claus negligee or lying down in front of our Christmas tree with only a giant red bow around my waist has provided good practice for when the time comes for us to put our talents together and make a baby.

The quilting club continues to meet once a week. I sit by Adanna or sometimes by the young doctor with the ponytail who brings his girlfriend. The quilts, everyone decided, should go to foster children in our county. Since it is Christmas, we are putting in long hours for the kids.

We meet at my workshop, it is still potluck, and we regularly have forty people come. Needless to say, we make a lot of quilts. Our recent quilts have featured giant reindeer wearing tuxedos, snowwomen in purple dresses, and dancing elves.

And once a month, Ed Surbanks, Evie's Mr. Sugarmissile, her Sugar Pistol, makes his Baked Alaska, the flames shooting high.

Family Blessings

Deborah J. Wolf

Acknowledgments

Truth be told, when my editor and agent encouraged me to write a piece for this book, I had little desire to do so. My father had passed away three weeks after Christmas and we were facing the first year without him. The idea of finding a story that represented the jovial, fun-loving memory I have of his booming voice caroling through the holidays seemed nearly impossible.

But every story comes from somewhere, and this one was no different.

I grew up the daughter of an army colonel. We moved frequently and pulled up roots faster than we could put them down again. But my grandparents had a wonderful home in West Hartford, Connecticut that I often thought of as my own, and which we would travel to nearly every Christmas. Some of my fondest memories started in their basement during the holidays when my brother and I would roll out our sleeping bags and giggle the night away with our cousins.

I'm so grateful to have been able to partici-pate in this holiday anthology. Writing proved to be a vital part of the healing process for me. But even more important was the wonderful walk down memory lane this story afforded. So, big thanks to Audrey and Richard for rooting me on . . . they were right, as always.

For Bill, Elizabeth, and Laura, this one is for you.

Chapter One

My mother had always been a bona fide Christmas fanatic. It was, by far and away, her very most favorite holiday. She loved everything about it—the ritual, the tradition, the customs. She was usually caught humming carols by Halloween. And Black Friday—the day after Thanksgiving, the busiest shopping day of the year—was practically a national holiday, holding more credence than the turkey itself; she was usually at the mall, extensively planned shopping list in hand, by five AM.

This year she had dragged all the Christmas decorations out in early September, just after Labor Day. The leaves had already turned; brilliant, golden foliage tinged with red and orange, and burnt at the ends. We were having an Indian summer and the thermostat read eighty-six when I arrived at the house at 9:30, same as always, to pick her up for our weekly coffee and pedicure. By that time, my mother was sweating, panting, as she heaved box after box of baubles and trimming down from the attic. The artificial tree was set up in the middle of the living room, stuffed from tip to trunk with three decades' worth of ornaments—ornate glass bulbs, hand-stitched dolls, jeweled trinkets. The plastic singing Santa Claus belted out "Jingle Bell Rock" and started dancing the minute I walked into the entry hall, giving me a minor heart attack. Lighted garland lined the banister, woven in and around every other baluster. Two large wreaths had been placed on either side of the stone fireplace. By all accounts it looked like Christmas Eve.

My mother stood in the middle of it all, humming "Carol of the Bells." She was wearing her red tartan skirt and a black sweater. And she looked busily contented; joyful, as if she'd waited all year for Christmas to begin.

"Ma?" I questioned, standing amidst the boxes. "What's going on . . . ?"

She stared at me blankly at first, as if she was trying to figure out what I was doing in my white shorts and tank top when apparently we were supposed to be walking in a winter wonderland.

"Oh, hello, Kacey. Where are your brothers and sister? Supper will be on soon. Paddy wanted lamb stew, of course. You know how he loves lamb stew on Christmas Eve. Although I'm making a vegetable quiche as well. You know Maureen won't touch the lamb." Her eyes danced with the magic of Christmas, the impending holiday in her mind.

Maureen was traveling when I called her later that afternoon. My sister was nearly always traveling and usually we had no idea where she was. Luckily, her global satellite phone worked nearly anywhere in the world and although she rarely answered, she always picked up her voice mail. In this case it was Sunday morning where she was and she was two hours and knee-deep into a detailed and exceedingly specific expedition at the Bazaar of Isfahan, searching for a hand-woven silk Persian rug the color of cadet blue, the very color her client had pulled out of the Crayola box two weeks earlier. It was hopeless and her frustration level was growing.

I left her a fairly pointed and explicit message. With Maureen, there was no beating around the bush. Anything past thirty seconds and she was likely to delete your message without ever having made it to the pertinent details.

"Mo, it's me. I'm calling about Ma. She's decorated the whole house for Christmas. She's singing carols. And she's baking Granny's fruitcake. God, there must be half a dozen fruitcakes. Call me, okay? Clearly things have gotten worse."

My sister is seven years older than I am. There are four brothers in between the two of us. Michael, Sean, Thomas, and Timothy. My father calls Mo and me his bookends, one on either end of the four strapping boys he'd always wanted. My name is Katherine, but everyone calls me Kacey. Six kids in seven years; my family is Catholic, as if you couldn't tell. Irish Catholic.

My mother's name is also Maureen. When Mo was born, my mother was so distraught over the fact that she hadn't given Paddy the son that he'd prayed for that she told my father to name his daughter. My father, not possessing an original creative bone in his body, named her Maureen Rose, after his wife and his own ma.

Mo called me later that afternoon. She was sipping tea and eating one of the Balance Bars she had brought with her. Mo could survive an entire two-week trip on Balance Bars and turkey jerky. She was rail thin and jittery and consumed by work at all times.

"How bad is it?" Maureen asked me in a rather accusatory tone.

"I mean to tell you, Mo, there are decorations everywhere. *Every*where."

"What did you say to her?"

"I didn't know what to say. I don't just mean she's decorated. I mean she has pulled every last thing out of every closet. Every bulb, every ornament, every nutcracker, every piece of the snow village, candles, stuffed angels, satin ribbons, blow-up snowmen. Everything."

"Can't you just put it away? Can't you just tell her it's too early? Tell her she can get that stuff out in a couple of months, after Thanksgiving. But this is September 6th, Kacey. It's ridiculous."

"I know it's ridiculous. I understand that,

Maureen. But she doesn't. And, well, quite frankly, she seems happy. Happier than she's been in a few months. You know how much Ma has always loved Christmas. It's her absolutely favorite time of the year. What's it going to hurt for her to have the Christmas decorations out for a few months longer than the rest of the world?"

Mo was pacing, I could tell, back and forth across her small hotel room. "It's awful, Kacey. It's just unbearable. It's worse than a fucking Hallmark store. Even they wait until after Halloween before they drag everything out and start stuffing their shelves."

"It has nothing to do with the date on the calendar, Mo. Nothing at all. In her mind, it's Christmas."

"What'd Paddy have to say about it?"

"What do you think Paddy has to say about it? Paddy doesn't talk about these things. You of all people should know that."

"You need to pull Paddy aside and point it out to him. Make sure he's paying attention, Kacey. Make sure he's looking you in the eye. This can't go on; he has to do something."

"Yeah, Mo, I know."

"I mean it, Kacey. Make sure you've got

his attention before you confront him. He can't just ignore this. Paddy has got to take control of this. He doesn't have a choice."

"Somehow I don't think he'll be able to ignore this, Mo. Ma's spent the entire weekend baking Christmas cookies. She's got hot cocoa on the stove and a turkey ready to be stuffed. 'I'll Be Home For Christmas' is pouring out of the stereo speakers."

Mo was quiet on the other end of the phone. She was waiting for me to reassure her, to promise her that I'd deal with it, that there wasn't anything for her to worry about. We ended most of our conversations in the same way: Mo lecturing me about what I needed to do and then waiting me out until I finally told her I would take care of things.

We hung up after that. I placed the receiver back in its cradle and stood in the middle of my postage stamp–sized kitchen. I live alone. I'm not married and I have no children. No pets, no houseplants, no commitments of any kind. Last year I broke up with my boyfriend, a passive-creative type who couldn't commit to living in the same city as me. We had been going out for three years, but there was no future, not really. Even our breakup was unimpressive.

Like it or not, my family was the center of my universe. My mother and father celebrated their forty-sixth wedding anniversary last year. They defined everything you would expect about their generation. My mother raised us with a strict hand, a thick accent, and a warm Irish heart. For thirty-eight years Paddy's heating and air-conditioning business had kept the residents of Leominster, Massachusetts, warm in the winter and cool in the summer, and our family with food on the table.

Michael followed Paddy into our family business right out of high school, but Sean and the twins—Timothy and Thomas—they all went to university first. Notre Dame, of course. Including the nieces and nephews, we were batting six for eleven at the university.

We all live in Leominster. Everyone except for Maureen, that is. Maureen lives in New York now; in Manhattan. She has a refurbished three-bedroom flat on the Upper East Side that she won in the divorce from her second husband. He got her kids, but she let them go fairly willingly. She sees them for a couple of weeks during their summer break and gets them every other holiday.

I'm what you might call the midfielder for our family. I set the pace and tempo for what's going on at any given time. Everyone comes to me with their problems; they line up one right after the next. Some nights the phone calls come in on top of each other, someone complaining about something that someone else has done, another person ratting someone out. My brothers are all married, each to a woman as distinct and individual as you could imagine. But for some reason, they all seem perfectly comfortable confiding in me.

My sister-in-law Mary Beth was the first to notice that something about Ma was, well, off. Mary Beth and Michael had married right out of high school, just after graduation. I was only thirteen and I thought their wedding was like a fairy tale. It wasn't. Mary Beth was three months' pregnant and had to have her dress let out the week before the wedding.

"Kacey," she said to me one morning over lattes, "something about Maureen isn't right.

It's as if she's lost her balance and can't quite find it."

We all had a rule about Ma and Maureen. Because they shared the same name, everyone referred to my mother as Ma and to Maureen as Mo. Everyone, except Mary Beth. She refused to call my mother Ma. And she hardly ever talked about my sister at all. It was always throwing me off.

"Maureen? When did you talk to her? I thought she was in Vietnam?"

"Your *mother,*" she said with emphasis. "Something is wrong with your mother."

"Oh, right."

"Haven't you noticed?"

"How do you mean?" I asked her, licking the chocolate off my fingers from a filled croissant.

"She's not making any sense these days. She and Paddy were over for dinner last weekend and she insisted that we should be eating breakfast. It was seven o'clock in the evening and she wanted pancakes."

I laughed. My mother's favorite meal of the day had always been breakfast. When we were growing up and Paddy was out late on an emergency call, Ma was famous for putting a whole chicken back in the icebox and cooking up a pot of oatmeal or scrambling a dozen eggs.

"Ma's always loved breakfast," I told Mary Beth. "She probably just had a craving or something."

"No, Kacey, it wasn't like that at all. She and I were out on the sunporch. You remember, it was that weekend we had the warm spell and I had taken all the covers off the outdoor furniture and we decided to sit out there and enjoy the late afternoon. Michael was barbecuing and Joseph and Elaine were home for the weekend. It was really quite perfect, quiet and sweet with the smell of spring in the air. But try as I might, I couldn't get Maureen off the subject of pancakes. She was fixated on the damn things."

"Where was Paddy?"

"Oh, God, Kacey, I don't know. Where he always is, I guess. Fiddling with something in the house, I suppose. Maybe he was down in the basement watching the ball game with Joseph."

"Well, did he notice? About Ma, I mean? And the pancakes."

"She seemed to snap out of it when he finally came out to the porch. He sat down right next to her and she looked at him for a few minutes with this blank stare until he took her hand and said to her in a very clear voice, 'Maureen, we'll be having *dinner* soon.'"

"I'm sure it was nothing, Mary Beth."

I told Mo about it later that evening, when I finally tracked her down.

"Pancakes? You woke me up at 3:30 in the morning to talk about pancakes? God, Kacey, can't you check the time zone website before you call my cell phone at all hours?"

"I'm sorry. I thought you were due back last night. I can't ever remember if you're coming or going, Mo. How's Vietnam?"

"I'm not in Vietnam," she yawned into the phone. "Bangkok. We're in Bangkok. Anyway, about Ma—Mary Beth *always* makes more out of everything than she needs to."

"Oh. Well, still sorry. I don't know, you're probably right. Mary Beth's probably blowing things way out of proportion."

"Of course she is, Kace. Of course she is."

*   *   *

Two weeks after the pancake incident Paddy called me.

"Katherine?" Paddy asked, yelling into the receiver.

"Paddy? What's wrong? Is everything okay?" I couldn't think of the last time Paddy had called me. In fact, I wondered if he had ever initiated a call to my apartment. That would have been a job for my mother.

"Have you seen your ma?"

I looked around my apartment, confused, as if I might find her there. The television was on in the other room, but otherwise everything was quiet.

"No. She isn't here, Paddy, why?"

"Well, she isn't here, either, and it's getting to be time for supper. I'm getting hungry and, well, I don't know where she's run off to."

"Didn't she leave you a note or something? Did you check the icebox?" Ma never carried a cell phone; she had never touched a computer. Her main form of communication was the front of the icebox where she stuck notes about her whereabouts right next to the running list she kept for groceries.

"No, there's no note."

Alarm ran up and down my spine, setting my nerves alive.

"Are you sure she didn't have an appointment this afternoon? What day is it? Thursday? She goes to gardening on Thursdays. Maybe she's running late from gardening."

Paddy grumbled something indistinguishable into the phone.

"I'm sure she'll be home in a while, Paddy," I said, trying to sound upbeat. I checked the clock on my microwave. Paddy was right, it was nearly dinnertime and it wasn't like my mother to be gone this late in the afternoon. Paddy often ran late from work, dragging himself in after a heater needed fixing on the coldest night in January. Ma would have supper heating on the stove, something warm and nutritious that she'd pour into their best china and serve with homemade bread. My mother was the finest of chefs when it came to staples. She made a mean lamb stew and could whip together shepherd's pie or corned beef faster than Paddy could finish his pint.

I called an hour later, after dusk had settled on our town. Paddy answered the phone, gruff and full of worry.

"Did Ma make it home, Paddy?" I asked him, wasting no time on niceties.

"I can't talk right now, Katherine. You mother's down at the Market Basket. I need to go and pick her up."

Paddy rarely called me Katherine; he had never been very keen on my given name. I could smell his sour mood from here but I couldn't just let him go.

"What's wrong? Doesn't she have the car?"

"Yes. Yes, she does," he said more softly. "But she wants me to come and get her anyway."

"Well, call me later when you get home, okay?" I asked him quickly before he could hang up. "Call and let me know what's going on, Paddy." The phone buzzed dead in my ear. I held it there anyway, hoping Paddy would answer me. Nothing made sense. My mother didn't shop at Market Basket; she'd been a loyal Shaw's Supermarket shopper for thirty years. And if she had the car, why did she need Paddy to drive down there and get her?

I shook my head and called Tommy's wife, Veronica. V was my age, thirty-four. She'd been my roommate before she fell for my brother. Tommy swooped her up in a whirl-wind romance that consisted mostly of Friday and Saturday nights at Billiards 7 or the Palace Bowling Alley. I loved my brother, but he had to be the worst date in central Massachusetts. Fortunately for him, V's existence up until the point she met him was equally as pathetic, and they made the perfect couple. I still shudder to think that he actually proposed to her in rented shoes on New Year's Eve in front of a bevy of his jackass high school friends. What's more shocking is that she said yes.

Veronica had just pulled her van in the carport when she picked up the phone. Her boys were arguing in the back; something about the Red Sox acquisition of Javier Lopez.

"*Shut UP!* Honestly, you two, can you get out of the frigging car before you start in on the goddamn baseball stats again? I can't stand it." V held her hand over her cell phone but it did little to help muffle her frustration level. Mother of the Year, she was not.

I waited for her to come back on the line before I said to her, "V, have you heard from Ma today?"

"God, no, Kacey, I've been running my ass off chasing these two all afternoon. I had a conference with Justin's principal about his crap-ass attitude and then had to drag the two of them off to separate fields on opposite ends of town so Chase could make batting practice and Justin could see the trainer. I'm just getting home now. And"— she paused to unlock the side door—"not for nothing, but I see your brother hasn't bothered to grace us with his presence yet. Nearly eight o'clock and I have no clue about where he is, although I'm fairly sure it has something to do with the bottom of the seventh inning and his friend Jack Daniels."

Veronica and Tommy had veered off track; one going east, the other west. Justin was born three years too early, before they'd drained all the fun from their systems. Chase followed only sixteen months later, putting a further strain on their finances and their lifestyle. Veronica found herself at home alone with the boys more often than not. She grew to resent her husband, her children, and everything about herself. I felt sorry for V; nothing ever seemed right anymore, and there was little I could do but listen.

"I'm sorry, V."

"Hey, it's my life. You'd think I'd be used to it by now."

"I don't mean to cut you off, sweetie, but I'm trying to figure out what's going on with Ma. Paddy just called and she's down at the Market Basket. He had to go down and pick her up. I'm just wondering if you talked to her, or maybe saw her, sometime earlier today."

"The Market Basket? That's all the way across town. What's she doing over there?"

"I couldn't tell you. I have no idea, really. But something's not right, Veronica. Something with Ma really is wrong. I should have listened to Mary Beth when she brought this up two weeks ago. She was all bothered because Ma wanted pancakes for dinner when she and Paddy were over. I laughed her off, but I'm telling you, V, I'm beginning to think that maybe Mary Beth was onto something."

"Don't be ridiculous, Kacey. Mary Beth will find any opportunity to raise a stink about anything. She's probably floated that story out there to every mother in her bridge group. I'm surprised she hasn't ordered a psych evaluation for Ma. Christ, if you believe what she's got to say about things, I'm going to have *your* head examined."

Needless to say, there was no love lost between Mary Beth and V. Mary Beth had an opinion about everything and everyone, and her opinion about Veronica was that she was a fool to stay with Tommy. Tommy drank too much. Tommy ran around too much. Tommy sucked as a father and role model. And most of all, Tommy was a drain on the family business. It wasn't necessarily that Mary Beth was incorrect in her assertions, or that she was pointing out something that Veronica didn't readily know herself. But V certainly didn't need someone—especially someone with such a perfect life, married to the perfect brother—pointing out the obvious. V had as much as told Mary Beth so at the last family gathering (Easter) while Tommy was at home sleeping off a nasty hangover.

"I don't know, V. Paddy didn't sound at all like himself tonight. Something's definitely up. I'm on my way over there now. I want to make sure they get home, you know. I want to make sure she's okay."

"Call me later, Kace. Call and let me know

what's going on. Let me know if you need me, okay?"

I hung up and changed my clothes. I lived only a few miles from my parents' home, the same house we all grew up in, and on spring nights like tonight when the weather was warm, I liked to ride my bike over to their house. It reminded me of 1982. Sixth grade. The year I was permitted to ride on my own for the first time. I went everywhere as if struck by a freedom lightning rod.

The house was dark when I got there; even the porch light was off, and I couldn't recall a night when Ma hadn't left the porch light on. I climbed the front steps and felt around for the handle on the screen door. Behind me the moon illuminated the porch, sending shadows dancing across the worn wood.

Paddy was shuffling around the kitchen in a thin white undershirt and his flannel pajama bottoms. He was barefoot and wore a long shadow, the white prickly ends of his beard poking through his skin. I startled him when I came in and he jumped back, drawing a deep breath. He looked old to me, older than I had noticed in a long while. He was in need of a haircut and the ends of his comb-over stood on end.

"Kacey, you startled me. What are you doing here?" Paddy whispered this to me harshly, as if reprimanding me. I shrank back in his presence, leaning against the doorjamb.

"I came to check on Ma. You didn't call me back and I wanted to see how she was doing. What happened tonight, Paddy? And what was she doing way over at the Market Basket?"

He was making a sandwich, spreading thick layers of bologna and American cheese on white bread. He dipped his knife in the French's mustard bottle and ran it across the top slice. Paddy didn't make eye contact easily; he was often accused of having an entire conversation with someone without ever looking them in the eye.

"Your ma's fine. She just got a little confused is all."

"Confused about what?" I asked. I helped myself to a handful of nuts from the open jar on the countertop.

"Just confused. It's nothing to worry about, Katherine. It's just that sometimes your ma gets a little out of sorts. It just made her feel better for me to come down there and let her follow me home rather than driving on her own."

Again with my formal name. Something was most definitely wrong.

"But I don't understand, Paddy. Ma knows where the Market Basket is. She doesn't shop there very often, hardly ever, actually. But the Market Basket is right over by the Helping Hand. And that's practically her second home." Ma had been volunteering at the Helping Hand for years, sorting through clothes that came in from those eager to clean out their closets and dump their old styles; she was a regular there.

"Like I said, sometimes she just gets confused is all." Paddy walked past me and into the living room. He settled into his favorite chair, a leather recliner that needed to be recovered or replaced, and reached for the remote, signaling that our conversation was over. Paddy wouldn't mind if I stayed; he liked company as long as they were quiet and respectful during prime time.

"Is Ma sleeping?" I asked him.

"She's resting. She's in her room."

I wandered up the back staircase. Paddy and Ma lived in a rambling old Cape

Cod–style house that we'd added onto when I was six. The back staircase came as an addition for us kids so we'd stop tracking mud through the front room.

Ma lay in the bed with her eyes open and unblinking. It took her a minute to focus on me, but when she did, she sat up and said, "Kacey, hi. What are you doing here?"

"Hi, Ma," I answered her and crawled up onto the bed next to her, settling against one of the down pillows. "I just stopped by to check up on you."

Ma laid her head back on the pillow and sighed deeply. She laced her fingers together and placed her hands on her chest where they rose and fell with her breathing. She cleared her throat as if she was trying to remember what had transpired.

"What happened today, Ma?" I asked her, running my fingertips over her forehead and pushing back the graying curls that fell in short wisps around her face. "Paddy said you were over at the Market Basket."

"Well, I just don't know, sweetie. It was the strangest thing, really, just so odd. I started off on my way to Shaw's but then I remembered that I needed spackle for Maureen's room. It's just been in such bad straits since she left, you know. And, well, you know how badly Timothy wants to move into her room. I just think we need to fix up all those holes. Maureen had so many holes in her walls from all those posters. Posters everywhere; it's just not fair to your brother. So I thought maybe I'd spackle up the walls first, and give it a fresh coat of paint. Timothy can move in after I've got it in order. He'll be so thrilled."

Goose bumps ran over my skin, crawling across my arms and down my back like spiders. I stared at her openly, my mouth gaping.

"Ma?"

"Hmmm."

"Ma. Maureen moved out years ago. Timmy never moved into her room. You remember; Tommy took it because Tim said he didn't want to go through all his crap and shuffle it up and down the stairs. Remember, Ma, we spackled and painted the room over the Fourth of July. You remember; it was so bloody hot that weekend."

Her eyes narrowed, confusion creeping across her forehead in worried, wrinkled lines. She sat up on her elbows and looked around the room for a minute, as if she was taking everything in for the first time. My parents' room hadn't been redone in years; it might as well have been 1984, the year my sister had left home for NYU and Tommy had painted the pale pink walls in Maureen's room a solid navy.

"It was a long time ago," I said to her.

She sat back on the pillow and put a hand to her head, covering her eyes.

"You remember, Ma. Maureen graduated in mid-June that year. It poured the day of her graduation and they had to move everything inside. Tommy and Timmy argued for a couple of weeks about her room, but in the end Tim had so much junk that we all figured it would take months for him to get it in order. You and Paddy finally just told Tommy to haul his stuff up there. Remember, we spackled it and painted it all in one day."

She didn't flinch, my mother. She remained as still as she could, fighting the memory until it overcame her, flooding her head to toe and dragging her back into the present. It was as if she was possessed, as if the demon had been chased away again. She heaved a sigh and sobbed, her large frame shaking the wrought iron bed she and Paddy had owned their entire married lives.

"Kacey," she wailed. "Why can't I remember these things?"

"It's okay, Ma, it's okay." I cradled her head and stroked her cheek, wiping away the hot tears.

"I must have given your father such a scare today. I, well, I just couldn't figure out how to get home. *From the Market Basket, Kacey.* I've lived in this town my entire married life and I couldn't figure out how to get home."

I sat with her for a long time, until her breathing finally slowed and an even, deep snore filled the room. Before I left, I dimmed the side light and draped a chenille blanket over my mother. She looked old to me, older than I'd realized. The lines in her face weren't many, but those that were there were deeper and more pronounced, creased around her eyes and at the corners of her mouth. Somehow she looked frightened, even as she lay peacefully unaware of what was going on around her; somehow she seemed to know that something wasn't right, that part of her was slowly beginning to disappear.

*   *   *

In the den, Paddy was sunk low in the worn leather recliner, his bare ghost-white feet propped up in front of him. He greeted me with a low grunt, and put up a finger to signal for me to remain quiet until the segment on *CSI* was over. He muted the set during a commercial before looking up at me.

"She's sleeping," I said to him before he could ask me how Ma was.

"Well, that's good." He turned up the set again.

"Paddy? We need to talk about this."

He waved me off then, his large callused hand pushing me away. He didn't want to talk about it, not then, and not weeks later when the doctors finally said the word Alzheimer's out loud for the first time.

Outside, I caught the very last of the summer light, a streak of gray-orange that ran from one side of the sky to the other as if someone had taken a Magic Marker and ran it across the horizon. The air was light, translucent, and I breathed it in slowly, waiting until I felt my head clear. Then I boarded my bike and pedaled home.

Chapter Two

Labor Day, when Ma started decking the halls, everyone was thrown off.

Michael and Mary Beth had driven over immediately. They stood in the middle of the living room staring at the tree, shaking their heads in unison, struck by the abnormality and absurdity of my mother's actions.

"Something has to be done, Michael. If your father isn't going to do anything, then you need to step in," Mary Beth whispered in harsh tones that could be heard in the kitchen. As with her refusal to call my mother Ma, she had dismissed the idea of calling my father Paddy like everyone else had for years. He was always *your father* or Paul.

Michael was far too emotional to do much of anything. Michael and Ma had always been close. She was his first boy, the gift she had finally presented Paddy.

"Michael?" Mary Beth's incessant whine cut through the bottom floor of the rambling house. "Michael"—she tugged on his shirtsleeve—"are you okay?"

My brother stepped toward the tree, his hand outstretched toward the manufactured branches. His hand brushed a large blue ball, a third-grade masterpiece covered in glitter and stuck with small, colorful crystal beads.

"I made this one. In Mrs. Newsome's third-grade class." He turned and looked at Mary Beth, a blank look on his face. "I can't . . ." He stopped and cleared his throat. "I can't believe she's kept it all these years; all of this. God, it's got to be more than thirty years old."

Two days after Ma had strung the lights and hung a piece of plastic mistletoe over the archway that led into the kitchen, I went to the house and began the tedious chore of removing each ornament, rewrapping every gold and silver ceramic ball. I'd always hated the burden of putting everything away after the holidays, but in the middle of September, the ominous task was even more dismal.

I'd asked Maureen to make the four-hour

drive from Manhattan to Leominster to help me but she was in the middle of a redesign for a client who'd bought a three-bedroom, seven-figure condo on the Upper East Side.

I told Paddy to take Ma out for a long lunch and a movie, a decoy of sorts, while I righted the house again. But nothing about it felt right.

"Paddy won't move her, will he?" Maureen asked, more accusingly than inquisitively, when she called me on my cell phone. "He won't put her in a facility."

"Not yet," I answered, dislodging a candy cane from one of the top branches. "We haven't even considered that possibility yet, Mo. Not really, anyway."

My sister paused, letting dead, flat air fill the space between us. "She isn't going to get better, Kacey. You understand that, don't you? She's going to get worse, not better. All the studies say she'll get more forgetful, more confused. The more confused she gets, the angrier she's going to get. She's not going to be anything like the Ma we know."

"I know what the studies say, Mo. I've been to the doctors with Paddy. I've read the write-ups online. But there's no reason to jump to the next step. We can manage this," I answered her firmly. And then, as if to make my point, I said, "Paddy and I can manage this."

"Well, I'm glad to see that you've come to your senses and are putting the Christmas decorations away. I can't imagine how un-nerving that is."

"We need to keep her as present as pos-sible. That's what the doctors said to us. Remind her of what time of the year it is. Remind her about what year it is."

"It's the right thing to do, Kacey."

"I don't know, Mo. Christmas seems to be the only thing she wants to talk about these days. It makes her so damn happy to think about everyone coming home for the holi-day. It makes her happy to think about *you* coming home for the holiday."

I was packing away the manger, wrapping each delicate ceramic figurine in bubble wrap and placing it gingerly in the large box that I'd hauled down from the attic.

"How do you stand it, Kacey? How is it that you're able to watch over them every day, day in and day out? Especially now? How can you stand to watch her deteriorate like that?" Mo asked me, her voice rising in a high pitch, a cry of sorts.

"How could you walk away? Just up and leave them? How could you leave all of us?"

We'd been having this discussion as long as I could remember, my sister and me. It was pointless by now, diametrically opposing views of the world, of our family. After Mo had moved to Manhattan years ago, she assumed a lifestyle that was mostly foreign to those of us who were still getting together after Mass every Sunday for a late hearty lunch, crowding around the television set to watch the Patriots take on the Jets. I had never gone farther than Holy Cross, in Worchester, a mere 25-mile drive up Interstate 190.

"There was nothing there for me anymore, Kacey."

"We were here, Mo. We were all here."

It took me all day, a combination of pulling things down from the spot my mother had set them year after year and carefully packing each breakable item in tissue or Styrofoam peanut pieces. By the time I was done, I was sweating; beads of perspiration glistening on my top lip.

I missed my sister, the energy she infused

into our family as if we were addicted to her like a drug. With it came controversy, always plenty of controversy, but without her it was like we'd missed the first note in a song and were forced to spend the rest of the time trying to catch up to the beat of the melody. Mo was like Paddy through and through. She shared his quick wit and tenacious drive, his insatiable desire for learning and his ability to charm a roomful of people. While the rest of us borrowed from my mother's robust physique—big bones and pale, ruddy, freckled skin—Mo favored Paddy's tall, slight frame, long legs, and narrow hips. She'd been blessed with his copper-colored curly hair and on Mo, it hung in thick, chunky waves down to the middle of her back.

Although the similarities didn't stop there, it may have been the thing they shared most in common—the inability to compromise on nearly anything—that drove the deepest wedge between them. It had taken me a long time to realize that my sister's biggest fault was her selfishness. That quality alone she did not take from Paddy. In fact, it was a rare thing to find in our family.

By the time Paddy brought Ma home, she

was disoriented and confused, clammy and sticky from the humid afternoon. She went immediately to her room to lie down.

"We should have made her change. She never should have gone out in this heat dressed like that," I said to Paddy accusingly, referencing the thick wool stockings and heavy black velvet party skirt my mother had insisted on wearing. Despite our insistence to the contrary, Ma had thought Paddy was taking her Christmas shopping and then to tea at Copley Plaza, one of her favorite holiday traditions. "Was everyone staring at her? They must have thought she was half . . ." I'd wanted to say *half-crazy,* but I'd held my tongue. Paddy didn't look much like he was in the mood for my full assessment. In fact, he'd left me standing amidst the boxes and bows, bubble wrap and tissue, and walked down the hall. I saw him lift his hands to his face and cover his eyes, rubbing them deeply.

I took Ma a cup of tea made the way I knew she liked it best: mixed with just a splash of whole milk and honey. Despite her large size, she seemed very small on her bed, shrinking against the pillows and disengaged. Her eyes darted quickly around

the room as if she was looking for something, as if she was searching for familiarity.

"Ma," I said sharply to make sure I had her
attention. "I took the decorations down. Remember, it's not time for Christmas just yet.
We can put them back up in a couple of
months when it's a little closer."

Her face was blank, unemotional. Her
mouth was open, as if she might be ready to
say something but she was unsure of what
that might be. She stared at me as if she
was looking right through me.

"Oh, Kacey," she answered me quietly.
"It'll be here before you know it."

Chapter Three

When I was little we spent nearly every Christmas with Ma's family. Paddy didn't so much mind, at least that's what I'd always believed. His parents had passed away at a young age and he had only one brother, a workhorse who'd remained in Dublin when Paddy had come to the states. Paddy went to see him every summer when they'd steal away to Galway to hunt fox for a week together.

Ma had one brother, too, but he'd followed on the heels of seven girls and three miscarriages. Daniel was seventeen years younger than Ma, a miracle in the making, and closer in age to my siblings and me than he was to his own sister.

Christmas at my Granny and Pa's was a series of celebrations, laughter, and confessions and was usually followed by some

sort of drama that lasted at least a year until we all got together the following year. As
far back as I could remember Daniel was
usually the source of consternation. He'd
dropped out of college two months into his
sophomore year, fathered a child out of
wedlock, married a Jamaican woman darker
than a starless night, and had been in and
out of rehab more times than I could count.
He'd far from grown up, still preferring to
pass his summers waiting tables at the
shore and his winters giving ski lessons on
the slopes in Upstate Vermont. Ironically,
the most fiercely independent and driven
member of my immediate family—my sister,
Mo—was most often Daniel's crutch. She'd
hauled him out of a ditch, or a jail cell, more
than once, funding his next stay in some
posh clinic, convinced that she could turn
him around. She was wrong.

When we—Ma's sisters and their families,
Daniel, and my family—were all assembled
at my grandparents' house for the holidays,
we were packed in like new recruits in a bar-
racks. Couples would stake out their rooms,
each sister reclaiming her childhood twin
bed, an equally uncomfortable rented rollaway set up right next to it for her husband.

Ma and Paddy shared a room with Ma's sister and brother-in-law Caroline and Stew, and what nearly always followed the first night in that tiny room together was a discussion about whose snoring had worsened over the year.

No one would have ever considered a hotel.

There was one place and one place only for the children, the next generation, in this equation and that was the basement. Vast and spacious, Ma's parents had bought the house in the early thirties for the basement, a cavern they could count on to send their own brood on snowy Connecticut days when school was cancelled and children were forced to spend the day inside.

The basement, or as it had been renamed, *the club,* spanned two large rooms, a tiny bathroom with merely a toilet and a sink, and a small, secluded bedroom. The large rooms on either side were as distinct in their purpose as my grandparents were. On one side, my Granny's washroom, you'd find the washer and dryer, ironing board, sewing machine, and a wall-to-wall closet filled with relics like the Girl Scout uniform my ma had worn and the sheet music from my Aunt Vi's first piano recital. Granny's side of the basement was papered in fading yellow wallpaper peppered with lilacs. The room smelled perpetually of Tide and Clorox and hints of dried lavender wreaths. Despite the cold tile floor, the room was warm and inviting as if you'd found yourself in my Granny's arms and weren't easily to be let go.

Pa's side was as different as the other side of the world. Dark, thick paneling worked its way about three-quarters of the way up the wall and was met by a strip of checkered plaid wallpaper that bordered the ceiling. Pa's desk, a large, ominous oak rolltop stuffed with papers that dated back forty years, had been placed against the far wall the first year they'd moved into the house and never moved since. His favorite chair, a worn leather wingback with peeling armrests that desperately needed to be replaced, sat in the corner; an aging television set topped one of the bookcases. Whereas light and life danced on my Granny's side of the basement, mystery and intrigue hung on Pa's.

Counting Daniel, who oftentimes would spend his Christmas break in the basement with the generation that followed his, there were nineteen children who took up refuge in the basement. We came with sleeping bags and pillows, favorite blankets and stuffed toys, overflowing backpacks, stories and games, and a sense that this holiday would be like none that had preceded it; a grand expectation considering they had *all* been memorable.

Daniel's soft spot for my ma started at an early age. She might as well have been his ma; surely she'd been old enough to have born him herself. Daniel arrived on the scene the summer before Ma's senior year in high school. Being the eldest in a series of girls that ranged from seventeen to eight, she assumed second-in-command to Granny. Already a whiz at changing diapers and bathing infants, Ma was often the first to Daniel's crib, picking him up and gently rocking him back to sleep predawn in the only boy's room, painted the softest shade of pale blue.

I called Daniel on Halloween, from the closet in my old room at Ma and Paddy's house. Not surprisingly I caught him in a bar, a small Irish pub he liked to frequent in Boston. He was with friends and the swell of merriment made it hard to hear him.

"Daniel?" I asked, practically screaming into the phone. I cupped my hand around the receiver so he could hear me better.

"Yeah. Who is this?"

"It's me, Kacey."

"Kacey?" he asked, laughing. "I didn't recognize your voice. Happy frigging Halloween. Did ya get a little treat in the sack?"

A female voice faded in and out of the receiver, laughing in a high pitch and calling out his name. *"Daniel,"* the voice whined. *"Come dance with me."*

"Is everything all right? What's going on?" I imagined him shrugging off his companion, shaking free of the clutch she had on him. "Where are you?"

"Home, Daniel. I'm at home. At Ma and Paddy's house." I paused then, letting the weight of my heavy voice fall on him. I needed to talk to Daniel. I needed to know what to do next.

"What's wrong, Kacey?" The voices around him dulled, then were silenced altogether as he stepped outside the bar. "I'm here. Tell me what's going on. I can hear you better now."

"It's Ma."

Ma had decorated the house for Christmas again, in a day, no less. When Paddy called to tell me, he said she'd even managed to string the lights over the garage this time, and in order to do that, she'd have had to pull down the ladder and used the staple gun to secure the strands together. I could only imagine what the neighbors must have thought; Ma outside with the heavy steel staple gun in one hand groping her way along the shingles.

It was just past seven when I arrived at their house and trick-or-treaters flooded the neighborhood, ninjas and princesses ducking in between cars and around the light posts. Ma had chosen the white icicle lights and they twinkled against the outline of the eaves. Around the garage, she'd strung a double strand of colored bulbs—solid red, blue, green, and yellow. I stood staring at the house, my hands on my hips.

From behind me, I heard someone whisper, "Never too early to get ready for Christmas, I suppose."

I turned around to glare at the voice. I was angry; hurt and embarrassed and scared by my mother's antics. Immediately I felt the urge to protect her, to ward off the harsh criticism of a stranger.

"She doesn't realize what time of the year it is. And Christmas makes her happy," I snarled at the stranger.

"Kacey? Is that you?" the voice answered.

I looked up, suddenly aware that this might not be an outsider after all, and blushed fiercely. I was grateful that long, dark shadows had crept over the yard, making it difficult to distinguish features. He was tall, as tall as Paddy, and as unfamiliar to me as a stranger in an airport. He held the hand of a little girl—Belle from *Beauty and the Beast*—who I didn't recognize, either. I cocked my head to the side, unknowingly.

"Cooper. Cooper Stewart."

My eyes grew wide and I dropped my arms to my sides, causing my handbag to fall and hang loosely at my wrist. Cooper Stewart.

"Cooper Stewart?" I asked, not because I couldn't recall the summers we'd spent diving from the wooden raft anchored in the middle of Mirror Lake, but because I couldn't believe he was standing here, standing in front of me, my mother's Christmas lights twinkling around us. I hadn't seen Cooper Stewart in years.

"Yeah. Wow, imagine that. All these years and I'm standing in front of the stunningly beautiful, always collected, Kacey Flanigan."

"I think you're thinking of my sister," I countered, shuffling my feet. "Maureen. You must be thinking of her."

"No. I'm sure that I'm not."

"Cooper Stewart," I said again, trying to convince myself and gain my composure at the same time. "And who is this?" I bent to come face-to-face with his companion, a sweet child who was a dead ringer for the costume she'd chosen. Her auburn hair was pulled up tight and had been curled into perfect ringlets, her lips painted cherry red.

"I'm Belle," she exhaled, exasperated by my apparent ignorance of her costume.

"Of course you are," I answered, looking up at Cooper for help.

"Ah, my niece. Olivia Spencer. Also known, at least for tonight, as Belle. I don't suppose you've seen the Beast roaming the streets, have you? He seems to have gotten away from us again." He swung Olivia up on his hip and winked at me.

"No, I'm so sorry that I haven't. I'll keep an eye out for him, though." I whipped my bag up on my shoulder and looked around me, altogether visibly uncomfortable with the lights, too obvious to ignore. I nodded toward the house. "My mom. She's, um, well, she's not herself these days. I'm afraid she's got her dates a bit mixed up." I ran my hands through my hair and sighed. "Cooper Stewart. God, it has been years. What are you doing with yourself? What are you do-ing *here?* The last I'd heard you'd moved to California and were never coming back."

"Never is a very long time, Kacey."

I nodded my head. "Indeed it is."

At his side, Olivia tugged on his arm, pulling him along. "Uncle Coop, we gotta keep moving. C'mon . . ."

"Ah, Halloween beckons. Are you cele-brating?"

"No. Not really, anyway. I've come to check up on my mom. Come on, despite the appearance that we're on the verge of waiting for carolers, I'm sure she'll have a bowl full of candy fit for any princess."

We climbed the front steps together, Olivia leading the charge and storming the porch, ringing the bell wildly. Paddy answered, dressed in faded jeans and a flannel shirt, Ma close by his side.

"Merry Christmas, darling," she greeted a confused princess. "Oh, don't you look just precious. Did Santa bring you that beautiful outfit?"

Paddy reached into the bowl and plucked out two large chocolate bars, dropping them into the girl's pumpkin-shaped bucket. When he spotted me, his face relaxed, if only a little. He looked from me to Cooper and back again, as if trying to figure out who I'd brought with me.

"Hi, Paddy," I said, and pulled the screen door open a little wider.

Ma's eyes grew wide with recognition. "Cooper Stewart," she declared, clear as a church bell. "Heavens, child, what are you doing here? Are you home from UCLA for the holidays? How's your mama? And your daddy, too? I am so looking forward to seeing them at the holiday bazaar and auction next weekend. Your daddy is always so supportive and generous of our efforts."

Cooper stood next to me, temporarily stunned as if he'd been stung by a bee. His mother had died years earlier. His father had long been remarried and moved away.

I shuffled my feet and tried to think of something to say when Cooper took two steps forward, took my mother in his arms and hugged her tightly. When he pulled back from her he held her firmly at the shoulders. "I'm sorry, Mrs. Flanigan, my mother passed on."

"Oh," my mother gasped audibly, and put her hand to her mouth. "No, that's just impossible. Gloria Stewart? I just saw her a few months ago. We had the nicest time at the Autumn Treasures luncheon. I am so sorry, Cooper. And at the holidays, too. Oh, honey, that's just awful." To my father, Ma said, "Paddy, we'll have to send flowers. Something beautiful for the service." She shuffled back into the house then, leaving us all silent on the porch.

"I'm sorry, son," Paddy said to Cooper. "She gets a little confused these days. It's nice to see you." Then he let the screen door close behind him, and drifted back inside.

I stood uncomfortably on the worn wood planks and let silence fall between Cooper and me. It had been more years than I could count since I had seen him. In fact, I couldn't recall the last time. In the light, he looked nearly the same; angular jawline, glassy hazel eyes, a mash of freckles that swam together over the bridge of his nose.

He fell somewhere between Maureen and me; I couldn't remember where. Three years younger than her, two or three older than me. He'd been in the same grade as my twin brothers, a regular fixture in our house after school; but among the two baseball teams full of boys that had drifted in and out of our kitchen, drinking our milk by the gallons, he'd been unmemorable to me.

"I'm sorry, Kacey," he said, quietly.

"Yeah, me, too. It hasn't been easy."

"How long has she been like this?"

"It varies, depending on what you mean by *this*." I shrugged my shoulders. "Forgetful and sort of living in the past for about six months. Living as though every day were Christmas Eve since about September. She's always loved Christmas. So I guess we should be glad that she's in a place in her head that makes her so happy."

"It's sweet, actually."

I looked at him quizzically. "Sweet?"

"Sure. To be locked in the magic of Christmas. There isn't a better time of the year, is there? Really, when you think about it, there's nothing like the few weeks leading up to Christmas, the hum of the holidays approaching. It's one of my favorite times, too."

I had to laugh, which I did out loud. "'Hum' would be an understatement. We've been eating turkey and stuffing, spiced nuts and pie for the last two months."

Cooper stared at me intensely until I felt so self-conscious that I had to clear my throat. I hadn't remembered a time when someone had looked at me that way; surely not the entire time Peter and I had dated. An electric shock took me by surprise, leaving me a bit weak.

Around us, trick-or-treaters streamed into the yard, heading for the porch. Olivia grew tired of waiting and began to whine. "Uncle Coop . . . C'mon . . ."

"Kacey? Can I see you again? I mean, I'm not in town long, only a few days, but it would be nice to catch up again."

I shoved my hands in the back pockets of my jeans. I hadn't even stopped to consider how I must look, dressed in low-slung denim and a khaki corduroy jacket. I was in need of a haircut and, for that matter, an overhaul tip to toe.

"I, um, well . . ."

"C'mon, Kace. I'm betting you could use a break from all of this," he said. "Let me take you to dinner or something." He paused then, waiting, before he said, "Oh, unless, of course, you're seeing someone. God, you're not married, are you?"

I held up my left hand, devoid of any sort of significant jewelry. "Nope."

"Okay, then."

"Okay, then," I answered him, not sure of what I was getting myself into. I scribbled the number to my cell phone on a small piece of paper and handed it to him.

"I'll call you. Tomorrow night okay?"

"Sure. Tomorrow night it is."

Chapter Four

As it turned out, Cooper hadn't remembered much about me, either.

"You were older than me, right? Three years or so? God, between all of your brothers, I can't remember who came where."

"Younger. I'm the youngest. My sister, Maureen is older. She's an interior designer in New York now. She decorates overpriced flats for the super rich and charges them a fortune, which they readily pay."

He raised his eyebrows, impressed. "Really?"

I nodded my head. "She has great taste. And the ability to find the most unique treasures."

"And your brothers?"

"They're all here. Married, with children and working for my dad's business. Michael, that's my oldest brother, he's got two kids that have already been through college. And Sean and Tim and Tom are all married, too. Everyone's here. Everyone but Mo. She's always been a bit of a black sheep. She's got a soul that has to wander."

"And Kacey Flanigan? What's her story?"

I spread my arms wide and shrugged my shoulders. "Not much of one, I'm afraid. I work in publishing, editing manuscripts. It's been a good gig, especially lately because it gives me the flexibility I need to help Paddy with Ma. You know, Mo's got her business; and the boys, well, they're busy keeping the company going, dealing with their kids. It's sort of been Paddy and me on this one."

He nodded his head. "That's very responsible of you, Kacey."

"I don't know that responsibility has much to do with it. I don't see that there's much of a choice in the matter." I reached for a piece of bread and buttered it generously. Despite Mo's insistence to the contrary when I'd called to tell her I'd run into Cooper and he'd asked me to dinner, I'd refused to consider this a *date*. We were simply catching up.

Earlier that afternoon, I'd caught Mo on the phone. "Oh, God, Kacey, I wish I had my yearbook here. I know the name, but I can't put a face to him. Was he one of Sean's friends? Redhead, right?" Mo questioned me on the phone, drilling for details.

"Nah. He's got brown hair. And he was the same year as Tim and Tommy, but I think he knew Sean, too. Frankly, I can hardly remember," I fibbed. After I'd called Daniel on Halloween night, breaking the news to him about Ma, I'd rummaged through an old box in the back of my closet until I came up with my yearbook from my freshman year. There he was, on page 53, standard black tuxedo for his senior portrait, a stern and rather serious look on his face. He was thinner then, and his hair had touched the edges of his tux, leaving him looking very boyish.

Stewart, Cooper: Baseball: V, JV;
Lacrosse: V; Debate, Student Council.
Future plans: Attend UCLA. Motto:
One day at a time.

I'd stared at the photo, remembering the smile he'd had on his face when he asked me to dinner, the electric current that had passed between us. Then I shut the yearbook and filed it away.

"How long has it been since you've been on a date, Kacey? Honestly, you are long overdue," my sister prodded.

"It's not a date, Mo. For God's sake, Cooper Stewart lives three thousand miles away. Next week he'll go back to California and I won't ever hear from him again."

"Kacey, is it physically impossible for you to see promise in anything?"

"What's that supposed to mean?"

"It means that maybe there's some reason you're supposed to go on this date. Maybe, just maybe, Cooper Stewart sees something in you that you can't see in yourself."

"We're just having dinner, Mo."

But it was a date, no question about it. "So, Cooper, what's your story?" I asked him over the bottle of Cabernet he'd ordered. "What are you doing back here, anyway? Contrary to popular belief, it isn't Christmas yet."

He smiled, acknowledging Ma's current state. She'd spent the morning baking him a chocolate Bundt cake topped with peppermint glaze and two dozen Christmas cookies. "My sister, actually. She's going through a nasty divorce and, well, she needed some help settling into her new place. She's got Olivia, but really no other family to speak of. So it was big brother to the rescue."

"That's very responsible of *you,* Coop," I said, teasing him.

He sat quietly for a minute, thoughtful. "Actually, I think it's less about responsibility and more about commitment. I'm all Nicole has, especially now. I tried to get her to come to California after she and her husband split, but she's hell-bent on staying here. I guess she figures this is home."

"I can understand that."

"No desire to leave, Kacey? Even a little bit? I mean, it's the same thing, all the time. Same people, same stores, same predictable traffic lights."

"The traffic lights have never much bothered me, Cooper. Besides, I don't even commute."

"So, about your mom . . ." he started cautiously, lacing his fingers together and resting his elbows on the table between us. "Tell me how it came about. You said you first noticed something last spring?"

"Mmm-hmmm, yeah. It was Mary Beth who noticed it first; that's Michael's wife. She kept insisting something wasn't quite right but we couldn't put our finger on it, not at first, anyway. It was as if she'd drift off a bit, every now and then. She began confusing things, like all of us kids. She'd mix us up constantly, calling me Maureen, or confusing Michael and Sean. Or Sean with his sons. After a while we couldn't ignore it any longer, really. She doesn't get around on her own anymore, and she really can't be left for long periods of time by herself. Paddy takes care of her most of the time, and me, of course. I go most nights now so Paddy can get out and have a break. It's funny, you know where he goes? To the office. He can't get it out of his system. He ran that business for over forty years and he just can't let it go, even though all my brothers are there. You'd think he'd go out with his friends, maybe join a bowling league or see a movie. I wouldn't even blame him if he took a stool down at the pub, but nope. He goes to the office."

"I suppose there's something very cathartic for him there. Otherwise he'd probably do exactly what you're suggesting. But the relationship he has with the business is probably as tight as the one he's had all these years with your mother."

"I hadn't thought about it that way. But, yes, I think you're probably right. God, Ma used to get so angry when he would come home late, having lost time staring at the books or making a late-night customer call for someone when it wasn't an emergency. She used to say he was having an affair with the business."

I shook my head back and forth, thinking about the nights she'd been left to fend for herself, six kids counting on her for dinner, help with their homework, baths. Even when Paddy was home, he hadn't been much help in the child-rearing department, except to lend a severe tone, reminding us of a chore that needed to be done, an expectation that needed to be met.

"I'm glad we got to do this, Kacey," Cooper said to me, pulling me back from the daydream I'd slipped into. He'd raised his glass in a toast and was waiting for me to clink mine alongside his.

"Me, too." And I'd meant it.

Chapter Five

The year I was ten, the snow had started in earnest three days before Christmas, and our normal two-hour drive to my grandparents' house had taken nearly five hours. By the time we'd gotten there, crammed into the wood-paneled station wagon that barely held all of us, never mind the luggage and gifts we had stuffed in every corner of the car, Tim was carsick and Ma and Paddy were barely on speaking terms. Paddy opened the back door of the wagon and we popped out like a jack that had been stuffed in his box for far too long.

Pa poured Paddy a scotch and my Granny forced a potato masher and a pot of boiled potatoes at Ma. The six of us kids slinked down the stairs with our gear in tow, thrilled to be the first on the scene and determined to stake out the best sleeping spot.

Daniel was stretched horizontally on the firm hunter green daybed on Pa's side of the basement watching MTV. He wore torn jeans and a black cable-knit sweater and his hair was parted in the middle and combed back slick against his head. It was 1983 and Daniel had come home for the holidays, hitchhiking his way from Boston where he'd been crashing for the last few months on a friend's couch.

"Daniel!" I cried, and ran to pummel him where he lay on the couch. He scooped me up and pulled on my braids roughly.

"Kacey Kangaroo . . . What kind of trouble you find yourself in lately?"

I shrugged my shoulders and pushed him back onto the couch playfully. "I'm not the one who finds trouble, Daniel."

It was a game we'd been playing for a long while. At ten, I craved Daniel's adoration. He'd never treated me like the last in a line of six, the baby. Daniel had always included me, always found some way for me to feel as if I was as important as my older sister and brothers.

But now he stood and nodded at Maureen. Always tall to begin with, in the last year Maureen had finally grown into her lanky figure. Now her pleated plaid cargo pants and the hot-pink sweatshirt she'd carved up to match that of the dancer in *Flashdance* looked intriguing, inviting.

"Hey, Mo," Daniel said, staring at her in a way that I'd never seen before. "You're looking good."

My sister bowed her head demurely and bit her bottom lip. "Hi, Daniel," she managed before my brothers wildly trampled down the curved flight of narrow stairs, tossing sleeping bags and pillows across the room so they landed haphazardly on the open cots they would claim as their own for the next few nights.

Mo and I ducked into the other side of the basement, Granny's side, where familiarity seeped into my senses. I ran across the room and snagged the bunk I knew was most desirous, a lone single against the back corner of the room. From here you were shielded from a late-night visit from the boys; from here you were the last one to be attacked in a pillow fight that could ensue at any moment.

My sister sauntered across the room slowly, running her fingers through her hair as if she were primping. *Primping!* And in the basement of all places. Sure, Mo had changed this year—her last in high school—and boys and makeup and a permanent use of the phone had all proved to have besieged her senses, but this was the basement. These were her siblings, her cousins, and in Daniel's case, technically her *uncle*.

I looked up to find Daniel standing in the doorway, his hands shoved deep in the pockets of his jeans. "You girls need any help with anything?" he asked when I looked up and caught him watching Mo struggle to drag her oversized makeup bag across the room.

"No, we're fine," I reassured him, bouncing up and down on my rollaway. I had shoved my meagerly packed duffel under the cot with a push of my heel. As far as I was concerned, that constituted unpacking.

Mo folded herself onto her rollaway and tucked her long legs under her like a swan. She leaned on one arm and cocked her head to the side. "The drive down was a complete nightmare," she said to him in an overexaggerated whine. "My mother wouldn't let me drive so we were smashed in that god-awful station wagon like we were sardines."

Daniel nodded at her sympathetically as if

he understood the injustice she'd been forced to endure.

"You only just passed your driving test, Mo," I jumped in with emphasis, and watched her glare at me. "Ma says, 'Pity the people on the freeway when Mo is on it.'"

Daniel broke in and with a grin, announced, "Granny's got me on shoveling duty. She'll be down here yammering at me any minute if I don't go out and clear the six inches that have accumulated in the last hour."

I laughed at the idea of my Granny busting Daniel's chops about the snow, as she was likely to do. But I had kicked my boots off upstairs and in stocking feet was ready for a game of hide-and-seek or, better yet, Pong on the Atari console my brothers had insisted we haul with us. If I was lucky, I wouldn't have to go upstairs again until someone forced us to surface for dinner.

Mo, on the other hand, scrambled off her cot faster than I'd seen her move in a long while. "I'll help you, Daniel. I could use some air," she said to him and scampered into her boots, pulling on her fur-lined down parka.

Years later I'd remember that Christmas

as the last time we went to my Granny's house, the last time I spent the holiday in the basement, hope and wonder creeping in with every minute ticking closer to Christmas morning.

Chapter Six

I hardly recognized Daniel when I opened my apartment door a week after Halloween. He wore a full beard, and from it, poked the first few forlorn gray hairs that made him seem as if he'd fast-forwarded through a few birthdays. Still, he picked me up in the doorway and swung me wildly around and around before dropping me back where I'd started, a wooden spoon in my hand.

I was cooking; the start of a bevy of feel-good, homemade recipes that I'd pilfered from Ma's beat-up cookbook. They were staples of my youth; a perfectly seasoned, hearty meatloaf, baked scalloped potatoes made with heavy cream and Gruyère cheese, Brussels sprouts topped with a glaze so sweet you hardly noticed the vegetable, and an apple pie made with rum and a half pound of butter. Cooper was due for dinner within the hour and I was behind schedule.

I'd hoped Daniel would come; it was the reason I'd called him in the first place. And true to his nature, he'd done so unannounced, without a plan or a schedule or even a phone call to let me know that he'd be arriving.

"Daniel! What are you doing here?"

"Come on, Kacey, you wouldn't have called me if you hadn't wanted me to come."

I smiled at him. There was no fooling Daniel, not ever.

He heaved an oversized backpack into my apartment with a thud and left it sitting in the middle of the room, next to the dining table that I'd set with candles and two place settings. "And by the looks of it, you were expecting me, anyway. What's for dinner?"

I began to object, looking for a plausible excuse, and then stopped abruptly. "I'm cooking for a friend. It's his last night in town."

Daniel made his way into the kitchen and retrieved a beer from the refrigerator. He was lucky, I'd shopped earlier that day and since we'd had both wine and beer over the last few nights when I'd been out with

Cooper, I'd bought both, not really sure which he preferred.

"Guinness?" Daniel asked me with a raised eyebrow. "Since when does my lager-drinking niece drink stout?"

I blushed furiously, a deep red tinge growing up my neck and connecting my freckles in a blotchy pattern the way it was known to do when I was embarrassed. "It's for my dinner date," I answered, looking at my watch nervously. "And he'll be here in less than an hour."

"A date? An honest-to-goodness date?" he ribbed me furiously. "Geez, Kace, we all had you pegged for the life of a single woman after you threw what's-his-name out last year."

I stood my ground, hands on my hips, before I went back to the potatoes, trying to recall where I'd left off on the recipe. Had I added the two tablespoons of flour or hadn't I? "Cooper's just an old friend. He's out here visiting his sister. He used to live in the neighborhood and hang out with Tom and Tim. I ran into him on Halloween."

Daniel grew silent, nursing his beer. He'd hoisted himself up on the kitchen counter and was watching me measure the sour cream to the precise cup. "How's your ma, Kacey?" he asked me, changing the subject, thoughtful all at once.

I looked up from my recipe and wiped my hands clean on the striped dishtowel next to the sink. "It's not good, Daniel. She's not very well at all."

He took a long swig on his beer, finishing it off and opening another. "What do the doctors say?"

I shrugged my shoulders. "Not much, to be honest. There's little that can be done for her. They encourage us to keep her as present as we can, to bring her back when she falls into one of her episodes or when she forgets something that seems so black and white to you and me." I paused, collecting my thoughts. "Last week she couldn't remember where the bathroom was. She and Paddy have lived in that house forty-two years and she couldn't remember where the bathroom was. She was standing in the middle of the kitchen staring off into nothing when I asked her what was wrong. A little puddle had formed under her skirt and when I asked her why she hadn't gone to the bathroom, she said to me, 'Well, I just couldn't for the life of me remember where to go.'"

Daniel hung his head low beneath his shoulder blades. "How often?"

"How often what?"

"How often does she get like this? Where she can't remember or she doesn't know where she is?"

I held open the refrigerator door with my foot and put the milk, butter, sour cream, and cheese back on the shelf. I took out a beer for myself, figuring if Daniel was going to have a few, then I should probably join him. "It's not so much a matter of how often she gets like this anymore, D. It's more like when is she *not* like this."

"Does she still know you, Kacey? When you're there, I mean? Does she know who you are?"

"Sure, yeah, sometimes. And sometimes she confuses me with Mo. Or with Granny. And sometimes she doesn't know me at all. Sometimes it's like I'm not even there."

"It's so damn depressing, Kace. How do you deal with it? How can you possibly deal with it?"

"Well, now you just sound like Maureen. She asks me the same question all the time.

How can I not deal with it? Paddy can't do this alone. We've been trying to get him to put her in a home, you know, somewhere that he can go and visit her but that she gets the kind of care that she needs. And he could have a break."

"Don't suppose there's any way in hell your father is going to do that," Daniel interrupted. "No way he'd let someone else take care of her."

"No," I concurred. "Not on your life."

Cooper was beyond prompt. In the five days since we'd reconnected, he'd made this annoying little habit—his penchant for being exactly on time—as evident as possible. I'd begged Daniel to clean the kitchen for me while I showered and applied a little makeup and when I reemerged from my bedroom, Daniel had Cooper cornered in the kitchen and was on his third beer. Cooper looked helplessly at me and then at the oversized bunch of flowers he'd brought, before he said to me, "Those are for you, Kacey."

"They're beautiful. Thanks," I replied and went in search of the only presentable vase I owned, which dwarfed in comparison to the bunch. I separated half the bunch and set them in the vase, choosing a smaller plastic pitcher for the hydrangea. "Sorry," I mouthed to Cooper from behind Daniel's back. In response, he stared at me intently, following my every move across the small kitchen and back again.

Daniel announced that he would take a shower and then be out for the night. "Is it okay to crash here, Kacey? I can call a friend if you'd rather."

"No, no, it's fine. We'll go see Ma tomorrow if you'd like. She'll really like that, D. She'll be really, really happy to see you. Paddy, too."

"We'll see," was all he answered.

I knew Daniel wouldn't venture to Ma and Paddy's without me. I was trying to remember the last time Daniel had seen my father, the last time they'd been in the same room together, and all I could come up with was Mo's first wedding. She was twenty-two then, just out of NYU, and head over heels for a long-haired, greasy guitar player named Ian who was both a native New Yorker and a Jew. Paddy could hardly stand it.

"Let me get this right, he's your *uncle?*" Cooper asked me, dragging me back from the memory.

"Yeah. My mom's brother. There's seventeen years between them. She was practically out of the house by the time he was born. He was the ring bearer in my parents' wedding and I don't even think he was out of diapers. He's always been closer to us—my brothers and Mo and me—than he has to any of his sisters. Except Ma. He loves her."

"Yeah, you can tell just by listening to the guy."

"I couldn't decide if you'd want beer or wine so I got both," I said to him, checking on the potatoes.

"Hmmm. Seems more like a wine night tonight, doesn't it?"

Cooper helped himself to the bottle of wine I'd chosen and I handed him a corkscrew.

"Your last night in town, Cooper. Tomorrow you'll be back in that condo of yours staring at the Pacific Ocean, barefoot after a walk on the beach." Cooper had told me all about where he lived, Santa Monica. He'd told me about his Lab, a playful chocolate-colored puppy named Fenway, in honor of the park where his beloved Red Sox played. He'd described the smells in the air, so different from New England—leaves being burnt (on the appropriate day of the month)—but smells that signified the start of a new season all the same.

"And you'll be here," he said, handing me a glass filled with deep red wine. I circled it in my hand and backed against the corner of the counter.

"I will, indeed."

He'd grown on me, this old acquaintance who'd materialized out of nowhere. We'd been inseparable the last few days, finding an excuse to spend a least part of an evening together every night. As a decoy, Cooper had even called Tommy, catching him completely out of the blue, and managing an excuse when Tommy invited him to a dinner that Cooper knew I was going to be at.

"I'd have brought you along," I'd told him, "if I knew you'd wanted to go."

"I hadn't wanted it to be awkward for you," he'd answered. "Besides, Tommy was my friend, you know. I should have at least made the effort to see him while I was in town," he lobbied.

It shouldn't really have come as much of a surprise when he kissed me that first time, wedged up against the countertop there in my kitchen, the smells of all my favorite childhood meals percolating around us. But first kisses have a way of doing that, a way of being the nicest little surprise, even when you are, in some way, expecting they might happen at any given moment.

Cooper had a wonderfully unique way of kissing. He had squared me off in the corner and balanced himself with one hand on each of the countertops that I was wedged against so that he could lean his entire body into me. And that's how it felt to be kissed by him, as if the kiss itself came from everything he had in him, straight from the bottom of his toes.

"Kacey," he said when he came up for air, his face and body still very close to mine. "I want you to promise me that you'll come out to California. It doesn't have to be for a while from now, but sometime, okay? Maybe in early spring when everything here is so dreadfully drippy and gray that you can't stand it here anymore. Just say the word, then get on a plane and come out and see me."

I hesitated for no particular reason other than I was still trying to get used to what it felt like to be kissed again. It had been over a year, and even then, the last kisses I'd racked up hadn't been worth chronicling, anyway. This was different.

The last thing I had on my mind was starting a long-distance, never-see-you, sit-at-home-and-pine-after-someone relationship. If I didn't meet a guy who lived here, what was the point? What could come of it? I wasn't going anywhere anytime soon. Not with Ma in the condition she was in and Paddy needing me at home.

I'd already had a talk with myself, just this morning, over this very thing. I wouldn't get attached to Cooper. I wouldn't wish for him when he was gone, or want for him when he called. I wouldn't allow myself that luxury, surely not now, when there were so many other things to be concerned with.

I set my wineglass down on the counter and smiled up at Cooper. At six foot two inches, he towered over me. "Oh, Cooper. I'd like to, I really would. But there's so much going on here. I couldn't possibly make that kind of promise. Not right now, anyway."

"I'll be back to convince you, Kacey. I

booked a ticket this morning. I'll be back for Christmas."

I spied him curiously. "You're coming back?" I asked him and he nodded his head and kissed me again. "At Christmas."

Chapter Seven

I gave Paddy the courtesy of a call first thing in the morning and he told me he'd take the liberty of going to Mass on his own when Daniel and I arrived. Ma wasn't much in shape for Mass anymore and Paddy would arrange for Father Gregory to stop by the house later so that she could take communion.

When Daniel held out his hand, Paddy looked long and hard at it before he finally took it in his own and shook it firmly. Then he took his winter coat, the one he'd had for as long as I could remember, and left the house without saying a word.

Ma was sitting on the couch, propped by three firm pillows. "The Little Drummer Boy" poured out of the old black stereo speakers.

"Hi, Ma," I said to her and placed the thick

ring of keys I carried with me on the coffee table. I bent down to kiss her forehead.

She looked past me at Daniel, who was waiting patiently behind me, unsteady on his feet. Recognition flooded her face immediately. "Danny boy!" she cried out and clasped her hands together. "You've come for Christmas! I knew you'd make it."

I'd warned Daniel about Ma's penchant for holidays, how she had found herself locked in the month of December as if she couldn't get past the Twelve Days of Christmas. He'd listened intently as I described how it had started a few months earlier with the tree and the cooking. My brothers and I had long given up on tearing down the ornaments by now. We preferred to believe that it was better to leave the house decorated, since Ma was so insistent on it. What difference did it make if the nutcrackers were already lining the mantel the first week of November?

"Hi, Moo," Daniel said to my ma, choosing to use the childhood name he'd given her when he couldn't pronounce Maureen. "How're you feeling?"

"I'm fine, sweetheart, just fine. I'm better than that. Only a few days to Christmas now. You know how I love Christmas. Well, we'll all be heading down to Granny and Pa's soon and everyone will be in. Sarah and Katherine and Granny told me that even Ginger is coming home this year. It was so lonesome without her last year, but she'll be there this year. I've just heard from her myself and she'll be there."

"It will be a grand celebration, Moo. It's always such a grand time."

"Oh, Danny, where are my manners. Can I get you some tea? Kacey, see if your Uncle Danny would like some tea. I've had it on the stove all morning."

True to her word, we could smell the spices simmering from where we sat. I rose from the side of the couch where I was perched and left the two of them together, glancing back only briefly to make sure that Daniel was okay on his own.

From behind me, I heard my mother say, "How is school, darling? You know, Maureen is due to graduate this year."

Chapter Eight

In my family, there was no getting around midnight Mass on Christmas Eve. You practically had to be on your deathbed to miss it, which had happened only one year when I was three or four and the basement had to be quarantined with an outbreak of chicken pox. Other than that, and the year my cousin Billy ended up in the emergency room with sixteen stitches in the back of his head after he missed the bunk he was jumping onto, there were few, if any, excuses for missing midnight Mass.

In 1983, the year my sister was prone to helping Daniel shovel snow every few hours as if she'd found a new calling, Mo spiked a fever around six o'clock in the evening, Christmas Eve. She lay lethargically on her cot moaning that her side felt as if it was going to split open and Ma began muttering something about her appendix until Paddy said that her appendix was on the other side and they determined it must be a bad case of the flu. Ironically, the closer the clock crept to midnight, the worse Daniel claimed he felt as well, complaining that the back of his throat felt as if it was on fire. Having just found the both of them whispering about plans for later in the evening, I stood dumbfounded in the foyer, dressed in a purple cord skirt and matching sweater set, wondering why one of the dozen adults couldn't identify the sham I'd so easily put my finger on.

It was easy to see what enticed Maureen into taking the risk to worm her way out of midnight Mass. Daniel had never resembled anything very unclelike. Rather, he'd taken the role of cooler, older big brother, one with a slightly off-kilter view of the world. While the "adults" in our world spoke of Daniel in hushed tones, shaking their heads back and forth as if to dismiss his crazy ideas and bohemian lifestyle, there was something about him that made even them all long for a piece of the freedom that he wore like a badge of honor. Daniel had few cares, little worry, and an entirely optimistic view of the world. And at twenty-one, just four years older than my sister, he was able to get away with it.

I don't know what it was that possessed me to cover for Maureen that night. We'd returned from Mass, cheeks pink from the cold and excitement of what the morning would bring: a sea of gifts so vast and wide it was hard to know where to begin. Ma sent me downstairs to check on my sister and report back, which I did dutifully, informing her that Mo was, in fact, resting comfortably in her bed below. I'd taken it upon myself to line her cot with two pillows and pull the covers up tightly, so that if anyone glanced over, if any of my less sophisticated, less than cool cousins, suspected a thing, their inquisition would easily be quelled knowing Mo had just pulled the covers up over her head to shield any light that might have disturbed her.

I suppose I felt as if by covering for Mo, I was in on their game; as if, in some way, they'd allowed me to play along. Truth be known, my feelings had been hurt and I'd been stung by my first instance of true jealousy, so sharp a pain that it had left me angry at first. Up until this year, I'd been Daniel's favorite, the one with whom he'd spend countless hours playing cards, maneuvering chess pieces so that I could win a game. Up until this year, Maureen had been less interesting, less enjoyable, less everything.

The world was blanketed in a fresh coat of snow, with more coming down in soft drifts. If I stood on my tiptoes on top of one of the bunks, which I did that night, I could see the street from the small-paned windows that bordered the ceiling in the basement and ran flush with the ground outside Granny and Pa's rambling house. I waited for Maureen, checking the snow conditions by the light of the streetlamps, my heart beating harder and faster with every passing minute, every slow toll of the chimes from Pa's towering clock that stood in the hallway outside the door to the basement, bonging every fifteen minutes.

I woke, disoriented, sometime near four, hot from my thermals and the exchange of heavy breathing nine girls put out. Across the room, I could make out the shape on Mo's rollaway, looking the same as when I'd left it hours earlier. I groped my way across the room toward the bathroom, realizing I had to pee something fierce and alarmed that my sister was still not in her proper place. Guilt washed over me in giant waves, fear that something had happened to her and I was to blame for it.

I crossed into the hall that separated Granny and Pa's sides of the basement and stumbled toward the small bathroom and the bedroom that none of us kids ever used, despite the more comfortable double bed, that had been a perfectly acceptable guest-room for guests who had visited my grand-parents throughout the years. Someone was in the room and whoever it was had meant to close the door and unsuccessfully left it ajar.

My sister's laugh, unmistakable in its pitch, floated out in the hall like a flute and filled my ears. Music, louder than it was meant to be played, punctuated the floor-boards beneath my feet, causing them to vi-brate in rhythm with the beat. And the fra-grance of marijuana—something I wouldn't recognize until years later when I smelled it at a concert—mixed with whiskey, sent a pungent odor wafting into the hall.

I stood barefoot in purple- and pink-flow-ered pajamas, my hair spilling loosely around my shoulders, listening to what I could only identify as something that clearly shouldn't have been happening. Not here. Not on this night.

I squeezed my eyes shut. Memories of earlier days flooded my mind. My sister and me hiding and surprising unsuspecting cousins as they ambled their way down the stairs into our hideout; endless games of Twister, checkers, backgammon, Monopoly; notes passed back and forth from the girls' side to the boys' side of the basement; KEEP OUT signs posted on the doors in between the two.

I'd forgotten that I had to pee, the urge disappearing like a shooting star. Something in the back of my mind urged me back to bed and I took a few steps in that general direction before something else seized me; curiosity, I suppose, for all these years later I'm unable to describe it as anything else but just that. *Curiosity killed the cat,* my sister would be famous for saying, years later when I would pry, even slightly into her private matters, shooting me a look that would take me back to that night, that Christmas Eve.

It was shocking that they hadn't woken a soul.

I pushed open the door, lightly at first, until the old rusted hinges gave way and it creaked, causing everyone and everything within sight to stop abruptly. Only the music played on, Prince's "Little Red Corvette," from a small boom box I suppose Daniel had toted home with him.

My sister straddled the lap of a boy I did not recognize and wouldn't ever lay eyes on again. Her short jeans skirt had been pushed up around her waist and she was without her shirt. In the room dimly lit only by the moon that shone through the small windows behind her, her dark nipples lay flat like quarters against her full, round white breasts. The boy, a scrawny, long-haired blond kid with pimples that ran across his bare chest, encircled my sister's waist with his hands, helping her to gyrate over him up and down. Until the minute when the hinges creaked and gave me away, I don't remember having seen Mo quite as happy as she appeared to be at that very moment. Her face relaxed, her head bent back so that her back arched toward the boy, she wore an almost angelic look on her face.

Not far from where my sister and her Christmas companion sat, Daniel lay spread across the bed, nursing the head of a woman who appeared to be sucking him hard like a lollipop. She, too, was naked, and her bare ass pointed skyward as she worked over him. I knew only her first name, and only because when Daniel opened his eyes and spotted me standing in awe, my eyes as big as marbles, my mouth hung open as if I was trying to catch flies, his deep voice rang out, "Goddammit, Shelly, get off of me, we've got company."

It was Maureen who made it to the door first, dislodging herself from the boy and yanking her skirt down in one fell swoop. She held one hand over her chest to cover herself and with the other, pushed the door shut in a single thwack that echoed throughout the bottom floor. Before I knew it, I was staring at the paneled door, images of what I'd just taken in floating before me.

I scrambled up the stairs as fast as I could, taking them two at a time, and slipping on the last two when I had neared the top. My Granny and Pa's bedroom was on the first floor, just down from the basement door, but their door was closed shut and from the other side, Pa's deep, heavy snore reverberated in the hallway. They were both dead to the world.

I flew up the second stairs and through the door that led to Ma's room, bursting forth with such ferocity that Uncle Stew sat upright on his cot, his bald head glistening in the moonlight. Paddy rolled over drowsily, then alarmed, his socked feet hit the floor and he reached for his robe.

"What is it, Roo?" he asked me, using the nickname that Daniel had given me, a match to the one he used for my mother.

I shouldn't have come, of that I was certain. I knew it the minute he sat up and looked at me that I should have crossed the hall back from the bathroom, from the guest bedroom that had been so infrequently used, and pulled the covers up tight over my head. But there was no going back now, no easy way out. Below us, footsteps, the distinct *clip-clop* of high heels crossing the wood floor.

My father rose from his rollaway and pulled his robe tight, cinching it at the waist.

"Who's down there, Kacey?" he asked me. I couldn't move, couldn't speak to let him know what I'd found, or to reassure him that it was nothing. I was frozen in place, unmoving only until he brushed past me and clomped his way down the stairs.

In the morning, even before light began to creep its way across the afghan of white that had been laid in my grandparents' front yard, my father had gone outside to begin the arduous task of shoveling out after a night of constant snowfall. Ma crept her way down the curved stairs that led to the basement. Her back was rigid and she held firmly to the railing so that she wouldn't lose her footing and fall.

"Pack your duffels," she said firmly to my brothers and me, her mouth a thin, creased line. To Mo, she simply said, "You, too."

We left before the first gift had been opened; even before some of my cousins had roused sleepily and ascended to see what had materialized under the tree. Mo wouldn't speak to me; she wouldn't even look my way. The storm was far from blowing over; it had only just started.

But Daniel pulled me aside, just before I lugged my bag back up the stairs, and hugged me tightly, his muscular arms wrapping around me. I was stiff against his chest, wary of his actions, and unsure of what possessed him to ruin what we'd had.

"It's okay, Roo. I know you didn't mean any harm."

"Me?" I choked out, trying unsuccessfully to hold back the tears. "What did I do? I didn't do anything."

"No, I suppose not. But someday you'll think back on this Christmas fondly. You'll see; they all have their own special bit of magic. Someday."

After every Christmas comes the New Year, full of promise, ready to be opened like one last gift you'd missed under the tree. The year we left my grandparents' house at dawn, the thing I remember most about the New Year was how much of the past it pulled along with it.

Our house was quiet; quieter than it had ever been. Paddy had stopped talking to nearly everyone, unable to verbalize what it was he'd lost the night he sailed past me and down the stairs to find my sister half-clothed and stoned, Daniel trying his best to shake her so that her head might clear and she'd somehow magically appear coherent again.

It was a long time before Maureen forgave

me, if, that is, she ever did. I'd never really known. The following June she turned down a full scholarship to Notre Dame, opting instead to tally up a heap of student loans at NYU. We got a letter from her—a LETTER, no less—in mid-November. She was staying in New York for Thanksgiving and wouldn't be home for Christmas, either. My sister had gone. And it'd be a long time before she came back.

Chapter Nine

After his first trip to see Ma, Daniel's visits became more and more regular, even frequent. It was as if Daniel realized that Ma's time was slipping away and he was willing to try nearly anything to ensure he could squeeze as much out of whatever she had left.

Sometimes I'd open my apartment door and Daniel would be standing in the long hallway, a bag of groceries and a six-pack of beer in his arms. Other days I'd stop by my parents' house in the afternoon and find him sitting with Ma, holding her hand and talking with her quietly, unfailingly patient when she would drift off.

The days ticked by and crept closer to the holidays. Around me, the world changed, autumn slowly giving way to winter. Frost settled on the wide expanse of lawn that

bordered my apartment complex; and be-
grudgingly I dragged my wool sweaters and
boots out of the plastic bags and boxes
where they'd been stored. When it was too
cold or too icy to ride my bike anymore, I'd
warm up my clunker of a car—an old Volkswagen Beetle—and drive it, sputtering in
fits and starts, over to Ma and Paddy's
house.

Ma's Christmas decorations had become
so commonplace that no one really men-
tioned them anymore. They remained where
she had set them, nutcrackers with round,
frozen painted cherry cheeks; glass angels
with hollow, clear eyes. I hardly noticed
them when I went to visit; they'd completely
lost their charm.

The year after Mo had shamed my family
into packing the station wagon and heading
home Christmas morning, we stayed home
for the holiday. No Granny and Pa, no
cousins, no Daniel, and no magical basement. The feeling was so odd, so out of
place, that none of us knew what to make of
it. Mo had refused to come home, taking
refuge instead at the Colorado ski lodge of
a wealthy NYU coed she'd met in her first
semester.

Paddy grieved his way through the holiday, exuding all the classic emotions as if someone had died. He denied anything was amiss; he was angry. He begged Mo to come home, then he moped around the house when she refused. Finally, as if he had no other choice, and just before Christmas present turned into Christmas past, he solemnly accepted his fate.

But somehow this year I'd convinced Mo to come for Christmas. She arrived on the scene Christmas Eve morning, bringing with her the first snow of the season, which blanketed our town in a thin sheet, barely enough to coat the streets. I was elbow-deep in the first of two turkeys we'd be cooking the next morning, pulling out the neck and giblets and wondering how Ma ever managed to cook for all of us, when Mo burst into the kitchen in a fit of angst over the town car that was supposed to have picked her up and hadn't. Someone on the other end of the phone, most likely Mo's devoted assistant, Priscilla, was getting her ass chewed out over this one.

My sister had cut her hair; a lightly layered, chin-length style that set off her features and left her looking more angular than ever. Not surprisingly, she was overdressed, fashionable in black slacks and a still-crisp white shirt even though she'd been in it since before dawn. Over this, she wore a black Marc Jacobs cropped cashmere coat.

"God, Kacey, why didn't you just have me *order* the dinner?" she exclaimed when she saw me. "That carcass is practically nauseating." She clicked her phone shut with a clap and air-kissed my cheek.

"Why didn't you just let me pick you up, Mo? I'd have come to the airport," I answered her.

Mo waved me off, dismissing me instantly. She stopped in the middle of the kitchen and turned slowly, taking in everything around her. From the ceiling, Ma had hung pretty silver stars from fishing wire. They turned slowly and bounced off the reflective light in the kitchen. The stars had been one of our favorite decorations as children. I'd always thought they brought just the right sparkle to a dull room, but Ma told us they reminded her of the clear, starry night on which Jesus had been born. In the center of the room hung the large North Star, the biggest and brightest, the one that had always been placed above Mo's chair, her place at the breakfast table. For years, Ma had been saying to me, "Perhaps this year the star will help your sister find her way home."

Now Mo stood in the middle of the room, her fingertips reaching to brush the worn foil that covered the five points. "She's really done it, hasn't she?"

"Hmmm?" I answered her, blankly, trying to reconstruct Ma's family recipe for stuffing. The worn three-by-five card on which the ingredients had been written was yellowed and stained from years of being handled by one too many people.

"All this, this . . . God, Kacey, it's worse than I thought."

I glanced at her briefly. "It's been up for months, Mo. I hardly even notice any of it anymore. I'll admit it was more than a little disconcerting in the middle of September. But now? At least it's the right time of year." Outside, the snow was falling lightly, tiny flakes drifting in soft waves before they hit the ground and disappeared.

Mo removed her coat and sighed deeply. She looked visibly uncomfortable.

I wanted to cross the room and hug my sister, pulling her close to me so that I could feel every piece of her bony body against mine. I wanted to hold her at arm's length so I could study her face, memorizing every feature all over again. I wanted to pour us steaming cups of hot cocoa and top them with tiny marshmallows and thick whipping cream and settle into the two stiff armchairs in the living room, trading secrets. I wanted to know everything about her all over again, all of the intimate details I'd long forgotten plus all the new things that made her who she was today.

"She's having a good week," I said to my sister. "She's happier than she's been, and much less confused. You picked a good time to come home; she's beside herself with excitement that you're here. Go on," I encouraged her. "Go on and find her. She's upstairs folding the linens for Christmas dinner."

When she left the room, I felt the need to set things in the kitchen in order. I righted the two turkeys, each in their own roasting pan and covered them with foil, leaving them to sit on top of the stove. Then I replaced every ingredient I'd pulled from the icebox, stacking them on the refrigerator shelves neatly. With a clean dishtowel and a

can of disinfectant, I scrubbed the countertops and fixtures, polishing them until they
shone.

Ma would want tea, and if I brought hot
cups with some of the biscuits that she
liked, I figured I might be able to keep Mo
and her together in one room for more than
the five minutes that my sister would be
willing to give her. Mo was likely to grow im-
patient, uneasy with the way Ma's speech
had slowed or how she sometimes stopped
midsentence, to take in everything around
her.

I climbed the stairs with a tray in hand,
stacked with the good china, silver, sugar,
and creamer, and a plate of tiny cookies. In
Ma's room, my sister sat at the end of the
bed, her knees pulled up and tucked under
her chin. She was watching Ma intently,
hanging on her every word as if she couldn't
get enough.

Ma had stacked a dozen or so red-and-
green-plaid napkins on the side table. I'd
pressed them earlier, not trusting Ma with
an iron any longer, and she had folded then
neatly, precisely in the way she had always
taken to her chores.

"Kacey, would you look at what the cat dragged in?" she asked me, and grinned.

"I know, Ma," I said, setting down the tray on the firm mattress. "It's great, isn't it? Can you believe that Mo's finally come home?" I smiled at my sister to insist that I meant no harm by my comment, but she didn't seem to notice. Mo's eyes had drifted to the window. She stared out at the acreage that bordered my parents' home, the barren trees that ran flush to the gray sky.

"We've got so much to do to get ready. The cooking, of course. We must get to the cooking."

"Everything's under control, Ma. I've been cooking all morning. There's nothing you need to worry about."

"The pies, Kacey? Have you done the pies?"

"Veronica's bringing the pies; she ordered them from Shaw's. You don't need to worry about the pies."

"Store-bought?"

"It'll be fine, Ma. We've had Shaw's pies before. Shaw's makes a good pie, Ma. Great, really. It'll be fine." I went to her side and rubbed her back. Since Ma's diagnosis she had a tendency to repeat herself over and over again until it nearly consumed her. Now I knew the signs to look for, the way Ma's face grew wide with awe, the wrinkles in her forehead becoming deep creases. I ran my fingertips along her spine, reassuring her.

"I just think it would be nice to have a homemade pie."

"I know, Ma."

"I'll make you a pie, Ma," Mo said quietly, but defiantly. "What do you want? Pumpkin? I'll make you a pumpkin pie."

I stared at Mo with my lips pressed together in a thin, disapproving line. She wasn't helping, not at all. Ma didn't need a pie. She didn't need to worry about whether she wanted pumpkin or apple or mince, for God's sake.

"It's okay, Mo," I answered her firmly. "V's bringing pumpkin. Apple, too," I threw in before she could change her mind.

"It's no problem, Kacey. What else am I going to do? I can make a pie if that's what Ma wants."

"We don't need any more pie. We really don't. We have enough pie. We have enough breads and stuffing and green bean casserole. We've got Jell-O salad and a green salad and two kinds of potatoes. Mary Beth's bringing the squash casserole with brown sugar and cornflakes and marshmallows." I tried to keep my voice calm but I was unsuccessful. It was really downright futile.

"Okay, Kacey," my sister egged me on, sarcasm seeping into her voice. "If you don't want a pie, what is it that you need?" Mo poured two steaming cups of tea and left them on the tray. She went to Ma's side and took her by the elbow, encouraging her to take a seat in the worn armchair in the corner. Ma settled against the cushions and took the saucer from my sister.

"Have you made the pies, Kacey? Should we start them now?"

Ma's question stopped Mo dead in her tracks. She sat on the edge of the bed, staring. "We were just talking about it, Ma," she said, quietly, unsure what to make of my mother's request.

I was hardly rattled. Ma's episodes came on that quick, and left you feeling that strange. I knew how my sister felt; the first time Ma had said something similar to me, I'd felt as if I was the crazy one. But I hardly felt obligated to rescue Mo. Not when she'd come in so presumptuous, as if she knew what was what.

"No, Ma. I just told you. Veronica is bringing the pies. She ordered them from Shaw's."

"Oh, yes, you did say that, didn't you?" my mother answered me quietly, as if she knew she'd said something to startle the room, but hardly knew what it was.

"She'll bring them in the morning. They'll be great."

I took Ma's teacup from her and set it on the tray, offering her one of the biscuits. She took it eagerly and nibbled on the end, watching the snow fall outside the window.

Mo worked her way next to my mother, settling in against her side and drawing her arm around her shoulders. "It's Christmas, Ma. You love Christmas."

My mother smiled shyly, a little half-grin that lighted up her face like a child. "Oh, sugar bean, you're right. I do love Christmas. All the hustle and bustle. Everyone getting together. Kacey?"

"Yeah, Ma?" I answered her.

"Did you ask your father what time he wants to leave?"

"For where, Ma?"

"For Granny and Pa's?"

"We're not going to Granny and Pa's, Ma. Not this Christmas," I answered her without missing a beat.

Mo closed her eyes, defeated.

"Remember, Ma. Everyone's coming here this Christmas. Mo came home from New York. And the boys will all be here, too. Michael and Mary Beth, and Tommy and Veronica. Sean and Stephanie, and Timmy and Betsy. And all the kids will be here, too. It's going to be a wonderful Christmas, Ma." I went to stand in front of her and my sister, pulling them both to me in a tight bear hug. "Just wonderful."

"Kacey," she said again. "When will we make the pies?"

Chapter Ten

Mo clutched her coat closed and exhaled the cigarette smoke into the cold afternoon air. Her cheeks were pink and they stood out against her monochromatic wardrobe; it was the only color she wore besides the deep, burnt-red lipstick that she'd reapplied carefully. She was standing on the front porch, her cell phone permanently stuck to her right ear, and from the front room I could hear her barking orders to New York. My sister was relentless, even on Christmas Eve.

Paddy anchored the Cadillac in the driveway, taking his time to gather his things before he lumbered out of the car and shut the door firmly behind him. He trudged up the driveway, two brown paper grocery bags in his arms.

My sister paced the length of the front

porch, back and forth, careful not to make eye contact with Paddy until he was on the top step. Then she stopped and glanced up at him, smiling curtly and motioning that she was on the phone, just in case he missed it.

Paddy stood on the porch waiting for Maureen. My father looked older to me, vulnerable and defenseless. He looked uncomfortable, even as he entered his own home, waiting for his eldest daughter to acknowledge his presence with more than just a nod.

Mo carried on. Her voice was audible even from inside the warm house. I watched her turn her back on my father and pace the worn wooden planks until she came flush with the end of the railing. She stopped there and leaned over, no intention of ending her conversation anytime soon. Paddy dropped his head between his shoulder blades and shook it slowly, resolved that nothing would be different, not this time, not this trip, than any other time he and Maureen had spent time in the house together.

I greeted Paddy at the door and relieved him of the bags he was carrying, unburdening him of the load.

"How's your ma?" he asked me.

"Not too bad." I nodded. All things considered, Ma had had a decent day. Lately,
Paddy and I had devolved into short de-
scriptions for each other. *Good day. Not so
bad. Not all that great.* It had become our
way of giving the other person a heads-up
for what they were in for. I was happy to report that Ma had been up and around, current, calm, and pleasant to deal with. On
days when things weren't so optimistic, I'd
hardly be able to look Paddy in the eye before I'd mutter, "Not so great today, Paddy.
She's pretty confused." Or frustrated. Or
angry. Or just downright checked out. Those
were some of the worst days of all; when
Ma's disease robbed her of every personality trait that made her who she was, and
she'd sit on the chaise, forlorn and lost,
staring across the room as if she was looking at nothing in particular.

I was grateful for Ma's good days, especially thankful that she had been able to
string two or three of them together this
week. I'd been praying nearly every minute
of the day that it would last through the
weekend, so we could enjoy Christmas Day
together without everyone fussing over her,

jockeying for a position of importance in the caretaking of my mother.

Paddy and I had decided to keep Christmas to just immediate family, determined that this would be the least overwhelming for Ma. Even so, my immediate family—the wives and children that accompanied my brothers, along with Mo and me—totaled twenty-three people. It would be a houseful. With my family it was always a houseful.

Even though Ma had changed the linens on Mo's old twin bed, my sister insisted she stay with me at my apartment. I knew this had nothing to do with me. Clearly the time away from Ma and Paddy was part of her salvation. And, quite honestly, although Mo hadn't dealt with Ma for even a smidge of the time I had, I couldn't blame her. We fed them dinner, a pot roast with roasted carrots and potatoes that Mo refused to eat, and then tucked them into their chairs in front of the television. "I'll see you tomorrow, Ma. For Christmas," I whispered in her ear and draped her favorite afghan over her lap.

In the car, Mo settled into the passenger seat next to me and leaned her head back against the headrest, sighing. "It's so damn depressing," she said to me.

I started the engine but was quiet. I drove back and forth between my apartment and my childhood home so often that I practically expected the car to know the way. We pulled out of the driveway and headed east on Walnut Street, past the homes of families Mo and I had known our entire lives. Some of them were gone now, their children grown and moved on to other cities, the parents choosing to retreat to the sunny, warm beaches in Florida. Their houses stood out from the rest, overtaken by a new crop of newly married couples or families with young children, renovation projects under way.

Mo stared out the window at the neighborhoods, the STOP signs and streetlights that we passed along the way. It was more than familiar to me; it was my home. But for Mo, who hadn't been here in more than a year, and before that even longer, it was like falling into a time warp. The more Leominster changed, and the change was slow in coming, the more it stayed the same.

Houses glittered, cheerful and dressed up for the holiday. An oversized snowman waved from one front lawn, a plastic Santa led eight reindeer, rocking against the wind, from another.

"She seems okay, doesn't she?" Mo asked anxiously, looking for me to reassure her. "I mean, she slipped up here and there, but for the most part, she seemed pretty good."

"Today was a good day, Mo. She was in good spirits today," I replied, rubbing my eyes. "She's excited about Christmas. It's been a long time in coming."

"And tomorrow, Kacey? How will she be tomorrow?"

"You just never know. That's the problem. You just never know what tomorrow is going to look like." Short of detailing for Mo the drastic changes Ma was apt to take on, there was no way she'd understand it other than to experience it herself, as she had today, in small doses.

At the apartment, when I struggled to open the door with my key, Daniel pulled it open from the other side, greeting us with a wide smile. He was dressed in jeans and an oxford, barefoot and at home. I'd finally broken down and given him a key; he came and went as he pleased now, popping in and out to spend time with Ma when he could make it. I hadn't expected him this weekend, though, and, standing there in front of me, I wasn't altogether sure I was so happy he was here. The holiday had set me on edge; everything carefully planned to the last detail. The last thing I needed now was a landmine.

Mo, on the other hand, was ecstatic and squealed when she saw him, practically jumping into his arms. In turn, he picked her up and swung her around until they both fell dizzily into the room, unsteady on their feet.

"What are you doing here?" she cried out, reaching up to tousle his hair.

"Waiting for you, love bug. All my life I've been waiting for you."

"Right," she retorted, laughing. "Hardly. Seriously, Daniel, what in the world are you doing here? When did you get here? Kacey, did you know he was coming?" She eyed me accusingly.

I shook my head. Truth was I hadn't told Mo that Daniel had started visiting Ma on a frequent basis; that he would show up at will every few days to check on her. First off, I hadn't wanted to face the barrage of questions I knew would come from my sister. Second, I didn't want Daniel's visits to be an impetus for Mo's arrival on the scene. But even more, I guess I hadn't wanted to share Daniel with my sister, not this time. I liked the fact that lately I'd arrive home, only to find the television on and Daniel showering in my bathroom, or that I'd have someone to talk through what a bad day Ma had had, how her mood had shifted so drastically south. Having Daniel around was better than talking with one of my brothers. Having Daniel around was better than talking with Mo.

Daniel sensed the critical tone in my sister's voice and recovered quickly. "Kacey didn't know I was coming, Mo-deen," he answered on my behalf, and Mo laughed at the childhood name he'd used for her.

"Well, what are you doing here? When did you get in?" Mo pushed her bags aside and tugged on Daniel's arm, dragging him to sit beside her on the couch.

"You know me, Mo. I come and go." Daniel shrugged his shoulders. "But where else would I go for Christmas? It's Christmas, Mo!" He reached over and tickled my sister until she laughed, kicking up her feet and giggling uncontrollably.

It was as if they were teenagers all over again. No one could make my sister laugh like Daniel. And it had been a long, long time since I'd seen her like this. Goofy and giggly and silly. Mo simply didn't lose her composure like this; not anymore.

"You mean you're going to come with us tomorrow? To Ma and Paddy's?" Mo eyes were wide with surprise, of course they would be. She didn't know that Daniel had spent the last two months visiting our mother, comforting her and tracing the days with her, easygoing and even-tempered with her mood swings. Mo hadn't known that Daniel had seen some of Ma's worst days; that he had been there to help Paddy carry my mother up the stairs and place her gently on the bed, reassuring her that everything would be okay. Mo didn't realize that, in doing so, Daniel had begun to repair the damage between him and Paddy, wreckage caused so long ago. Mo took a deep breath and sighed, "You better know what you're in for."

I thought about the first time, a few weeks ago, that I'd seen Daniel extend his hand to Paddy. And how Paddy had taken it, tenuously at first and then warmly. Then I remembered the look on Paddy's face, standing on the porch earlier this afternoon, when Mo had completely disregarded him.

"Yeah, sure," Daniel answered her. He got up and crossed the room, opening the refrigerator and looking for something to eat or drink. He came up empty-handed, turning to face both of us.

Mo was quick to decipher the situation. She looked from me to Daniel and back again, studying our faces intently. "You've already seen her, haven't you? You've seen her recently."

Daniel leaned against the kitchen counter and crossed his arms over his chest. He shrugged his shoulders. "Yeah, sure, Mo. I've been down now and then. It's been okay, you know. It's been good, actually."

"Oh," Mo answered, stunned. She folded her hands in her lap, studying them. "I didn't realize."

"Daniel's been visiting Ma," I said, trying to fill in the dead space, searching for the right words. "He's been helping me and Paddy now and again." I crossed the room and went to sit on the couch opposite my sister. I felt immensely guilty, as if I had betrayed her, cheating on her simply by omission of details. I should have told her.

"Well?" Daniel asked Mo. "What'd you think? Of your ma, that is?"

Mo was quick to recover, never one to let any emotion show. "She's not gonna get any better," she said defensively, as if she could push off the anger she felt onto Ma's condition. "She should be in a center; I've said that all along. She should be somewhere where people can take care of her. You know, people who understand what's going on in her head and can help her." She'd made her point, but just to reiterate how she really felt, she said, *Real people who know how to help her.*"

After that, my sister proclaimed she was exhausted and needed sleep. I'd set out a towel and washcloth for her, anticipating that she wouldn't stay under Paddy's roof and that she was going to end up at my apartment, as she had. She rose from the couch and pulled her suitcase behind her, blowing us an air kiss from across the room. I watched as she disappeared around the corner into my bedroom, closing the door behind her.

"You didn't tell her?" Daniel asked me immediately, turning to study my face.

"No."

"Why not, Kacey? You knew she was coming down. You knew she should know."

"I didn't expect you'd be here, Daniel. And explaining to Mo that you'd come home to help us with Ma, after all these years, well, it just doesn't work its way easily into a phone conversation. Especially not one with Mo. You know that."

"Even still, Roo. You should have told her." He ran his hands through his hair, long waves of auburn curls that brushed the top of his collar.

"You could have told her yourself," I fired back. I was tired of being the glue that held everyone and everything together. These were adults for Christ's sake. I got up and pulled a cotton blanket from the oversized basket in the corner of the room. I threw this and two small square pillows at him. Then I turned and left the room, adding "Merry Christmas" as I walked out.

Chapter Eleven

In my room, Mo had left the small table lamp burning. She lay on her side with her back to me, the duvet and sheet pulled up tightly to her chin. She said nothing, but I knew she wasn't sleeping. Her breathing was shallow, her shoulders were rigid.

"Mo?" I whispered. "C'mon, I know you're not asleep."

She didn't move. She never even flinched. I stripped naked and pulled on an old set of pajamas, crawling in bed next to her. "Mo. C'mon, you can't stay mad at me." I reached out and touched her shoulder blade, hopeful that she might turn toward me so we could talk. I would apologize to her, explain that it wasn't that I didn't want her to know that Daniel had been down, but just that I hadn't exactly gotten around to telling her.

"You can't stay angry at me, Mo. It's

Christmas. It's been so long since we've spent Christmas together."

"How could you keep that from me, Kacey? Why didn't you tell me?" She kept her back to me, refusing to turn around. Her voice came out in harsh whispers as if she was afraid Daniel might be able to hear us from the other room.

"I didn't keep it from you. I just hadn't exactly gotten around to filling you in."

Mo rolled over and looked at me, squinting against the light. "Right."

It was easy to understand why Mo's feelings were hurt. Daniel was the one person she counted on Paddy holding a grudge with worse than the one he held with her. If our uncle and father had found a way to patch things up, where did that leave Mo?

I took a deep breath and sighed. "Okay, all right. I'm sorry. I should have told you. The thing is that Daniel's been so amazingly helpful. I don't know how I could have gotten through the last few weeks without him. And Ma really likes having him here. He's been really great for her. He is patient and kind and he seems to arrive on scene exactly when Paddy and I need him to rescue the both of us."

Mo scoffed and shook her head. "I can't believe it. I just can't believe it. Paddy and Daniel. After all this time, you mean to tell me that he and Paddy have found a way to put all . . . all *that* behind them? Not a day goes by that Paddy won't forgive me, but after a couple of weeks Daniel has managed to win him back? God, Kacey, do you realize how that makes me feel? Do you have any idea in the world how that makes me feel?"

I swallowed down the large lump that had grown in my throat. It wasn't my fault, not really. Mo hadn't even tried to make amends with Paddy. And if my sister had a beef with the way Daniel had wormed his way back into Paddy's good graces, she should take it up with him, not me. I wanted to tell her so, too. I wanted to unleash the resentment I felt, exhaustion from months of dealing with Ma virtually on my own. Daniel had come along at exactly the right time. He'd made the effort, filling in the gaps when we needed someone to do so. Where had Mo been? What had prevented her from making the four-hour drive from New York? Hell, she could have hopped a commuter flight and been here in an afternoon.

In my apartment, nothing twinkled. There was no Christmas tree, no decorations, not even a pile of gifts. I'd had no time to shop for anyone, no desire to do so, either. Mo had arrived with bundles of professionally wrapped gifts, treasures she'd probably had Priscilla pick up on her lunch hour. She'd come with beautiful matching outfits and ideas about what should be on the menu for Christmas dinner. She'd come in a flurry of activity and drama that swirled around her no matter where she went, and left her little time to see what was really right in front of her.

"You could try, Mo. You could really try with Paddy. You know, more than just a passing glance or a nod or a ten-minute conversation. He'd give you a chance. Paddy's always wanted to give you another chance."

"I hardly think so, Kacey."

I lay down next to her, curling my hands under the pillow. I was tired and I desperately needed sleep, but this was Mo. This was more time than I'd had with my sister in more years than I could remember. She was closer at this very minute than she had been in a long, long time.

As children we'd been the best of friends,

despite the years between us. Mo had been my keeper, the person who protected me from the relentless teasing our brothers had bestowed on me in giant heaps. The year she left and never returned had rocked my world. I was ten, gawky and clumsy and un-sophisticated. I'd driven her away, not on purpose, of course. But I'd always felt as if I'd set off a tidal wave that took on a life of its own and tumbled upon the shore, leav-ing devastation in its wake.

"I'm sorry, Mo," I said to her, quietly. "I hadn't meant to hurt you."

My sister settled her freshly washed face on the pillow next to mine. She smelled of Noxzema and an expensive moisturizer that I didn't recognize. Mo was classically beau-tiful; the kind of woman that made men lose sight of themselves.

She grasped my hand and pulled it toward her lips, brushing my knuckles lightly with a kiss, and holding it there. "I know, Kacey," she said to me. "I know."

I'd have thought her words would have made me feel better but they didn't.

Chapter Twelve

The next morning I woke in my apartment—Christmas, at last—my sister was not in bed by my side. She was not sitting in the small chair in the corner on which she had heaped the pile of clothes she'd brought with her for the forty-eight hours she was due to be in town. I rolled over and read the clock: 8:42. Not only was I surprised I'd slept so soundly, and for so long, I was shocked that I hadn't heard the rise and fall of voices coming from the adjacent room, laughter that grew and fell in soft swells.

I pulled on my chenille robe and cinched it tight at my waist, pushing my matted hair back away from my face, and stumbling into the living room, yawning widely. Daniel was stretched out on the long couch; Mo curled up into the chair opposite. She held a large mug of tea, the warm scent wafting across the room.

"Merry Christmas," I said to them both, feeling immediately as if I'd interrupted them.

Daniel was clearly waiting on Mo to say something to him; to answer a question he'd posed, perhaps. He studied her face intently, patiently. When she didn't answer him, he said to her, "I don't think you've given Paddy the credit he's due, Maureen. I don't think you've even begun to understand this from his perspective."

"What perspective is that? Huh, Daniel? You know what I see? I see an old man set in his ways. I see someone who's not willing to take a bit of the assistance that's been offered to him. So I'll beg your pardon if I'm not looking at this from Paddy's perspective and encourage you to take a look at it from Ma's perspective." She set down her mug on the table with a thud, meaning business. And, as if to add injury to insult, she finished by including, "Or are you so set on making things right with Paddy that you've forgotten what's best for your own sister?"

I made my way over to the couch and lifted Daniel's feet, settling myself under them. In turn, he sat up and let his feet drop to the floor with a thud, his fists balled at his sides. Daniel was angry; this was no way to start Christmas morning.

"What's best for your ma starts with Paddy, Maureen. They're a package deal. Whether you realize that or not, they're a package deal."

Daniel was right about that. I couldn't remember a time when Paddy and Ma had been on separate pages. Sure, they'd disagreed. In fact, when Ma was in her right mind, she was the only person who could ever give Paddy a run for his money. But even when they disagreed, even when they were on opposite ends of a discussion, they'd found a way to respect one another. If Ma and Paddy were two aging tree trunks, bent and disfigured by the years, they still grew toward each other, their branches intertwining.

Mo started to object. I wasn't sure what it was she was planning to use to defend her opinion and I never did find out. The phone rang and bolted us from their argument. I went to answer it, wondering which one of my family members was calling with news that couldn't wait.

"Katherine?" my father asked frantically. "Is your ma there?"

"Paddy?"

"Yeah, yeah, it's me. Is your mother there, honey? Did she make her way over to your apartment?"

"No," I said slowly, panic gripping me at the middle. "No, Paddy, she's not here."

The alarm in my voice stopped Daniel and Mo cold. They both stared at me from where they sat on the couch. I gripped the phone in my right hand, my fingers clenched on the receiver until I thought they might cramp.

"She's not here, either, Kacey," he said slowly, anticipating that it might take some time for me to comprehend his words and their meaning.

"Then where'd she go, Paddy?" I replied, an edge to my voice. It wasn't meant to be an insolent reply, but as I stood there, a sense of urgency washed over me in a giant, uncontrollable wave. It was just like me to get defensive and lash out.

Mo was at my side in an instant. *"Is it Ma? What's wrong? Where is she? Doesn't Paddy know where she is? What's going on, Kacey?"*

I brushed her off, waving my hand frantically in front of her face and walking away with the receiver glued to my ear. She followed like a loyal, but annoying, pet.

"Kacey, please? What's going on?" she asked me again.

I whipped around and covered the receiver with my hand. "I DON'T KNOW, MO. I DON'T HAVE A FRIGGING IDEA. GIVE ME A MINUTE TO FIGURE IT OUT, WOULD YOU?"

Daniel rose, wadding up the blankets into a giant heap that he left on the end of the couch. He pulled on a pair of jeans over the boxers he was wearing and yanked a sweatshirt over his head. He was searching for his shoes when I turned my attention back to Paddy.

"Paddy? When did you last see Ma? Are you sure she's not down in the basement? Did you check the garage? What about upstairs? Did you go in the hideaway space in Mo's old room? Are you sure she's not there?"

"Kacey," he said, clearing his throat and all of a sudden sounding very old and frail to me, "she's not here. I've been through the entire house; upstairs, downstairs, around the perimeter, out into the front yard. I've been calling her name for the last hour."

"The last hour?" I cried. *"She's been gone for over an hour and you're just calling us now?"*

"I, um, uh, well, I'm sorry, Kacey. I guess I thought I could find her on my own. But, um, well, she's taken the car. I don't know how she got her hands on the keys, but it's gone. And so's your ma."

"She *WHAT?* She took the car? She's been gone this long and she's out some-where in the car, Paddy?"

My eyes met Daniel's. Only Daniel would understand the magnitude of what this meant. Ma hadn't been permitted to drive for two months. Paddy drove her every-where now, catering to her every whim. He'd been ultracareful with the keys, stash-ing them in places Ma wouldn't find them. Though not easy to enforce, we'd all agreed this was the best—no, the only—option. The thought of Ma out there on her own, a car at her disposal, was an entirely different scenario.

"Do you have any idea where she might have gone, Paddy? Any idea at all? Did she mention anything to you after Mo and I left last night? Did she talk about wanting to go somewhere or see someone?"

"No, Kacey. We watched a television program after you left, and your ma, she fell asleep in the chair. She was snoring pretty loudly, actually. I had to keep turning up the volume just so I could make out what they were saying. I got her up around ten and we went into bed. She didn't say a word. She just went about her business and went to bed. When I got up this morning, I went looking for her, calling her name. Then downstairs, then outside, then just about everywhere. Oh, Kacey, where in the world could she have run off to?"

There was no way to know; Ma could have been anywhere. She could have been around the corner at her favorite diner or out on the interstate somewhere.

"Was she dressed, Paddy?"

"How the hell would I know, Kacey? I didn't see her leave." Paddy was agitated with me, his voice gruff and gravelly. I imagined him standing in his flannel pajama bottoms, his hair uncombed and unruly. There were a million questions I could ask him, but the truth was, none of them was going to do us any good.

From behind me, Daniel's voice was strong and reassuring. "Get off the phone, Kasey. Tell Paddy we'll be over in a few minutes. Tell him he oughta call the police and get someone to come out."

I repeated Daniel's instructions to Paddy and hung up the phone. My mouth hung open. I was speechless and not altogether sure about what I should do next.

"Get dressed, Kacey," Daniel ordered, picking up his wallet and keys from the countertop. "C'mon. We need to get going."

I followed Mo into the bedroom and we each dressed quickly, in silence. We were both just far too stunned to talk. Our ma was missing. There was no telling where she might have run off to or how she'd get home again.

"She should have been in a facility. This is exactly what I was afraid of. This is exactly what I told Paddy would happen," Mo finally said.

"Don't start, Mo. Don't start with Paddy and don't start with me," I answered her, pulling a sweatshirt over my head. "It sure as hell won't help us find Ma." I turned and

left her standing in the middle of my bedroom.

Daniel insisted he drive my car so that Mo
and I could scan the sidewalks and parking
lots for any sighting of Ma. He drove slowly,
purposefully, as if we might miss her along
the way.

"Daniel," I said, fidgeting in my seat.
"Can't you go any faster?"

"Why, Kacey?" he asked me.

"So we can find her? We've got to hurry
up and find her."

"Going any faster isn't going to bring her
home any sooner, Kacey. If I knew where
she was, I'd risk breaking the speed of
sound to get there. But we don't know
where she is. We have no idea where to go,
so it doesn't matter how fast we go to get
there."

His words fell over me like a wool blanket,
itchy and smothering. I wanted to slap him.
I wanted to send him back on the high
horse he'd ridden in on. How could he be so
calm? *My mother was missing!*

At Ma and Paddy's house, nothing seemed
right. Paddy seemed more confused about
things than Ma had ever been. He couldn't
quite get his words to line up right, stum-

bling over them one by one. The authorities had promised to send someone over, but so far no squad car had come to sit in our driveway, its red and blue flashing lights swirling and bouncing off the garage door.

Think, think, think. Where would Ma have gone? What made sense? At the house, I wanted to be in the car. In the car, I wanted to be back at the house. There was no good answer; there was no good place to start.

Daniel was inquisitive but firm with Paddy. "Are you sure she didn't mention wanting to go anywhere in particular, Paddy? Maybe just something in passing that you wouldn't have given another thought to until right now? Anything at all?"

Paddy shook his head and slumped down into his chair. He'd gotten dressed; tan corduroy pants and a white turtleneck. In the corner of the room, the artificial tree looked the same this morning as it had for the last fourteen weeks, but something about the decorations was lackluster, something about the house seemed more artificial than it had.

"We should be out looking around for Ma," Mo insisted. "We should blanket the neighborhood and canvass the entire area. We should split up. Paddy can stay here in case she comes back, but the rest of us should be out there looking around for her. We're wasting time. We have to get out there now. There's no reason for us to sit here and talk about where she might have gone. We just need to go and find her." Mo's shrill voice rang through the entire downstairs. She was frantic; panic had begun to set in.

"Mo," Daniel said sharply. "Calm down. There's no sense in going out there until we have some idea about where she's gone."

"She's out there, Daniel. Our ma is out there somewhere. We need to go right now. Right N-O-W!" Mo held one hand on her hip, the other outreached toward Daniel, palm up, waiting. She was waiting for the car keys.

"If you think I'm going to put you behind the wheel of a car, you're crazy. Not on your life."

"Goddammit, Daniel. She's out there. Standing around here isn't going to do us a damn bit of good."

Daniel took two steps forward so that he was standing squarely in front of Mo. He reached out and put one hand on each of her shoulders. "Maureen," he said to her, "we're going to find her. I promise you that, okay?"

Numbly Mo nodded her head.

"I promise you that," he said again.

Chapter Thirteen

Cooper rang my cell phone just past noon. By then, we were standing-room only at Ma and Paddy's house. *Everyone* was there. And anyone who wasn't there was in their vehicle searching for Ma. In total, we had two SUVs, three minivans, and one VW Bug roaming the streets of Leominster.

I was commandeering the entire event, taking calls on my cell phone on regular intervals. Ma was nowhere to be found.

I explained the situation to Cooper. He listened without interrupting me, as so many other people had done all morning, repetitive advice and questions spewing from every person I'd connected with.

"What can I do, Kacey? How can I help?"

"I wish I could tell you, Coop."

"I'll be there in twenty minutes."

"It's Christmas, Cooper. You don't have to come."

"I know that."

Cooper cleaned up well. He came dressed in black slacks and a cream cashmere sweater and I imagined he'd already endured a morning of gift giving, colorful wrapping paper flying off Olivia's gifts.

I was a mess. Hair pulled back, no makeup, a ripped pair of old sweats, and worn tennis shoes. He kissed me on the cheek and settled in by my side.

"You've called the authorities?"

"Yes."

"You've called the entire family? All of her friends?"

"Yes. They're all out, in one pocket of town or another."

"And nothing?"

"Not yet."

"She hasn't just disappeared, Kacey. She's somewhere. We just need to find her."

"She hasn't called, Cooper. And she doesn't carry a cell phone, so it's not like we can call her, either."

"She's somewhere, Kace," he repeated. "Don't worry. We'll find her."

My cell phone rang again, a number I didn't

recognize. I stared at it, unable to move, and then yanked it open and clicked it on.

"Hello!"

"Um, hi, hello. Uh, you don't know me, but I think maybe your mother is, um . . ."

"Is she there? Oh, God, is she there? Maureen Flanigan? About five foot six inches? Gray curly hair? An older woman?"

"Well, yeah, she is."

"I FOUND HER. I FOUND HER. SHE'S OKAY!" I shouted, covering the receiver with my hand. Around me, chaos erupted. My family, those who weren't out scanning the streets, rushed forward and surrounded me. It was impossible to hear a thing. I covered my other ear and turned my back on everyone, turning my attention back to the person on the other end of the phone, the stranger who had called.

"Is she okay? Oh, God, please tell me that she's okay."

"Yeah, she's okay. At least I think so. We finally got her to come inside. She's, um, well, she's been standing outside our house all morning. On the front lawn. And I know this is going to sound crazy, but, well, she's in her housecoat and a pair of slippers. We were really concerned because, of course, it's so cold, and well, it is Christmas and all."

Oh, God. My mother was in her night clothes in the middle of God-knows-where. She was standing on someone's front lawn. It was shocking that someone in my family hadn't found her. Surely someone had to have passed her.

"I'm sorry," I said, "but she's not really herself these days. We'll come and get her, of course. We'll come right now. Can you tell me where you are? What's your address? I'll send someone right now."

Behind me, my family held hands and mumbled, a consistent, dull rumble that ebbed and flowed and reacted to my conversation. They hung on every word, waiting patiently for me to deliver the news.

"That's the thing of it, lady. I'm not really sure where you are. Your mom's plates are from Massachusetts, but we're in Connecticut. Just outside of Hartford, actually. I can give you directions and all, but your mother keeps mumbling something about this being her house. I'm not really sure what she's talking about. We've lived here for the last eight years and I've never met your mom. But she's insisting that this is her house."

I froze. My God. Ma was in Hartford, two and a half hours away. Ma was standing in her night clothes in the house she called home.

Ma was home.

"Three Bear Creek Lane? Do you live at Three Bear Creek Lane?" I choked out in a whisper.

"Well, yeah. Actually, we do," the voice quaked from the other end, in just as much disbelief as I'd found myself. "But, how'd you know that?"

"Ma's house. You live in the house my ma grew up in."

Paddy couldn't take it anymore. "Kacey?" he tugged on my sleeve. "Where is she? What's going on?" When I didn't answer him right off, he asked me again, more insistent this time. "Where, Kacey? What's going on?"

I turned my attention back to the caller, someone I hadn't even identified by name yet. "I'm so sorry," I said into the receiver. "She's not really herself these days. She has been suffering from dementia. And Alz-heimer's. I'll send someone right away. Can you keep her there?"

"Of course," the voice softened. "Of course we can do that."

"It'll take us a few hours. Oh, I'm so sorry. We've had our whole family searching for her. Our whole entire family. We'll leave now. Just make sure she doesn't leave."

"She doesn't seem in any hurry to do so, lady."

"I'm Kacey," I said into the phone. "Kacey Flanigan. You can tell her that I'm coming to get her. You can tell her that her daughter is on the way."

"Kacey," he said, committing my name to memory. "We found your number in her handbag. She said Kacey was her daughter and that you would know where to find her. She kept saying that you'd be coming, too. I'm John, Kacey. Don't worry about your mother. We'll keep an eye on her until you get here."

Chapter Fourteen

"She's *WHERE?*" Mo asked me, barking into her cell phone. She was out and about in Michael's caravan when I finally reached them, bubbling with the news that Ma had been found.

"She's at Granny and Pa's old house. In West Hartford. John said they found her standing out on the front lawn. She was just standing there in her nightgown and house-coat staring at the house."

"Who the hell is John, Kacey?"

"He lives there, Mo. He found my number in Ma's purse and he called us to tell us where she was. He's got her there, at Granny and Pa's."

Mo was quiet on the other end of the phone. So quiet, in fact, that I thought I might have lost the connection.

"Mo? Mo? Are you there? Hello?" I asked.

"Yeah, Kacey. I'm here."

"Oh. Okay. So, um, Paddy wants to leave right away, of course. There's really no reason for everyone to go. Paddy and I can go and get her. Daniel says he'll go with us, too."

"I want to go, Kacey. Wait for me there, before you leave. I want to go with you."

"Are you sure, Mo? You really don't need to. And under the circumstances, maybe it'd be better if you didn't. I mean we don't need to make a bigger production of the whole thing than we already have. Once Ma figures out what she's done, I'm sure she's going to be a bit hot-tempered and angry with herself over the whole thing."

"No, Kacey. I want to go, too. I should go."

Quite frankly, I wasn't so sure I wanted to spend two and a half hours in the car with my sister. And I knew if I wasn't so sure about the prospect of doing so, I could only imagine how Paddy would feel. Still, I didn't see much choice about it.

We waited for Mo by the kitchen door, Paddy in his heavy barn coat and wool gloves. When Mo arrived, he opened the storm door, crossed the carport, and settled himself into the front seat of Daniel's idling

Jeep Cherokee. Daniel seated himself in the driver's seat and Mo and I climbed in the backseat. We were off.

The car was noiseless, each of us lost in our own thoughts. Paddy stared ahead at the road and cleared his throat every few minutes. I imagined that he must be hungry; I didn't think he'd eaten anything all day.

Mo kept her Blackberry close at hand, punching out messages on the tiny keyboard. I couldn't imagine who she was conversing with. After all, it was Christmas Day. Couldn't she take a break, even for one day?

Daniel drove with one hand on the wheel. He leaned his right arm on the armrest and kept his eyes focused on the highway, the barren trees zipping by us.

I was anxious; timid and apprehensive about what kind of shape we might find Ma in. John hadn't said much more about her condition. On the phone he'd sounded kind and I was grateful that a tender-hearted family owned Granny and Pa's house so many years later. It seemed as if it should have been that way.

As we checked off the miles, I searched for familiarity. I hadn't been to this part of

Connecticut in years and nothing reminded
me of the trips we'd taken when I was a kid,
shoved in between Mo and one of my
brothers. Daniel exited the freeway and nav-
igated the neighborhoods. As we got closer,
Paddy began to grow antsy, shifting and
turning in his seat.

The house was small; smaller than I'd remembered. In fact, as I opened the car door
and stood staring at the front porch and the
wraparound deck that ran from one side of
the driveway until it disappeared around the
back side of the house, I wondered how in
the world we'd ever housed so much of
Ma's family under one roof. The outside had
been painted—no longer the traditional
brick red with black shutters that I'd been
accustomed to—brighter, now a brilliant
yellow and cream ensemble. The yard
seemed smaller, the driveway shorter, the
doorway much narrower, than I had remembered. I realized, of course, this was an illu-
sion. None of these things had dwarfed; I'd
gotten bigger. Everything about my perspective had changed.

Ma and Paddy's Cadillac was parked
askew in front of the house. No doubt about
it, she was here. It appeared Ma had come

with a mission in mind, abandoning the car in her wake. Paddy charged the front door and rapped on it loudly. He stood back and shoved his hands into his coat pockets, waiting.

The heavy front door opened and a ruddy-faced, stout, redheaded gentleman stepped out onto the front stoop. Irish, I thought. Thank God. I watched as my father shook his hand and then allowed the man I assumed to be John usher him inside, guiding Paddy with his hand on the small of his back. Daniel, Mo, and I followed before the door could close and we'd be left on the other side.

Everything about the house was different than I'd remembered. The kitchen had been updated; modernized and made current. The cabinets had been refinished, the stove and refrigerator and countertops had been replaced. The floors, wide stained cedar planks, were new. Long gone was the classic wallpaper that my Granny had loved. It had been replaced by warm, faux-painted walls topped with classic crown molding.

Still, it was *our house*. Oh, I realized someone else lived here. Apparently, someone with three children and a beautiful ten-foot

Christmas tree lived here. But regardless, it felt like our house. I'd grown up here; my secrets lay within the seams of the wood. It felt as if I'd walked right into my past. If I listened close enough, I could hear the shrill, joyful cries of my cousins and me playing hide-and-seek. If I closed my eyes and stood in the foyer long enough, I could imagine my Pa inviting guests in for a Christmas scotch, his warm, booming voice carrying across the entire bottom floor of the house.

Ma sat in a hard-backed wood chair that had been dragged from the dining room table and set in front of the television. She was prim and proper, even in her robe. Her legs were crossed at the ankle, her hands in her lap. She was completely absorbed in a repeat performance of *The Glory of Christmas,* one of her favorites, broadcast from the Crystal Cathedral.

Paddy approached her tentatively, placing his hand on her shoulder and speaking her name clearly.

"Maureen. It's about time we started on home."

I thought it was a funny thing to say right off, actually, after all of this. As if we would just up and go and never discuss Ma's trip again.

Ma looked up at him from where she was sitting and blinked rapidly. "But I've only started watching the show, Paddy. What's your hurry? Can we give it a few minutes? The children are having such a good time."

Paddy breathed evenly, holding his temper and emotions in check. I'm sure if he'd been given the opportunity, he would have taken Ma by the arm and escorted her right out of the house without another word. Paddy was a proud man; certainly this wasn't easy for him. It left me remembering that fateful Christmas morning twenty-four years earlier, when Mo had so badly disgraced the family and he couldn't leave fast enough.

"No, honey. Just Mo and Kacey are here. And they're not children anymore. They've grown up now. This isn't Granny and Pa's house anymore, Maureen. We shouldn't be here. It's time we let these wonderful people get on with their holiday now. It's time for us to be heading back now."

John's family had gathered around my parents, forming somewhat of a semicircle and watching. I wanted to usher them away.

I wanted to tell them that my parents weren't a circus act to be enjoyed, that they weren't an exhibit at the zoo. But I didn't move from where I was standing, my feet were glued to the floor.

Ma blinked a few more times as if she was adjusting her eyes. She followed Paddy's gaze around the room, taking in the people who were watching her, the unfamiliar faces that waited. Confusion clouded her eyes and she lifted her hands to cover her face. When she dropped her hands in her lap again, her shoulders dropped with them, defeated. She looked around again until her eyes rested on Mo and Daniel and me.

"Let's let these fine people get on with their dinner, Mama. It's time we got going now," Paddy encouraged.

"Kacey? Maureen?" Ma piped up, asking for us. We were both at her side in a second, scrambling over each other to get to her. "You thank this nice family and clean up any mess I may have made."

"I don't think that's a problem, Ma. But, yes, we'll take care of it. Don't worry," I reassured her.

Mo was visibly uncomfortable, nearly as confused as Ma. Clearly this was the last place she'd imagined she'd find herself on Christmas Day. She couldn't figure out which world she was in; the one in front of her, where no one knew her, or the one from the past where so much of who she was supposed to be had veered off course. It may have been the first time my sister was rendered speechless.

Ma allowed Paddy to take her hand and pull her up, walking her slowly to the door. John followed, his head bowed in deference. They shook hands again, and Paddy thanked him for everything he'd done to keep Ma safe.

Daniel twirled the car keys in his hand and waited for Mo or me to move. We were both sewn to the floor, incapable of simply leaving now. I hadn't ever imagined being back here, either, and I wasn't too keen about moving on. What I really wanted was the opportunity to wander off and explore every inch of the architecture I knew by heart. The house had clearly changed; a new set of clothes had replaced the old. But inside, the soul had remained the same.

"I know this will sound incredibly odd," I said, coming eye to eye with John, "but would it be okay if maybe we just took a look around a bit? Just for a few minutes. I know it seems like such a strange request, but we—all of us—we spent so much time here. Well, gosh, Daniel grew up in this house."

"Is that right?" John asked, turning his attention to my uncle.

"Indeed, it is. Knocked my front tooth out right on that corner of the stairs. Right there," he said, walking over to the base of the staircase.

John looked from me to Mo to Daniel. It was as if we'd stumbled upon an unopened Christmas gift, something left under the tree.

"Well, then, by all means. You should have a look. I don't suppose I need to give you the tour. You probably know your way around." He was kind, kinder than he needed to be. I thought about the crazy day they'd had; a strange woman and her family, former residents, showing up on their doorstep and wanting to look around his home, making it theirs for a few hours.

We all looked at each other and nodded in unison, heading immediately for the basement. It was the first place we'd gone as children; it felt like the only place I wanted to go now.

The stairs were narrow and steep and the ceiling was low. I remembered the sign Pa had posted on the slanted cement: *Duck, don't bump.* I hadn't understood it then, but now, much taller, it seemed brilliant. Naturally, as if the sign was still in place, I ducked my head and held on to the thin wood railing, taking the stairs one at a time. Mo followed me slowly, reluctantly at first.

"Why would she have come here? Of all places, why did she pick Granny and Pa's?" Mo's voice was barely a whisper.

"It was her home, Mo. Everything about this place was familiar. It was the place she never wanted to leave."

Around us, the basement walls were lined with boxes, stuffed with treasures that had been laid to rest and forgotten. John's family used the space differently than we had. No one could sleep here; no secrets could be kept. The room was filled with discarded riches, lost and forlorn memories.

"If only these walls could talk," Daniel said, laughing.

"The stories they would tell," my sister finished.

"We never talked about it," I said to both of them coldly, crossing my arms over my chest. "That Christmas. We never talked about what happened. Paddy packed up the car and made us leave, but we never talked about it. Everything changed that day. Nothing went back to the way it was. It was our last Christmas here."

"Actually," my sister said, turning on her heel and starting back up the stairs, refusing, even now, to talk about it. "Actually, I think *this* is our last Christmas here, Katherine. I don't expect we'll ever be back again."

We ascended the stairs then. At the top, I closed the door on my innocence; I closed the door on my past. Mo was right; we would never come back.

Chapter Fifteen

The snow began to fall in earnest on our way back, picking up enough to be purposeful. It stuck to the road and made the driving a bit dicey. Daniel kept both hands on the wheel and his eyes on the road. Mo sat in the passenger seat next to him, quiet and reserved.

I had the backseat to myself. My eyes followed the landscape outside the window, watching it change with the towns we passed through. The guardrail ran alongside the road, a constant silver barrier that held my attention and kept me mesmerized.

Behind us, Paddy and Ma followed in the Cadillac. Every few miles I would turn to steal a glance at them through the back window and make sure they were still with us. Paddy drove the same way he had for years, with one hand on the wheel, the other arm propped up along the back of the seat. Ma huddled in the passenger seat, her mouth unmoving. I imagined the silence that cut through their car was deafening.

Cooper was standing among the waiting crowd when we pulled into Ma and Paddy's driveway. He hung back while my brothers and their families crowded Ma as if she'd hit the winning home run in the World Series. I circumvented the crowd and found myself by his side, enveloped in a warm embrace.

"You found her, Kacey," he said when I collapsed against his chest. "She's home now."

"Yes, she is. Though I'm not sure she recognizes it as such. Frankly, I think she may have been happier where she was. You should have seen her, Cooper. She was so content, you know. It was like she was really, truly at home."

From the sidelines, we watched my family mill about in the frigid afternoon, patting themselves on the back and congratulating each other. Ma looked tired, worn and old. I watched Paddy take her at the elbow and walk her up the front steps into the house.

"Cooper," I said. "I want to come to California. Not right away, of course, but maybe in a few months."

"I think that would be a fine idea, Kacey," he said to me.

Chapter Sixteen

Mo left the morning after Christmas on a 7:30 AM flight. She was up long before the first light, dressed in a warm brown suit and soft pink silk blouse.

"I have a noon lunch and back-to-back meetings that will run through eight tonight, Kacey. I can't miss this flight," she said to me while we were racing to the airport.

At the curbside, I blew warm air into my hands and rubbed them together to keep warm. "You don't have to go, Mo."

"What would possibly keep me here, Kacey?"

I watched my sister walk away from me again, wanting so badly to pull her back but knowing that I never would be able to do so, not in the way I wanted to. Despite Ma's best efforts, there was no going back.

At the house, Paddy was up and dressed,

and removing the ornaments from the tree. I plucked a red and silver glittering ball from the tree and set it to rest in the box that lay open on the table.

"You're taking the decorations down already?" I asked him. Sure, they'd been up for a long time, but there was part of me that wanted to hold on to Christmas with all my might, hold on to everything about it.

"Kacey, these goddamn ornaments and lights have been up since Halloween. Earlier than that if you count the first go-round. I can't stand to look at them anymore. I think I'm entitled."

"Where's Ma?" I asked him, frowning.

"She's having her breakfast in the den."

I removed the hook from another larger ornament and placed it on the table.

"I always hated the day after Christmas. It's such a letdown," I said to him. Paddy's milky blue eyes met my own. He didn't say anything but continued with what he was doing quietly, solemnly.

I went to find Ma. She was sitting in a small, comfortable chair next to the fireplace, her breakfast on the portable card table in front of her.

"Kacey!" she said exuberantly when I walked into the room.

"Hi, Ma. How'd you sleep?"

"Pretty well, after all the excitement yesterday. Pretty well."

"That was quite a trip you took," I answered her and she blushed, bowing her head. "You had us all so worried Ma."

"Are you angry with me?"

"Of course not," I told her, standing by her side and petting her head, smoothing her hair. "But, Ma, I can't help but think you had a reason for going back there. I can't help but think you'd found your way there on purpose." It had kept me up all night, actually, the feeling that Ma wasn't so crazy, that it wasn't her dementia that had drawn her back to Granny and Pa's house after all. In fact, crazy as it sounded, I'd been wondering if Ma had, in some way, planned to go.

She winked at me then and smiled to herself. "It was a wonderful Christmas, Kacey. I got everything I'd ever wanted. How about you?"

I smiled back at her. "It was just perfect."